A FATAL PROSPECT

RIVER REAPERS MC, BOOK 3

ELIZABETH BARONE

Maietta
INK

ALSO BY ELIZABETH BARONE

RIVER REAPERS MC SERIES

A Disturbing Prospect

A Risky Prospect

A Fatal Prospect

A Lasting Prospect

RIVER REAPERS MC SPINOFF NOVELLAS

Her Mercy

Burning for Stixx

Contemporary romances are also available.

Visit **elizabethbaronebooks.com** to purchase!

MAIETTA INK

A Fatal Prospect

River Reapers MC, Book 3

Copyright © 2021 by Elizabeth Campbell, writing as Elizabeth Barone

All Rights Reserved

1st Edition

Cover photography by Period Images, kiuikson/Shutterstock, and lexaarts/Shutterstock

Cover designed by Natasha Snow

Edited by Traci Finlay

ISBN 978-1-7331197-0-2

 Created with Vellum

A FATAL PROSPECT

*The reapers of past and present are returning to put us in our graves.
Only death could keep us apart, but death isn't the only thing that's
fatal...*

Cliff

I've finally got Olivia, but she can't give me the two things I want
most: three words so I know I'm not in this alone, and a family so
I can redeem all the horrible things I've done. My past is still
chasing me, and the only way I can meet her halfway is if I stop
running and face it. I can't allow the monster in my blood to take
over, but it's rising to the surface and I can't fight it much longer.

Olivia

After all I've been through, I'm never giving away my heart,
even if my heart has other plans. War strikes before Cliff and I get
a chance to figure it all out. When a teen football player is
unspeakably violated, only my club can avenge him. A rival

motorcycle club from the past is also looking for revenge, just as I realize my true feelings for Cliff.

When someone betrays us, we'll pay the ultimate price, in both blood and love...

A FATAL PROSPECT is the third book in the River Reapers MC series, a dark romance with a body count. Some content may be disturbing to some readers.

For Noni.

FOREWORD

A *Fatal Prospect* continues Olivia and Cliff's story, and carries on dark themes from the River Reapers MC series.

Some of the themes in this book might make some people uncomfortable, and may even be triggering for people with personal trauma. I've made a list of potential trigger warnings that I'm including here.

For the sake of realism, I've depicted biker culture from my own experience and understanding. Although that culture and its attitudes toward women is changing, it has a long way to go. My goal for this book and its subsequent series is to help change that mentality.

TRIGGER WARNINGS

Here are the potential triggers for A *Fatal Prospect*.

Drug and Alcohol Use: Some characters use drugs and drink alcohol.

Childhood Sexual Assault: Several characters have a history of being molested as children.

Guns and Violence: My vigilante bikers use guns to fight the bad guys, as well as other violent means of taking out the trash.

PTSD: Multiple characters experience flashbacks, anxiety, anger, and other symptoms of PTSD.

Sexual Assault of a Minor: A character under the age of 18 is sexually assaulted (off page).

This book will break you. Have tissues ready.
(I promise, Cliff and Olivia get their HEA in the fourth and final book!)

If you feel that you won't be safe reading A *Fatal Prospect*, please don't risk your health. As a rape survivor and someone with PTSD, I wish many books came with a list of trigger warnings. No book is worth your well-being.

Please also note that I don't necessarily condone or endorse the themes contained in this book. I do, however, wish it was legal to kill rapists.

If you've read *A Fatal Prospect* and feel that I may have missed something, please email me at elizabethbaronebooks@gmail.com.

A FATAL
Prospect

1

CLIFF

"**Y**ou're on Bunny duty, Cliff," Olivia tells me as I set down the final box of decorations. I turn to find my cousin Lucy holding out her baby to me.

"Leigh," she says, narrowing her eyes at Olivia. "Her name is Leigh." She passes the baby Olivia nicknamed Bunny to me, and I cradle her in the crook of my arm.

"Easiest job in the house," I say. I'd never pass up on some uninterrupted Bunny time. It's a regular game my cousin and I play. Where we used to fight over turns playing Crash Bandicoot, now we fight over who gets to hold Bunny. Lucy always wins, of course.

Nothing has changed between us.

"I can't believe you two talked me into a biker Sip and See," Lucy says, climbing onto a chair. She wraps crepe streamers around the stripper pole, and I bite back a laugh.

I can't believe it, either.

I catch Olivia's eye from where she sets up the bar. She smirks. "Please. I wasn't about to let you sip tea. Whiskey's so much better, and we've got plenty of that."

"I told you to save it for your own baby," Lucy says.

"Not gonna happen," Olivia says. "And don't even start with that 'you'll change your mind' bullshit again. I'd be a horrible mother."

I swallow her statement. It lodges in my chest, wedging the rift between us even wider. Babies are a touchy subject between us, close behind marriage and Olivia's PTSD.

Bunny fusses. I look down at her, and I can't help but smile. "Hey," I soothe. She's existed for just about two weeks, yet she brings out the very best in me. I might never have my own children, so for me, Bunny is it.

"I'm gonna spoil you," I confess, rocking her. I swear she smiles. "I'll even buy your first motorcycle."

"Over my dead body."

I turn. Lucy holds out the tiny outfit she debated over for the last week, rolling her eyes at me but smiling. "I'll work on her," I tell Bunny.

"It might not take long." She holds out her arms. "Olivia talked me into a biker baby debut. The two of you could talk me into anything. Give me my baby."

"I can change her," I say, not ready to give up my niece.

"I need you to hang up the rest of the streamers," Olivia says, joining us. She barely looks at the baby. I've seen her hold Bunny twice, and both times were at the hospital.

"Sucks being tall, doesn't it?" Lucy teases, and I relinquish the baby, immediately missing her.

"She smiled at me." I grab a roll of streamers and tape, and get to work.

"We've been through this. It's gas." Lucy lays Bunny down and starts working her out of her tiny onesie.

My chest aches.

Olivia loves Bunny—*Leigh*. I know she does. She's the one who gave her that nickname while Lucy was pregnant. But once Lucy brought Bunny home, everything changed between Olivia and me.

The distance between us is complicated. She doesn't want to move in with me, she doesn't want to get married, and she definitely doesn't want to have my babies. She won't even let me tell her I love her.

It's not just that.

Sometimes when I close my eyes, I still see her on top of Greg, those fingers, currently stacking delicate shot glasses, wrapped around his throat. There's no doubt in my mind that she had to do it. I still wish I didn't have to see it.

I guess that's how Lucy must feel about me.

I finish up the streamers, my hands tingling, the muscles and nerves remembering what I want to forget. I made my father pay for his sins against Lucy with my bare hands. No regrets, that's how I live. Olivia, too.

It still changes you.

There are times when I can't look at her. The monster in me sees the monster in her. It stops me cold in my tracks. Our entire relationship is probably built on that thread that runs through us both. It makes sense that we can't have the things I want so badly.

Our world is no place for a child.

It's not her fault at all.

I just don't know what to do about it.

"It's time," Olivia calls, putting the final touches on the gifts table. Right on cue, the door swings open, and Donny and Esther shuffle inside with their herd of kids. Esther's three little sisters come with a plus-one, an older teen boy I've never seen before. Esther's oldest little sister, Cierra, breaks off from the group with him and they dip their heads together. Cierra points to Olivia, and my eyebrows furrow.

"Who's he?" I ask Donny.

His jaw tightens. "Cierra's seventeen-year-old 'friend.' She's fourteen, for fuck's sake. I wasn't ready for this shit."

"She's in high school, brother," I say, clapping him on the back. "It was bound to happen."

"I ain't a fan." Donny eyes the boy. "They're attached at the hip, and I swear, if they attach anywhere else, I'll kill him." His dark eyes meet mine, softening as his threat dies.

Donny fell in love with Esther and didn't skip a beat when she got guardianship of her little sisters. They've all been through a lot and, teen boyfriends aside, I'm glad things are getting back to normal for them.

More guests pour in, mostly teachers Lucy works with at the elementary school. I spot her chatting with friends, rocking Bunny in her arms. Motherhood looks good on Lucy. She reminds me of my mother, dedicated and tender.

I'll probably never know the truth behind Ruth's death.

It's a loss I feel every day, but especially today when she should be here. She'd love Bunny. She'd love Olivia.

I glance around for my woman, but she's gone. So are Cierra, the boy, and Esther.

"Olivia will fill you in later," Donny says, gripping my arm.

"Fill me in on what?" Before I can get an answer out of him, music fills the clubhouse.

"What's going on?" I stand in the hall with Esther, peering into the office where Cierra and her friend sit.

"I'm so sorry to do this here," she says, "since it's Lucy's day and all, but they just told us this morning."

"Told you what?" Music pours into the hall, and I hover between playing host and hearing out my best friend.

She drops her voice, and I have to lean in close to hear her whispering. "Cierra told Bryce that you can help with his situation. She doesn't know exactly what you and the club did for us, but she's smart enough to know Toci and Josué didn't just take off," she says, referring to her sexually abusive parents.

The hairs on the back of my neck stand up.

"Bryce is her friend, in there?" I nod toward the office, where dark haired Cierra touches her forehead to the boy's.

"He's on the football team at their high school. There was an incident in February . . ."

His cotton candy pink hair looks too soft and fluffy for a football player, but I bite my tongue. "What incident?"

"Some of the football players went to the National Conference in February. It's a clinic where they improve their skills. Alumni from the high school mentor their team's current players. Technically it was a school field trip, but only specific athletes went. Not the whole team."

I shrug. Football is boring. Lately it's all Cliff can talk about. Every damn week, he can't wait to see his Raiders play. Blah, blah, fucking blah.

"It was chaperoned," she adds.

"Okay," I prompt, twirling a finger in the air.

"Some of the mentors assaulted Bryce."

"You mean like a hazing thing?" Men. I roll my eyes. They can't do anything without violence. Every year there's a story about some college frat who got his ass beat in some caveman ritual.

"No." She swallows. "Bryce said they held him down on a pool table and . . . raped him with cue sticks."

My entire body stiffens. I want a shot from the bar more than anything now, but I stay composed. "What did the school do?"

She shakes her head, her lips pressed into a tight line.

"No one reported it?"

"Bryce went to the chaperones, but they told him they couldn't do anything since they didn't see it happen. None of the other teammates saw anything—supposedly." Her nostrils flare.

My stomach clenches. "Wasn't there . . . damage?"

"They took him to the hospital out there. They didn't even call his mom. He called her himself. He had to have surgery. Every student had to bring in a form giving the coach and chaperones permission to make medical decisions during the trip—as a precaution. It's not unheard of." Her teeth sink into her lower lip. "It was bad, Olivia. He was really hurt."

Memories crawl up, clogging my throat with a thick, fuzzy burn. Even though there are no hands chaining my neck, for a moment, I struggle to draw air. I shove it all back down into its box. "Why are you telling me this?"

"His mom went to the coach when he got home, who gave her the same bullshit line: Didn't see anything. She went to the principal, who took the coach's side. She filed a police report, and the police said the hospital's medical report wasn't enough because no one would talk." She sucks in a shaky breath, tears slipping down her cheeks. "Bryce finished out the year from home, and came back after summer break, but the boys who did this to him have been stalking him around town to keep him quiet."

"Why are you telling me this?" I ask again. My throat is so dry. I glance into the office, at the teenagers huddled together.

"The club can help Bryce the way you helped us." Her brown eyes search mine. "Right?"

I jolt upright. "Are you asking me to have my club make a bunch of eighteen- and nineteen-year-olds disappear?"

"I'm asking you, Cliff, and Donny to ask your club to look into it. Maybe you guys can put some pressure on the police department. Just look at him."

I do. Through the doorway, his blue eyes meet mine, pleading.

"He's all alone, Olivia. All his friends and teammates ditched him. Cierra met him through cheerleading. I think she's his only friend. He could use friends like you and the River Reapers."

I close my eyes. My club barely made it through what we did for Esther, and then what I did for myself. Esther's parents and my ex had it coming. I wouldn't change a thing. We're supposed to be on the straight and narrow now, though—or at least as legit as a club can be, selling guns and drugs.

"Livvie, I know this is hard for you. You're the only one who can help him. You and the club. Please? For me?" She pauses, letting the music fill in the silence between us. "For Cierra?" she tries. "For Bunny?"

My eyes snap open. Someday too soon, my niece is going to be a student at that same high school. I can't make the whole world safer, but I can at least try to help this boy. I can make sure this never happens again.

"We'll take it to the table," I tell her. "But no promises." I return to the party, my blood boiling even as I try not to think of what they did to that sweet pink-haired boy.

3

CLIFF

"**W**hiskey and babies," Stixx says, joining me. "Nothing about that can possibly go wrong."

"We'll just keep her away from the bar," I quip. I give him a once over. His blond hair is pulled back into a half up, half down man bun. Beard wax holds his otherwise unruly beard in place. A black short-sleeved button-down leaves most of his tattoos exposed.

Nothing could cover all of the ink he has. Dude's face is the only thing untouched. Right now, he isn't even wearing his cut. He looks like a hipster.

"What's with the getup?" I ask, instead of what I really want to know: *What the fuck are* you *doing here?* I hadn't expected to see any of the guys here. It's our clubhouse, of course, but it's a baby shower. The only reason Ravage is here is because Shannon helped Olivia put it together.

His beard twitches as he lifts one corner of his mouth. "I'm toning it down."

"Toning it down?" This from the man who gleefully burned down a house just a couple months ago—and not for the first time.

His eyes dart toward a booth in the corner. I follow his line of vision to where Lucy sits with her parents.

I glance from Lucy back to Stixx, then back to Lucy. "Huh?" I'm the picture of eloquence right now.

"We're just friends," he assures me. "For now."

"Friends?" I peer at him. I cannot remember a single time when Lucy and Stixx were even in the same room.

"We ran into each other at Big Y."

I wait for more. He doesn't give it to me. "And?" I prompt.

"She asked me if I'm a River Reaper."

Again, I wait for him to continue. Several beats pass. His pale blue eyes dart back to Lucy. I clear my throat. "She recognized your cut?"

He nods. "We were in the wipes aisle."

"You were buying wipes?"

His gaze slides back to me. "Dude, if you're still using toilet paper, you're not living."

Stixx just gave me hygiene advice. Between the converted strip club and this doppelgänger, I'm starting to think I stepped into *The Twilight Zone*. "So what, you traded tips?"

"I have sensitive skin. Baby Leigh has sensitive skin. I told Lucy to try the water wipes."

She did *not* mention this. I need a cigarette. "So now you're friends."

"For now. She invited me. I figured the cut and tattoos were too much." He ducks his head. "I don't know how to dress for her."

The rest of his earlier statement hits me. I gape at him. "For now?"

"She's nice. And she's pretty." He straightens and looks me in the eye. "But I know she's your family. I wanted to make a good impression . . . on both of you."

I glance around The Wet Mermaid at my two families and all

of Lucy's friends. I knew it'd be a little awkward for everyone. I just didn't think it'd be weird for me.

"Do I have your blessing, if I pursue her?" Stixx asks.

"I don't know, brother." I run a hand through my still damp hair. "She's been through a lot."

He nods. "Bastard."

I forgot the whole club knows Lucy's history. It's not just my history, it's club history. My father Bastard was President until his brothers found out what he was doing to Lucy. "She needs a fresh start," I say carefully.

"Baby daddy not in the picture?"

"Far from it." My hand goes to the pocket in my cut where I keep my cigarettes. If this wasn't a baby shower, I'd light up.

Stixx is my brother, but I don't want him dating Lucy. I want to keep her as far from the club as possible. If I'd known Stixx has a thing for her, I never would've backed up Olivia on throwing this at the clubhouse. But Lucy is a grown woman, and I am not her keeper. She probably doesn't even feel the same way he does.

"You don't need my blessing," I tell Stixx.

"But if I hurt her, you'll kill me. I'll hold myself to that." With a quick bow of his head, he turns and heads toward Lucy's table.

"Jesus Christ," I mutter.

My aunt and uncle eye Stixx with open disdain, while Lucy beckons him to sit down. A smile tugs at my lips. Maybe it'll happen, maybe it won't, but it'll be fun to watch her parents squirm for a little while.

A hand clasps my shoulder. The thick fingers, void of any tattoos and decorated only with a wedding band, give him away.

"Hey, Pres." I pat his hand. "Any word?"

A few weeks ago, I made small talk before asking about Olivia's parents, out of respect. Ravage isn't an iPhone; you can't push his button, tell him what you want, and then put him back in your pocket. But every time I cross another day off my calendar, my nerves coil tighter. Something is wrong. Either Mercy didn't find Bree, or trouble found them.

"Not yet." Ravage's shoulders slump, only for a second. Then the hard muscle contracts back into place.

"Should we be worried?" I watch his face. No one knows Mercy better than he does.

He blinks, ice blue eyes distant. The black stubble on his face is flecked with more gray than the last time I saw him—just a few days ago. "I don't know," he says finally. He turns to me. "She never asks, you know."

She doesn't ask him about hers, and I never ask about mine.

Ruth's death still weighs on me. I might never know why she stayed with Bastard for so long, when he clearly didn't love her. Ravage might be able to give me those answers, but maybe the past is better left buried. Learning the truth won't bring her back.

I glance over at the bar, where Olivia is showing Trish how to make the shower's signature drink, a Rob Roy. Even though this isn't the first time she's had to show this to Trish, she doesn't even look fazed. Her face is closed, disconnected, somewhere else.

I don't know what Esther told her, but it can't be good.

4

CLIFF

I slide the key into the lock, turning it so that it won't wake
Lucy. "We're gonna bring everything into the living room," I
tell Stixx.

Lucy may not have gotten a proper baby shower, but she and
Bunny sure made out today. There are boxes and boxes of
diapers, bags of tiny outfits and socks, several gift cards, plus a
couple bigger items, like a walker and some contraption for
"tummy time." Bunny is basically set for the first year of her life,
and then some.

"Is Lucy up?" Stixx asks, pushing strands of blond hair back
from his face.

"I don't think so." I step into the silent condo, glancing around
the living room for Dio, Olivia's cat. Instead I see my woman,
sitting on the floor, her back against the base of the couch. "Hey,"
I greet her, keeping my voice low. "Lucy and Bunny napping?"

"Yeah."

I'm about to ask her why she's sitting on the floor in the dark
when I actually see her.

The smudged makeup around her eyes.

The dark circles underneath.

The way her curly hair is thrown carelessly up into a messy bun.

Casting a glance at Stixx over my shoulder, I go to her, dropping to one knee in front of her. "What happened?" I smooth my hands down her arms, checking her for . . . I don't really know what.

"Cliff," she sobs.

The vodka on her breath hits me like a wall. I tip my head back. Relief floods through me. She's just drunk. I never pegged her for a crier. Then it occurs to me: *Why* is she drunk?

Something must've happened to Bree and Mercy. I can barely form words. I sputter a series of half questions. I pull her close, arms wrapping around her. "It's okay," I say. My voice is hoarse. It's not just concern that's robbing me, though. It's the realization of *how* worried I am. How much I love her.

I lead Olivia to Lucy's couch and turn on a lamp. In the soft glow, I can see the haunted look in her eyes, the red around her nostrils. "What's going on?" I ask Olivia as Stixx carries a tower of diaper boxes inside.

"I'm not even here," he says, setting them down and hustling back out.

Olivia shoves her phone into my hands.

I fucking hate smart phones. When Lucy gave me one, I tried. I really did. But I can't figure out the damned things. There are two-year-olds whipping around on these and I'm a thirty-eight-year-old man who can barely text.

Olivia snorts softly, but her eyes are kind. She takes the phone from my hands and unlocks it. Then she drops it into my palm again with an app I've never seen. "Just scroll down."

"Scroll?"

Her forehead tightens. "Sometimes, it is *really* painful how old you are."

"Thanks," I say dryly. I'm not old. I'm just a felon who missed everything while I was inside.

She shows me how to move the screen up and down with my fingers. "I've showed you this a thousand times. It's really not hard to do."

I laugh. "That's what she said."

Olivia glares at me. "This is serious, Cliff."

I frown down as the page loads. Bold text proclaims that I'm looking at @RapedAtUSAFootball's profile. Next to the name is a circular photo of a deflated football, and the image spanning the top is the Naugatuck High School team logo. "My name is Bryce. I was raped at football clinic," the bio reads, "and everyone wants to pretend it didn't happen. Spoiler alert: It happened."

"What am I looking at, Olivia?"

"This is his Twitter," she says. "Strangers are the only people who listen to rape victims."

"*His* Twitter?"

"It happens to boys, too."

Sobering, I scroll through the Twitter profile. I keep having to hand her back the phone when my big fingers accidentally touch an advertisement and a whole new page loads up. She shakes her head at me every time.

As I read, my chest rises and falls with shallow breaths. Maybe it's a hoax. There's no way an entire high school administration *and* police department could legally ignore something like this.

Then again, everyone ignored Lucy.

Even my opinionated Olivia kept her story to herself, for fear no one would believe her.

I glance over at her. "Is this for real?"

She stares at me with mascara-smudged eyes. "Scroll to the bottom. That's the beginning."

"Why is the beginning on the bottom?"

She shakes her head at me.

I scroll through dozens of tweets until I get to the bottom. The beginning.

@RapedAtUSAFootball: I was a football player at Naugy High. I was raped at our hotel during a clinic last winter.

I scroll through the thread, my eyes scanning across line after line of text.

@RapedAtUSAFootball: There were several parents chaperoning. Coach and assistant coach. None of them took my complaints seriously.

@RapedAtUSAFootball: The first person I told was Coach. He told me to stop being so dramatic.

@RapedAtUSAFootball: I could barely walk. No one called my mom. I had to call her myself.

I look away from the screen. "Are you sure this is legit?" I ask Olivia.

"He's friends with Cierra, and told her," she says. "Cierra told Esther and Donny, and Esther pulled me aside at the Sip and See. The school's keeping it hush-hush," she says, fresh tears—tinged with black—gliding down her porcelain skin. "This really happened, and no one is doing anything."

I think of Lucy, imagine how different things might be if someone had done something sooner. If I hadn't walked into that kitchen. My cousin would be a completely different person—or she might be dead.

My chest tightens. This boy's life is ruined. Sports are supposed to be an adventure for kids, a way to get out of their heads and into their bodies. A ticket to a better life, sometimes. I hand Olivia's phone back to her.

There's no point in saying something banal like *That's horrible.* "What do you want to do?" I ask, meeting her eyes.

"I'm glad you asked." She wipes away her tears. "Esther wants us and Donny to take it to the table."

Stixx re-enters, another tower of diapers balanced in his arms. "Take what to the table?" he asks, setting it down.

Olivia passes her phone to him. He doesn't need Twitter 101. He scrolls through and reads, his pale eyes darkening. "This happened here?"

She nods.

"He's Naugy—he's one of us," Stixx says.

Olivia rests her head on my chest, and I kiss her temple. "They *raped* him," she says. "No one is doing anything about it."

My fists curl. It reminds me too much of Lucy. Another man who won't stay dead flashes through my mind, his face too much like mine. My stomach clenches.

"He's all alone," Olivia mumbles into my chest.

Even with my eyes open, I can see back to Lucy in that kitchen. Part of me will always see her as that little girl huddled in that corner. Part of me will always hear her screams. I've never regretted what I did.

I only wish I did it sooner.

I don't have words to comfort Olivia. In this world, there aren't many promises of justice.

"I'll back you up at the table," Stixx says.

I cup Olivia's chin and lift her head so that our eyes are level. "Let's do it."

She presses her lips to mine. They're as cold as ice.

5

OLIVIA

I spend the night holed up in my room, Cliff by my side, Bryce on FaceTime. He sits in his bedroom at home, band posters I don't recognize on the walls.

"Where's your mom, Bryce?" I ask, slightly more sober than when Cliff found me.

"At work. She works doubles at Cara's," he says, naming the diner we frequent.

I take a deep breath. "This is going to be hard, but I need you to tell me *who* hurt you. I need names."

Cliff squeezes my hand.

Bryce's blue eyes sharpen. "It's not that it's hard at all . . . It's just that two of them graduated before I started playing. Alex and Kyle graduated in June. I don't remember the other two guys' names."

I scribble them down on a notepad.

"Would you recognize them if you saw them?" Cliff asks.

Bryce switches to screenshare and scrolls through Instagram. "They're on Insta but their usernames aren't their names." He pulls up profiles and pictures, and I jot down usernames while etching their faces into my brain.

"How old are they?"

"Eighteen, nineteen," he says. "Can you help or what? My mom's gonna be home any minute. She doesn't know I'm talking to you. Cierra said I should . . . keep this secret."

"She's right. Listen, Bryce, we have a friend at the police department." Sort of. Finn doesn't know that I killed his brother. "My club has to vote on this," I prepare him. "If they say no . . ."

The last time I broke protocol, Ravage made me a full member, with a stern warning to never pull that shit again.

"My hands are tied," I finish.

Desolation flashes in his eyes, and I can't take it.

"I'll do whatever I can," I tell him. "I'm also a social worker."

He rolls his eyes at me, and I can't blame him. "My mom's home. Gotta go." He disconnects the call without a goodbye.

I turn to Cliff. "I don't wanna make promises I can't keep." I search his eyes for comfort, but there's none to be found.

"I think I should sit this one out," he says, looking away.

"What do you mean?"

"Last time I saved a kid, I scarred her for life."

"You also saved Esther's little sisters," I remind him. "They're not scarred. They're telling their friends to come to us with their problems."

At least this town's thinking of my club in a positive light.

"That was mostly you," he reminds me.

"If we do this the right way—follow club protocol, go to Finn —no one will be traumatized and no one will end up in prison." I grin. "We won't even have to bury any bodies."

He snorts softly. "You okay? This is some heavy shit."

"We've always got heavy shit." I peer at him. "Are *you* okay?"

He nods, chasing the clouds from his eyes. There are a lot of things we avoid talking about. I know being back here is all he wants, but there are ghosts everywhere—for both of us.

❧

SUNDAYS ARE FOR SLEEPING IN, throwing my hair up in a messy bun, and dragging my ass into Church. At least, they usually are. This Sunday is different. I get up early, wash my hair, and organize my materials for Church. I wish I had more than just Bryce's story and some Instagram pictures. Luckily, the MC has a really good hacker. If I can convince the club to take this on, we'll have it cracked open and handled within a couple of weeks.

Still, I take a deep breath and slide my hands over the copies of @RapedAtUSAFootball's tweets.

Lucy pads into the kitchen, Bunny wrapped snugly to her chest. *Her* hair is in a messy bun. I sigh, just a little bit jealous.

Her eyes flick down to the stack of paper I'm holding. She hands me a manila folder. "Perks of having a teacher for a sister: endless office supplies," she says, pouring a mug of coffee. She holds the carafe up toward me.

I shake my head. "I'm so wired, I've got that nervous buzz now." I probably shouldn't have told her what we were doing, but I didn't have a better story for why I used her printer to print out a bunch of boys' pics.

"Cliff's backing you, right? And Stixx?" The corners of her mouth curl up, then fall back into place so quickly, I might've imagined it.

"Donny, too." I pluck a cigarette from my pack and stick it between my lips.

"Livvie," Lucy warns.

"Relax, I'm not lighting it."

"You really should quit. Bunny's gonna need her Auntie around for a long time."

"Don't worry," I assure her. "I'm too bitter to die any time soon. All this rage keeps my blood pumping."

Lucy rocks Bunny while humming a Tool song. I take a shaky breath. I'm happy for her. I really am. Still, every time I look at the two of them, my eyes burn and my throat tightens.

I have a few good memories of my mother, Bree: dancing to

Prince in the living room, listening to her read me the Shannara books, eating pancakes on the Sundays she was actually around. Sometimes she left for days and the only meals I had were the hot lunches at school, *if* I could scrounge up the change.

I have fewer good memories of Lucy's mom, Nora, but even less bad memories. She never made me feel unwanted, but didn't exactly make me feel loved, either. I was more of a knickknack in the living room that needed to be dusted every so often.

Lucy is her real daughter. By being with Cliff, I've incinerated any chance of her ever accepting me.

Lucy is a completely different mother. She's both the mom I never had and the mom I could never be. When she looks at Bunny, her eyes soften. She's got this whole changeling thing going on. One minute she's laughing at some raunchy joke I've made, and the next she's staring down at that baby like there's nothing else in this world.

Motherhood suits Lucy. Bunny is her everything. It should be beautiful to watch, but instead it hurts.

Almost as much as it hurts to watch Cliff with Bunny.

I know that all he wants is a family. I thought her birth would fill that hole for him. Instead, Bunny has only widened it into a tunnel straight out of Olivia-ville. Eventually, he's going to get bored and he'll find a woman who will birth as many babies as he wants. Someone like Trish or Pru—beautiful and warm. Not someone like me.

Her lips flatten into an unconvinced smile. "Maybe you should leave this alone." She gestures to the folder.

"Someone's gotta help this kid."

"I just worry," she says slowly, "that you're using this as a distraction from Bree being MIA."

I look away. "I should get going."

"Livvie . . ." She reaches across the table and squeezes my hand. "She'll be back. They both will."

Lucy knows me too well. I can't fake my way out of this. I don't want to talk about it, either. I stand. "I've really gotta go." I hurry out the door, shoving the folder into my backpack purse. It doesn't exactly fit, and the whole thing bends. Scowling, I kick the Street Glide into gear, then tear out of the driveway.

Cliff, Donny, and Stixx are on my side. That's four votes, at least. I just have to convince the six other guys. It'd be seven if Mercy had stayed instead of chasing after Bree.

I pull into The Wet Mermaid's parking lot right behind Vaughn. He slides into a spot and takes his helmet off before I've even picked out my own spot. As I pull in between him and Cliff's bike, he grins.

"You look nice."

"Thanks," I say cautiously.

"More like a social worker than a biker," he continues with a smirk, "but it looks good on you."

I hop off the Street Glide and swat at him. "I was born a biker. Can you say the same?"

He lifts his eyebrows in a "Got me" face. "You know I love you, Olivia."

"I'm probably the only girl you ever say that to. Besides your mother." I turn toward the club, Vaughn falling in behind me.

"Do you all really think I have no life?" he mutters.

As we reach the entrance, some guy approaches us, his baseball hat askew, facial features obscured by a scruffy beard.

"We're not open yet, buddy," I say.

"But I can put some coffee on," Vaughn adds.

The man straightens, facing me, blue eyes bright under messy red hair.

Bile crawls up my throat.

My hand goes to the small of my back, where I normally keep my gun. My nails only scrape chiffon underneath my cut. I left the gun at home.

The morning light catches his eyes, bringing the rest of his face into view.

I swallow the nausea. It's only his brother. Greg is dead.

"Finn," I rasp.

"Just the gal I wanted to see," he says.

Vaughn glances from me to my rapist's brother. "Olivia?"

"It's cool. He's a . . . friend."

Giving me a nod, Vaughn heads in. "I'll be right inside. We'll *all* be right inside."

I wave him on, then turn back to Finn. He's wearing a stained Naugatuck PD tee—probably had it since he was a cadet or whatever—and sweatpants. Actual '90s style sweats, complete with the agonizing elastic band on the bottom of each leg. I wrinkle my nose. "What are you doing here?"

He steps closer to me. On reflex, I step back.

"I have some questions for you," he says, shoving his hands into his pockets. "Off the record."

"Okay." I take a deep breath, wait. I knew eventually he'd have questions. When I called him the night I killed his brother Greg, he didn't know that Greg lured me there. He just knew our history, that Greg raped me when we were dating, and he knew that Greg was stalking me. When I asked him to call off the police that were surrounding Greg's house, he thought he was being a good ally.

"Why were you at my brother's house? I just want to know. Was he drunk? I'd told him a million times to update his smoke detectors."

I relax—only a little. "I just wanted to put the past to bed." As I say the words, I see Greg motionless in that bed, his eyes cold and staring into nothing.

"How did he seem when you left?" His eyes—so like Greg's—search mine.

I relax even more. This is a grieving brother who just wants closure. He's not here as a cop.

"Not much," I tell him. It's the truth. Dead men don't talk. "I wasn't expecting an apology or anything. I just told him that we were over, and that I wanted him to respect that." The lies flow one after another.

"He and Cami were having problems," he says, referring to Greg's wife. "She'd just left him." He peers at me. "He had to have been drunk, to be so careless. The fire department said the place went up so quick, there wasn't much left. I told him that house was too old. He should've upgraded his doors."

I shrug. "He wasn't drinking while I was there. I'm really sorry, Finn. I know you loved him."

He bows his head. "Yeah. I did love him, but I guess karma caught up with him. Thanks for your time." He turns and walks to an older model Subaru, and then he's gone.

Hands and knees shaking, I smooth my cut, my shirt, my slacks. I walk into the bar and grab a shot glass and a bottle of vodka. No—not vodka. I pour a shot of whiskey instead.

For a moment there, I thought he was going to arrest me. Looks like he's still leaving me out of the investigation—not that there was much to investigate. My nose wrinkles as I down the shot.

If there's one thing Stixx is good at, it's arson.

"It's like I was never there," I whisper to myself as I set down the shot glass. I've got the whole club to back me up. Stixx's fire destroyed all of the evidence. The only thing that ties me to the house that night is the phone call I made to Finn.

As long as I've got Finn on my good side, that night will soon be a blurry memory for both of us.

I didn't think things through enough that night. I let fear and fury take over. I won't make that mistake again.

Straightening, I turn toward the Chapel.

This time, I'll be careful.

That is, if I can convince the club to help this kid.

6

CLIFF

I drum my fingers on the polished wood of the Chapel table. The seat to my right remains empty. "I thought you said she was right behind you?" I ask, turning to Vaughn.

He shrugs, chomping on gum like his life depends on it. "She was talking to some guy. She said he was a friend, but I don't know, dude. He was wearing a Naugy PD shirt."

I press my palms into the wood, ready to stand, when the oak double doors open. Olivia strides through holding her head high, her dainty chin raised. Her eyes are another story. Cold fury blazes in them. Must've been some guy. I light a cigarette, watching her as she takes her seat next to me. "What happened?" I stage whisper.

Ravage bangs the gavel, calling the meeting to order. "Now that we're all here," he says, eyeing Olivia, "let's get started. Beer Can, where're we at with the Bastard Brothers ride?"

Our Sergeant-at-Arms lifts his head, his caterpillar eyebrows knitting together. "I've texted their SAA. Nothing yet."

"Bastard Brothers ride?" Abraham echoes. He sets his muscular arms on the table, his long blond hair trailing on the polished wood. He gives me a sidelong glance.

Ravage twirls the gavel between two thick fingers. "The Bastard Brothers supported us during our benefit for Shannon's Haven. I want to extend that olive branch."

I exhale a stream of smoke. "Even though they betrayed us?"

Everyone at the table freezes, all eyes trained on me.

"Come on, I know my history. They were against taking Bastard to the river. When I killed him, they split. We're really gonna kiss and make up?" I look each of my brothers in the eye.

Olivia lights a cigarette, shaking her head. "They supported a rapist," she says, exhaling. "We're really gonna forgive that?"

Ravage's ice blue eyes meet mine. "We're not forgiving anything. Mercy wants—"

"How do you even know what Mercy wants?" Olivia interrupts. "He isn't here. Is he?" Underneath the table, her leg bounces against mine. She's winding up.

I hold up a hand. "Everyone just hold on, here."

"What about you, Beer Can?" Olivia turns to the stocky man. "I heard you're the one who packed up a bag for Mercy and got his bike ready. Which means you knew he was leaving."

"Reynolds," Ravage warns.

"Don't *Reynolds* me," she continues. "I'm done with the secrets. This should've been a vote."

The men around the table mutter. She has a point. Still, even I know she can't talk to Ravage like that. I reach for her arm, hoping my touch will calm her, but she stands before I can reach her.

"We *vote* on things. No more of this whispering in the dark bullshit. We're a club. We should be all in, together."

Ravage leans back in his seat. The light from the window catches the grays in his otherwise pitch-black hair. "You done?"

Olivia's always outspoken, but she's never talked to Ravage like this. I don't know what's gotten into her, but I back her up before he kicks her out of Church. Or worse. "She's got a point, Pres. We should vote on this," I say, going for diplomacy.

"Agreed," Abraham rumbles, folding his thick arms across his chest. "I want a vote."

Ravage holds up his hands. "Fine. We'll vote now. I say yea."

Olivia slaps her palms onto the table. "You didn't answer my question, Beer Can. You knew Mercy wasn't staying?" Her voice shakes.

I stand, too, touching the small of her back. "Let's get some air."

She yanks away from me. "No!" She turns back to Beer Can. "Answer me. You knew?"

He nods. "He called me to let us know he was getting out. He asked me to pack a bag. He wanted to find your mother, Olivia. None of us had heard from Bree—"

"Fuck Bree." Tears drip from her eyes onto the table. "And fuck you." She tosses a folder onto the table, and storms out, slamming the doors behind her.

"She doesn't mean it," I tell Beer Can.

"Oh, she does." He sighs, running a hand over his face. "I probably deserve it."

"She was only a Prospect," Ravage says. "She wasn't privy."

I turn to Ravage. "She's your goddaughter."

"Which does not give her the right to do whatever the fuck she wants," he growls.

"I know that. She's missing the father she always wanted. She loves you." I look them each in the eye. "She loves all of you. Can we cut her some slack?"

"Mercy's got his hands full," Ravage mutters. He sets the gavel down. "Let's table it for now. We'll vote next week. I need a ride."

I hurry outside, my brothers exiting behind me. I scan the parking lot until I find Olivia in her usual smoke spot, off to the side of the building. She leans against the hot brick, a cigarette dangling between her lips.

"That's not what we planned," I say, leaning next to her.

The corners of her mouth twitch. "Nope."

"Wanna tell me what happened?" I smooth back a strand of hair that's fallen out of her careful bun.

"I ran into Finn outside." She shrugs. "I tried to shove it down, not think about it. Instead, I did that thing where I start a fight." Her lips close around the filter of the cigarette.

I want to wrap my arms around her, but right now, I think she needs me to just listen. "What does your therapist say?"

She scowls. "It's internal chaos. Or external chaos. Whatever. When I feel mixed up inside, I lash out at the people around me and create something else to focus on."

Not for the first time, I'm amazed that she's even able to keep it together at all. Not after what she's been through. "I think you might be a little mad at them, though."

"I am." She sighs, deflating. "Are they voting me out?"

"The opposite. We're going to vote on the Bastard Brothers thing."

"And how do *you* feel about it?" She turns knowing brown eyes on me.

I lean against the wall, too, and light another cigarette. "I don't like it. The Bastard Brothers backed up my father, Olivia. Maybe they didn't believe he was capable of such a thing—I don't know. Lucy suffered for it."

It still burns me from the inside out, how my club could be so fixed on following their rules back then, but now it depends on what we're voting on.

She grips my bicep, running her thumb back and forth in a soothing tempo. "I'll vote nay, too."

"Maybe Ravage is right, though. Maybe it's time to let shit go, look to the future. They did ride with us." I shake my head, clearing the whirlwind. In some ways, I know how Olivia feels. The smallest things take me back to that night. Back to my time in Lewisburg. I need to change the subject; if I think about it too long, it'll consume me. "You wanna talk about Finn?"

Her lips part. She freezes for just a moment, but it's enough.

The roar of eight motorcycles drowns out the space, and her lips purse. Our brothers pour out of the parking lot. I watch them go, wishing I was with them. I could use a ride right now, clear my head.

"You can go, you know," she says when silence falls again.

"Nah." I wrap an arm around her and draw her in. "Wanna get breakfast at Cara's?"

"Is there any other place to get breakfast?" She stands on her tiptoes and kisses the stubble on my jawline. "Feed me, Seymour."

I head to our bikes with Olivia tucked under my arm. I don't even bother asking if she's riding with me. When we reach the bikes, we break apart, but she pulls me in for one more kiss.

"Be safe," she whispers against my lips. It's the closest to an *I love you* I'll ever get. I need to hear it so badly, to know I'm not alone in this. I've got to know that I didn't just trick myself into falling for the first woman I saw outside the pen, that the way I feel isn't all in my head. I let her go ahead of me, wondering how long it'll be before she's out of my sight forever.

7

OLIVIA

As soon as I get out of work on Monday, I head over to The Wet Mermaid. I don't have a shift tonight, but I do need to talk to Ravage. Apologize, too, I guess. I don't do apologies. Maybe it's because the people who hurt me never apologized. I'm trying to break the cycle, though, even if only for myself. So I swing my leg over the Street Glide, straighten my lame ass social worker uniform of buttons and collars, and walk in.

"There she is!" Shannon shouts from behind the bar.

I can't help but grin as I make my way over. "Hey there, stranger." I set my bag down and plant my elbows on the bar. In the three years since Shannon started her shelter for survivors, I've barely seen her. Running a non-profit is a full-time job, and then some.

"I never see you anymore." She blows blonde bangs out of her face, brown eyes crinkling.

"You're never here!" I glance around. "Why *are* you here?"

"Trish is out sick, and I didn't want to call you in. Besides, I kinda missed this." She pours a beer for the man down at the other end.

"Really," I deadpan.

"Really." She carries the beer over to him, then saunters her way back. "How are you holding up?"

I shrug. "Waiting on Bree is my superpower."

"You know, I hired and trained her, too." She slides me a glass of more ice than water.

I take a sip. I don't want to talk about Bree, and I'm dying to talk about Bree. It's the tug o' war I've been playing my whole life.

"You here to see Ravage?" Shannon asks.

I wince. "You heard?"

"Olivia, Ravage tells me everything."

"Are you really here to fill in, or are you here for damage control?"

"Yes." She flashes me an angelic smile. "He's in the office."

I glance at the door. "Alone?"

"Mark is at a Chamber of Commerce meeting," she says, referring to our Treasurer.

"Fun." I grab my bag. "How mad is Ravage?"

"Olivia . . ." She sucks in her cheeks. "We're your godparents. We're never mad for long."

"My godparents?" Now that I know Mercy's my father, it makes sense that his sister's my godmother. I think of all the times Bree disappeared, of all the foster homes I hopped from. I try to imagine growing up with Ravage and Shannon instead. "Can I ask you a question?"

She tilts her head at me. "Since when have *you* been shy?"

I swallow. "Why didn't you two foster me?"

"Oh," she says. She takes a deep breath. "Sit. I'll pour you a shot."

"I'm good. I just . . . I just need to know. Why didn't anyone want me?"

"We couldn't," she says sadly. "Not with Ravage's record. We could've gotten married—there's a loophole in Connecticut—but I didn't want to. I . . . had my reasons, at the time."

I glance at her ring and wonder what made her change her mind. "You and me both," I say instead.

"You used to stay with us a lot, though, before DCF stepped in," she says.

My eyebrows knit together. "Why don't I remember that?"

She shrugs. "You were so little, Olivia. Memory is funny."

"I figured it was Mercy who taught me how to ride and took me out shooting. Was that Ravage?"

"Sure was. Beer Can, too." Her sad smile returns. "If Bree worked with us instead of running away, DCF probably wouldn't have gotten involved and the state would've been none the wiser. We could've made it work."

"Well," I say, turning toward the office, "it worked out anyway. And, shocker, Bree is still out of the picture."

"Don't count her out," Shannon calls after me. "Bree always loved you. I never questioned that."

I did. I don't say so. I give her a smile over my shoulder, then knock on the office door.

"Come in," Ravage calls.

Pushing the door open, I step inside. "Hey."

He does a double take. "Hey." He straightens in his seat, the light catching the grays in his hair as he moves. Shannon once told me he dyes it black. Looks like he's been letting it go gray.

I sit across from him, studying the lines in his face, the crow's feet at his eyes. My godfather. I sigh. "I'm sorry about yesterday."

"It's okay." The ice in his eyes softens. "Listen, Donny and Stixx gave me the rundown. I told Vaughn to help you dig into things."

"Really? Even after the fit I threw?" My cheeks blaze with embarrassment.

"It's hard to stay mad at you."

"Is that why you made me a member?" I joke.

"Partially." He stretches out an arm and closes the door. "It was always the plan: you and Cliff, inheriting the club. Bastard and Bree really fucked that up."

I stiffen. How can Shannon love my mother so much, while Ravage clearly hates her?

"I don't mean that Bree is anything like Bastard," he says. "I just mean nothing is the way we planned." He lights a cigarette. "I've got a dead President, a split club, and two kids who really should still be Prospects."

I light up a cigarette, too, mostly to cover the awkward pause.

"Cliff's mother wanted him to have nothing to do with the club," he continues. "Your mother wanted nothing to do with us. Cliff went to jail, and then your father went with him, then DCF took you . . . But I guess it all worked out the way it was supposed to."

I take a long drag. Ravage has *never* opened up this much to me. Usually he drops like two sentences and then keeps being surly. I don't want to say anything, don't want to break this spell. So I listen.

"We're a family, Olivia—no matter how much time we spent apart. That includes the Bastard Brothers. I can't change the past, but I can make a better now. I want your father to come back to a better now."

I swivel in my chair. "You know these guys better than I do," I say, choosing my words carefully, "but aren't you worried they'll want revenge? They hate Cliff."

"The Bastard Brothers? I'm not gonna let anything happen to Cliff." He lifts his chin, eyes regarding me with a tenderness I've never seen. "You have to trust me."

"It's not you I don't trust," I say, taking a drag. "What if they're still holding a grudge?"

"Olivia, it's been twenty years. It's time to let shit go. They thought they were doing the right thing, backing their President." He lifts an eyebrow at me.

"I can't vote yea."

"I know." He sighs. "They weren't protecting what Bastard did to Lucy, you know. They really thought Mercy and I were making a grab for the gavel. In some ways, Cliff made things worse. Don't get me wrong," he says quickly. "Bastard needed to go. Cliff did what he had to do. But things were complicated. We needed more time. If Ruth hadn't kept Cliff from the club, he would've been in the loop. I want to clear the air for once and for all. Your children don't need to inherit an enemy."

I scoff. "I'm not having kids."

He holds up his hands. "All's I'm saying is, someday this club is going to be yours and Cliff's, and hopefully someone else's after you're dead and gone, too. Maybe your sister's kid."

"Over her dead body," I say with a laugh.

Ravage chuckles. "But you get my point, right?"

"I do," I say with a sigh. I look down at the hand holding my cigarette. "I'll try to keep my outbursts to a minimum."

"No," he says. "I don't want you to change. You're a warrior. You fight for all survivors. The world needs that. But—" He holds up a hand before I can say anything. "Next time, *talk* to me, the way we're sitting here, talking now."

I nod.

"We're a family. You can always talk to me." His eyes meet mine. "If they hadn't taken you, maybe we'd have a better relationship. I hope we can still have that, and I hope you'll have that with your father. Bree, too." He shrugs. "I don't love her choices, but I love Mercy, and I love you."

Tears sting my eyes. "Jesus, Ravage. Don't get all soft on me."

"Shannon will tell you there's a softie under all this leather." He jabs a thumb into his cut, the leather creaking. "If things had been different—if I hadn't fucked up—we'd have our own kids. You're the closest thing to a daughter we'll ever have."

"*You* taught me how to ride," I whisper.

"And shoot." He grins. "DCF would *love* that, a biker taking a five-year-old into the woods to hit cans."

I grin back. "Well, it paid off." I think of the way the bullet slammed into Eli's forehead, how he hit the floor. The smile slides from my face.

"Hey," he says, reaching across the desk. He cups my chin and lifts my face so that our eyes meet. "Sometimes, it's them or you. Don't let it be you."

I press my lips together to staunch the flood of tears.

"That son of a bitch got what he deserved. Both of them. I know you're having trouble with that. That's the Mercy half of you. But the Bree half of you wanted to live."

My eyes widen. "Bree killed someone?"

He snorts. "Hell no. Her weapon is that pair of legs, walking away from everybody who loves her. We're the ones always cleaning up her messes. My point is, you've got a good heart, Olivia, and you're a survivor. Remember that: Don't let it be you."

"Eli's got a family looking for him," I blurt, "and Finn might figure out I killed Greg."

"They won't find him," he counters. "And Finn can think whatever the fuck he wants."

"He might make things difficult for us. I'm sorry, Ravage. I didn't think—"

He holds up a hand. "When it comes to them or you, I don't want you to think. I want you to live. We'll take care of the rest. Just . . . maybe ease up on us for a while. We don't want to run out of places to hide the bodies." He grins, and I grin back.

For the first time in my life, I get an idea of how it'd feel to actually have a father. If things had been different, maybe I would've had conversations like this with Mercy. Ravage is right. Things can still be different.

"I'm still voting nay," I say, blinking away tears.

"I expect it. You've got your own mind. You should always stand for what you believe in." He pats my hand. "Now get out of here. I gave you the night off. Go live."

~

GO LIVE.

Ravage's words echo in my head as my phone rings in my hand, Cliff's name on the screen. Usually on a Monday night, we'd grab G's Burgers and hang out at Lucy's, maybe go for a ride, swing by his apartment for a quickie. Not tonight.

Tonight I stand on a tidy front walk, struggling to reconcile this house that looks straight out of a magazine with Vaughn, who so doesn't fit the image, with his messy hair, constant smirk, and all black attire.

It just gives me one more thing to bust his balls about.

Ignoring Cliff's call, I pull up Vaughn's number and call him.

"I'm outside. I think."

"I see you. I'll be right out." He hangs up, leaving me searching for cameras. I spot one tucked under the gutter and give it a tiny wave. A moment later, he cracks the front door open and waves me in. "Just be quiet."

My heart tells me Vaughn would never hurt me, but experience taught me paranoia.

"Why all the secrecy?"

"Just come on."

I follow him into a living room lit only by a muted TV. He rushes me through and I catch only a glimpse of a woman sleeping in a recliner. Reaching the door to the basement, I hesitate. "You first."

He nods and ducks as he passes under the doorway. It's an older house, made for smaller people. Even I have to watch my head as I near the bottom of the stairs and pass what I can only describe as a hanging wall with a lightbulb that's too close to my hair for comfort. The basement smells like laundry, though, and it's well lit and clean, aside from the Red Bulls and packs of Juicy Fruit scattered all over the L-shaped desks.

"I'm trying to quit smoking," he explains.

"So this is your lair." I wriggle out of my jacket and hang it over the back of a chair.

"Sorry about the secrecy. My mom . . . She needs her rest." A pained look crosses his features before he replaces it with a grin. "So what can I do for you?"

"Nothing too illegal. Just hack into the police department and get a copy of a report that was filed . . ." I check the notes in my phone. "Back in February."

"That's my specialty."

"That's what Ravage said." I watch him for a beat. "I always wondered what it is you do for the club."

"Now you know." He stretches his arms over his head, brushing the ceiling of the basement. Then he plops into a chair in front of more monitors, keyboards, and laptops than I'd know what to do with. "Just watch."

My phone buzzes with a text as he types.

Cliff: Whatcha doing?

"Is that lover boy?" Vaughn asks.

"Yeah." I send him a reply, barely looking at the screen. Even though this is work, I feel a little bad. I don't want Cliff to think I'm not interested. I'm very interested. I freaked out a little this summer but I want to give this my best shot.

I just don't know how to.

Olivia: Just hanging out in Vaughn's basement while he does some digging for me.

I put my phone on silent.

"You can sit, you know."

"Right." I take the chair next to him. "So . . . your mom's sick?"

He nods, fingers flying over the keyboard. "I'm gonna run a script that'll log us into the PD's internal system."

I nod like I know what he's talking about. This must be how Cliff feels.

"I don't wanna pry, so tell me to fuck off if you don't wanna talk about it. What's going on with your mom?"

He hesitates, fingers hovering. "Cancer," he says finally.

"Fuck. I'm sorry." I give his shoulder a quick squeeze. "Anything I can do to help?"

"Nah. Thanks for asking, though."

I spot several bottles of white pills among the clutter. It's hard to make out the labels, but I put two and two together. "Is *this* how the club gets their Percs?"

"Too many questions, Olivia," he says.

I hold up my hands. "Hey, I'm just as incriminated, sliding all those baggies across the bar. I just never realized . . . Is she gonna be okay?"

"I hope so," he says softly. He reaches for a Red Bull, finds it empty, then sets it down.

I change the subject. "All right, walk me through the scripts."

He snorts. "A magician never reveals his secrets." He tosses me a cocky wink, and my heart swells with love for this guy who's like the little brother I never had. He sits back, watching the screen flash as usernames and passwords are automatically tried in the login. One after another sends up a red INVALID USER-NAME OR PASSWORD warning, and he rocks back in his seat, calm as fuck while I practically twitch for something to *do*.

I think of Bryce, chased out of school by the very people who were supposed to protect him.

"Bingo," Vaughn says.

I lean forward. He clicks around, muttering to himself. A second later, a PDF appears on the screen.

"Good, good, here we go." He scrolls down through scrawled notes with sections blacked out. He frowns. "The victim's name is censored. So are the suspects' names."

"The fuck? Where's the original?"

"Good question." He clicks around the internal website some more, coming to a bold red warning that tells us this user doesn't have clearance.

"They buried it," I say.

"Seems so." He knots his hands behind his head and tips back in his chair. "What do you want to do?"

I skim through the handwritten report. The officer used words like *allegedly* and *claims*, yet there's an attached medical report describing the vicim's injuries. Every name is blacked out.

"This should be enough to get the votes we need," I say. "Can you print that?"

"Piece of cake." He presses a couple keys and a printer tucked under the desk spits out copies. When they're done, he hands the warm stack to me.

"Thanks, V. I owe you one."

"Pleasure's all mine. This is the best Monday night I've had in a while."

I think of his mom out cold from painkillers in the living room, and nod. "Let me know if you ever need anything."

"I appreciate it," he says.

He walks me out, waiting on the stoop while I call Cliff. There's no answer.

"Guess he's already asleep," I say, swinging onto the Street Glide.

Vaughn starts to say something, then lifts his hand in a wave instead. "Ride safely."

I start the bike and ride home, but the engine isn't loud enough to drown out my insecurities.

8

CLIFF

I roam town, my thoughts drowned out by the sound of the Screamin' Eagle. Ruth's been gone a long time, yet more and more I wish she were here so I could talk to her. She'd give me advice, help me cope with being in love with someone who doesn't love me back.

I know Olivia cares for me, because she wouldn't have taken me back this summer if she didn't. Everything she's been through made her guarded, cautious. Brick by brick I take down her walls, burying myself in the process.

How did Ruth stay with Bastard for so long when he treated her like nothing?

My early memories are hazy, blurred by grief. She was a good mom, giving me a stable foundation. I now know she kept me as far from the club as possible, because she must've had at least an idea of what Bastard and the rest of them got up to. Even back then, they weren't exactly ninety-nine-percenters.

But why did she stay?

She must've loved him, and that blind loyalty ultimately cost her life.

I find myself at the cemetery, kneeling at her headstone and brushing away leaves that have already fallen. I haven't been here nearly enough.

"Cliff?" Shannon approaches the headstone, her phone shining a path in front of her.

"Hey." I go to stand, but she shakes a hand at me.

"No, stay." She sets down a bouquet of sunflowers and sits beside me. "I like coming here at night, too."

"It's peaceful." I tip my head back, gazing up at the stars.

"It is."

"I didn't realize you knew my mom." I stick an unlit cigarette in the corner of my mouth.

"Not very well. She kept her distance."

I nod, still watching the stars blinking back at me. "You knew Bastard pretty well, though?"

"Mostly from what Mercy told me. Women weren't really allowed near the club back then."

I snort. "Of course not. Bastard was a pathetic excuse for a man."

"He wasn't always that way," she says carefully.

"What do you mean?" I light the cigarette and face her.

"My brother served with him in the Gulf War."

"Don't make excuses for him." I flick ash into the grass. "Everybody comes back from war fucked up. Not everybody rapes little girls."

"You're right." She smoothes her long skirt. "Mercy and Bastard go way back, even before the war. They were tight. Bastard loved your mother, Cliff. I think she kept some of the darkness at bay for him."

"Darkness?"

She sighs. "Have you ever heard the phrase 'hurt people hurt people'? Bastard was sexually abused as a child."

I tug at my beard. "By who?"

"An uncle."

I rock back on my heels. "Jesus."

"Yeah." She exhales. "I think he struggled for a long time, and eventually he became the monster he always feared."

"Doesn't change how I feel about him." My thoughts churn, fury roiling with grief. "He had something to do with Ruth's death. I know it."

"Maybe." She leans back onto her elbows, her blonde hair curling around her arms. "I've always had a hard time believing Ruth killed herself. I wonder if Bastard was truly responsible, though. He loved your mother," she says again, quickly. "He was broken, and he wasn't an attentive father, but he loved her. Most of the men stayed at the clubhouse, fucking around on their women—Todd included. Never Bastard, though. He went home to you and Ruth every night."

"I wish I could talk to her," I confess. It's the first time I've admitted it out loud. My chest hitches and I take a long drag to compose myself.

It's weird to hear these things, to see the man I hate the most in a different light. Knowing that he was abused doesn't excuse the things he did, but it explains it.

Hurt people hurt people. The cycle continues—unless we do something about it.

I want the chance to break the cycle. I want to be a good husband, and a good father. I want to pour the love my mother gave me into my own legacy. I want to be more than the anger trapped in my hands.

Shannon touches my arm. "I know I'm not your mother, but you can talk to me."

"You're the club mother," I tell her, giving her a grin.

She waits, giving me space to collect my thoughts.

I frown, circling back to something she said earlier. "Ravage fucked around on you?"

"It's why we didn't get married for so long. I couldn't forgive him for that shit."

"But he loves you."

She nods. "He does."

"Did you ever feel like he didn't love you?"

"Give me one of those," she says, pointing at my cigarette.

I light a fresh one for her and pass it over. We smoke in silence for a several minutes, each lost in our own thoughts.

"You know," she says, "even when he was blatantly cheating on me, I knew he loved me. He got caught up in the life, in the freedom of the road. He wanted it all, and no one can have it all." She gives me a pointed look. "Every relationship has its problems. The strongest relationships are built on compromise, sometimes even sacrifice."

I absorb her words, not comforted or convinced.

I spent twenty years surviving day by day. There was no room for negotiation. Every hour was a cage fight, either with another man or my own mind. Days and even weeks in seg were a fight for sanity.

After twenty years of no guarantees, *I* need the words.

"Let me put it this way, Cliff," Shannon says. "If you don't get what you want, are you willing to walk away?"

My eyebrows furrow. "No."

"There's your answer."

My frown deepens. Twenty years in Lewisburg was nothing, compared to the prison of love.

9

OLIVIA

On the next Sunday, I take my seat at the table between Cliff and Stixx. The file lies open in front of me, the bullet points of what I want to say to my brothers scrawled on a Post-it. This time, I won't let my emotions get the better of me. I don't know what's wrong with me lately. Every barrier I've so carefully erected over the years has been washed away. I don't know how to rebuild.

Ravage seats himself at the head of the table, the gavel in one hand, a cigarette in his other. "Before anyone asks me, no, I haven't heard from Mercy."

I nod in appreciation. It isn't anything I wasn't expecting, but I'm grateful he understands how I'm feeling.

"Olivia, Cliff, Donny, and Stixx have something they wanna bring to the table, but first we need to vote on the Bastard Brothers situation." He clears his throat. "I know a lot of you have misgivings." His eyes sweep over both Cliff and me. "Your votes matter to me. I also think it's important that we attempt to let the past go. Our ex-brothers thought they were doing what was right at the time: protecting their President from a power play. People don't always believe what's right in front of them. I'm at a place where I'm ready to forgive them for that. But I want to hear all of your thoughts. Skid?"

Our Vice President rests both arms on the table, one covered in ugly scars from a motorcycle accident when he was a Prospect. Every time I see them, I can't help but wince.

"Bastard took me under his wing when I was a Prospect," Skid says. "I looked up to him. I loved him. We all did. That doesn't change what he was doing. I've never been more conflicted about a vote in the years I've been a member."

Donny scoffs. His badges—Enforcer and Sludge Specter—are in bad need of cleaning. Not that he'd let even Esther anywhere near his cut with some OxiClean. "Where's the conflict? Those motherfuckers betrayed us. When the shit hit the fan, they walked. There isn't any forgiveness in my heart."

Several of the men around the table grumble their agreement.

Ravage sighs. "I don't want to make any peace without all your support. We'll table this for now." His eyes meet mine.

I nod and pass the copies I've made around the table. "You're looking at a police report for a minor from town. He's a high school football player."

"Was," Stixx corrects emphatically, his eyes blazing with fury.

"Was," I agree, "right up until his mentors raped him during a conference for high school athletes." I let that sink in, then continue. "He reported it to the chaperones and his coach, but no action was taken against the mentors. He dropped out. His life is ruined. He deserves justice." I look around the table, meeting each of their eyes. "I want us to give him that justice."

Skid frowns at me. "You want us to take out a bunch of high school kids?"

I lift my chin. "They're eighteen, nineteen now. Bryce didn't know all of their names, so we need to do some more digging."

"We're not doing anything without due diligence," Ravage says. "Vaughn, can you get deeper into the police system?"

Vaughn grins, cradling the back of his head with folded arms. "It's a challenge but I'm up for it."

"We'll go from there." Ravage's eyes meet mine. "Fair?"

I nod.

"All right," Ravage says. "So it's decided: We'll let the Bastard Brothers be, Olivia and Vaughn will dig into the PD's progress with this case." He bangs the gavel and releases it from his grip. "Let's get the fuck out of here. It's a beautiful day for a ride."

I relax into my seat. I should've known better than to doubt them, that all of them would have my back. I finally have the family I've always longed for. Maybe it doesn't matter if Mercy and Bree never come back.

Maybe everyone I need is right here.

10

CLIFF

Olivia hangs back as the rest of our brothers filter out of Church, watching me.

I glance toward the door and beyond it, the parking lot, where my Screamin' Eagle and freedom wait. When I look back at Olivia, her lashes are lowered, the tip of her nose a faint pink. "What's up?"

"I don't want to be my mother," she says softly.

"You're not Bree, babe," I assure her. "You know how I feel," I add.

"I do. And I . . ." She licks her lips.

I wait, breath stilling in my lungs. I so badly need to hear her say those words. I'll wait forever if I have to. I still need to hear them, to know I'm not in this alone.

"I don't want to lose you," she finishes. "You've been kinda distant lately."

"I'm good," I lie. I draw her into me, leaning down and kissing her. The same fire that always engulfs us, always consumes me, flickers to life as her mouth moves against mine. She curls her arms around my neck, pressing her body into mine. I open my lips, coaxing hers to part. Hers are so warm, a white-hot heat. She opens to me, my lips melding to hers, following her lead. Her tongue traces my lower lip, then eases into my mouth. I sigh, breaking the kiss. "Let's catch up to those guys before they ditch us."

"And maybe make a pit stop at your place?" Her brows lift in a suggestive wiggle.

I palm her ass, bringing her close to me so she can feel my answer. "Ditch the ditchers? I dig it."

She slips her hand into mine, and together we walk outside. The guys whistle, already straddling their hogs.

"Next baby in the family oughta be coming soon, at this rate," Mark teases.

Olivia throws him a glare.

"I dunno, Essie and I are gonna give 'em a run for their money," Donny says.

"Yeah?" I grin.

"That's how many kids now?" Olivia ribs, straddling her Street Glide.

The mood is high, so I don't let my own pain spoil it. I hook a leg over my Screamin' Eagle and strap on my helmet. As if rehearsed, all ten bikes roar to life, the sound echoing off the buildings lining the street.

"Down 63 into Watertown," Ravage calls out. He rolls out of the parking lot, and we fall in behind him.

The air is heavy with the three words I can't say, caging me, making the monster restless and agitated. If this ride doesn't soothe the fight out of me, I won't be able to contain it. Seven months out of prison and I still crave the sensation of my fists hitting flesh and bone when it all becomes too much to bear.

Olivia pulls up even with me, the two of us trailing the rest of our brothers. Out of the corner of my eye, I appreciate the wide rips in her jeans, the way the denim hugs her thighs and calves.

Through the visor of her open-face helmet, I catch a wink before she faces back to the road.

I'm so focused on Olivia that I almost miss the three bikers surrounding us. Two cage us at either side, a third behind Olivia and me. My brothers ahead seem oblivious.

I veer closer to Olivia, trying to catch her eye. Her subtle nod tells me she sees them, too. Before I can alert the others, the biker to my left speeds up toward Ravage, and I can finally read the patches on his cut.

Bastard Brothers MC.

Rage boils in my veins. I don't care what Ravage wants. These three men loved my father so much, they named their club after him. The anger fills me until it spills over and I'm no longer on 63, I'm in the kitchen standing over Bastard, my fists pummeling his face, smashing bone, blood bursting from his nose. Lucy cowers in the corner, her screams echoing off the walls.

"Cliff!" Olivia shouts, calling me back to the here and now. The rider on her right pulls up even with Ravage, but the one behind us remains. It takes everything in me not to whip my piece out and shoot them all.

Up ahead, Ravage seems unconcerned. He rides between the two Bastard Brothers, his shoulders relaxed.

I've never felt so tense on a bike before.

It's too open, and I don't like how they snuck up on us. Olivia glances at me again, and I read the same mistrust in her eyes. By backing my father, they betrayed hers, and sentenced Lucy to more abuse.

My neck and shoulders remain tight until we reach the point where Route 8 forks off from 63. The Bastard Brothers lift their hands in a wave and take the right onto the ramp, speeding out of sight.

"The fuck?" Olivia shouts.

Donny joins Ravage at the lead, his head shaking. His body language is clear, mirroring Olivia's words. Beer Can joins them, gesturing back to where they split. I can't hear a word they're saying, but I don't need to.

I don't give a fuck if they rode with us during the benefit for Shannon's Haven. The monster inside of me holds them just as responsible as Bastard. When I get my chance, they'll join him in hell.

11

OLIVIA

By the time we get to Cliff's, the rage pouring off of him is thick and alive. He swings a leg off his bike and yanks his helmet off. A second later, a lit cigarette dangles between his lips. He paces the parking lot, shoulders drawn.

I want Mercy here for an entirely different reason now. I can't believe that he would be cool with making amends with the Bastard Brothers. Especially not after today.

Explaining it aloud is intangible. It's not *what* they did. It's the way they did it.

"Ballsy motherfuckers," I mutter. I light a cigarette too and take long strides to catch up to my man. "There're only three of them?"

"I don't know." He clenches the cigarette between his teeth.

"And Ravage was just fine with it." I exhale a stream of smoke.

He lifts his chin, hard eyes staring out into the distance. "I understand why he wants to make peace. But they can't be trusted." His eyes meet mine, softening a little when our gazes meet.

"I'm right there with you." I tap ash onto the ground. "I wonder what Mercy would think of all this."

"Mercy isn't here," he growls, a low sound that sets my spine straight.

"No," I say softly. "He isn't."

He closes his eyes. "I'm sorry, babe." He puts his hands on each of my arms, rubbing my shoulders and biceps. "I know you need him." His eyes turn to stone again. "This is completely fucking upside down. I'm almost questioning whether Ravage told them where we were going to be."

I scoff. "Cliff, you sound paranoid. Ravage knows how we all feel. He wouldn't do anything to betray us. Besides, 63 is a state road. Everyone rides that route."

His head hangs. "I know. I . . . I can't see straight. Not when it comes to this."

I nod, stepping into him. I drop my cigarette to the ground and, standing on my tiptoes, wind my arms around his neck. "It's okay," I soothe.

He melts into me, the tension draining from his body. "I'm never going to be okay with this."

"You're not the only one. Donny and Beer Can looked pretty pissed, too."

"What the fuck was that Skid said today? That he looked up to Bastard. Skid and Abraham . . . I don't trust them either."

I curl my fingers around his beard, tipping his head down so that he looks into my eyes. "You can't let them wedge between us like this. Skid said what Bastard did was unforgivable. None of us condone that. As for Abraham . . . He's just a quiet dude."

"He doesn't like me."

I bite back a laugh. Cliff sounds like a middle school girl. I can't say that, though. I reach up and run my fingers through his hair. His lids lower and he shrinks to his normal size—huge, but without all the male rage hulking. "They're our family. We'll bring it up next weekend. For now," I say, tracing his jawline, "let's go upstairs."

His eyes flash with desire. Before I can take his hand and lead him like I planned, he places a palm on each cheek of my ass and lifts me into his arms. I laugh, my legs dangling in the air as he carries me to his building. He throws the door open and ducks inside, taking the stairs two at a time. Somewhere between the stairs and the landing, his lips lock onto mine, urgently seeking comfort.

I've lost count of how many times Cliff gave me comfort sex. He's done everything for me. I'd do anything for him—*almost* anything. I can definitely give him comfort sex, though.

He keeps his eyes cracked open as his tongue sweeps into my mouth, but he still misses the next step. He stumbles, holding tight to me. He actually laughs. "Sorry," he says. "You kind of make me dizzy."

Whatever was left of the walls I've so carefully built evaporates. Warmth spreads through my chest, my limbs tingly and my head floaty. I want to say something that expresses this adequately, but the words don't come. So instead I kiss him in answer, hoping that my lips will do the talking for me.

We reach his apartment, and he stops. "Keys," he breathes against my neck between kisses. "Pocket."

I reach down between us and grope for them. My hand finds something else hard. I grin. "That's one key."

"You gonna let me in?" he asks, nipping at the delicate skin of my throat, and I know he's not asking about the door.

I shift my hand over until I reach his pocket. I pluck the keys out and search for his hand. His fingers close over mine, our hands joining without sight.

"Let me in, baby," he whispers, his voice husky. My jeans cling to me, my pussy wet and aching for him. He fits the key into the lock and kicks the door open. When we're inside and hidden from the rest of the world, he carries me through the front hall. "Where?"

I consider it. We've been slowly christening his place. The bed has seen more than enough of us. So has the couch and living room floor. "Counter," I say, grinding against him.

"Bathroom or kitchen?"

His cock twitches against me. I feel it even through his Dickies and my jeans. "Don't care," I reply. "Bathroom's closer."

He steps into the bathroom, not bothering to flick on the light. Setting me down on the counter, he steps back, checking me out. "Your hair's all messy. I love it."

"My hair is always messy." I unzip his jeans and wrap my hand around him. He tips his head back, a moan vibrating in his throat and sending warm tingles down my spine. Lifting up, I give him enough space to unzip my jeans and pull them down.

He pauses at my ankles. "Boots on or off?"

If I could get out of these jeans without taking off my boots, I'd keep them on. The picture of them pressed against his ass while he fucks me is almost too perfect to pass up. But that would involve getting partially dressed again.

"Fuck that," I say, and he unzips them and slides them off. They hit the tile with a thud. I squirm out of my jeans and he takes them before I can throw them onto the floor. With quick movements, he folds them, then puts them aside.

That warm sensation floods my chest again. I've never been with anyone who cared enough to fold my clothes as he takes them off. Cliff does little things like that all the time.

"No panties, huh?" He grins, running a finger down my slit. He rests the pad of his middle finger against my clit, pressing lightly.

"I like to think positive," I tell him, and pump my hand up until I'm fisting his crown. I bring him to me, and he moves his hand.

"Ready?" He tucks a stray curl behind my ear, brown eyes adoring.

"Not quite." I need his skin on mine. With Cliff, that's always been important to me. I release him long enough to take his shirt off. He tugs mine over my head. Neither of us folds anything.

We cease—him standing, my legs wrapped around his thighs. His eyes rove from my face to my breasts, down the flat plane of my stomach, to where his tip rests against my clit. In turn, I take him in: the black ponytail curled over one shoulder, his tight nipples, the swell of his desire.

His eyes are dark and hazy, his lips parted.

I place my hands on either side of his face and bring his lips to mine. Between us, his thumbs graze my nipples. He pinches them lightly between his fingers, his mouth locked to mine. His crown rubs my clit and I shiver. I need him inside me now. I also need this moment to last forever. I draw his lower lip into my mouth, sucking and running my tongue over it.

"One of these days," I say between kisses, "I want to make out for a straight hour."

"With who?" he teases, kneading my breasts and nipples with his huge hands.

I shift, taking his crown into me in answer. "There's nobody else, baby."

I don't know when we started calling each other *baby*. I think he just let a *babe* slip one day and it stuck.

I lean back against the mirror and he slides deeper into me.

"God, I wish you could see yourself right now," he rasps.

"I don't know, my view is pretty magnificent." I lift an eyebrow at the muscle he's built up. He's always been fit—what else is there to do in prison?—but ever since he started at the factory, he must've been sneaking in lifting sessions.

He sheaths himself in me, leaning forward a little, putting pressure on my clit. "All in," he says, and I know he's not just talking about what we're doing.

I grip his ponytail in my hand. He catches my wrist and kisses my fingers. Then he slides out, stretching me, setting a slow pace. He places my hand on his shoulder and his hand over mine. I put my other hand on his other shoulder as he glides back in, filling me.

"You good on that hard-ass counter?"

I nod, eyes locked onto his. If I speak, I'll break the spell.

We move together, connected in every possible way. My limbs go slack and I spasm against him. A second later, he fills me, spilling onto the counter. Even as my muscles protest, I wish we could stay this way forever. He slides out and pulls me into his arms, setting me on the floor. I can't help but pout.

Smirking, he turns and twists the shower faucet. He holds a hand out to me, and I climb into the shower and under the warm water with him.

12

CLIFF

I n the past two days I've done my best to let the ambush on 63 go. Logic tells me Olivia is right. It's a main road. Everybody rides it. Despite that, I can't ignore the anger churning in my gut—anger born of fear. It's unreasonable, I know that. So I do the only thing I can when nothing makes sense: I bury myself in work. Which is why, on a Tuesday night, I'm bouncing for The Wet Mermaid after working a thirteen-hour shift at the machine shop.

It ain't just me.

Olivia plants herself behind the bar, burying herself in bossing around the other bartender Trish and the shot girls. Both of us are on edge, but she's doing a better job of hiding it.

"ID," I growl at a guy who looks barely old enough for high school. He blanches, fishing his wallet out of his pocket. I give him the up and down, and he drops his wallet. I can't help myself. He's barely five-foot-five. I fold my arms across my chest and eye him while he picks it up.

"I—I left it in my car," he mumbles over his shoulder as he turns and books.

I bark out a laugh. It's the first thing I've felt in days, apart from apprehension.

"That was fucked up," Beer Can says. He claps my shoulder, chuckling. "I almost wish you'd let him in so we could mess with him some more."

"What are you doing here?" It's a Tuesday."

"Erik is gonna take over for you in a sec," he says, referring to one of the non-members who works at The Wet Mermaid.

My spine stiffens. I widen my stance, boots and shoulders forming a perfect stack. "What's going on?" I look over Beer Can's head and at the bar. Olivia is gone. My pulse ticks up, blood pumping through my veins at lighting speed. "Where's Olivia?"

Beer Can pats my arm. "It's all good, brother. Just come to Church."

I push past him and stride to the Chapel, Trish and some of the cocktail waitresses giving me curious looks as I pass. Hands and legs shaking, I throw open the doors. They clatter against the wall. The only person in the room is Olivia. She doesn't even flinch. She just sits with her hands on top of the table, a cigarette between her lips, the smoke trailing a thin curl into the air. I don't stop moving until I'm at her side. I put my hands on her shoulders, and she places hers on top of mine.

Beer Can hurries in after me. "Ah, shit," he mutters. He closes the doors, then runs a hand over the scuff I've put on the wall. "Ravage is gonna be pissed."

"I'll pay for it." I lean down until my lips are at Olivia's ear. "What's going on?"

My other brothers file in, looking just as confused as I feel.

"I don't know." Her face is pale. "When was the last time we had emergency Church?"

"Look at me," Beer Can says, dropping into a seat. "It's all good."

I do a quick head count. There are only nine of us in here. "Where's Ravage?"

Olivia sucks down her cigarette, putting it out and lighting another. I light one, too. I hate to see her rattled, but I'm kind of relieved I'm not the only one who's frayed. I remain behind her, my hand linked with hers.

"Where *is* Ravage?" Vaughn echoes.

"Is this about the other day?" Donny asks.

Olivia's grip on my hand tightens. That must be it.

"Fuck," I growl. "I knew something wasn't right about that."

"You and me both, brother," Donny says.

Beer Can scoffs. "Come on, guys. Listen to your grandpa here. Everything is okay."

"Then where's Ravage?" Abraham asks.

He's got a point.

Beer Can holds up his hands. "I don't know any more than you do. I just know all's good. I *trust* my President. He told me to get you all in here and that everything was okay."

I study his face. Ever since I washed up here seven months ago, Beer Can has never steered me wrong. He's been just about the most forthcoming guy here, apart from Donny. Still, the last-minute Church has my gut in knots. This wouldn't be the first time Ravage kept us in the dark, either. *Something* is wrong.

13

OLIVIA

One minute I'm serving drunk guys who just want to see some pussy on a pole, the next I'm in Church with a bad case of the jitters. I squeeze Cliff's hand again, wishing he could just wrap me up in those big arms of his. PDA has never been my thing, though, and I'm not about to get all touchy feely in front of these guys. Not when something is so obviously wrong. As the newest and youngest River Reaper, I've got to keep my cool.

So I light a third cigarette.

We've just been sitting in this room, waiting, for twenty minutes. No one knows anything. No one knows where Ravage is. Beer Can said all he got was a text.

A fucking text.

I tap my foot against the floor, thinking. I call Ravage but there's no answer. I send him a text, my mind going off the rails.

It just reminds me of how little I can control. I took my power back from my past, but there's so little I can do about right now.

I take a long drag. I want to give Bryce more than this. I want to put hope in the space his heart was ripped from. I can't guarantee anything, but I've got to do more. I type a text to Bryce with one hand.

Olivia: How are you holding up today?

"Well, since we're all here," Vaughn says, stretching in his seat. "I got some info on the football team."

Skid clears his throat. "Let's wait for Ravage."

I scoff. "Wait for Ravage? It's been twenty minutes."

"Olivia," Beer Can soothes. He pins me with a firm but loving look from across the table. "Just trust that whatever it is, it's worth the wait."

I can't. I need to know what's happening, and I need to know now. I can't just believe that everything is fine. Why else would Ravage have yanked us from our stations, from our beds in some cases? Not for good news.

Cliff drops into the chair next to me, our hands still entwined. The only comfort here is that everyone in this room is just as in the dark as I am. I'm not alone. *That* I can trust.

It's not even that I don't trust Ravage. I *love* my godfather. We've become so much closer lately. The thought of something happening to him while I'm just sitting on my ass in this room is too much.

I try his cell again but it goes straight to voicemail.

I untangle my fingers from Cliff's and jump out of my seat. "I'm going to look for him."

"I'm coming with you," Cliff says without skipping a beat. That's the kind of man he is: ride or die. I turn toward him, the hardness in my face softening just a little.

Donny stands, too. "Just the three of us. It's my job as Enforcer to protect our President."

I cast him a surprised glance. So Cliff and I aren't the only ones who are worried about the Bastard Brothers.

"Just give him a few more minutes." Beer Can glances at the clock on the wall. "He said he'd be here."

"You guys can wait here in case he shows," I say. I nod to Cliff and Donny. "Let's go."

I stride toward the doors, reaching a hand out as I near them. They swing open and I freeze in my tracks.

Ravage stands between Bree and the man I've never seen in person. Ravage's eyes widen just slightly as we nearly collide. His lips begin to turn up into a teasing grin, but I rip my gaze from him. There's only one person I see.

I take in her worn boots, her ripped and stained jeans, the crocheted poncho she's huddled in. My eyes meet hers and before I can stop myself, a sob ripples through my throat.

I take a step back, stumbling a little. Cliff catches my elbow, holding me steady. I never stop staring at Bree. I count the new wrinkles, retracing and re-memorizing her face.

She lifts hands adorned in silver rings, silver bracelets tinkling as she reaches out to me. "Olivia," she breathes, her eyes filling with tears.

"It's good to have you back, brother," Beer Can says from beside me, clasping hands with the man next to Bree. The sound breaks the trance I'm in. I turn toward the man I've been longing for my whole life.

He looks the same as he did in the photo, except older. More lines etch his eyes, but they're the same wide brown eyes. *My* eyes. I swallow.

Cliff places a hand on my back, his touch grounding me.

"Hey, kiddo," Mercy says, and he sounds exactly the way I always imagined he would. Warm whiskey and honey, his rumble moving through me. Suddenly I'm seven years old again, standing in Lucy's parents' foyer, uncertain. My lips tremble, and I step toward him.

"Dad?" I breathe.

He gives me a warm smile, his eyes crinkling. He opens his

arms, and I don't hesitate. I step right into them. Cliff pulls his hand back, and then I'm surrounded by my father. I inhale the leather, the sweat of the road, searching for something familiar, anything to tie this man to my childhood, anything that marks him as mine. *His eyes*, I remind myself. *We have the same eyes.*

Mercy hugs me tight, his chin resting on the top of my head. "God, it's good to see you." He pulls me away from him. "Let me get a good look at you," he says, eyes teary. Bree touches his arm, her own eyes filled with tears.

All I see is Mercy.

"Okay, that's enough," he says, pulling me back in for another hug. "I missed you, kid."

I should say something. I know I should. What should be a beautiful moment is quickly overshadowed by years of pain. All I can think about is how they both left me. How, when Mercy had the chance, he went after Bree instead of coming to see me. I stiffen in his arms as the betrayal stings all over again. How many times are these two going to leave me?

I break the embrace, my eyes hardening. I pin Bree and then Mercy with my hardest look. "Where the fuck have you been?"

They glance at each other.

I glare at Bree. "Don't give me that confused face, *Bree*." I turn to Ravage. "And *you*, always covering for these two. What the fuck?"

Ravage bows his head almost apologetically.

I wheel on Bree. "You fucking disappeared. You—"

From the table, Skid clears his throat. "I hate to break up the family reunion, but Ravage, you called us all here." He spreads his hands.

I turn back to Ravage. "We thought you were dead or something!"

He smirks as he makes his way to the head of the table. "I told Beer Can to tell you all everything was fine."

"See?" Beer Can says. "But no, nobody wants to listen to Grandpa!"

Ravage casts an apologetic look at Bree. "Give us a few minutes."

With a nod, she slips out of the room, glancing at me over her shoulder before the club swallows her. I shake off her sad eyes.

I stalk back to my seat, lighting another cigarette as I sit. Mercy hovers behind Beer Can and Donny, as if he's unsure where to sit. There are only ten seats and they're all full.

"Oh, for fuck's sake." Ravage scowls. "Olivia, go get your pops a chair."

I scoff. "Me? I'm not a Prospect anymore."

He glowers at me. "You're about to get us all drinks, while you're at it."

My lip curls. I do *not* want to go out there, not with Bree sitting at the bar, looking all wounded.

"Drinks sound nice," Skid says. "A round of whiskey in honor of our Mercy!"

They all look at me, amused expressions on each of their faces. Even Cliff looks entertained.

Rolling my eyes, I push back my chair and leave the room in a huff.

I emerge into bass, the scent of booze, and the laughter of the girls on the poles. All of the noise is enough to dull my swirling thoughts.

"Let me help you," Mercy says from behind me.

"I've got it," I say, moving to the bar. It's been a while since I was a shot girl, but it's like riding a bike.

Mercy follows me anyway. As predicted, Bree sits on a stool, nursing a soda.

"I'm really glad you're not up on that stage," Mercy says.

"Me too," Bree adds.

I glare at them both as I grab a tray and eleven shot glasses. I plunk them down a little too hard and mutter, "Not like you get a say."

"Olivia, come on," she pleads.

Trish appears at my elbow, her eyes curious and wide. "Can I help?"

"I got it." I pour the whiskey and pick up the tray, balancing it with one hand. I don't spill a single drop, not even when I grab a stool from the bar.

"Do you got anything more, ah, supportive?" Mercy asks, taking long strides to keep up with me.

I make the mistake of looking at him. He limps as he walks. I can't help but soften a little. I'm mad at him, but I'm more pissed at Bree. She wasn't behind bars all these years. She could've stayed in Connecticut. Instead she chose to leave me—over and over.

I set down the stool and scan the bar. "Not really," I say with a sigh. "You can have my seat."

Mercy grins. "Thanks, kiddo."

I pick up the stool and get moving again. He holds the doors for me and then we step back into the hushed Chapel. I slide the tray onto the table and take the stool over to my seat. Grabbing my chair, I carry it toward the head of the table. I don't know where to set it. I hover between setting it down next to Beer Can and Donny, or between Ravage and Beer Can. I bite my lip.

Before he went in twenty years ago, Mercy was President. I don't know what he is now.

"Next to me is fine," Ravage says. I drop the chair into place and head over to my seat. Lighting yet another cigarette, I take Cliff's hand. He gives me a squeeze.

"Thank you," Mercy says. He sits slowly, stiffly, like he's hurting.

"The musical chairs Olivia just played makes a good segue," Ravage says. He grips Mercy's shoulder with a smile. "It's really good to have you back, brother. I've been keeping this seat warm for you, but it's time to pass the gavel back."

Mercy goes still in his seat, his gaze dropping to the table.

"What do you say? You want this back?" Ravage asks, and extends the gavel to him.

14

CLIFF

Several beats pass without anybody speaking. I wasn't a part of this club when Mercy was President, but I can't imagine Ravage stepping down. Not when he does it so well. Judging by everyone's stunned silence, I'm not the only one who thinks so.

"I'm dead serious, brother. This was never mine." Ravage holds the gavel out to Mercy, his pale eyes warm but hard, his jaw set.

Mercy chuckles. He drums his fingers on the table, brown eyes even wider than usual. They're so like Olivia's, it's a bit unnerving. Those big eyes of hers are one of my favorite things about her. I look away from Mercy, instead looking at her.

I wish Ravage hadn't sprung this on us—on her. He must want out of that seat real bad. I'm still green, but there's usually a procedure to this, a conversation behind closed doors. A vote.

It can't be easy, sitting in that chair, making decisions for the good of everyone. Ravage has been holding it down since Mercy went in—not too long after I went in. It has to have taken a toll on him. I glance at Olivia again, putting myself in his shoes. If we were married. If I were constantly putting the club before her. Where would we be?

I take a deep breath in through my nose. Whatever happens, I'm backing Ravage on this. He deserves to step down. He's done everything for this club, for Olivia, for me. If this is truly what he wants—not something he's doing out of obligation to Mercy— then I support him. I owe him that.

Mercy chuckles again. Reaching into the pocket of his cut, he pulls out a pack of smokes.

"The ol' lady know you're smoking now?" Skid asks, smirking.

"No." Mercy lights up, exhaling smoke. "If any of you tell her, I'll kick your ass."

"Sure, old man," Donny ribs. He claps Mercy on the back. "God, it's good to have you back."

"I think we all agree on that," Skid says, "but this ain't how we do things. We discuss. We vote."

Ravage scoffs. "We're discussing it now. We all know this seat doesn't belong to me. So unless you've got another candidate in mind . . ." His gaze passes over me for a beat, then returns to Mercy.

I shift in my seat. He's mentioned before that this club is my birthright. Olivia's, too. He can't really mean to pass it to me now. I just learned how to ride.

I remember my promise to Bastard. Someday, that seat will be mine. Today isn't that day. Not yet.

"You and Cliff sacrificed everything for this club," Ravage continues. "We all owe the two of you more than we can ever repay. The least I can do is get the fuck out of your chair. So, what do you say?"

Mercy takes a long drag. "Brother, I've still got the grit of the road on me." He smiles, but it doesn't reach his eyes.

He doesn't want it.

"I think it's safe to say we could all use a shower," Ravage says. "Except Olivia."

We all laugh. Olivia lifts a shoulder, tips her chin toward me. "He isn't so bad."

"All right," Skid says, holding up his hands. "We don't need to hear no more."

"I would *love* to hear more." Vaughn reaches across Abraham and gives my arm a nudge off the table. "How good does this guy smell, Olivia?"

"Wouldn't you like to know."

I glance at Abraham, who's been oddly quiet this whole time. Then again, that's just him. Or is it? I study him. Even though he's ridden beside me, cut my hair, even shaved my beard, I know little to nothing about him. I don't even know where he fell in the split. Doing the math, he has to be the one who voted against taking Bastard to the river. He just didn't go with the Bastard Brothers.

The question is, why not?

Ravage clears his throat. "All right," he rasps, bringing our attention back. "What's it gonna be, Merce?"

Mercy bows his head. His shoulders lift then fall as he takes in a deep breath. When he lifts his head, his eyes are dead on Ravage. "I can't thank you enough for stepping up when it all went down. From what I've heard, you've done a great job." His gaze sweeps the table. "Isn't that right?"

Everyone nods, shouting agreement.

"He's all right," Olivia ribs, her lips twisted into a bittersweet smile. She looks at Ravage with tears in her eyes. I smile, too. I'm glad she's had him all this time, even if she didn't really know it.

Ravage ducks his head. "Cut it out." Even then, we can all tell he's pleased at the compliment.

"I love you all," Mercy continues, "and if you really want me to take that seat back, I'll do it. But I think I'm good with sitting on the sidelines."

"Sidelines." Skid scoffs. "You're one of us, brother. Whether you're in that chair or not."

"We love you, Daddy." Vaughn smirks.

"Who the fuck is this kid?" Mercy asks, chuckling.

"Your long-lost baby boy!" Vaughn holds his arms open.

"Far as I know, I've only got one kid." Mercy gives Olivia a soft smile. She returns it with a tight smile. If it bothers him, he doesn't let it show. "That seat is yours, Ravage. You've earned it."

I want to wrap her in my arms, to help her sort through all this. Ravage could've given us a heads up, especially given their complicated history.

"A'ight," Ravage says, setting the gavel down. "Just remember, I asked." He stands from his seat. "Listen, a lot of us were either on or off tonight, but this is a celebration now. Whoever took over for you is there 'til close. Let's get reacquainted with our brother, Mercy!" He lifts a shot then passes the tray around. Once we all have one in our hands, Ravage holds his up in the air. "To returns and sacrifices, past, present, and future!" He downs his shot, and we all follow suit. "Now get outta here and get wasted."

I turn to ask Olivia if she'd like a drink, but she's already gone.

15

OLIVIA

I slip through the doors before anyone misses me, heading straight for the parking lot. I need air. I sneak under the darkness of the club, grateful for the first time ever that I work at a strip club. There's too much going on for anyone to notice me. I go out the back door for members and employees only and light a cigarette. I don't drop into the chair. Instead, I pace the lot, mind whirling.

Bree is back.

Mercy came back with her.

I thought I'd be relieved when they finally came, but I'm not. Instead, I'm angry. Seething, burning pissed. Bree thinks she can waltz back in here and pick up as if nothing's happened, like I'm still that seven-year-old waiting for her to get back after a few days.

I don't know why I expected an apology.

At least I wasn't alone all the time. I didn't remember Ravage and Shannon taking care of me. My memories are muddied, a product of childhood and trauma. Now that I know they cared, I can look back at that time with a little less hurt. They tried. Bree didn't.

And Mercy, he might've been protecting the club, but by doing whatever he did to go to prison, he abandoned me. He could've stayed when he got out, but he went after Bree. I take a long drag, blowing smoke Os into the sapphire night sky. He gets a break from me, but only a little one. If they're here, they better be here to stay.

I finish the cigarette, dropping it to the ground and turning. I'm going in there and I'm telling them to their faces. I don't need them to tuck me in at night, but I do need them to stick around. I yank open the door and march back inside. As I pass the office, the door open only a sliver, I hear voices.

Laughter spills through the crack. I pause, not meaning to eavesdrop but the party should be out there, not in here.

"I don't mean to kill the moment, but you should talk to Olivia. You owe her the truth." Shannon.

"We're going to tell her. I promise." Bree.

"We're just waiting for the right time. We just got back, Shan." Mercy.

"And it's a lot more complicated than you know." Bree.

I frown, trying to hear what they're *not* saying, and failing.

"How complicated can it be? She'll understand," Shannon insists.

Mercy sighs. "It's going to hurt her."

"How will it hurt her? Is there something you haven't told me?" Shannon asks.

I don't give myself time to wonder. I push open the door and step into the office. "What's going on?"

I glance from one shocked face to another.

Shannon gives me a warm smile. Standing next to Mercy, I can definitely see the resemblance. They have the same soulful brown eyes, the same bone structure. The only difference is Shannon is blonde and Mercy has dark hair like me.

I have no idea where I got these curls.

"You've got some catching up to do," Shannon says. She

presses a kiss to Bree's cheek, giving her arm a squeeze. "It'll be okay." As she leaves, easing the door shut behind her, Bree pales.

"Something you've got to tell me?" I ask.

"Maybe now isn't the time," she says.

I scoff. "It's never a good time for you, is it?"

Mercy spreads his hands between us. "Let's all just take a breath."

Bree's eyes meet mine. A tear slips down her cheek. She blinks it away, then takes a deep breath. My stomach clenches, my body bracing for what she's about to say.

16

OLIVIA

Mercy wraps an arm around Bree. She glances over at him, and he gives her a single nod. My frown deepens. Grabbing my cigarettes, I pull one out with my teeth and light it. I hold the pack out to Mercy.

"No, thanks," he says, voice rough.

"So," I say between drags. "Let's hear it."

Bree licks her lips, her eyes begging me. To do what, I don't know. Let it go? Understand?

"When I met your mother," Mercy begins, "she washed up here at the club. Shannon took her in, gave her a job as a cocktail waitress."

I wave a hand. "I know all that."

"I lied about my age," she blurts.

I lift an eyebrow. "Do you think I'm an IRS auditor or something? What do I care?"

"I was fourteen," Bree says.

I glance from her to my father. Eyes widening, I take a deep drag. "Oh," I say on my exhale. "How old were *you*?" I shake my head. "You know what, I don't want to know. It was another time, right?" I shudder.

They exchange a heavy glance.

"Is that what you wanted to tell me?"

Bree sits on Mark's desk, setting her shaking hands in her lap. Mercy reaches over, twining his fingers through hers. The hardness in me softens a bit. Why would he have stayed for me? He barely knew me. I was an infant when he went in. Of course he went after her. For all her flaws, he loves my mother. If it were Cliff and me, he'd go after me. Without hesitating.

"You should tell her this part," Mercy says quietly.

She nods, letting out a shaky breath. Slowly she lifts her eyes to mine. "When I got here . . ." Her voice is so low, I have to lean in to hear her. "I was fourteen. I ran away from home. And . . . I was already pregnant."

"So you already knew each other?" I suppress another shudder. I never, ever want to know how old Mercy was. There's a mega age gap between Cliff and me, but at least I'm legal, even if related by adoption.

She shakes her head.

"No," he confirms. He begs me with his eyes to understand, to have mercy on my mother.

"So this guy," I say, pointing my cigarette toward Mercy, "isn't my father?"

She opens her mouth, but I cut her off.

"I need to hear you say it. *He's* not my father?"

"My name is on your birth certificate. For all intents and purposes—"

I laugh. "Purposes? What am I, some court agreement? What are you telling me right now?"

The puzzle pieces keep shifting, more that I didn't have falling beside them. If I could put the brakes on, I could probably figure it out. If I could just stop the ground from shaking underneath me. If I could just have a minute.

Because whatever it is, I already know I don't want to hear it. Not out loud.

Instead of listening, I lash out. All of my therapy and trauma training flies out of my head. "Do you even love each other?"

I have no idea why I asked that. Why it's even important. What is love when we're all just running around with secrets?

Mercy kisses her forehead, his eyes closing for a fraction of a second. "I've always loved your mother, Olivia. But the circumstances—"

"Fairytales aren't real," she says sadly. She wipes away more tears. "But we can all still have a happy ending." She watches me, hope spilling from her eyes.

I don't feel hopeful. All I feel is betrayed and lied to, over and over. "Who is my father?"

She pales again.

I shake my head slowly. The cigarette in my hand died out a long time ago. I drop it into Mark's ashtray and light another. "Do you even know who he is?"

I hate how scared I sound, how my voice matches how unsteady I feel inside. It all makes sense, why neither of these people have my hair, why Mercy didn't feel like home when he hugged me. He isn't my father. He isn't anything to me at all.

She swallows. "Yes," she whispers.

"He wasn't a good person, Olivia," Mercy says.

I stare at Bree, blood pounding through my veins. My heart aches for her, for me, for all of us. Mostly for me, the baby neither of them wanted.

That's why it was so easy for them to leave.

"In what way?" I suck on the cigarette like it's my lifeline. It is. Because history repeats, and instead of having guidance when the loop came back around, I had no one.

I stand.

She swallows. Brushing away more tears, she lifts her chin. For the first time, I see some of myself in her. There's steel there, underneath all the flowers and flight.

"Your *father* is right here," she says, squeezing Mercy's hand.

His grip on hers tightens. "But the man who made you raped me."

I'm a rape baby.

I stare into my mother's face, her hazel eyes riveted on me, pleading with me to believe her.

"I'm so sorry," I whisper, the words inadequate. I back toward the door. "I just . . . I need a minute." My head spins, and I want to rewind, to undo what was done to her. Now I understand why she buried her pain in drugs and booze, instead of staying with me.

Someone stole those years from both of us.

"Wait," she says, but I pull open the door and bolt so that she doesn't see me cry.

17

CLIFF

"Essie wants to have you guys over for dinner," Donny says, one arm draped over the bar, the other slung across the back of his chair. "Now that we're all settled in and everything."

"That'd be good. I mean it." I sip my whiskey, scanning the club for Olivia. Her, Bree, and Mercy are all MIA, so I'm assuming they're holed up in Mark's office, catching up. I turn back to Donny. The question burns on my lips but I hesitate.

"What?" He runs a hand over his beard. "I got something on my face?"

I chuckle. "Nah man, you're good. I'm just wondering how you help Esther through her shit. I mean, Olivia's parents are nowhere near as bad as Esther's, but her mother was absent and she's just getting to know Mercy now." I rub the back of my head. "How do you help her through all that?"

He signals for Trish to bring us another round. "Well," he says once she's put our drinks down, "there's not a whole lot I can do. All you can do is be there for her, you know? Listen when she wants to talk. Hold her when she doesn't. Whatever she's feeling, validate it." He claps me on the back. "Basically, just keep doing what you're doing. I finessed all my moves watching you."

"Me?" I knock back the rest of my whiskey and grab the fresh drink. "You're kidding."

"I'm serious. Don't get me wrong, I got my own moves." He laughs. "But I see you with Olivia and I say to myself, 'That's the kind of man every man should be.'"

I stare at him for a beat. He lifts his eyebrows. I narrow my eyes. We both bust out laughing at the same time.

"Why're you laughing, man?" He takes a sip of his blackberry brandy. "I'm dead serious."

"Yeah, all right." I shake my head.

"Where *is* Olivia?" He glances around the club.

"Talking with Mercy and Bree, probably."

"Brother, Mercy and Bree are right there. They both look rough around the edges."

I turn on my stool. Sure enough, Olivia's parents are at the other end of the bar, their faces grim. Bree looks straight up sick.

"What the fuck happened?" Donny echoes my thoughts.

I stand, leaving the rest of my drink untouched. "Be right back."

"No, you won't," he calls after me. "Remember what I said. You're doing great."

I weave through the club, my gaze sweeping from face to face. All of my brothers, lots of club colors, dozens of pretty faces, but no Olivia. I step into the back hall, heading toward Mark's office. Shannon emerges from the storage room, face drawn.

"You seen Olivia?"

She shakes her head. "She took off."

I touch both her elbows. "What happened?"

She closes her eyes. "Honestly, I don't know."

"She talked to Bree?"

"Bree and my brother." She sighs. "I encouraged Bree to talk to Olivia, Cliff. I thought maybe they could smooth things over faster if Olivia understood."

"Understood what?"

"Why Mercy went away, why Bree kept her father a secret."

"And why's that?"

She fixes me with a flat look. "How old do you think my brother is?"

"Probably about as old as my father would be now."

"How old do you think Bree is?"

I frown. I'm not good at this game. "This feels like a trick question."

"She's thirty-five—three years younger than *you*, Cliff."

I rock back on my heels. "Ah." I pluck a cigarette from behind my ear and shrug. "I ain't one to judge. I mean, I'm a good twenty years older than Olivia."

"Bree was fourteen when she had Olivia."

I light the cigarette. "Explains why Mercy went away."

"A nurse didn't like their age difference, and she had connections. It was a done deal the moment Mercy signed that birth certificate."

"Christ." I rub my beard.

She takes a deep breath. "Cliff, I think there might be more to the story."

"Why do you think that?"

Shannon eyes me. "Come on. You and I both know Olivia pretty well. She's tough. Something like this would barely raise her eyebrow, never mind send her running. Besides," she says, reaching for my cigarette. "Bree *said* there was more to it." She exhales and hands the cigarette back to me. "Any idea where she might've gone?"

"I've got a few." I lean over and kiss the top of her head. "It's gonna be okay."

"I'll try and get it out of Bree," she says as I fly out the back door.

When I step outside, Olivia's Street Glide is long gone, which I figured. I'm going to have to use good old fashioned detective skills. Except I don't have any. I stand half in the gray shadows, half in the orange light, torn. She didn't come find me. Maybe I should just give her some space. I can't always go jumping on my motorcycle, chasing after her.

Donny's words flash neon in my head: *Keep doing what you're doing.*

I lift the cigarette to my lips, turning my options around and around. My phone dings in the pocket of my cut. I reach inside and pull it out.

Olivia: Can you meet me at Lucy's? Please.

I hold the phone to my chest, breathing a sigh of relief.

Cliff: Be there in seven.

I get there in five.

18

OLIVIA

I put my phone face down on the kitchen table, relief flooding through me. "He's on his way," I tell Lucy.

"Good." She pours me another shot of tequila.

I rake my hand through my wild curls. I didn't even stop to put my helmet on. Gripping the glass, I down the shot.

"You can smoke in here," she says. "Just this one time." She pushes open the sliding glass door and opens all the windows wide.

"What about Bunny?"

"She's upstairs. She'll be fine. Our parents did worse to us."

I raise my shot glass. "Truth." She pours another and one for herself. We clink glasses and drink in silence. The tequila burns all the way down, soothing the nausea. For now.

"I feel awful for Bree," she says after a moment. "It doesn't excuse her abandoning you, but it explains it."

"I can't believe Mercy took the fall." I light a cigarette, cupping the flame and guilt in my shaking hand.

"Liv . . ." She bites her lower lip. "Are you gonna be okay? No bullshit?"

I hold out my shot glass in answer.

"Okay, we'll drink," she says, frowning while pouring. "For now."

I lose track of how many shots I've done. By the time Cliff flings open the front door and rushes to my side, I'm gone. No more nausea, no more heartburn. I feel absolutely nothing. I lean against his arm, a sloppy grin planted on my face.

Cliff and Lucy exchange worried looks.

"It's fine, guys. I'm fine." I take a long drag and blow Os into the air. "Lucy said we can smoke."

"I said *you* can smoke," she chides. "Just for tonight."

"What happened?" Cliff asks her.

I put a finger on his lips. "Nope. Not going back there. Let's drink!"

He eyes the tequila and empty shot glasses. "There aren't even any limes."

"What the fuck do you think this is? San Marino?" Lucy rolls her eyes.

I burst out laughing. "No limes. We said that on our second first date."

"Second first date?" Lucy asks.

"At the benefit," Cliff explains.

I motion for Lucy to get pouring. "Cliff needs to catch up with us."

He holds up a hand. "I don't know, Olivia . . ."

"Please," I beg, giving him big eyes. Eyes that aren't Mercy's. No wonder I have these curls. I shove the thought away, but tears sting my eyes anyway. "Pour," I tell Lucy.

"All right, I'll drink." He shoots Lucy another look, and I catch the tiny shrug she gives him in return. The three of us clink glasses.

"It's like old times!" I smirk, thinking of the hole in the wall we all ended up at in Pennsylvania.

"Remember that old ass woman?" Lucy asks. She pours us more shots.

"She had to have been about a hundred," Cliff says.

"And you," I say, poking her in the arm, "were already knocked up, so you didn't even get to do granny shots with us."

"I didn't even get the chance. You two killed them!"

"And a station wagon," Cliff murmurs.

I meet his eyes. A silent memory passes between us: the feel of the upholstery on my skin, the squeak and rock of the vehicle, the cigarettes we smoked after. We grin at each other.

"The two of you," Lucy says with a laugh. "It was meant to be." She holds her shot glass up but only Cliff clinks with her.

I break eye contact with him and pour the tequila down my throat. I don't believe in fate. I don't know what I believe in anymore.

Cliff lets out a deep breath, sagging in his seat. "I could really use a cigarette now. I can't keep up with you guys."

"Come on, Luce. Let Cliff smoke, too." I give her little sister puppy eyes.

She caves like I knew she would. "*Just* this once," she warns.

Cliff lights up, exhaling in relief. "I'm getting too old for tequila."

"Please." I scoff. "You're only three years older than my mom."

He gives me a curious look. "So I heard."

Several beats pass between us but I don't say anything else.

"I have something else we can smoke," Lucy says with a mischievous grin.

I gape at her. "No fucking way you do."

"I do!" She stands and dances over to the counter, where she lifts the lid of the cookie jar and produces a perfectly rolled blunt.

"Luce," Cliff chides. "You shock me."

"Oh, please, you two." She rolls her eyes at us. "Do you really think I'm some kind of saint?"

Cliff and I exchange glances. "Uh, yeah," I say. "Since when do you smoke weed?"

"Since I started therapy and got my card for anxiety."

I blink at her. "You're in therapy?"

"I have an infant and an estranged baby daddy. Of course I'm in therapy." She dances back to the table and pulls a lighter from her pocket.

"I cannot believe we're smoking in your kitchen," I say, reaching for the bottle. "This calls for a celebrity shot!"

They both stare at me blankly.

"Wait. *Celibate* shot," I slur.

Cliff chuckles, sliding his arm behind me to rest on the back of my chair. "You're wasted."

"Let me do this." I whisper the word to myself a few times until I land on the right one. "Celebratory! Celebratory shot!" I pour for us while Lucy takes a big hit off her secret blunt. "This is the best worst night ever!"

Cliff presses a kiss to my temple. "It'll be okay."

That's the last thing I remember.

I wake up in bed, Cliff's giant body wrapped around me. It's gloomy outside, and my head pounds out a merciless beat. I slam my eyes shut again, groaning. I must've done a lot more shots. I groan again. I hate having a blank space in my memory. At least I know I didn't go anywhere, didn't have the chance to do any damage. I was safe.

It's an odd feeling.

Somehow, despite everything I've been through, I've found good people to hold me down.

My conversation with Bree and Mercy comes rushing back, along with a wave of nausea that gets me up and running. I fly to the bathroom, slamming the door behind me and kneeling in front of the toilet just as the first round shoots up my throat. I vomit until I'm empty, and then keep throwing up.

If only I could purge my heart so easily.

19

CLIFF

"**C**liff."

I crack an eye open, grimacing as the light hits me. Lucy stands over me, two mugs of coffee in her hand. "What's up?" I grunt, rolling onto my side.

She hands me a mug. "Olivia's in the shower."

Balancing the coffee, I sit up. "Okay?"

"We need to talk." She sits down beside me, her hands wrapped tightly around the mug.

I groan. "Can't it wait, Luce? I need at least another hour."

"Sucks getting old, doesn't it?" Her lips twist for a moment before pursing again, her green eyes dead serious.

I take a sip, the hot brew stinging my throat. "You're the ones who made me do tequila shots. Again." I tip my head back and close my eyes. It's too easy to get swept up in the two of them, to forget that I'm pushing forty hard and can't quite keep up with them.

"Did she tell you what happened?" she asks.

"Uh, no, Luce. There was a lot of drinking." I squint at her. "How are you even standing? You drank just as much as Olivia."

"Not even close. She took the bottle to bed with her." She points to the nightstand. Sure enough, there's an empty bottle.

"I want her to tell me what happened," I say, "but I need to know how bad it is."

She sighs. "Ordinarily, I'd agree. She should tell you. But . . ." She takes several sips, stalling.

"Fuck," I breathe. If even Lucy can't say it out loud, it's got to be cataclysmic. I put my hand on top of hers. "Just say it."

She cranes her neck, listening. "Shower's still running. Okay. Bree and Mercy talked to Olivia."

"Yeah, I got that." I eye my cigarettes on the nightstand, wondering if last night's rule applies to this morning or if Lucy would just kill me.

She takes a deep breath and says, on an exhale, "Mercy isn't Olivia's father."

I gape at her. "How do you figure? They told her that?"

Nodding, she gives my hand a squeeze. "There's . . . more."

I swallow coffee, but it does nothing to ease the shifting beneath me.

"Bree didn't say who Olivia's father is, but she did say he raped her." Her green eyes lock onto mine.

I blow out a long breath, setting my mug on the nightstand. "Holy shit." I close my eyes in an effort to stifle the tearing in my chest. My hands close into fists, but there's no one to hit.

She's the product of everything she hates.

"Cliff, what do we do?" she whispers. "I don't know how to make this better."

I peek at the room through the slits of my eyes. I don't have a fucking clue, either. "Why would they just drop that on her last night?" I turn, facing Lucy.

"Shitty, right?" She shakes her head, lips pressed into a line.

"I think," I say, holding her gaze, "we need to just give her some time. She talked to you—she'll talk to me when she's ready."

"The water stopped."

I cock my head in confusion.

"The shower," she whispers in a hurry. "Is she still in therapy?"

"I don't think so," I say, standing. I grab my smokes. Lucy gives me a look. "I've got to pull my shit together before she walks out."

"Go do that." She stands, too. "I'll get her some coffee." She grips my arm as she passes, then pads out of the room.

I follow her downstairs, turning for the front door as she heads to the kitchen. I step outside, lighting up the second I shut the door behind me.

I clench the cigarette between my teeth, fists curled at my side. A dozen questions fly through my head. All I want to do is swing onto my hog and find Mercy, shake him down for answers. Bree, Mercy, Ravage—the three of them and their bullshit. No heads up, just dropping bombs on Olivia's head. Shannon didn't know, but maybe Ravage did. Makes me wonder what other secrets they're keeping.

The door squeaks open and Olivia steps out, curls dripping down her back. She fists a towel closed between her breasts, her feet and everything else bare. She holds out her free hand for my cigarette.

"Morning." I pass it over. "How's your head?"

"Pounding." She takes a deep drag and blows a stream of white smoke up into the gray sky.

I shift my weight, wrapping an arm around her. "You wanna talk about it?"

"My headache?" She smirks over at me, eyes dancing. "Nothing breakfast at Cara's won't fix."

I chuckle. "Is that a hint?"

"Take it whatever way you want," she says. "I have to work, so if you wanna come, you better hurry."

My eyebrows furrow. "You're going to work?"

"Of course." She frowns up at me, flicking ash into the bushes. "What else am I supposed to do?"

"I get it if you wanna go in, get your mind off things."

She narrows her eyes at me. "Lucy told you."

I light up my own cigarette. "Yes." I steel myself for her anger, for her hurt.

"Then there's nothing to talk about."

I hug her tighter. "It's up to you. I'm listening when you're ready."

Stretching up on the balls of her feet, she cups my beard with the same hand holding her cigarette, the cherry a dangerous inch away. She presses cold lips to mine. I open to her, breathing heat into her, giving her the fire in my fists.

"Want me to kick anyone's ass?" I ask against her warming lips.

The towel drops between us, puddling at her feet. She stares up at me for a shocked second. Bending over, I retrieve it, giving it a shake. I wrap the towel around her.

"Let's get you inside."

"It's a little late for that. The whole complex saw my ass."

I usher her inside, my fists clenched with frustration. I'd never raise a hand to either Bree or Mercy without Olivia's blessing. That's her business and she's more than capable of taking care of it. I just need to do something other than hold my woman while she sobs all over me, drunk on tequila. She doesn't remember it, but I do. I'll never forget it.

20

OLIVIA

I get dressed while Cliff takes a quick shower. As I'm stepping into a pair of black jeans, Lucy knocks. She pushes the door open a fraction. "Coffee?"

"You're my favorite sister." I take the mug and sip.

"I'm your only sister."

"You're the only real family I have," I say.

She gives me a tiny smile that's more like a grimace. "Are you gonna talk to Bree?"

"What's there to say?" I hand the mug back to her and tug on a beige tee.

"Well, you're hurting now, understandably." She pauses, as if waiting for me to say more. I don't.

Tears sting my eyes, betraying my resolve. I blink them away, shoving it all down.

She sighs. "Go to work. It's good to stick to your routine."

"We're grabbing breakfast on my way in." I step toward my dresser and reach for the box of jewelry I barely wear. I turn my back to her while I comb through silver rings—rings that remind me of Bree. "You told Cliff."

"Yeah." She sighs. "I didn't mean to betray your trust. I just thought he should have a heads up."

"I don't like you guys talking about me like that," I say, picking up a skull ring. Hardly DCF appropriate. I drop it back into the box and keep digging. "But I understand why you did it."

"You're right," she says.

"After this, I don't want to talk about it ever again." I grab a long diamond-shaped ring engraved with gray crystals and tiny balls. A teardrop crystal decorates the top and bottom points. I slip it on.

"I think you should," Lucy says, "but it's up to you."

"Jesus. You sound like Cliff." I turn on my heels. "I'm not going to break. I just don't want to talk about it."

She nods again but worry clouds her eyes.

"Stop looking at me like that." I take the mug from her. "Seriously, I'm fine. Tequila can fix just about anything."

She twists her lips, skeptical.

"Your face is gonna get stuck like that." I tug my boots on one at a time, sipping while I balance on each foot.

"How do you not kill yourself doing that?"

"I don't have time to be careful. Not if I want breakfast—and I need something greasy before this hangover kills me."

"Well," she says, giving me a bright smile, "enjoy your breakfast." She watches me for almost a beat too long, then strides out of my room.

I turn back to the dresser, debating whether earrings would be too much, when the shower stops. A moment later, the bathroom door creaks open and Cliff pads into my room, wearing only a towel.

"Copycat," I tell him.

He closes the door behind him, then drops the towel. "Oops," he murmurs, dark eyes heated. His hard length points toward me.

I laugh. "I'd love to help you out with that, but I really need hangover food."

"Can't blame a guy for trying."

"At least the whole neighborhood didn't see your ass," I tell him, tossing a T-shirt at him.

"I don't think anybody saw." He dresses quickly, and I'm sorry to see him clothed again. I really do need to eat something, though.

"We'll find out when Lucy has her next HOA meeting."

"It's not your fault she buys such small towels," he says.

I grin at him. Leave it to Cliff to always find ways to make me smile. "Let's go. I'm gonna be late."

I take the Street Glide to Cara's, Cliff following me on his Screamin' Eagle. We park in the same space. As always, Cara's is packed. I just hope our food doesn't take too long. Harrison will find some way to punish me if I'm late, and it won't be anything as tame as running up a hill in my work clothes. I sigh, and Cliff takes my hand.

"If all else fails, I'll get it to go and bring it over to your office," he says.

We walk hand in hand to the door, which he holds open for me without letting go.

"My office?" I laugh. "I've barely got a cubicle there."

"You know what I mean."

I scan the diner for an empty table, but there aren't any. I spot a brunette with short hair, her floral skirt and worn denim jacket as familiar to me as my own hands. Mercy sits across from her, their hands joined across the table. "Fuck," I say.

"What?" Cliff follows my gaze. "Ah." His hand tightens on mine. "Don't," he says.

I stare at Bree and Mercy. They must feel my eyes on them from across the room, because suddenly his gaze meets mine and Bree turns in her seat. He smiles tightly, his hopeful eyes punctuated by dark circles. Bree doesn't look any better.

I stand straighter, glad I took the time to throw on some concealer. I release Cliff's hand. "I'm not hungry anymore." Turning, I walk out of the diner with my hangover headache pounding even harder.

"You're late," Harrison says as I slap down my bag on my desk. He leans on the wall of the cubicle, an arm draped across the top. His other arm rests behind his back.

I glance at the man I've been shadowing at the Department of Children and Families. I should've called out. I'm in no shape to help anyone, especially not kids, and I'm definitely not in the mood for his teasing. He's about Mercy's age, which doesn't win him any points right now.

I sigh. "It's been one of those mornings. What do you got for me?" I glance around the desk for a case folder, but there isn't anything.

"*I* don't have anything for you." He pulls a folder from behind his back and hands it to me. "Your orientation and disciplinary probation periods are up. This case is all you."

I stare at him. "You serious?"

"As a hemorrhoid." He tips an invisible hat to me.

"Oh, Harrison. Never change."

We grin at each other, and I swear for a moment he almost looks proud of me.

"Don't fuck it up," he says, and strolls out of my cubicle.

I drop into my seat and flip open the folder. My first solo case. I should be ecstatic. I don't have to follow anyone around anymore. I can do everything on my terms—within reason, of course. I probably shouldn't make any other single moms cry.

Now I can really help people without someone breathing down my neck, judging how I get things done. I've had so many cases since that first one, but I'll never forget how good it felt to cut through the red tape and actually make a difference.

I should be happy, but I'm not.

As big a pain in the ass as Harrison was, he was there for me. He was a guide. Now I'm on my own, and there's a good chance I *will* fuck it up.

There's no going back, though. I worked too hard to go home and go back to bed. I can't let the man who took Bree from me take this away from me, too. I can help these kids. I know I can.

With a sigh, I begin reading through the case, hoping it's an easy one.

It's not.

A nine-year-old girl was put into foster care when a neighbor noticed that she'd been alone for a couple weeks. DCF hasn't been able to track down the mother. I close my eyes, taking deep breaths. It's too familiar. I'm too raw. I stand, clutching the folder to my side. I have to go to my supervisor, Diane. I'm too close to this one. Ethically, it's the right thing to do.

Nine years old.

I open the folder again and find the photo of the girl. Big front teeth, freckles, sad eyes. She's too skinny, and the smudges under her eyes make her look sick. She's probably been alone for a while now.

I'm her future, if she isn't careful. She deserves better.

My eyes drop to her face again. She's all alone. The least I can do for her is give her a better chance than me. If I go to my supervisor and ask for a different case, I'm going to have to share why. I know I can't do that right now.

Wincing, I open my desk drawer and grab a pair of sunglasses.

I RIDE in circles around the girl's old neighborhood, not really sure what I'm doing. I should probably contact the foster family, or drop in for a home visit, but I'm in no condition to deal with people. The wind in my hair is soothing even though

I'm only doing about thirty miles an hour, so I turn and start another lap. I can't go home, and I can't face this kid yet, so I'm hoping I can get my shit together enough to call the foster mother. Or, bare minimum, try the biological mother's cell phone.

A police cruiser approaches me in the opposite lane. As it nears, I make out Finn's red hair and dull eyes.

"Fuck," I mutter.

The car slows, and he rolls down his window. Keeping one hand on the wheel, he motions for me to pull over. With his window down, I can see how much weight he's lost since I last saw him. Even his hair is less vibrant, the once bright red streaked through with gray.

I know my rights. He has no reason to stop me. It's not even illegal to ride without a helmet, not anymore. It's one of the few plus sides to living in Connecticut.

He probably just wants to talk about Greg again. I don't know how much longer I can keep this up.

He stops in the middle of the road. "Just the gal I was thinking about. You know anyone by the name of Eli Moretti?"

My grip slips and my heart damn near stops. I don't know what my face looks like, but I probably look guilty. "Doesn't ring a bell."

"He was in your . . ." He glances over at the laptop mounted in his car. "You had a photography class together."

"Oh," I say, lifting a shoulder. "That guy."

"He's been reported as missing. It's interesting, though." He leans out of his window. "We found a key maker in his apartment, and a photo of *you* on his wall."

It takes every ounce of my strength to keep the bike upright.

I'd wondered how Eli got into Esther's and my place, how he had so many copies of our keys. Now it makes sense.

The shaking of the bike hides the tremor in my hands. "That's freaky," I tell him.

"I'll let you know what we find out." He waits for a beat, then waves and takes off.

I maintain the speed limit as I continue in the opposite direction, abandoning the neighborhood. So much for clearing my head.

Heading back to 63, I keep an eye on the mirrors. I don't expect him to just let me get away. So far, he thinks he's protecting yet another victim that the system failed. He doesn't know that I took care of Eli myself. That doesn't mean he won't figure it out. Next time we meet, it might be on the other side of an interrogation table.

My mirrors remain empty all the way to Route 8. Once I'm on the highway, I push the bike to ninety.

I've never been so relieved to be in Waterbury.

21

CLIFF

As soon as my shift at the machine shop ends, I fly over to G's Burgers and get our usual orders. I pack everything into my saddle bag and head to my cousin's. When I pull up to her condo, I only see Olivia's Street Glide in the driveway.

I head straight in, eyeing the sky as I duck inside. "Liv?" I call. I stand in the dim living room. The only other soul in here is Dio, curled up on the back of the couch. He cracks open both eyes then hops down with a meow, all in what looks like one fluid motion to humans, but probably happens much slower for cats.

They're all ninjas.

He winds himself between my legs, his nose in the air and whiskers twitching as he sniffs. The burger bandit strikes again.

"Where is everybody?" I ask him.

"Hey," Olivia calls.

I turn toward the sound of her voice. She stands at the top of the stairs, wearing only a towel. Her wet curls trail down her shoulders. From this angle, she's all eyes and legs. "Hey," I tell her, my voice smoky.

She lowers her lashes, cheeks rosy from her shower. "What's that?"

I hold up the bag. "Grabbed G's. Where's Lucy?"

She gives me a cocky tilt of her lips. "Out."

"Out," I repeat, smirking back at her. "When's she coming back?"

She descends the stairs one slow step at a time. "Don't know."

"We better eat quick, then." I extend a hand to her and, to my surprise, she takes it. Her slender fingers are warm and soft in my callused hands. She glides down the last few steps and presses herself into my arms.

"Let's do that." Standing on tiptoes, she places a hand on each of my shoulders and captures my lips with hers for a moment. Instead of the hunger I usually taste on her, there's a softness, an openness. "You really got me G's?" she says, her tone adoring. She kisses me again, this time slower.

I place my free hand on the small of her back, my body reveling in her warmth. I move my lips against hers, savoring the simple sweetness. Every time her lips are on mine, I want to drink and drink. I pull back. I'm not here to take.

"You had a rough day," I say, tucking her into my side.

"You have no idea."

We walk into the kitchen with her curled against me, and separate only when we reach our seats, but she scoots hers closer to mine. I unpack the bag, leaving Lucy's food inside. "What else happened?"

She pops a fry into her mouth. I watch, dazed, as her lips and tongue wrap around it and it disappears into the velvet dark of her mouth. "Ran into Finn again."

I blink away from her lips. "Again?"

"He's looking into Eli's disappearance. I didn't tell him anything, but he knows Eli had a thing for me."

I don't want to break the mood between us, so I take a bite of my burger. "What are you gonna do about him?"

She sighs. "I mean, is there anything I can do? He's doing his job. I can understand that. If he crosses the line and becomes a creep, I'll handle it." Despite her words, her eyes don't linger on mine.

"He's making you uncomfortable." I set my burger down.

"He's not his brother," she says, more to herself than to me.

"He's not," I agree, "but if he approaches you again, we're gonna have a little chat."

"More effective than a restraining order." She holds her burger with both hands but doesn't take a bite. "Thank you," she says softly.

"It's nothing." I hold her gaze, bathing in the unspoken things passing between us. The moment stretches, suspending. I admire the flecks of gold in her eyes, the curl of her lips as she gives me a slip of a smile. Neither of us speaks a word, but we both move at the same time. She drops her burger and reaches for me, her hands cupping my face. Her exhalations warm my nose. I brush mine against hers and her smile widens. I close the distance between us, gliding my tongue across her bottom lip. She flicks her tongue against mine, drawing me inside her.

Without breaking the kiss, she slides onto my lap. The towel unfurls, puddling around her hips. I didn't even see her undo the knot. She's a ninja, too.

I trail the tips of my fingers from her hips up her side and over her ribs, my tongue tangled with hers. My palms mold to her breasts, cupping. She inhales sharply, back arching. She grinds against my thigh, her heat soaking through the thick material of my Dickies.

"Let's take this upstairs," I whisper. She nods and moves to get up. I stand and lift her. She wraps her legs around my waist and her arms around my neck, and I carry her upstairs.

In her room, I lay her on the bed. Her damp hair fans out around her face. She's regal, even on her back like this. I kiss my way down her throat, taking my sweet time on my way to a nipple. Taking it between my teeth, I give it a nibble, running the head of my tongue over it. I reach between us and palm her soaking heat. My cock twitches, straining against my work pants. If I can't *say* I love her, I want to fuck it into her until I'm empty so she can fill me up again.

Her fingers tangle in my hair, tugging. I glance up. "Please," she whispers.

I smirk. "'Please,' what?"

"Take your fucking clothes off already." She reaches between us and grabs my shirt.

Laughing, I pull the hem up and yank the shirt off over my head. I bear down on her again, pressing my skin to hers. "Better?"

"More." She cups me through my pants. "Now."

I stand and strip, kicking them to the side. I'm bare before her, and she looks at me like I'm a king. I part her legs wide and kneel between her thighs. She watches me, waiting, trusting. Gripping my shaft, I trace her. We both shiver at the partial connection. I glide my head over her hood, applying just enough pressure. Her eyelids lower, body relaxing into the mattress. She thrusts her hips up, begging me with her body. I shift, stretching my legs out behind me, hovering over her with a palm planted on the bed. She throws her legs around me, the heels of her feet digging into my ass, urging me. I ease my crown down, notching myself in her. She gives me another push and I slide in another inch.

"Please," she begs again, throaty, her lids heavy.

I thrust forward, feeling her clench around me, drawing me in deeper. I fill her until I hit the end of her, a low moan vibrating in my throat. Rolling my hips, I set the pace, sliding all the way back out until my crown brushes her clit. She gasps, legs locking around me. I thrust back in, gritting my teeth in concentration. She's so wet, I'm gonna have to be careful I don't come first.

I lower myself onto her until her nipples press against me, bracing myself with my palms. I give her all of me, driving her to the edge with everything I've got. Her nails dig into my back, her gasps closer and closer together. I thrust into her deeper than I thought possible, grinding against her clit. She twitches around me, letting me know she's close. I'm so in sync with her I can't tell where she ends and where I begin.

"Come on," I rumble into her ear. "Come for me, baby."

She shouts against my shoulder, her limbs going slack even as she clenches around me, falling. I go with her, emptying myself into her while my heart and arms are fuller than ever. We cling to each other, falling through the dark.

22

OLIVIA

For the first time ever, I'm dreading Church.

I don't want to look at Mercy. At least I won't see Bree. Throughout the past week I've done my best to move on. My head is as sterile as a hospital operating room.

Not a thing out of place. Nothing to see here. Move along.

That doesn't mean I want to revisit everything.

I stand in front of my closet, my hands tingling, chest tight. I don't know what to wear, what I'm trying to say with my body today. "Fuck you, you're not my dad" just doesn't cut it, and I'm a little old for that. All I can think of is the night Mercy was supposed to come home. Except this time there's no Esther to talk me down. Even Lucy isn't home—as usual lately. She must've joined a Mommy and Me group or something.

"Just grab clothes, Olivia," I mutter to myself, but I still can't move.

Dio rubs his face against my hand. I crane my neck to see down. He stands on his hind feet, his front paws in the air. He gives me a questioning meow, as if to say, "You okay?"

I'm fine.

I throw on the River Reapers hoodie I jacked from Cliff over my favorite leggings, a pair so soft they're almost a second skin. I tug on the motorcycle boots I just bought to replace my old ankle boots. I don't know if it's just me, but I've been burning through shoes since I started riding. I'll never ask the guys, though, because they'll probably bust my balls, saying I'm just using it as an excuse to buy shoes.

I've never needed an excuse.

Giving Dio one last chin scratch, I leave my room and the empty house. Nowhere feels like home, not right now, not anymore.

Nowhere except Cliff.

I push the thought away and ride to the clubhouse. I'm the last to arrive, which suits me just fine. In and out. Rip off the Band-Aid. We'll go for a quick ride together, and then maybe Cliff and I will check out the new coffee shop that opened up on the green. Some hot coffee and a change of scenery will be good for me after this.

I join the others in the Chapel, sliding into my seat next to Cliff. "Morning," I tell him, planting a sweet kiss on his lips.

He smiles, surprised, the crows' feet around his eyes crinkling. "Morning," he replies, slipping a hand onto the back of my neck. He draws me in for another kiss, just as sweet.

The other men make corny middle school noises.

"Look at you two lovebirds," Vaughn croons.

I give him the finger.

"All right," Ravage says, but he's smiling, too.

I do my best to avoid looking at Mercy.

"We've got a few items on the agenda. Shannon needs some canned goods for her place. Vaughn has some updates for us on the high school case. And the Bastard Brothers want to hook up for a ride sometime."

The air shifts in the room. Donny crosses his arms, his forehead wrinkled. Skid mutters something about where they can ride. Everyone looks pissed. Everyone except for Abraham.

"Well you sure slid that last one in nice and slick," Beer Can grumbles.

"One thing at a time," Ravage says.

I sneak a quick glance at Mercy, just to gauge what he thinks about all this. His face is unreadable.

"Shannon's Haven is getting low on nonperishables," our President continues, redirecting everyone. "I want us to throw together a quick food drive. Beer Can, Mark, you're taking point. We'll just do the usual."

"No problem," Mark says, but his eyebrows are furrowed.

"How soon do you think we can get it going?" Ravage asks him.

"We'll need at least two weeks' notice for the other clubs, flyers around town, that sort of thing," Beer Can says. He places both hands on the table. "We gonna talk about that ride last week?"

"Next on deck," Ravage drawls, "Vaughn's got some info for us. We might have a teacher we can talk to."

"Hold your horses," Vaughn says. "Let me get to that."

We all turn toward him. I sit up straighter in my seat.

"Okay, so." He clears his throat and bows his head toward the table. "I got deeper into NPD's system. Police report says each team member from the trip was interviewed, so were the chaperones. None of them saw anything. The police are continuing the investigation."

"Continuing how?" I ask, lighting a cigarette.

Vaughn shifts in his seat. "It doesn't say what their particular plans are. But it looks like they're following procedure."

"Loosely." I roll my eyes. "We need to put pressure on them."

"That's where this next part comes in," he says. "I also got into the school's email. Looks like all of the teachers and chaperones were asked to sign NDAs."

I lean forward. "Are you fucking kidding me?"

"But," Vaughn continues, "we might have an in with one of the teachers. If we could get a witness to come forward, even better. But teachers hear a lot."

I twirl my cigarette between two fingers. "An in?"

"Someone we know teaches at the high school. Someone who owes us a favor. You, specifically," he says, pointing at me.

"Me?"

"Remember Cami?"

"Whoa," Stixx says.

"She skipped town," I say.

"She came back," Vaughn says, "after . . . the house burned down."

"And you think she's gonna talk to me?" I shake my head. "After I told her that her husband was a rapist, scared her out of town, and killed him?"

"She owes you," Vaughn insists.

"I don't know." I reach for Cliff's hand. "That's a lot to ask."

The heat from Cliff's hand envelops my cold fingers. I don't know when we started holding hands, but I kind of like it.

"I know you don't want to do any more damage," he says. "But if there's a chance she can help us get justice for that kid, it's worth the risk."

Ravage nods. "It's a done deal. Talk to Cami. Find out why everyone had to sign NDAs. Find out if any of the chaperones saw anything, if any of the kids are talking."

I blow out a long stream of smoke. I have no right to go to her. If I were her, I'd want *me* to leave me the fuck alone. I'm only a reminder.

But my President has tasked me with this, and since I'm the one who brought it to the table, I've got no room to say no. Even if seeing her will tear me apart. Even if it undoes all of the work I've done to put myself back together.

My hands tingle. I turn them over, palms up. They look

normal—no blue or even red spots. I stare at them so long I forget to be snarky about the third item on the table today.

"Last week, the Bastard Brothers approached me," Ravage says.

Donny clicks his tongue. "If that's what you wanna call it."

"That felt more like an ambush, brother," Beer Can agrees.

"Ambush?" Ravage chuckles. "You all act like they had guns drawn. They want to go for a ride together."

"Didn't we already do that?" Vaughn asks.

"They're trying to bridge the gap," Ravage says. "It's only a ride. It's not making amends. It's not forgiveness. It's just two clubs riding together. Merce?" He turns to look at the man who is not my father.

Mercy's chest expands under his cut. He rubs his chin. "I don't like it."

"Come on," Abraham says. "Ravage is right. It's just a ride. How long are we going to pretend they don't exist?"

"Forever, as far as I'm fucking concerned," Cliff says, giving my hand a squeeze. His touch is comforting, reassuring.

"So we can't even agree to this." Ravage shakes his head. "The past is done and over. We were once a family."

"You know what we do to family who fucks us," Donny says, inclining his head toward Cliff.

Cliff smirks.

"Jesus Christ." Ravage grins. "You're all a bunch of stubborn motherfuckers."

"They chose their side when they walked," Mercy says.

"You're right, brother." Ravage sighs. "But we don't have to keep a line drawn forever. Bastard is dead. Cliff and Mercy are out. We should all move on. As far as I see it, it's best if we do that together."

Beer Can throws his hands in the air. "Fine. Fuck it. We'll take a ride with them."

"Yeah?" Ravage says, glancing around the table.
Donny clicks his tongue again but shrugs.
The other men shrug, too. I lift my shoulders.
"Cool," Ravage says. "How does right now sound?"

23

CLIFF

The whole table falls silent, but the vicious spinning in my head gets louder and louder.

"Right now? Are you fucking kidding me?" Olivia asks.

"It's just a ride," Skid says. "We all agreed."

Donny leans back in his seat, shaking his head. "Yeah—to a far off, future date that probably ain't ever gonna happen."

Beer Can nods in agreement.

"Might as well get it over with," Ravage says. "We're just gonna keep running into them."

I grip the edges of the worn table, torn. I see where my President is coming from. But I can't ride with these motherfuckers, not now. Now when I'm still so angry. Not when the Bastard Brothers carry on my father's legacy of pain and poison. Ravage has to see where *I'm* coming from.

He doesn't. He stands and stretches, a relaxed grin on his face. "Come on." He motions for us to follow him, like we're kids who need to be coaxed into a cold pool.

I don't want to defy him, not when he rebuilt this club and

strengthened it while I was gone. If this was my club, I wouldn't let the Bastard Brothers within a mile of us.

Donny whips his cut open for a second, flashing his piece. "Yo, they pull anything like they did the last time, I'm putting one of these in them."

Olivia and I glance at each other again. Her eyes tell me the same thing I'm thinking: I didn't think to bring my gun to Church.

"Do I need to remind you all that none of them knew what Bastard was doing? They thought Mercy and I were throwing a coup." Ravage plants a hand on Mercy's shoulder. "Tell 'em, Merce."

"If this club was that skittish, maybe we shouldn't be riding with them," I say.

Mercy lifts his brows. "He's got a point, Rav. I'm not really ready to deal with them. I just got back."

"Brother, you've been out for months." Ravage pats him on the back. "You've had plenty of time to get used to the idea. And so have all of you. We're going on this ride, end of story." He strides out of the room, leaving us all sitting in stunned silence.

It doesn't last long.

The rumble of three Harleys cuts through the air.

Jumping to his feet, Donny stomps to the window overlooking the front entrance. He parts the blinds with two fingers. "Motherfuckers, here they are."

I join him, glaring through the blinds. "I don't like this."

"You and me both," he says, "but what can we do?"

"Ravage means well," Mercy adds. "He's got a very different perspective on the whole thing, though."

I frown at Mercy. As far as I can tell, only Olivia and I know the truth. I wonder why he hasn't told Ravage and the rest of the club, or Shannon.

There's no time.

The Bastard Brothers are here.

I turn and face my club. "All right, none of us love this—except maybe Abraham."

He glares at me.

"But when we walk out there," I continue, "we're one. We're a family. We can't let them see any tension between us. We all agree?" I glance from Mercy to Olivia. Both give me slight nods.

Abraham rises from his seat, his eyes still narrowed at me. "As long as you quit throwing out accusations."

"You voted nay to taking out Bastard."

He crosses his arms in response, his biceps flexing. His eyes bore into me, challenging me to prove my accusation. I've never been able to get a good temperature on him, but I do know one thing.

I ain't afraid of him.

"The math adds up, brother. You voted nay, yet you didn't walk when the rest of 'em did." I step closer to him. "Anything you wanna share before we walk out there?"

Donny intercepts, holding his arms out. "We ain't got time for this. Abraham's one of us. Let's go take this fucking ride so we don't have to see these fuckers for another twenty years."

"Amen to that," Mercy says, stepping out.

The rest follow him, leaving me alone with Olivia. She turns to me, a thousand questions in her eyes.

"He's right," I say. "No time. Let's go." She steps toward the door, but I catch her arm. "I know you can handle yourself, but can you just give me the peace of mind and stay close?"

Stepping into me, she stands on her tiptoes and wraps her arms around my neck. "If by some crazy chance we get split up, we double back and meet at the cemetery." Her dark eyes are more luminous than usual, filled with anxiety.

"That's a good idea," I tell her. Then I lean down and kiss her, using my lips to fill her with calm. If we're going to make it out of this alive, we have to be the right level of paranoid. Just enough to plan ahead and pay attention. I want to tell her I love her, but that might be too much. So instead, I straighten and move my hand to the small of her back.

"Let's take a ride."

24

Somehow Cliff is a whole five inches taller as we walk outside, even with his shoulders tight, muscles coiled. The sun hits me in the eyes, everything going white for a moment as I adjust.

All three Bastard Brothers idle in a loose triangle.

"That's Gavin," Donny points out to Cliff. I follow his line of sight to a man with crazy eyes and wild gray hair. "He used to be our Enforcer."

I lift my eyebrows. "I wouldn't want *that* nutjob torturing me."

"You wouldn't," Donny agrees. He points to a man with short gray hair and a pointed nose. "That's Zed."

The man in question looks just as crazy.

"And that?" Cliff jerks his chin toward the last one, a red-haired man with a surprisingly kind face.

"Malcolm," Donny says. "Don't be fooled. He used to get too handsy with the girls at the Mermaid."

I shudder.

Ravage stands in front of two of Malcolm and Gavin, his body relaxed. From back here, I can't hear a word they're saying, but everyone looks calm.

Giving them a wave, Ravage turns and saunters toward the line of River Reapers bikes. Donny follows right on his heels, his hand still on his piece. But the Bastard Brothers stay where they are, giving all of us plenty of room.

"Come on," Cliff says in my ear. I follow him to our bikes, heart thumping against my sternum. I'm ready for anything, and really regretting leaving my gun at home. Ever since we burned Greg's house down, I haven't felt like I need it.

One by one engines turn over, rumbling into the autumn sky, the echoes circling us in ominous booms.

"Remember the plan," Cliff calls to me. I give him a nod, and then we're off.

Ravage lets the Bastard Brothers take the lead. I guess the stubborn motherfucker isn't as blind as I thought he was. The three of them fan out as they hit the street. With their backs to me, I can finally see their colors.

It's a simple insignia. A circle—the kind normally on memorial type shit. It's a circle of chains, those big thick ones like prison shackles. A banner across the middle displays their name —*Bastard Brothers*, with the *MC* on a separate patch. In the background there's a screaming skull, its head tipped back, jaw open wide in protest.

None of them even have officer patches. It's the weirdest MC I've ever seen. I turn to tell Cliff but we're all moving, falling into formation as we chase the Bastard Brothers. Donny motions to Beer Can and they flank Ravage and Skid. There are definitely some perks to having a bunch of ex-mil members.

Vaughn and Abraham ride behind them, with Cliff and me taking up the rear, as usual. Luckily we outnumber the Bastard Brothers, and this time there are no surprises.

At least, there shouldn't be.

The Bastard Brothers ride in an arc, the three of them almost equal with each other. Normally I can tell the pecking order in a club just by watching its members ride. There's no hierarchy here at all.

They pick up speed, leaving quite a gap between our clubs. From the back, I watch Ravage, waiting to see what he does. If we leave it open too long, a car will turn in and split us up. During our usual rides, we stick close together. Safety in numbers and all that. Too many motorcyclists are hit and even killed every year, all because some cager got impatient. By right, the Bastard Brothers should hang back a little, let us catch up.

Instead, they surge forward again.

"They're trying to get us hurt," I yell. "Vaughn!"

"What?" Cliff veers closer to me.

"Help me flag Ravage." I yell for Vaughn again, but between the wind and all of these engines, he doesn't seem to hear me.

"Ravage!" Cliff yells.

It's too late.

At the front, Ravage leans forward, pushing his motorcycle faster. He gestures to Beer Can and Donny, and one by one we all rush to close the gap. My speedometer creeps to fifty, then sixty. The Bastard Brothers rush forward again. I push to seventy, and it still isn't fast enough.

"We can't just play follow the leader!" I glance at Cliff to make sure he's heard me.

"Just stay with me," he yells back. "No matter what."

"I don't like this." I don't need to say it, but I do anyway. I scream it again: "I don't like this!"

My gut has been telling me since last week that we can't trust these fuckers. It can't be a coincidence that they've come around now that both Cliff and Mercy are out. It's not amends they want. If that were the case, they wouldn't be making us chase them.

There's nothing I can do. I'm just the newest member in a club that's been around since before I was born. We do have a pecking order, and this is not the time for me to take charge and do whatever I need to defend myself.

Or is it?

This is *my* club, too. I should do whatever it takes to protect it, even if it means once again breaking the rules. All my brothers have forgiven me before, because they knew I didn't have a choice in killing Eli, that I needed to save myself from Greg.

Ravage can't see what I see from back here. It's up to me to be his eyes.

I swerve out of line, blipping the throttle so that I can get enough speed to pass Vaughn and Abraham.

I swear I hear Cliff call out my name, but I can't look back. There's no time. We can't keep playing this game, letting them lead us to some kind of death trap.

I lean into the wind, my thighs squeezing the Street Glide, my body connecting with its power. Just like when I rode to my graduation, except this time I'm less reckless, more in control.

"Where you going?" Vaughn yells as I pass him.

I hold up a hand, then blip the throttle again, blowing past them both. The speedometer creeps to eighty, then hovers just under ninety.

Donny spots me in his mirrors. He signals to Beer Can, and they put some room between them, giving me space. I maneuver my way in, white-knuckling the handlebars. I don't have nearly enough experience to be doing this. One wrong move and I could give us all road rash or worse. But I've also spent a lot of time practicing moves I shouldn't have been, and it's finally come in handy. I squeeze between Donny and Beer Can, my entire body thrumming with adrenaline.

And pride.

I can't believe I just did that.

"They're doing this shit on purpose!" I yell.

"No shit," Donny calls back. "That's what you came up here for?" He glances at me, shaking his head.

I frown. I'm just trying to help. "I couldn't tell if you guys realized. We can't keep chasing them. It's the middle of the fucking day!"

Donny points a gloved finger toward Ravage just a few paces ahead of us. "You don't think he doesn't know that? We're gonna veer off, take a different route."

"Get back there with Cliff," Beer Can adds. "We've got this."

I slow, letting them outrun me. My hands tingle as I drop back, my chest getting heavy. I thought I was doing the right thing. Instead I've been spanked and sent to my room.

By the time Cliff catches up to me, Ravage is already taking us onto Route 8, away from the Bastard Brothers and toward Torrington—one of our usual routes. Tears sting my eyes as I watch Ravage's back. I blink them away.

I'm embarrassed, but I'd do it again.

25

CLIFF

R avage is President and I have to trust that he knows what he's doing, that he's trying to do right by all of us. That doesn't stop my emotions from getting the better of me.

As soon as we're off the road, I yank off my helmet and toss it to the ground. "What the fuck were you thinking?" I demand, stomping toward Ravage. "What the fuck was that?"

"Easy, brother." Donny grabs for my arm, but I yank away.

"Ravage? Answer me!"

Ravage and Mercy dismount at the same time. Mercy steps in front of Ravage, blocking me.

"Move. Now." I jab a finger into his chest.

"Whoa." Beer Can steps out of my blind spot, hovering at my side. "Let's calm down a minute, here."

"Everybody's fine," Mercy says. "The last thing we need is to fight each other."

I laugh. "Yeah? *That's* the last thing we need?"

Olivia shoves herself between me and Mercy, ducking under my arm and getting in my space.

I stare at Ravage over her head. "What the fuck was that,

Ravage? None of us wanted this ride! We could've been killed. Or arrested. Or who fucking knows what their end game was!"

He crosses his arms over his cut, tipping his head back. Ice blue eyes stare me down.

"I'm with Cliff, man. What the fuck was that?" Stixx asks, closing up the haphazard circle we've somehow formed.

"Yo, we're all pissed. Let's take it down a notch." Donny pulls a blunt from the inside of his cut and lights it. "Yeah?"

I exhale, limbs shaking with unspent cortisol. "Fuck!" Nostrils flaring, I turn and take several paces away from them. I light a cigarette and keep moving—back and forth, spending the unused adrenaline, purging it from my system.

Olivia joins me, a cigarette dangling between her lips. "Cliff?"

"And you," I shout, wheeling on her. "What the fuck were *you* thinking?" Underneath my rage is fear. She scared the shit out of me, taking off like that. If the Bastard Brothers want revenge for me killing my father, there's nothing stopping them from using her.

I'd die if anything happened to her.

She flinches as if I've hit her. "At least I *did* something," she snaps.

"Will you guys please come and hit this before we all kill each other?" Stixx begs.

I keep pacing, ignoring them all. Fury burns through me, narrowing my vision, torching me to the marrow. I clench and unclench my fists, dousing the fear with white hot anger. Because if I let in the fear, it's all I'll feel, and I'll freeze.

This anger isn't doing me any good, either.

I gulp in deep breaths of nicotine, taking drags so big my lungs hurt. At least I'm not hurting anyone else.

In my peripheral vision, I see Olivia take two big hits off the blunt. She holds it out to me.

I take it from her and bring it to my lips. As I inhale, I finally take in my surroundings. We stand in the grass next to a swampy looking pond. Insects buzz around our heads. Exhaling, I glance toward the direction we came from. I don't think we're supposed to ride in here. It's just a small pond right off 63 in Middlebury. Technically this is just an access road.

I take another hit, focusing on everything around me. The light breeze. The warm sun. The wide path leading under an umbrella of trees. The algae dotting the water.

It'd be a great place to dump a body.

Coughing, I pass the blunt to Stixx.

"Everybody calm?" Ravage asks, smirking.

I sigh.

"Obviously," he continues, "that was some shit. I wanted to give them the benefit of the doubt, but I think it's safe to say we won't be riding with them again."

"All respect, but we all told you we don't trust them," Donny says.

I keep my mouth shut, nursing my cigarette instead. It's not just me demanding answers anymore. We're all pissed.

"I know." Ravage sighs. "Now we know for sure."

Olivia scoffs, but says nothing.

"It's clear where we stand with them," our President says. "I know you're all pissed, but I want you to keep it in check. We're rivals, but no River Reaper is going to aggravate this." He looks directly at me, then Olivia. "Understood?"

"Crystal fucking clear," I say, throwing my cigarette at the ground. I grind it out with the heel of my boot.

"Vaughn," Ravage says.

"Yeah?"

"I want a new surveillance system wired up for the Mermaid. How long you think that'll take?"

Vaughn motions to Stixx and Abraham. "Send these two to Best Buy with me, give us a few hours, and I can have it up tonight."

"Do it," Ravage says.

"Not like I have a social life," Vaughn mutters.

The three of them climb back onto their bikes. The thunder of engines drowns out any further conversation as they maneuver out of the access road and back onto the street. The rest of us stand in silence, staring after them.

"I guess it's safe to say the Bastard Brothers are off the invite list for Shannon's thing," Beer Can says finally.

"Indefinitely," Ravage agrees. For a moment, he dips his chin, his eyes closing. His chest rises and falls in a silent sigh. He turns back to us. "I want everybody carrying from here on out, too. You don't have a piece, talk to Donny." He swings back onto his motorcycle. "Now let's get the fuck out of here."

For the first time all day, I agree with him.

26

I charge into Lucy's condo, slamming the door behind me. The driveway is empty, so at least I know I'm not waking Bunny. The door opens behind me and Cliff steps inside, his head bowed. I wheel on him.

"What the fuck, Cliff? Since when do you go off on me like that—especially in front of other people?"

He runs a hand through his tousled black hair. "Since when have you become so reckless? If anything happened to you, I'd—"

"That's a garbage apology," I tell him. "What the fuck came over you?"

"Me?" He scoffs. "What the fuck possessed you to ride up on Ravage and boss him around?"

I fold my arms across my chest, straightening my spine.

"No answer, huh?" He smirks at me.

Cocky fucker. Of course I don't have an answer. I really don't want to hear what I know is under his anger. So instead, I pull a classic Olivia. "No one tells me what to do. Not Mercy, not Ravage, not you."

He averts his gaze.

I can't help but think of when he lured Greg to the clubhouse, to how terrified I was, how close he was to blowing his parole away.

"You can't be starting fights with Ravage and Mercy," I continue, stepping closer.

He laughs. "No? But hiding bodies is allowed?"

I roll my eyes. "You know what I mean. What the fuck is wrong with you?" I squeeze my hands, nails digging into the tender flesh of my palms. I want to punch him. I want to hammer my fists into his chest. Why does he do this shit?

"What the fuck is wrong with me?" he repeats. He closes the distance between us, catching my wrists in his hands and pulling me into his chest. "You tell me, Olivia," he murmurs into my hair. "You tell me."

All of the fight drains from my body, but the beast inside me fuels the flames. My mouth keeps moving. "Don't start with that shit again."

He laughs again. "'That shit.' Oh, Olivia. You're killing me. Do you really expect me to be with you and not love—?"

"You can't fight Mercy because he's still my stepfather," I blurt, cutting him off. "He's still my family, and he's your godfather. We have to work it out."

"You want me to work it out, but you won't even talk to Bree," he says.

There he goes, calling me out again.

I shake my head, curls bouncing against my forehead. "I can't."

"Why not? Because you're afraid you'll find out you have more in common with her?"

He knows me so well.

"Are you my fucking therapist?" I pat myself down, hunting for my pack of cigarettes. This is the thing about Cliff that drives me crazy. He always cuts right to my marrow, seeing me with a crystal clarity.

As irritating as it is when he's right, it kind of feels good that he knows me so deeply, that he cares so much, he'll never lie—even if it's something I don't want to hear.

My phone vibrates in my pocket. I tug at it, gritting my teeth as I wrestle it free. I don't want to read texts. I want to keep fighting. I want to burn us alive until all we have left is ashes, then rebuild on top of them. Because that's what we do. No matter how hard I push him away, he springs right back.

Even though I'm afraid one day he *will* leave, it'd be for the best for him. I'm only slowly breaking him. He deserves all of the beautiful things in the world.

By the time I get it out, my phone is dark again. I press the home button to wake it up, and the text displays across the screen.

"Fuck me," I mutter.

"What is it?" He glances down at the phone in my hand.

I hold it up for him to see.

Vaughn: You free to meet up with Cami?

"I thought he was setting up new cameras," Cliff says, grabbing his cigarettes.

"Apparently he's even faster than we thought." The last thing I want to do is sit across a table from Cami. I ruined her life. But if it means firming up all the research Vaughn and I have done, then I'll do it.

I glare up at Cliff. "We're not finished here."

"Well that's a relief," he jokes. "I thought you were gonna break up with me again."

I frown at him. "Break up with you? No, I just wanted to fight. I don't want to break up with you."

"Ever?"

Even though he's right, I roll my eyes at him and step around him. "Don't push it."

I glance over my shoulder, and he's grinning. I hold his gaze for a moment, and then I leave before I say something even more stupid.

I ride out to The Beanery, a hole in the wall coffee shop that's been in downtown Waterbury for decades. It's annoying that Cami picked a place out of town, but I get it. I wouldn't want to be seen with me, either. Not with my reputation.

I stroll through the door, lifting a hand in greeting to a blonde barista I don't recognize. I used to ride the bus out here during high school, always on my own. This was my spot. Not even Greg knew about it. I liked that it was out of town, that no one here recognized me. It was my escape.

Behind the counter, a guy wearing a backward baseball cap holds a phone between his ear and shoulder. He isn't the owner, but they've got the same nose, just younger. So much has changed since I was last here.

I spot Vaughn and Cami at a table tucked into a corner, and sigh. I'm going to need something stronger than coffee.

"What can I get you?" the barista asks. She's perky but there's an edge to her, a fraying around her eyes.

"Give me your strongest drink in your biggest size," I tell her. "And no pumpkin anything."

"So, a nitro. Except I can't give it to you in anything bigger than a medium. It's that strong," she says with a wink.

"Do it." I turn away while she makes my coffee, pouring it from a tap like at a bar. I try not to watch Cami—not in an obvious way, anyway—but I can't help it. She still looks whole. Her blue eyes crinkle at something Vaughn says, her lips tipping upward in a smile. There aren't any dark circles under her eyes. No signs of nightmares that keep her awake.

I watch as Vaughn leans into her, his dark eyes intent on whatever it is she's saying. They're so comfortable sitting there. By walking over, I'll ruin it all.

I almost tell the barista to make my drink to go. Then Vaughn spots me and jerks his chin at me. Sighing, I take the nitro she holds out to me and traipse over to them.

"Vaughn. Cami." I don't know what else to say. "Hi" seems a little too chipper, considering. I've never been a chipper girl.

"Hi Olivia," she says. Of course *she's* a chipper girl. She's still shiny.

Vaughn slides over a seat, motioning for me to sit where he just was. This puts me directly across from Cami. I chuckle nervously, setting my nitro down. An awkward moment passes as I stand here.

That's when I notice the shiner he's sporting.

"Dude, what happened to you?"

"Ah, it's nothing," he says with a smirk.

Cami's cheeks turn pink, and I tilt my head at the two of them.

"I won't bite," she promises, avoiding him and glancing at the open seat.

"Olivia might," Vaughn jokes.

Even though it's at my expense, it snaps me back into the moment. I pull the chair out and sit. This close to Cami, I can see the details I missed from way back there: the way her clothes hang on her a little, the tightness at the corners of her eyes, the slight tremor to her hands.

"Thanks for coming," I say, because what else can I say? "I thought you skipped town."

"I did," she says on a long exhale. "After what you told me, I panicked." Her bright blue eyes cloud over a bit. "I always knew something was off about Greg. Another one of his exes said something similar to what you said, and there were a couple times he got a little rough with me." She swallows. "So I ran," she finishes.

"But you came back," Vaughn says. His hand slides toward her then halts.

I smirk, then quickly pull my face back into neutral. I can't wait to bust his balls about this later.

"I came back," she affirms, but she doesn't elaborate. I don't push, because it's none of my business, and it isn't what I came here for.

"Cami, we thought you might be able to help us with something." I spin my cup around.

"That's what Vaughn said. I don't know what I can possibly do to repay you, but I'll try."

I blink at her. "Repay me?"

She nods, but again, she doesn't say any more about it. "So what's this about?"

"There was an incident earlier this year," I say, "with the football team." I wait for a flash of recognition.

Instead, she pales. "Oh."

"Cami, we're hoping you can help us with some information," Vaughn says, his tone soothing. I cast a quick glance at him. I never would've pegged him for a sweet talker. Not like this.

"We all signed NDAs," she says.

"Why?" I lean forward, but she crosses her legs away from me. We're losing her. I look at Vaughn again, hoping he's got another smooth card up those black hoodie sleeves.

"People talk," he says casually. "We've heard some things. We just want to confirm what we've heard."

"I don't know a lot." She reaches for her car keys, uncrossing her legs.

"Please don't go," I beg. "We just want to talk."

She stands so suddenly she bumps the table, the cups of coffee sloshing liquid over their sides. "The last time you 'just' talked to me, Olivia, my house burned down." Without another word, she storms out of the coffee shop.

I turn to Vaughn. "What the fuck?"

"Subtlety really isn't your thing, is it?"

"What do you mean? I thought she knew why we were meeting." I narrow my eyes at him. "How did you get her here?"

He runs a hand through his hair. "I kinda told her you wanted to check in with her."

"Fuck, Vaughn." I pick up my cup and take a sip of the nitro. Despite its dark appearance, it's actually creamy. It could use a little more sugar, though.

Kinda like me.

"She'll be back," I tell him, and hope I'm right. So far, she's the only lead we've got.

28

CLIFF

The alarm on my phone goes off, letting me know it's time for my lunch break. Unlike in high school or prison, there are no bells to keep me on track, so I had to improvise. Turning off my machine, I remove my safety glasses and hook them onto my T-shirt. I hate lunch break. If I had it my way, I'd work straight through.

Grabbing my backpack, I head outside. It's still early autumn, still warm enough to sit outside without freezing my balls off. I walk several paces away from the building, keeping my back to it, and sit down in one of the lonely patches of grass. Ever since I got out, I appreciate shit like this even more.

I still can't believe Olivia didn't tell me to go fuck myself yesterday. After the way I lost it on everyone, I expected her to cut me loose real quick.

She's still here.

I don't know what's changed between us, but I'm not about to jinx it. I pull out my phone and start writing her a quick text asking about her day. My thumb hovers over the send button. That might be too much.

My phone dings, but it isn't Olivia.

Lucy: Can you watch Leigh tonight? Olivia has a shift. Pretend I'm six and still super cute. Pretty pretty please, Cliff?

The kid sure knows how to get me. I couldn't say no to her even if I wanted to. Not after everything she's done for me since I got out.

It also gives me an excuse to be around whenever Olivia gets home tonight. I haven't seen her since yesterday afternoon, when we argued at Lucy's.

Cliff: You got it.

Now I've got uninterrupted baby time to look forward to, which I'll never say no to since I'll never have one of my own. Shannon said to compromise, but I don't know how to give up the picture in my head. Some shrink would probably say it's because I'm idealizing my childhood.

I say it's because I already gave up half my life for someone I love. Now I want to live. I just don't want to live without Olivia.

WHEN I WALK into Lucy's, she presses a crying Bunny into my arms.

"She just needs a diaper change," she says, looping a hoop earring into place. She leans down and checks her lipstick in the mirror.

"Got a hot date?" I joke. She glares at me, and I take Bunny over to the couch. "Somebody's touchy."

"I won't be any later than midnight," she promises, slipping into black heeled boots that hit at just above her knees.

"Are those Olivia's?"

"Tell her and I'll slit your throat."

"Wow," I tell Bunny. I start unsnapping the buttons on her onesie, my huge fingers clumsy on the tiny things. It's going to take me 'til midnight, at this rate. "Your mom really needs to get boned."

"Cliff!"

"Oh, *that's* where the line is. Good to know."

She gives me another dirty look, holding it only for a few seconds before she bursts out laughing. I join her, shaking my head.

"I do," she says between giggles. "I really do."

"I see you've already hit the fun pen."

"I'm nervous!" She sighs. "I can't believe *I'm* nervous. I don't even care about dating. Who am I right now?" She leans toward the mirror on the wall, checking her makeup again.

"Luce, you're so awesome, you're probably making *him* nervous right now. Any guy who isn't nervous around you will have to answer to me." I work at a tiny button with one hand, making a fist with the other.

Lucy smiles but goes quiet.

I return my full attention to the baby, finally finishing unbuttoning her. "Do I know this guy?" I ask, bracing myself before I open up this diaper.

"Gotta go," she says, and becomes a whirlwind as she grabs her keys and a clutch I'm pretty sure is also Olivia's. She bends down and kisses Bunny on the forehead, leaving a red smudge. Then she kisses me on the forehead, and I'm positive I've got a matching lipstick mark.

"Hey!" I call after her as she hurries out. "You better take this off! Your sister will kill me!"

She's already gone.

I look down at the baby, who's watching me with wide green eyes. "The biker and the baby," I say with a sigh.

I've never watched Bunny before. Suddenly it's a little hard to breathe. I don't know what I was thinking. It's been so easy, caring for Bunny under Lucy's watchful eye. If I had to do this for more than a few hours, I'd be completely lost.

"Let's just hope we don't run into any snags," I tell her, taking the diaper off. I clean her up and get her in a fresh diaper in just a few minutes, and she's calm by the time I'm finished dressing her. I sit back on the couch, Bunny in my arms. "We're gonna be just fine."

It feels like an omen.

29

OLIVIA

"Last call," I tell my cocktail waitresses. "Go make the rounds."

It's 12:41 a.m. and I'm ready for this day to be over. Thankfully we've been pretty slow, even for a Monday. The girls fan out and I turn to the register, hoping I can close out and we can just leave when the clock strikes one. It never goes that way, but I can dream.

My phone buzzes with another text from Bryce. It turns out that I'm really good at connecting with people. Maybe it's my months as a bartender, listening to drunk old bikers lament over my drinks, but Bryce opens up to me without much pressing. Maybe it's just that he needs someone to listen.

I think that's what we all need.

Olivia: We're gonna figure this out. I've got you.

Bryce: thx

I open the drawer and start counting.
In the mirror behind the bar, I catch a glimpse of Pru heading

toward me. Abandoning my count, I close the drawer. "What can I get you?"

"Got anything that will calm my nerves through the rest of the week?" she jokes.

I tilt my head to the side, lifting an eyebrow at her.

"Ravage and Mark asked me about Cervical Caves playing on weekends."

When I still look confused, she explains.

"My band. I guess Cliff suggested they ask me," she says, propping her elbows on the bar.

A twinge of jealousy grips my stomach. Fucking Cliff—always a ladies' man. A moment later, it fades. I kind of love that he's always willing to do for others.

"You know, since the old band didn't work out." Her violet eyes appraise me.

"Oh Vile Eye," I say, the taste of copper filling my mouth.

She nods. "It's a real shame about their lead singer," she says, her tone sardonic.

"You know," I say, mixing her a Long Island iced tea, "Oh Vile Eye was an anagram for Olivia. Most people wouldn't catch it, but I knew. Greg was obsessed with me." I slide her the drink.

"He deserved to burn." She takes a sip. "I once had a boyfriend who did some unspeakable shit to me. I pulled a knife on him the last time and he never contacted me again, but he still posts poetry about me on Instagram."

I don't know what to say. I don't want to be the poster girl for PTSD. I grab a rag and start wiping the already clean bar top.

"You're a lucky girl."

I glance up, my hand freezing. "Huh?"

"Cliff got me this gig. Well, not *this* one." She motions to the thong and bra she's wearing. "If I can start playing more shows, I might be able to stop dancing. He's one of the good ones, Olivia. One of the very few."

My lips part to say I don't even know what when Bree climbs onto the stool next to Pru.

"You missed last call," I tell her without looking at her.

"I don't drink anymore. I'm clean," she says.

"Then what are you doing here?"

Giving me a curious look, Pru takes her drink and leaves us to it.

"I came to talk to you," Bree says.

"I'm working, Bree. If you aren't ordering a drink, I can't talk."

"I'm staying at the house with Mercy. You should come by for dinner sometime."

When she should've been taking care of me, I took care of her.

And it's never enough.

I hate what happened to her. I'm even starting to understand why she couldn't even look at me. But we can't get those years back, and I don't know that I can trust her not to leave me again when things get too hard.

It hurts.

I grip the bar top, willing my lungs to just take the air that surrounds me. As always, I come up empty.

"Just think about it," she says, giving my hand a squeeze before walking away.

30

CLIFF

I 'm on the couch when Lucy slips inside, Olivia's shoes slung over the crook of her arm.

"Hey," she whispers, glancing around the living room.

I hold up the baby monitor. "She's upstairs."

"You're my hero. Thank you so much." She inches toward the stairs.

I can't help it. I have to bust her ass. "I take it things went well."

She whips her head around, red hair flying everywhere. "Huh?"

"It's after one. You said you'd be back no later than midnight." I smirk.

"Oh." Even in the dark, I can see her blushing.

"Luce," I tease, "did you get boned?"

"What? No!" She glares at me. "I don't bone on the first date. Usually."

"So you *did*." I place the baby monitor on the coffee table.

"You're such an ass." She freezes, sniffing the air. "What is that?"

"That," I tell her,"is my own special boning recipe. Olivia's getting out soon," I explain.

"I'll leave you to it, then." She turns for the stairs again.

"Not so fast, young lady."

"Yeah?"

I drop the smirk. "Did you have a nice time?"

Her mouth tugs up a little at the corners. "I did."

"Good. Goodnight, Luce." I smile as she ascends the stairs. Her happiness is worth every year I spent in the pen. I'd do it all over again, just to see her so free, living her life by her own terms.

I hope I can do the same now.

Switching off the baby monitor, I glance at my phone. It's almost 1:30 a.m., so Olivia should be home any minute. Stretching, I haul myself to my feet. I stretch again, wringing out muscles and tendons. I haven't been sitting long but that's what the late thirties do to a guy.

I shuffle into the dark kitchen, turning on a light as I enter. Lucy's oven is still on warm mode, so with any luck, I haven't ruined dinner. Pulling it open, I peer inside. Nothing is burnt. Relieved, I close the door again and straighten. There's not much else for me to do. The table is already set, except for one final touch.

I grab Lucy's emergency candles from the top of the fridge and flip on the switches. Like magic, I've got romantic flickering. Olivia's either going to stab me or swoon. I can't wait to find out which.

As I place the candles in the middle of the table, I hear her Street Glide rumble up the driveway. It's go time.

I rub my hands on my jeans, wondering for the thirtieth time if I should've worn a different T-shirt. Olivia likes when I wear V-necks, though, and black is my signature color.

I don't know why I'm so nervous. It's just dinner.

Except I've never cooked for her before.

The rumble of the engine fades and I imagine her walking up to the front door. I glance at the candles again, the sunflowers in a vase. It's too much. She's going to think I'm proposing or some crazy shit. I reach for a candle but it's too late. The door opens.

I stand over the table, frozen. From the other end of the hall, her gaze meets mine. She takes in the scene, her eyes widening slightly. Fuck.

"The power went out," I blurt, and immediately regret it. She's going to know I'm full of shit the second she sees what I made.

She sniffs the air, delicate nose turned up. "That smells good. Did you get pizza? I'm starving." She closes the distance between us and there's nothing left for me to do but keep going.

I pull out a chair for her.

"What is this?" she asks, dropping her bag onto the floor. Smiling up at me, she sits. "Did you *cook*?"

"Is it too much?"

She reaches for me, bringing my face to her level. She gives me a ghost of a kiss, but it's sweet and warm. "It's nice."

I kiss her back, moving my lips against hers. I almost want to say fuck dinner, but this *is* nice. I break the kiss, caressing her chin as I pull away.

"What's in the oven?"

I pull out the dish and carry the food over to the table. "Spaghetti squash," I say, setting it down. I serve each half to us, then sit across from her.

She gapes down at the spaghetti squash I stuffed with ground turkey, stewed tomatoes, mushrooms, and garlic. "I figured you made chicken nuggets. I didn't know you could cook!"

I shrug. "After my mom died, I spent a lot of time with her aunt. She was already up there, but she could still boss me around. I did her gardens, cooked for us, cleaned her house. She lived there until the day she died. Unfortunately I was inside when that happened." I stare down at my plate.

Olivia reaches across the table and places her hand over mine. "You were close with her?"

"Yeah. My mom was her namesake. She was cool. You would've loved her." I'm not sure Aunt Ruth still loved me at the end, but I don't say so. I push away the memories.

"You don't ever talk about your mom," Olivia says, watching me.

I shrug.

"I mean, you know all about Bree. I don't anything about . . ."

"Ruth." Even saying it is a knife twisting in my sternum. I'll never know the truth about her death, but I'll always wonder.

Giving my hand a squeeze, Olivia picks up her fork. "So how the fuck do I eat this?"

My shoulders relax a little. Olivia never pries, even though I can tell she's dying to know. Not because she's nosy, but because she genuinely wants to hear about my mom.

"I already did some of the shredding," I say, picking up my own fork. "But you just kinda reach in and drag your fork down, making spaghetti strands." I demonstrate, raking the filling and squash with my fork.

"This is pretty fancy for a felon."

"I told you. Aunt Ruth kept me busy." I frown down at my plate. "That's why I didn't know what Bastard was doing to Lucy until it was too late."

She sets down her fork. "Hey. It wasn't too late. You saved her."

"Damage was done," I say with a shrug. "You should've seen her tonight, though, Liv. She went on a date."

"Whoa, what?" She chuckles. "Lucy? Are you sure?"

"She stole your shoes, too."

"Which ones?"

"The velvet boots that come up to your thighs, with the heels." I grin.

A sly grin spreads across her face. "She did, huh?"

"She barely gave me any details. She was locked down." I plunge my fork in, coming back up with a huge bite.

Olivia mirrors me, grabbing her own bite. She slides the fork into her mouth, lips closing around the metal. Her eyes fall closed. "Oh," she moans. "This is good."

Thank Google for helping me fill in the blanks.

"The trick," I say, swallowing, "is seasoning the inside of the squash while it roasts. It has zero flavor, otherwise."

"Look at you," she muses, looking up at me from under sooty lash. "All kinds of talents."

"Keep me around, you'll see what else I can do." I lift a cocky brow at her.

Her cheeks flush. "God, I hope so."

We fall into comfortable silence, working our way through the squash. After a few minutes, I put my fork down. I almost forgot about the wine. "Thirsty?" I ask, standing and walking to the fridge.

"Very."

I glance at her over my shoulder and find her watching me as if *I'm* the glass of water. I pull the wine out and pour two glasses. "This'll have to do for now." I carry them back to the table.

"For now," she purrs.

When I'm seated again, I ask, "So how was work?"

Her eyes darken. "Bree came by."

"Shit. Did she say anything?"

"She wants to talk. She wants me to come over for dinner." She takes a sip of wine, then another. "Damn. You're even good at pairing wine."

I take a sip of mine. "I went on the packy guy's recommendation." When she nods, I wait for her to continue. She doesn't. "So Bree," I prod.

She sips more wine. "I can't picture going there for dinner, Cliff."

"I don't blame you," I say slowly.

"But? I heard a 'but' in there."

I sigh. "She's your mom. If Ruth was still alive, I'd do whatever it took to save our relationship."

She scoffs. "I never had a relationship with Bree, Cliff. She read me a couple books, maybe tucked me in ten times total. Usually when she was high on Percs. She was a lot more nurturing on Percs."

I tap my fingers on the table. "I know," I soothe. "At least now you know why she was the way she was."

She sighs into her wine glass. Taking another sip, she sets it down. "I don't want to talk about Bree. I want to talk about the fact that you made me dinner with candles and . . . Are these flowers for me?" She runs a finger along the petals of one of the sunflowers.

"Just to dress up the table a little," I say quickly.

"Uh-huh." She smirks at me. "Why all the dressing up?" Her eyes drop to my collarbones, exposed by the V-neck.

I stammer a little, gathering our dishes to buy me time. "I don't know."

"Yeah, you do." She stands too.

I carry everything to the sink, feeling her eyes burning into me. I scrape the dishes into the garbage and turn on the hot water.

She bumps me with her hip. "Step away from the dishes. You cooked. I'll clean up."

I turn and her face is just a few inches from mine. All I have to do is bend down and take her lips. It's not kissing Olivia that's distracted me. It's the idea of a future where this is a regular occurrence, where we have a life together.

"I figured we could use a few minutes of normal," I say.

"Right." She reaches a hand under the stream of water, then flicks several warm droplets at me.

"Hey!" I duck, but it's far too late. Beads of water hit my face, land in my beard. I go to wet my hand, but she's already turned off the water. Laughing, she darts away. I chase after her.

She runs through the kitchen and up the stairs. I keep on her heels, grabbing for her leg but she's quick and it's late. I don't want to wake Bunny or Lucy.

At the top of the stairs, she pauses.

31

OLIVIA

I stop at the top of the stairs and look down. Cliff stands a few steps below me, his frame silhouetted by the porch light shining in from the front door. He's all shadow, except the whites of his eyes. I swallow, waiting. He comes up the last few steps and takes me into his arms. I rest my head on his shoulder, my heart pounding against his chest. The house falls into a hush around us.

Wordlessly, I take his hand and bring him to my bedroom. I don't bother turning on any lights. As soon as he closes the door behind him, we find each other, touching everywhere possible. Our fingers twine through each other, our palms touching. His heart races against mine, the echo booming in my breasts, reverberating through flesh and bone. I don't need light to find him because he is my light.

Somewhere between this breath and the next, his lips find mine. I breathe him in, his oxygen infiltrating my lungs until the tingling in my hands disappears. Clothing falls to the floor, and I don't know who's removing what. He lays me down on my bed and comes to rest between my knees. The moonlight filtering through the blinds highlights his cheekbones, his nose, the quiet worship in his eyes.

He wraps his body around mine, his hands cradling my back, his thighs hugging mine. I spread for him, hugging him with my legs. There's a brush of fingers at my center, a slow caress of his head against mine. Then he's inside me, sliding in deep, fingers curling into my shoulder blades. His lips zero in on mine again, and all I can do is hang on as I fall into him.

He's the only thing that can catch me.

The heat of him thaws my icy limbs, his kisses mobilizing my lips, each thrust of his hips sending ripples of warmth through my nerves. I soar, hovering between the fall and a crash, and for a moment I hang in suspension. But he moves his hands from underneath me, captures my hands in his, holding them above our heads, flush against the mattress. His tether keeps me steady, and I let go.

In the fall there's a kaleidoscope rush, a sudden cutoff of air as I gasp. I tumble through forever, and all of my insecurities and doubts disappear for a sweet moment. I cling to him, taking him with me. In this suspension my heartbeat is crystal clear in my ears, an ebb and flow as he pumps into me. He spasms inside of me, and together we are full.

Hot tears fall from my eyes. There's no going back. I can't rebuild the dam he's broken, but the damage isn't damning. It's a permanent door, marked with his name on the plate.

My lips move with the words, but there's no sound.

He pulls out, rolling to the side and gathering me into him. I lie curled against him, my pulse amplified in the dark. I want to speak, to put a name to this, but my voice catches in my throat and I'm frozen again, always the rabbit girl.

He cups my shoulder with a warm hand, pressing a kiss to my forehead. "It's okay, Liv. I feel you."

I shatter into countless pieces, held together only by his arms.

I wait for him to say more, but he doesn't speak again. Minutes tick by, and his breathing slows, steadies, deepens. The tears keep rolling.

I lie awake all night, cocooned by him and the rapid beat of my heart. I don't feel tired or awake. I just lie in awareness.

The shadows of night turn to gray. The sky lightens. Streaks of orange brighten the sapphire black, accompanied by pinks and reds. An old nursery rhyme plays on a loop through my head.

Red at night, sailor's delight. Red in the morning, sailor's warning.

I stare at the sky through the blinds, my pulse picking up with every bit of sky the sun gains. By the time the birds start singing and the crickets go to bed, I'm full of a dread so deep, I can't move. When his alarm goes off and he rises, I close my eyes and feign sleep, wishing I could turn the clock back.

Because for a moment everything felt right, and now everything has changed.

He slips from the room and I hear him start the shower. Bunny fusses in her nursery and Lucy sings to her, soothing her. The velvet sweetness of her voice does nothing to calm me. Instead, it rings through my veins, a warning punctuated by each beat of the war drum in my chest.

I turn my alarm off before it joins the symphony and remain in bed, wishing desperately to rewind. I can only listen as the house rises around me, the day beginning whether I want it to or not.

I know it as deeply as I know my own history. There is no changing fate, and right now it spins around me, snaring me. There's already a subtle steady thrum, a faint flutter that I can only barely detect. I brace myself, but this time there's no one to catch me.

My eyes slip closed. The tears dry. The sun shines and birds sing. Someone starts a pot of coffee. I swim down into the deep, hoping that when I wake up, it will all have been a dream.

I can't control my dreams any more than I can control anything around me, what's already in motion. My body does the work while I lie here, unable to stop it. I opened the dam and now I am damned. The red of sunrise pulls me in, muddying to a deep, bottomless black.

32

"So," Lucy says, giving me a smug look over her coffee. "It sounded like there was some mighty boning going on last night."

I groan. "God, Luce."

"Oh, what's the matter?" Her grin widens. "Don't want to talk about boning my sister?"

I all but squirm in my seat. "Jesus Christ."

"How does it feel?" She takes a long sip, pleased with herself.

"You've made your point," I concede. "We'll never discuss our sex lives ever again."

"Seriously, though," she says. "Seems like you two are doing pretty well."

Leaning back, I nod. "Yeah. Things are a lot different now. Better."

"I'm honestly shocked. I mean, I love you both, obviously, but I thought there was no way it would work."

"People change," I say with a shrug. "Or it's my magic dick."

"Cliff!" Reaching over to the tabletop bouncer where Bunny is snoozing, she grabs a stray pacifier and chucks it at me. "I thought we called a truce!"

"People change." I smirk.

"Look, it's Olivia," Lucy says loudly. "Want some coffee?"

Straightening, I crane my neck to get a good look at Olivia. Our eyes meet, but she ducks her head.

"I'm good. I've got to get going."

"Hey," I say, twisting in my seat. "I'll see you later?"

"Yeah." Tucking a curl behind her ear, she grabs her keys from the table. She hurries out with her head down, shoulders drawn.

"Uh-oh," Lucy intones.

"Watch it." I frown as Olivia shuts the door behind her.

"I thought things were better. What happened?"

I lift a shoulder and shove down the doubt clawing its way up my throat. It doesn't go anywhere, though. Instead, it just settles in my stomach. "People change," I say.

She sighs. "I really don't want to see you get hurt."

Olivia rides off, taking my heart with her. "Too late." I lift my mug in a salute. Lucy clinks hers against mine. "To the broken hearts club."

"Pfft, please. My heart is unbreakable. *I'm* the one who does the breaking."

"You two deserve each other," I tell her with a wink, but my chest is tender and bruised. "Luce?"

"Yeah?" She regards me with soft eyes.

"Can you show me how to hook up my phone to the Bluetooth thing in my bike?" This morning I need to ride into work with my music blasting, and if that means swallowing my pride and asking my little cousin to hook me up, then so be it.

"Of course," she says, putting her hand over mine for a second. She gives my fingers a little squeeze. "Of course."

I ride to work with Deftones drowning out my thoughts. Before I can take off my helmet, my phone goes off with a text from Ravage.

Ravage: Meet me on your lunch break.

A second later, he texts me a location. I don't bother to ask for details. Ravage never elaborates.

I have no idea what I'm walking into.

33

OLIVIA

I call out of work.

My entire body aches with dread as I ride over to Esther's. I brake hard at the curb and climb off the Street Glide, hands shaking. She's almost always here in the mornings, sending the girls off to school, throwing dinner into the Crockpot, and logging into her online courses—all with a big ass smile.

Her car isn't in the driveway.

"Fuck."

I pace the front walk, debating whether or not to light a cigarette and sit on her front porch like a stalker. I couldn't sit still even if I wanted to. Anger and hurt and fear churn through me, making my limbs heavy and clouding my mind. This is what I get for shoving it all down, for pretending everything is fine.

I'm so far from fine, I'm on fucking Mars.

Esther is probably the only other person on this planet who can understand how I'm feeling. And now I've called out of work, probably blowing my career in the process.

I light a cigarette and continue pacing, tears burning my eyes. I need to calm down and look normal, but all I want to do is sit in the middle of the street and scream.

The bright green of the lawn pitches up toward me. I stumble, righting myself at the last second. Panting, I trudge to the porch and lower myself to the steps, knees shaking. I squeeze my eyes shut, willing my heart to stop racing, begging my lungs to just take the air. I don't understand why this keeps happening. It's only a panic attack—I know that—but it feels like I'm dying. I open my eyes and realize I've wrapped my own hand around my throat.

"Get a grip, Olivia," I whisper, lowering my hand to my lap. This body isn't even my own right now. I'm just floating, a blurred glitch disconnected from flesh and blood and bone. In therapy, Eva taught me a dozen techniques for this, but I can't think of a single one. I curl against the railing, eyes shut, nostrils flaring as I suck in deep breaths.

I don't even hear Esther pull into the driveway.

Instead, I hear Greg, the black velvet of his voice as he crushes the breath from my throat. "I love you, Olivia. I'll always find you, even if you run away."

"Olivia?"

The wooden rail bites into the side of my head, but all I feel is the hard box spring beneath me. I reach for his chest, trying to push him off me, but he's too heavy. I scratch at his hands, legs thrashing, but he doesn't budge. He's going to kill me. He's going to kill me and when they find my body, they'll think it was just a sex game gone wrong.

"Olivia?"

I wrench my eyes open. Esther crouches in front of me, her brow furrowed with concern.

"Olivia, what's going on?"

The words swirl through my head, but I can't remember how to speak. I beg her with bleary eyes, black tear tracks racing down my cheeks.

"Panic attack?" she guesses.

All of my strength goes into a single nod. "Can't breathe," I whisper, tapping the side of my head with a finger.

"Flashbacks, too?"

I nod again.

"Come on." Hooking a dainty arm under mine, she hauls me to my feet and leads me inside. She sits me down in a living room framed by large windows and bright green plants. I sink into the plush couch, running my hands over the corduroy.

"How come we didn't have this nice shit?" I croak. My thoughts slow. My breathing normalizes. With a quick dose of sarcasm, I slip back into my body.

"At our old apartment?" She hands me a cold bottle of water. I didn't even see her duck into the kitchen. "I thought our couch was nice."

I take a swig of the water. "If I'd known you were getting new shit, I would've made you leave me the couch."

"I didn't know," she swears, expressive eyebrows lifting. "My grandparents got us these as a housewarming gift." She motions to the matching love seat.

"What happened to the old couch?" I keep sipping water, my throat parched.

"It's in Cierra's room," she says, referring to her oldest little sister. "That way when she has friends sleep over, they don't have to sleep on the floor."

"What ever happened to sharing a bed?" I screw the cap back onto the bottle. It's still hard to get a full breath, but the distraction is working. I'll have to remember this the next time I have a panic attack: think about couches.

"Teenagers have gotten awfully prissy," she says with a shrug. "I'll admit, she's only got a twin, so it *is* a tight squeeze for two." She sits next to me, brown eyes still worried. "You wanna tell me why you were crying on my porch?"

I swipe at my cheeks. My fingers come away smudged with

mascara. Esther hands me a box of tissues. "Bree's back," I hedge, rubbing at my hands with a tissue.

"Yeah," she says warily. "What did she bring with her?"

This is why I love Esther. She gets it, without me having to explain. Fresh hot tears roll from my eyes. "Mercy isn't my father."

"Oh, Livia." She pulls me into a hug, rubbing my back. "I know you really loved the idea of him."

"That's only half of it," I say into her shoulder. "Bree was already pregnant when she met him. She was raped. I hate that that happened to her, but I still can't forgive her for leaving me. Am I a monster?" My own shoulders shudder as I let go of the words. I sob into her, and she lets me, rubbing my back until I'm empty.

She hands me another tissue. "Are you still seeing your therapist?"

I pat at the tears on my face. Somehow there's *still* more mascara. "Waterproof, my ass," I mutter. I meet Esther's eyes. "I don't have time to see her anymore. Greg is dead. Eli is, too. They can't hurt me now." I press my lips together.

"Doesn't make it suck any less." Her fingers sift through my hair, gentle and soothing. The last person to stroke my hair was Bree. How can I have good memories of someone who has hurt me so much? My feelings for her are fucked up, never mind complicated.

"Did Toci ever make you feel safe?" I ask.

Esther clicks her tongue against her teeth. "Nope." She continues smoothing my curls. "But Abuela always did. She and Abuelo stepped up every time Toci fucked up. All of my good childhood memories are because of them."

I sigh. "All my childhood memories are fucked up. I thought Mercy taught me how to ride a motorcycle and shoot a gun. Turns out that was Ravage."

"That's common with childhood trauma," she says. "There

was some truth to your memory. It might not have been Mercy but it was still someone who cared about you."

"So you're saying I should adopt Ravage and Shannon as my new parents?"

"Olivia." She laughs. "You've already been adopted."

"Look how that turned out," I mutter.

"I know you feel like everything in your life is a lie, but you still have me. You still have Lucy. You still have Cliff."

The sound of his name sends ribbons of tingles through me. I shut it down. In its place another emotion springs to the surface. I picture a shadow man holding my mother down, his hands around her throat like Greg's on mine. "I came from everything I hate," I whisper into her shoulder. More tears soak her shirt.

"I know." She rubs circles into my back.

"I wish . . . I wish she'd had an abortion."

"But then you wouldn't be here, Olivia, gracing us all with your dirty mind and itchy trigger finger." She cups my face and lifts my chin so that our eyes meet.

"I don't care," I sob.

"I had to make the same choice," she says. "I couldn't do what Bree did."

"How could anyone? It's an impossible decision that literally no one wants to make. The first thing I did after Greg was take a pregnancy test and an HIV test. I'm lucky. I didn't have to make that choice." I sink back into the couch and close my eyes.

"Bree made a lot of mistakes, Olivia. Believe me, I know that. But you aren't one of them."

Even though my eyes are shut, it isn't enough. I cover my face with my hands. "I don't know what's happening to me."

"I think you're used to burying your emotions and now they're spilling over. You've got to deal with them, sooner or later."

The night before flashes through the velvet dark: Cliff's arms around me, his lips on my neck, his heart beating inside me. I press the pads of my fingers into my eyes, blurring it all to red.

"Olivia?" Esther touches my knee. "What else is going on?"

I swallow nausea. My hands fall into my lap. I can't look at her. "How did you know you wanted to be with Donny?" I rasp.

"I don't know . . . It was just right, with him. He loves me, and I love him. Why are you asking me this?"

"Was he your first love?" I stare hard at my fingernails.

Esther tips her body until she's practically lying with her head in my lap. "Olivia?" A smile spreads across her face.

I bite my lip.

She lies on her back, her head still cradled on my thighs. My limbs become wood. "Well," she says slowly, "I didn't really do a lot of dating. Neither have you, really." She peeks up at me.

I tear away my gaze, staring down at the corduroy couch. I drag my nails up and down the fabric. The sensation of it under my nails is a soothing distraction.

"I just woke up one day and knew I loved Donny. And it was terrifying, don't get me wrong. He's twenty-six years older than me. And he's a man. He could be using me. But have you seen him with the girls? He loves them like they're his own little sisters. You can't fake that." She squares me with a look. "You and me are different people," she continues. "My heart was soft and open because of my grandparents, because of the girls. It was easy for him to get in. I used to dream that a dark knight would ride in and save me," she says with a little smile.

"You saved yourself," I point out.

"So did you. But who's been right by your side?"

I try to push it away, but there's too much already in there. "Fuck," I whisper.

She snickers. "It isn't the worst thing, you know."

I massage my temples with my knuckles. "Fuck."

Sitting up, she pats my leg. "You'll get used to it."

I gape at her. "It doesn't go away?"

"Girl, I'm about two seconds away from laughing at you. You can't control who you—"

I hold up a hand. "Uh-uh. It's just strong feelings because of his magic dick."

"Sure." She stands from the couch. "There's micellar water in the bathroom, and more mascara. Get yourself cleaned up. I need to go grocery shopping, and you're coming with."

I make an emo face at her. "What, you don't like my makeup?"

"I'll buy you a G's burger."

I stand in a hurry. "I'm gonna need your face wash, too."

"Mi casa es su casa, but hurry up. I want to get back here in time for *General Hospital.*"

"Jesus, Esther. The Donny feelings are ruining you," I call over my shoulder on my way to the bathroom.

She scoffs. "I was already a hopeless romantic. I'll have you know, my GH obsession is Abuela's fault."

I arrange the supplies on the counter. "Next you're gonna tell me you guys are trying to get pregnant."

In answer, she says nothing. I scrub at the mascara on my cheeks and try not to think about a tiny baby in a River Reapers onesie.

34

CLIFF

I hook up the spot Ravage sent me to the Bluetooth on my bike, proud of myself for figuring that one out on my own. It's getting easier, living in this world of screens and GPS. Some of it's even useful.

I pull up even with Ravage, the engine idling. We're on the border of Naugatuck and Waterbury, just in sight of the old Platt Brothers factory. I've already killed half my break riding out from the machine shop.

Ravage leans against his bike, smoking a cigarette.

"What's up?" I ask him when I kill the engine.

"Vaughn did some combing on Instajam or whatever the fuck you call it. Those little fucks hang out here brown bagging it." He straightens and drops his cigarette. "Come on."

We approach the abandoned factory on foot, circling around so they don't see us coming from the street. As we near, the sound of glass shattering cuts through the air.

"No jobs, huh?" I keep my voice low.

"You should see their rant posts about people on welfare."

We stop at the opposite end of where they hang out on the ground floor, Ravage holding his hand up to halt me.

"If we can see them, they can see us."

I nod. Through the window, I can only make out their shapes as they move around. "So what's the plan here?"

"I wanna watch 'em, see what their habits are. There's a few photos they must've taken at night, so we might be able to catch 'em here."

"'Catch 'em'?"

He doesn't respond, not right away. We creep closer, staying at an angle where they wouldn't see us out the window. At this range, the random shouts become words.

"I saw that little fucker at Cara's," one of them says.

"He's always hanging out with his mommy," another replies.

"Only a matter of time before he names us on Twitter. We gotta shut him up for good."

My hands curl into fists, rage drawing me forward. Ravage pulls me back, and I realize I took a step toward them.

"What do you wanna do about it, Chad?" one of them asks.

"I don't know, *Patrick*. My father said to keep a low profile, that just because the cops let us go, doesn't mean they aren't watching us," Chad says.

"I'll be your alibi if you'll be my alibi," Alex says with a laugh that makes me want to break his neck.

"Little fucking bitch. We were just having fun. He just had to go and cry to his mommy," Patrick says.

"I personally think Kyle did great work," Chad says.

"Why, thank you." More glass shatters.

"Don't forget," Chad reminds them. "Bonfire tomorrow night, right here. Got a few high school girls coming. Let's see how many V-cards we can collect."

"Is this what you wanted?" I say to Ravage, voice strained. Blood pounds in my ears. It's taking everything in me to not bust in there right now and pound flesh 'til those vile mouths stop moving.

He pats my shoulder. "I think we're good." Gripping my arm,

he leads me away from the factory and back to where we left our bikes.

I light up, crunching over fallen leaves as I pace and smoke, hands and limbs busy.

"Finn's working tonight. When you get off work, I want us to ride down to the PD and ask him *nicely* to re-open that case."

I stop. "Us?"

"You, Mercy, and me," he says, straddling his bike.

"Three of our best felons, walking into the PD." I shake my head at him.

"I'll let Shannon know I'll be home late."

I take a long drag. If there'll ever be a time to ask him about Shannon, it's now. Exhaling smoke, I study him. "You and Shannon didn't get married for a long time."

He sighs. "Not for lack of trying. I'll be straight with you, son. I fucked up, big time."

"She told me a little about that." I don't wanna pry, but I've got so many questions. Ruth and Bastard were horrible role models. Shannon and Ravage, on the other hand, managed to build a healthy relationship, despite all of his fucking around.

"I wanted to marry her when Olivia was staying with us. It was the only way DCF would've let us foster her, with my record. It's a weird fucking loophole. Tell me how a man like me is a better man just because he's married." He scoffs.

"Bastard wasn't." I die out my cigarette on the heel of my boot. "Yet Ruth married him." I shake my head.

"Love ain't never simple, son. You know that, don't you?" He eyes me. "I see the way you look at Olivia—hell, I see the way she looks at you."

I shrug. "She doesn't love me." It sounds simple, coming out of my mouth, but saying it out loud twists the knife in my chest.

He laughs. "You think she doesn't love you just because she doesn't say it? Because she doesn't want the same things you want? You've got a lot to learn," he says, but his tone is kind.

"I know *why* she feels the way she feels," I say. "She doesn't trust easily. Marriage is a trap. I get that."

"Shannon felt the same way. The difference is, *I* shattered that trust. So did Bastard. We aren't the same, but we weren't good to our women, in different ways." He pins me with pale blue eyes. "You've learned from your father's sins. You're *not* the same man, Cliff. I don't know what it's gonna take for you to know that. Maybe I gotta beat it into you."

"You think you can take me, old man?" I rib.

His eyes flicker to ice. "I know I can take you, boy." A moment later, the warmth returns. "Bastard was all twisted up inside. You're morally gray, but you've still got morals. Even if she never says the words, she ain't going nowhere. You and I both know how whip smart that woman is."

The alarm on my phone goes off, signaling the end to my lunch break.

"Shit."

"You better fly," he says as I swing a leg over my bike. "I don't want to hear you're in hot water with your P.O."

I rev up the engine, and shout so he can hear me. "Thanks, Rav. I love you, brother."

"And I love you. Now get the fuck outta here."

He and Shannon gave me a lot to think about. Maybe the problem really is me. Maybe I just need to let go of the fantasy I've been clinging to and live in the reality. Maybe I just got to re-train my brain, reframe my views of love.

If I can figure out connecting GPS to Bluetooth, I can figure out modern love.

35

OLIVIA

I sit on Lucy's back deck, a cigarette between my lips. A chill permeates the air, raising goosebumps across my skin, but I don't move. Here I'm cradled, suspended above the ground. It's a small comfort in a world with so many jagged edges.

"Hey," Cliff calls.

I turn my head and there he is, holding a throw blanket. "Did Lucy see you take that outside?"

"Nope." He unfolds the blanket, throwing it over my shivering body.

"She'll kill you," I tell him, but snuggle beneath it anyway. I focus on the cigarette between my fingers, the heat spreading through my limbs—anything except his face. I don't want to explain.

"I brought you something else," he says, shifting on his feet.

"Cliff," I begin, but I don't really know where to start.

"I got all their names."

I sit up straight. "The football team?"

"Four of them are responsible: Patrick, Alex, Kyle, and Chad. I didn't get last names."

"How did you get them?" I push the blanket aside and stand.

Cliff takes me into his arms, pulling me close. He brushes my hair out of my face with a big hand. "Ravage and I did some recon."

"Would you recognize them if I showed you the pics Bryce sent me?" I ask, closing my eyes as his fingers feather across my cheek.

"We didn't see their faces. I'd recognize their voices anywhere." His jaw tightens. "They admitted to all of it."

I sigh. I'm too emotionally connected. This isn't something I can be calm about.

He cups my chin. "Ravage and I are going to the PD tonight to talk to Finn."

"Just the two of you?" I don't want to deal with Finn again.

"Us and maybe Mercy." He hesitates, and I finally open my eyes and look at him.

"I'm glad to sit this one out—not because of Mercy. I can't see straight. I just wanna burn the world down if it means making it safer for this kid."

"Olivia." He holds my face with both hands. "*I* can't even see straight. While we were spying on those motherfuckers, all I thought about was crushing each and every one of their skulls. They were proud of themselves." His jaw tightens. "How can kids be so coldhearted, so vulgarly cruel?"

I shake my head. "That's the problem. They aren't kids. They're plenty old enough to know better. They need to be held responsible for their actions."

"If we can talk Finn into bringing them back into the station, putting more pressure on them—"

"Pressure?" I drop my cigarette. "Maybe *we* need to put pressure on them."

"More than happy to," he says, his eyes hardening.

"I know." The grass and sky spin around me.

"I wish we could make them disappear, too," he says.

I pull away from him, turning away as the tears burn my eyes.

"Your probation," I remind him. "This isn't just a stalker. This isn't just one rapist. It's four boys, with friends and families. With coaches and staff. We can't just make them all disappear." I fumble for my cigarettes, hands shaking. I don't know what difference I thought I could make. This isn't simple, not at all. "I don't know if you should be involved."

He laughs. "How many times have I violated my parole in the last year? Don't you get it by now, Olivia?" He clasps my arms, turning me so that I'm looking him in the face again.

"Don't," I warn.

"This is bigger than you and me," he says. "We have to change things so that this stops happening."

"What are you going to do from behind bars?" I wrench away, pacing a few steps from him.

"If we plan, if we're careful—"

"If you get caught, you'll be right back in prison." I jab at the air with my unlit cigarette. "We've already taken too many risks."

I am tired. Tired of losses, tired of fighting an avalanche.

His phone rings, cutting us off.

"Yeah?" he says, answering it. "Yeah, I'm on my way." In the fading light, I see his eyes skitter to me. He hangs up.

I watch him expectantly.

"I've gotta go."

It's only the PD, I remind myself. Talking to Finn won't get him into any trouble. I pat my pockets down for my lighter, but come up empty.

He pulls one out of the pocket of his cut, flicking the flame to life and holding it out to me.

I stand there for a moment, watching the flame dance in the September night air. Then, for better or worse, I walk toward it.

I drop my cigarette to the ground and swing onto my bike. The scream of three motorcycles surrounds the Mermaid, where we met up.

"Straight to the PD," Ravage shouts. With a twist of his throttle, he rolls out. Mercy follows, leaving me to take the rear. I straddle the motorcycle for a moment, watching them go. It feels good, that Ravage chose me.

I urge the Screamin' Eagle forward, pushing it 'til I catch up. When we pull into the police station's parking lot, there isn't exactly space for three motorcycles. I follow my President into an adjoining lot behind the station. It's narrow, but down at the end, near some storage containers and other miscellaneous garbage, there's enough room for us to park without being harassed or getting any of our bikes damaged. I swing off my bike and join the others in a loose circle.

"We've got about fifteen minutes before we're towed," Ravage says. "We better convince Finn fast."

"How exactly are we supposed to do that?" I ask, crossing my arms. I don't think we can talk Finn into anything. Part of me feels we should avoid him at all costs. The less we see him, the less a chance he'll suspect we had anything to do with his brother's death.

"We *talk* to him," Ravage says. "You're so used to settling everything with your fists. You ever try to just talk to somebody?"

I arch an eyebrow at him. He's got a point. I pull out my cigarettes from my cut and slide one out of the pack. Finn shouldn't see my face here. I'm too close to Olivia. We shouldn't be reminding him of his dead brother. "I'll hang back," I volunteer.

"You're taking point," Ravage says.

I damn near drop my lighter. "Me?"

He and Mercy exchange a glance.

My eyes narrow. "You just said I'm too used to settling shit with my fists." I'm not dumb, but I am big, and I'm no smooth talker. Only when it comes to women who aren't Olivia.

"That's why you're gonna do the talking." Ravage claps me on the back, and I have no choice but to follow the two of them inside.

"Can I help you?" a young officer asks from behind the front desk, his tone bored.

"Can we speak to Officer Byrne?" Ravage asks. "It's urgent."

The officer looks us up and down, noting our cuts and colors. "What exactly do you boys consider urgent?"

Boys. I smirk at him. He looks half my age.

Ravage remains calm. "We have concerns about a case he worked. We'd like to speak with him."

"Concerns?" The officer shakes his head. "What are you, his boss?"

"Technically, we pay the taxes that pay you," I say.

Ravage shoots me a sharp look. Turning to the officer, he pats his cut. "What my brother's trying to say is, if I wasn't wearing this, would you take my concerns more seriously?"

"It's about a child who's being abused," Mercy adds.

The officer picks up the phone and punches in an extension

number. "Byrne, there're a few concerned *citizens* out here who want to speak with you."

"Keep your comments to yourself," Ravage mutters to me.

I nod, clasping my hand over my wrist behind my back. I haven't been a fan of the police since the night I killed Bastard. Arresting me—they were doing their jobs. Scaring Lucy—completely unnecessary. They used her—the victim—to get me to comply, and I'll never forgive them for it.

Finn sweeps into the foyer. Stubble obscures his usually clean-shaven face. The bags under his eyes are even more prominent than the last time I saw him.

He shakes his head when he sees us. "Well, well, well. To what do I owe this pleasure?"

Ravage gives me a nod.

I clear my throat and step forward. "Officer Byrne. We're hoping you can help us."

Finn barks out a short laugh. "You want my help? The last time I helped a River Reaper, my brother died."

The officer behind the desk gives us an uncertain look.

"I read that Greg's death was an accident," I soothe. "Something about a cigarette?"

Finn's empty eyes meet mine. "Incidentally, the fire started after *your* girlfriend called me and asked me to cancel the response."

I try to put myself in his shoes, see things from his perspective. I open my mouth to deny it. Ravage holds up a hand.

"From what I know," he says, "Olivia stopped by your brother's to ask him nicely to stop stalking her at her place of work."

"Another interesting incidental," Finn continues, "is your tattooed Viking. Did you know *Stixx* has a juvenile record back in the homeland? Something about arson?"

I knew this, but I don't think Mercy did. He looks surprised for a moment, then fixes his face. Ravage, on the other hand, is as cool as always.

"If you have questions about that night," he says, "feel free to bring us in. My understanding is that the case is closed."

"We're here about another closed case," I say.

"So many mysterious closed cases," Finn says. He sighs. "Let's take this to my office." He leads us to a cramped corner of the pit of cubicles and sits on his desk. "How can I help you?"

Neither Ravage or Mercy say anything.

"A Naugy High student named Bryce . . ."

"Jensen," Ravage supplies.

"Bryce Jensen was sexually assaulted by his football mentors during a school field trip," I continue. "The boys who assaulted him were questioned, but no charges were filed. Why was the case closed?"

"Why are you asking me?" Finn crosses his arms.

"Because you took their statements when Bryce's mom filed a report here in town," I say, crossing mine.

"Why did you scrub all the names from the police report?" Mercy asks.

Finn huffs. "Because the alleged victim is a minor, and we didn't have enough evidence to press charges."

"He had injuries clearly indicating sexual assault," I remind him. "How is that not enough?"

"Are *you* really telling me how to do my job?" He sighs. "I interviewed them personally. They were just playing pool." His eyes don't meet mine, and my bullshit detector blips. "What do you want me to do here?"

Ravage holds up his hands. "Look, I know you think we're just a bunch of bikers, and we're shit to you. I know you've got your hands full. We want the same thing you want: a safe town. Can we at least agree on that?"

"I won't argue that," Finn says. "My hands are tied, boys. The DA shut it down."

"What if they come in and confess? Would that be enough?" I ask.

"That'd be a different story. I guarantee you, that's not gonna happen."

"Finn . . ." I glance at Ravage and Mercy. "Maybe we can work together on this."

"Sure," Finn says with a chuckle. "I'll just hire a bunch of outlaws to do my job."

Ravage gives his head a shake. "Time's about up. Wouldn't wanna get towed."

"I'm genuinely sorry, boys. I'm an ally." Finn spreads his hands. "I've got no witnesses, four suspects who all had the same story. I feel for the vic, but I can only work within the constraints of the law."

"Thanks for your time, man." I extend a hand to him, and we shake.

"Not bad in there," Ravage says once we're outside.

"Minus the working together bit," Mercy adds. "We don't work with pigs."

I light up. "I was spitballing."

"You did good." Ravage claps me on the back. "Time to fall back on Plan B."

In the dimly lit parking lot, we grin at each other.

"What am I missing?" Mercy asks.

"We just happen to know where those shits are gonna be illegally drinking tonight," Ravage says.

I flick my cigarette into the darkness. "How about we outlaws make a citizens' arrest?"

37

CLIFF

I f all goes well, we can take care of this tonight. Ravage, Mercy, and I rush into the Mermaid, Olivia close behind us.

There's hardly anyone in the strip club tonight. A lone dancer halfheartedly moves around the pole, a handful of men surrounding the stage. All of their movements are stilted and subdued.

"How'd it go with Finn?" she asks me as we go into the Chapel.

"He said if they confess, he can reopen the case." I pull out her chair for her and she sits at the table.

She reaches for my hand, and our fingers twine. Her hope thrums against my pulse. Lifting her hand to my lips, I kiss the back of it.

Ravage bangs the gavel, calling us to order. "Thanks for coming in so last minute. We've got names, we know Finn'll take their confessions, and we've got intel where they're going to be tonight." Ice blue eyes land on each face before he continues. "We're bringing them in."

Abraham clears his throat. "We are?"

"Everyone's on this?" Beer Can asks. He folds thick arms

across his chest. "Not that I've got a problem with helping," he says, eyeing Abraham, "but shouldn't someone stay here? In case there are any issues with the Bastard Brothers?"

"We've got both digital and real eyes on every square inch of this place," Ravage says. "Donny? What do you think?"

Donny dips his chin, brow furrowed in thought. "I trust our bouncers," he says, "but they're not patched in. This is only a job to them. We need people here who give a fuck."

I straighten in my seat. I'm ready to get my hands on those boys, to deliver them to Finn's door and make them take responsibility for what they did to Bryce.

"I'll stay," Mercy offers. "I've got fucked up joints, but I can still hit anything that comes through that door."

Olivia shifts beside me. I glimpse the tightening of her shoulders, the war in her eyes. She wants to be out there just as much as I do.

"All right," Ravage says. "Mercy, you'll stay. Everybody going down to the Platt Brothers place, leave your pieces here."

With a scowl, Donny unstraps his gun from his underarm holster and places it on the table.

Ravage fixes him with a look. "I know you've got at least one more on you, plus a couple knives. But you're staying here—Cliff, you too."

I meet his gaze. "The hell I am."

Olivia's hand tightens on mine. "Your parole."

"If it makes you feel better, brother, I'm hanging back, too. I can't risk anyone with a record. We're already on thin ice with Finn as it is," Ravage says.

"Don't worry about baby brother," Beer Can says with a hearty laugh. "He gives us any trouble, we'll give him a cremation, too."

"Courtesy of Stixx Funeral Services," Vaughn says, gripping Stixx's shoulder.

"We're playing by the rules this time," Ravage reminds us.

"Stixx has no record here, so he'll go with Olivia, Vaughn, and Abraham to have a little talk with those boys. They're going to turn themselves in and Finn is going to process them."

"Talk?" Stixx smirks.

"*Talk*," Ravage emphasizes. "Rough 'em up a little, but don't forget: we're trying this the right way first."

Vaughn passes printed out photos around.

"There'll be other people there," I tell everyone. "These are the guys you want."

Donny picks up a paper sack from the floor, upending its contents. Black ski masks and hoodies spill onto the table. "No cuts, lady and gentlemen. No one can know this was us."

Then it hits me: I won't be with Olivia. I know she can take care of herself. She's more than proven that to me. I just hate the idea of not being there to back her up.

We make a good team when we're taking care of rapists.

"What about me?" Mark asks.

"I need you here," Ravage says. "You're our Chamber of Commerce golden boy. If things go south, you can back up their alibi."

"I don't like this," Abraham interrupts.

"Which part?" I ask. "The part where we convince these motherfuckers to turn themselves in, or the part where they raped the athlete they were supposed to be mentoring?" I lean toward him, nostrils flaring. "They did it for fucking fun. So tell me: Which part don't you like?"

He glares at me. "You know I don't *like* that shit."

"We're making things right," Olivia says.

"We're not drawing any blood," Ravage reminds us. "As much as I'd like to personally put a hole in each of their heads, we've got to let Finn handle this. Grab the boys, scare 'em, drag 'em into the van, and dump 'em off on Finn. Stand over them in the interrogation room, if that's what it takes. Got it?"

It's simple. An easy task. So why do I got the feeling none of this is going to go as planned?

"Got it," Olivia says.

"Then let's roll," Ravage says.

Everyone stands at once, the room erupting around me. I shove my chair back and hurry after Stixx, who's already at the doors. I push it open for him, motioning for him to go through.

"What's up, man?" he asks.

I pull him off to the side, letting everyone pass us. Out of the corner of my eye, I track Olivia, pulse thudding in my throat. "I hate to be this guy," I say in a low voice, "but please watch out for her."

He pats a hand against my chest. "I've got you. She never leaves my sight." For a moment, he looks like he wants to say something else, but doesn't.

"Thanks, man."

Tipping his chin at me, he pats me one more time, then runs after Olivia.

Then it registers that we didn't say goodbye. I didn't even kiss her good luck.

Ravage stops beside me. "Go relieve Erik for a bit. Let everybody see our felons working tonight."

The last thing I want to do is stand at the door, but I don't have much of a choice. All I can do is hope everything goes smoothly, that I'm just paranoid.

38

OLIVIA

I take the weight that's pitted in my belly, wrap it in a kerosene-soaked blanket, and drop a match in. This pain has to have a purpose. I can't let anything like this happen to Bree, or Bryce, or anyone else, ever again.

Even though the air is crisp and cool, sweat soaks through the back of my shirt, the fabric sticking uncomfortably as I crouch in the back of the van. My pulse thumps in my throat in time with the swirl of fury in my heart.

Abraham signals a right turn, and Vaughn plants a hand on the metal wall for balance. Mimicking him, I place my palms on the floor. Lucky Stixx gets to ride up front, where there are actual seatbelts. I didn't even say goodbye to Cliff.

We pull onto Bristol Street, a spur off of Platts Mill Road. The old Platt Brothers factory is just a short walk over.

"Let's creep up on them, watch for a minute," I tell the men with me, passing around the ski masks.

"Rui's gonna fucking kill me if I get arrested," Abraham says, but yanks his mask on anyway.

We jump out of the van, closing doors gently so the sound doesn't echo over to the factory. The night presses down on us, lit only by the orange glow of old street lights. Out here, I can make out some of the stars.

"Let's get this over with," Abraham says.

"Olivia, you take point. This is your kill," Stixx tells me.

"Now, now," I remind him with an exaggerated wink he probably can't see. "Ravage said no blood."

Yet it's blood I want.

I lead them onto Platts Mill Road and over to the factory. I've driven by it before, but in the dark it rises up, lit only by street lights and the glow of a bonfire. I take them around the back, pushing through overgrown bushes until I peer around the side of the building.

A group of Naugy High students and recent graduates gathers around a portable metal pit, some on canvas chairs, others standing in small clusters. I pull the stack of photos from my hoodie pocket and point out each of our targets.

"Abraham, you're gonna take Patrick," I whisper, pointing to the largest, an olive skinned, muscular boy wearing a ripped up denim jacket.

Abraham grunts. "Sure, send the giant gay man after the biggest dick."

I laugh through my nose. Despite how he voted back in '97, Abraham has a wicked sense of humor. He's cut my man's hair and he's my brother. I want to trust him.

I point to the blonde wearing an old Naugy High team sweatshirt. "Kyle. He's all you, Vaughn."

"Did you really give me that ratty looking thing?"

The next target is tall and wiry, with a shaved head. "Stixx, you've got Alex."

He follows my finger and nods.

The fourth target bends to tie his shoe, his dirty blonde hair plastered to his forehead. He's the smallest of our marks. "I'll take dear Chad."

I tug on the ski mask, tuck my hair into my sweatshirt. I'd feel a lot better if I had my gun. "I'm gonna tackle that one before he finishes tying his shoe," I say. "Go!"

I don't look to see if they're moving, too. I sprint toward Chad, my body low and angled toward the ground. His white fingers flash in the dark, looping the last shoelace. I sprint, throwing myself at the backs of his knees with the balls of my feet, my calves tightened. My momentum carries me straight into him. His legs go weak and he goes down.

Not bad for a girl who's never even played football.

I press him down, scrabbling my knees to the ground for purchase. As they kiss the concrete, I remember the last time I straddled a rapist. I'm yanked back through time, to Greg's bedroom, to his surprised face. It superimposes over Chad's for a moment, long enough for him to flip me off of him like I weigh nothing. Which, considering the guys he plays with, I do.

I tumble to the concrete, my palms skinned. He stands over me, shoulders rising and falling with adrenaline. The soundtrack of girls' screams pierces my ears as everyone scatters.

Chad's fingers bunch around the top of my ski mask, tearing at my hair. My scalp screams. I lash out at him with the heel of my boot, aiming for his kneecap. It takes him on the inside of the knee instead, but it knocks him off balance just enough that he lets me go.

I scramble backward, giving myself space.

"Who the fuck are you?" he grunts, lunging toward me.

"Your escort to the PD," I say, rolling out of the way.

He catches my ankle and drags me toward him. I kick out at him with my free foot, but it only meets air. My eyes meet his and I read white male fury in them. Bile crawls up my throat.

He pulls me into him, planting a foot on my side. He throws all his weight into it, bruising skin. I bite down on my tongue to keep from crying out. He doesn't get to see what he's doing to me.

I'm the ghost of vengeance.

"Who the fuck are you?" he repeats, reaching for my mask

again. His other foot finds my knee, shoving my leg painfully into the concrete.

"I'm a friend of Bryce's." I reach into the back pocket of my jeans, curling my fingers around the palm-sized switchblade. Ravage said no guns. With it still concealed in my pocket, I press the button, releasing the blade. It slices into my ass, but it's no more painful than this jock standing on my body. Sliding my hand out of the pocket, I swipe it across the exposed skin of his wrist, dragging it hard against his flesh.

He yelps in pain, but his heels only dig deeper into me. He leans over me, snatching my wrist, twisting it with his good hand until my nerves and tendons give out. The blade drops, clattering. "I'm going to fuck you up," he seethes, and I believe him.

So much for taking the easiest target.

He kicks my legs apart, pinning me by digging his knees into mine. At least his foot isn't in my ribs anymore. His hands pin my wrists over my head, shoving them closer so he can hold them with one hand. His other hand yanks the ski mask under my chin, tugging it upward.

I squirm underneath him, but it's pointless. I can't move enough to free myself. Every self-defense class I've ever taken is useless. I scan the dark around us, wishing the city wasn't so cheap and this abandoned place had lights. I can't see any of my men. I can only hear them fighting the others.

I thrash my face to the side, determined to at least keep my identity hidden. If he sees me, we're all fucked. Panic claws its way up my throat, flashing images of Greg and Eli through my brain. This time I don't have the upper hand. This time, I'm fucked.

He yanks the mask up, exposing my mouth and nose. "Pretty little thing," he says.

"The other half of my club's on their way," I tell him, hoping he'll eat the lie. "We're taking you to the PD, and you're gonna tell them what you did to Bryce."

"Your club, huh?" He hesitates for a moment, and I take it.

I roll out of his grasp, yanking the mask back down and grabbing my knife. As he reaches for me again with a bloody hand, I stab. The blade hits bone. He screams, and the approaching sirens barely drowns it out.

"Time to go," Abraham yells, scooping me up and throwing me over his shoulder.

"Wait." I squirm in his grasp, but *he's* as strong as he looks.

"Cops are coming. We've gotta get out of here, unless you wanna lose your nice state job."

"We can hold them," I protest, but both Vaughn and Stixx run with us.

"The plan wasn't to get arrested, too," Vaughn says as we sprint into the woods and back to the side street.

Abraham dumps me into the van, slamming the doors shut as Vaughn jumps into the passenger side. Stixx guns the engine and takes off up Bristol Street, turning onto Highland Avenue just as a fleet of police cars passes on their way to the factory.

"Who the fuck called the cops?" Abraham yells from beside me.

"Definitely not any of those kids illegally drinking," Vaughn says.

I stare at Abraham, the mistrust in me building to a crescendo.

39

OLIVIA

With Vaughn's and Stixx's assistance, I limp into the clubhouse through the back entrance. They sit me down at Mark's desk, propping my leg up onto another chair. Everyone rushes into the tiny room, Cliff shoving through the throng of men.

"What happened?" he demands, glaring at Vaughn. He bends down in front of me, examining my leg.

"It wasn't his fault, babe. I underestimated that little fucker."

Shannon brings over a bottle of whiskey and pours me a shot. I hesitate. This isn't a good time to get drunk. Besides, it doesn't hurt that bad.

"We need a doctor," Stixx says.

"What the fuck happened out there?" Cliff stands and takes a step toward Vaughn.

"Holy shit." Mercy limps into the room, favoring his right hip. He bends down stiffly in front of me, peeling up the leg of my jeans. My leg is a raw mess of dirty bruises. "Who did this?"

I lift my shirt, showing him my ribs. "These probably need your attention more."

Cliff's face darkens. Lunging forward, he seizes Vaughn by his hoodie. "You were supposed to look out for her!"

"Anything else you wanna tell us?" Ravage demands of Stixx.

Everyone starts talking at once, the voices of nine men canceling each other out, drowning my thoughts. I try to take a breath deep enough to yell at them, to tell them to knock it off. A piercing pain stifles my voice.

My eyes meet Mercy's. He must see the startled distress in them, because he takes my hand. "It's okay, sweetie."

Shannon pushes the shot toward me and steps over to the light switch. She flashes the lights several times. "Everybody shut up!"

The room falls silent.

"I've got a strip club full of customers out there, and I'm not dealing with any cops tonight. Got it?"

Everyone nods.

"Good." She nods to Mercy.

He looks at Stixx. "Go get the first aid kit." Turning back to me, he gives me a gentle smile. "I think you might have a fractured rib, kiddo."

I glance down at the mottled purple and red covering my ribs. "I think you might be right."

"Todd, get the rest of them out of here."

It takes me a second to remember he's talking to Ravage. Todd. It sounds so normal. I chuckle, and it hurts. A lot. If I ever get my hands on that kid again, he's dead.

"Church," Ravage tells the rest of the club. "Now." He shepherds them out with a thick finger pointed toward the storage room across the hall.

"I'm not going anywhere." Cliff returns to my side, taking my hand.

I blink away tears. I don't want to shut out Cliff. If I have fractured ribs—and I'm pretty sure I do, judging by the pain—I'm going to have to go to the emergency room.

Our club needs him right now more than I do.

"Go," I tell him, forcing a smile. "I'm in good hands."

"You were supposed to be in Vaughn's hands," he mutters. He brings my hand to his lips, laying a kiss on my cold skin.

"It's not his fault. Shit just kinda hit the fan, as usual." I reach for him, and he bends down, kissing me.

"I'm right across the hall," he assures me. I nod, and he goes, but not before glancing back at me again.

The second he's out of the office, Stixx flies back in, first aid kit in hand. He, Mercy, and Shannon hover over me, uncertain.

"I'm sorry to do this," Mercy says, "but I have to set your ribs."

Giving him a nod, I pat my pockets for my cigarettes. I come up empty.

"I've got you." Mercy grabs one of his own, lights it for me, and hands it over.

"Since when do you smoke?" Shannon sighs.

"Not much else to do in prison, sis." He winks at me. "Ready?"

My chest hitches. He has no reason to be like this with me— so fatherly, so familiar, so tender. Like we've known each other a long time. "Ready," I rasp.

He presses my ribs with the pads of his fingers. Even though he's being gentle, the pain is blinding. My stomach roils. "Bruised, at the least. I can wrap you up, but if they're broken—"

Abraham clears his throat.

"What?"

"We don't do compression wraps for ribs anymore," Abraham says softly. "God, that was Rui that just came out of my mouth." He shakes his head at himself.

"A lot's changed. I only ever had basic field injury training, besides." Mercy chuckles.

"Ice and rest," Abraham says.

I stop chainsmoking long enough to shake my head. "I can't rest. You guys need me. And *you* should be across the hall."

"My boyfriend's a nurse in the ER," he says.

"I can't go to the ER. If those kids talk and I go in there with these injuries, I could be arrested."

"We can get you in for x-rays without anyone seeing."

I bite my lip.

"Better to know for sure what we're dealing with," Shannon agrees, running her fingers through my hair.

I know she's right, but still. I'd rather be across the hall, planning war with my club. "What if I just ice them for now and see how I feel in the morning?"

Mercy gives me a *look*, his eyebrows furrowing over brown eyes that I used to think looked just like mine. It's funny what you can see when you really want to.

"Here," Abraham says, cracking a temporary ice pack and handing it to me. Mercy turns his glare onto him. "For while you get her leg squared away," he explains.

I press the ice to my ribs, clenching the cigarette between my teeth. At first the cold makes it worse. I chomp down so hard on the filter, for a second I think the rest of the cigarette is going to fall out of my mouth and burn me. Then the cold starts to numb my ribs, and I sigh in relief.

"I'll take care of your leg," Mercy says, "but then we're going to the hospital."

I narrow my eyes at him, scrunching up my nose. Truth is, I kind of like how he's fussing over me. He might not be the father I imagined, but maybe none of that matters. Maybe there are things thicker than blood.

Shannon helps me clean up the slice on my ass while the guys look away. When she finishes, she squats down next to me, exchanging a worried look with Mercy.

"Want me to call your mom?" she asks.

I shake my head.

"She'd want to know," he says.

"She hasn't been my mom in a long time." I look past them at Abraham. "Can you let Cliff know Mercy and Shannon are smuggling me into the hospital?"

He nods.

"Have him shoot me a text and let me know what they're talking about in there." I have a million questions, but Mercy is right. I need to get these ribs checked out. I sigh and wave to him and Shannon. "Well, let's go."

40

OLIVIA

Mercy bundles me up into the backseat of a pickup, propping me against one of the doors. Shannon slides in beside me, another ice pack in hand. It's strange, being taken care of. Growing up, it was always Lucy bandaging my skinned knees. I always wondered who did it for her before I came along. Now I know. It was Cliff.

It's the people who bandage us up along the way that makes life less hard and more tolerable.

At one time, Mercy tried to make things better for Bree and me. There's something bothering me, and he might be the only one I can say it out loud to.

"Mercy?" My voice sounds so small.

"Yeah?" He glances at me in the rearview mirror.

"Someone called the cops on that bonfire. It's a bit back from the residential area, so it couldn't have been a neighbor. I think —" I take a deep breath. "My trust radar is so fucked. Do you think it could've been Abraham? He didn't want to go, and weirdly, when we were back in the van, he said someone must've called."

I stop. I have to start trusting people. I shouldn't have thrown Abraham's name out there like that.

"Hmm," he grunts. "I'll run it by Ravage. We'll keep an eye on him. Always trust your gut," he says softly. His eyes meet mine, and I nod.

I grab my phone from the pocket of my jeans, wincing when my ribs protest. I've never been this hurt. Panic bubbles up in my chest, but I shove it down. I can't freak out when I call Lucy. Otherwise *she's* going to freak out, and I don't want her rushing down to the ER with Bunny. That little baby's too new for all those germs.

"I'm gonna try to drive as smoothly as possible," Mercy promises. "I'm sorry if I hurt you."

"Can't get any worse than this." I pull up Lucy's name and tap it.

She answers on the first ring. "Hey! I've been wondering where you are. Listen, I got you a Juul. Cliff, too." Dishes clatter in the background, water running full force.

"A Juul?" I repeat.

Mercy backs the truck out of its spot. Switching gears, he turns out of the parking lot, and we're on our way.

"Instead of cigarettes. You really should quit," Lucy chides.

"Luce—"

"I know, I'm being a nag, but Leigh wants you guys around a long time." I can practically see her batting her eyes at me. "I'm leaving them on your dresser. Just give it a try."

"I will," I promise, wishing I had another cigarette. "Luce, I don't want to freak you out, but I'm on my way to get x-rays."

"What? Why? What happened?" I hear a coffee mug or something hit the stainless steel sink. She swears.

"Um," I stall, trying to think of a good story. I've got nothing. "Club stuff."

"'Club stuff,'" she repeats. "Stuff I don't want to know?"

"Probably not," I admit.

"Want me to meet you down there?"

"No!" I tell her. Mercy hits a bump, and I grunt. "I'm fine. Really. Shannon and Mercy are with me."

"Mercy, huh?" A smile threads its way through her voice. "So you're working it out?"

I glance at the rearview mirror. Mercy's eyes focus on the highway, his brow furrowed in concentration. His eyes do sort of look like mine, even if they aren't. "Maybe."

"Livvie, I can come down. It's no big deal. Leigh has all of her shots. The ER won't kill her."

"Why get her sick for nothing? I'm fine," I assure her. "Cliff will be down soon, anyway." I don't really know that, but I'll say anything to make her feel better.

"Was he involved with this 'club stuff,' too?" she asks.

"He wasn't there."

"Uh-huh." She sighs. "Who *was* there? Is anyone else hurt?"

I frown. She's never asked this before. Luckily, I don't have to answer. Mercy pulls into the parking lot of the Waterbury Hospital emergency department, angling the truck between an ambulance and a two-door sports car. "Luce, I've got to go. I'll fill you in when I get home, okay?"

"Fine. Just shoot me a text if you want me to come down. I love you."

"Love you too," I say in a hurry and end the call.

Mercy and Shannon help me out of the truck. The doors slide open and a familiar man in scrubs rolls an empty wheelchair toward us.

"I'm gonna go park," Mercy says, limping back to the driver's side.

I turn back to Abraham's boyfriend, Rui. "Right now I'm real glad you're a nurse."

"Nurse practitioner," he says proudly. "Hop in."

With Shannon's help, I ease into the wheelchair. The second

my ass hits the seat, Rui whisks me away, Shannon hurrying beside me.

"Thank you," she whispers to him.

"Don't thank me yet, honey." He flashes a grin at the security guard and pushes me through door after door, not stopping 'til we reach a small room of beds. The sign on the wall says urgent care.

Rui wheels me over to a gurney. "Can you hop up here on your own?"

"Just give me a hand up." I stand from the wheelchair, doubled over a little. Shannon supports my good side while Rui gives me a boost onto the gurney.

"Lie back," he instructs. Since my abs are shot, I cling to Shannon's hands while I maneuver onto my back. Rui pulls the curtain closed, then lifts my shirt. With one look at my bruised ribs, he shakes his head. "Probably sprained, maybe even broken. We need an x-ray for sure."

"Cool. Let's get it rolling."

"Not so fast. I gotta run labs on you."

"Labs?" I glance from him to Shannon. "Won't that blow this whole cover thing?"

"We run labs on every woman before x-rays," he says firmly, "even Jane Does." Turning away, he unlocks a drawer and pulls out supplies.

I huff.

Shannon smoothes my hair. "I know you want to get back," she soothes. "This'll all be over before you know it."

"I'm only doing this because I love Abe," Rui says. "Never again, Shannon. Do you hear me? I could lose my job. No offense," he says with a glance at me.

"None taken. I appreciate it."

Rolling his eyes, he runs an alcohol pad over the inside of my elbow. "Little pinch." He takes my blood, and I barely feel it.

Compared to the fiery, radiating pain splintering from my ribs, a little needle prick is nothing.

He removes the IV and sticks a Band-Aid to it.

"I'll be right back." He bustles out of the room, leaving me alone with Shannon.

"Did we really have to come here?" I complain. "I'm just wasting time."

"If your ribs are broken, are you going to stay in bed?"

"No."

She sighs. "Olivia . . ."

"Olivia?" Mercy calls.

"In here."

The curtain parts and he ducks in. "How're you doing?" He hovers by my side, his hands fluttering from the breast pockets of his cut, to his sides, to the loops of his jeans.

I give him a thumbs up. "I'm good."

Relief floods his face. His hand envelops mine, warm and secure. I blink before he sees the tears in my eyes. I was wrong to push him away. I see that now, clear as day.

"I talked to Ravage," he says, glancing at Shannon. "Do you want to hear this?"

She shrugs. "Todd tells me everything. That's how we work."

"I know, but you're not gonna like this." He clears his throat. "Vaughn ran through hospital records. The kid who crushed your ribs is currently at St. Mary's. You mangled his wrist."

Shannon pales. "Kid?"

"Hardly," I tell her. "Trust me." I take a shallow breath in through my nose. "Are they going after him?"

"Not while he's at the hospital," Mercy says. "Whatever happens next, Ravage is letting Cliff make the call." He watches my face.

"Cliff? Why?" Even though I want to be the one to dump those little bastards off at the police station, it doesn't really matter. What matters is they pay for what they did to Bryce. I sigh, closing my eyes.

"Ravage is looking to step down," Mercy says.

My eyes snap open.

"Since I don't want the seat, he's taking Cliff under his wing, showing him the ropes. It won't be right away," he says quickly. "Kid's got a lot to learn before he can be President. We're hoping that he's got what it takes and that when the time does come, he'll get the votes."

I let out a shaky breath. "Does Cliff know this?"

Shannon gives Mercy a sharp look.

"He will," he hedges.

"Look," I say, rising up onto my elbows. A sharp pain echoes through my sternum. Grunting, I lie back down. "Cliff wants this club. I know he does. You've got to be up front with him. No more of this secret agenda shit. Okay?"

"Secret agenda shit?" Mercy chuckles.

"You guys never lay your cards out. You're always calling shots before bringing it to the table, and it's fucking frustrating. We're a club, not a monarchy."

Sobering, he nods. "You're right. We should've been up front about a lot of things. I guess we're still stuck in our old ways."

"Yeah, well, let 'em go."

The curtain slides open and Rui steps in. "I have your labs," he says.

"Is my blood behaving?" I joke. "Can we just get this x-ray done already? I've got kids to wrangle."

Rui glances from Mercy to Shannon. "I think, uh, some privacy would be good."

I frown.

"I'll step out." Giving my hand a final squeeze, Mercy pulls out his phone. "I've got to call your mom, anyway."

"I'll go with you," Shannon says.

"Wait," I squawk, glancing at Rui again. His face gives nothing away. "Shannon, please stay? This guy looks too serious." I let out a nervous laugh.

"Okay." She takes Mercy's place by my side, her hand slipping into mine, her other hand smoothing my hair.

Rui waits until Mercy is gone. Then he looks at me. "Are you sure you don't want more privacy?"

"Spit it out, man."

He nods, then passes me a printout. "Everything looks good, except your hCG is positive. I can't sign off on an x-ray."

Shannon's hand tightens around mine.

"In English, please?" I don't need a translation. There's only one condition that will kill an x-ray.

"Olivia, you're pregnant."

I stare at him. Let the words sink in. Pregnant. I haven't even felt sick. I haven't even missed my period. I don't think. I don't know, actually. I blink at him, frowning.

"Olivia?" Shannon squeezes my hand.

"That's . . . You're funny," I tell him.

"The blood doesn't lie," he says.

"Ha." I laugh weakly. "I'm on birth control."

He bows his head.

"I don't want kids."

Shannon smoothes my hair.

"How did this happen?" I glance from her to him, then back at her. "Is this a joke?"

"I'll give you a moment," he says.

"No!" I struggle to a sitting position. "How . . . How long?"

"I'm not an obstetric nurse," he says. "The blood test we use here just gives us a yes or no."

"Run it again," I insist.

"Olivia—"

"Run it again!" My chest rises and falls. I squeeze Shannon's hand. "Run it again," I say, more calmly.

"I brought you some ibuprofen for your pain," he says, taking a packet of pills from the pocket of his scrubs. He holds it out to me. "That's all I can do for you, Olivia. You need to see an obstetrician."

I take the pills, cupping them in my hand. "Can I just have a minute?"

"Of course," Shannon says.

"Please don't say anything," I beg her. I don't even have to ask Rui, thanks to HIPAA.

"Never." She kisses the top of my head, and then she and Rui drift from the room.

I stare at the curtain, still swaying from the air conditioning. Esther's words replay in my head: "It isn't the worst thing, you know."

Tears dribble down my cheeks. I'd make a horrible mother. I didn't have one. I don't know how to be one. But . . .

I've seen Lucy with Bunny. Surely I can learn. I've got nine months. I laugh out loud. A family was the one thing Cliff wanted, the one thing I wouldn't give to him. Fate is laughing at *me*.

It isn't the worst thing, you know.

It isn't. I love Bunny. Surely I can love this baby, too. My past has been keeping me shackled, but it's time to let myself free. I take a ragged breath. This isn't exactly how I planned on telling Cliff how I feel, but I'm not about to keep any more secrets from him.

I'm going to tell him. For better or worse, we'll figure this out.

Because it isn't the worst thing.

Fuck me, I'm terrified.

41

CLIFF

Ravage's words echo in my head: "How we handle this is your call."

I'm starting to see why he's been pushing me. He's been mentoring me.

I stand in the parking lot behind the club, an untouched cigarette burning between my fingers. All this time I thought I wanted this club, but I never stopped to think about the actual responsibility. I don't know how Ravage held it together all these years.

The door squeaks open and Ravage steps out, his hands shoved apologetically into the pockets of his black jeans.

"Hey."

I nod in response.

"I just got off the phone with Mercy," he says.

Shit. Olivia. I pinch the bridge of my nose. "How's she doing?"

He tilts his head, eyebrows furrowing. "Oh—Olivia's all set. They're heading home now." He leans against the wall next to me, lighting his own cigarette. "We actually talked about *you*," he says. "He said I should be up front with you."

I chuckle. "It's kind of obvious, now."

"Yeah."

We smoke in silence for a moment.

"I don't know if anything I've done in the past twenty years was right," he admits.

I start to tell him I think he did the best he could, but he holds up a hand.

"Mercy's right. This club can't survive on secrets. Here it is: I want to step down." He levels his gaze with mine. "I want you to take my place."

I nod.

"You're not ready for it," he says.

"Can't argue that." I bring my cigarette to my lips, taking a long drag all the way to the filter. Then I drop it to the pavement. "I do want this club."

"It's your birthright." He clears his throat. "I want to teach you everything I know, so that in a year or two—or even three—when you're ready, you're ready. Is that all right with you?" His usually cool blue eyes search mine and, for the first time, I see vulnerability there.

"A year or two? I think that's fair. I want it."

He clasps my shoulder. "I love you, Cliff. I don't know if the choices I made were right, but I do know I love you like my own son. And I want you to have a good life."

I place my hand on top of his, my throat tight. "I love you too, Ravage." I give his hand a squeeze. "Given the circumstances, I think you did a hell of a job."

"Thanks."

My phone vibrates in my pocket.

"That's probably your Olivia. Go take care of her." Giving my shoulder a final squeeze, he drops his cigarette and steps back inside.

I stare at the now closed door. President. My promise to Bastard isn't just an empty threat anymore. This club *will* be mine. I hope I can do it justice.

I pull my phone out and read the text.

Olivia: Can you meet me at Lucy's? On my way now. I need to talk to you.

I bet anything she had a hand in this conversation I just had. Grinning, I text her back, letting her know I'm on my way too. Then I drop my cigarette and swing onto my bike.

Lucy's house is dark. Not even the porch light is on. I glide into the driveway beside her car, scanning the street for Olivia's bike. Then I shake my head at myself. Mercy and Shannon brought her. Her bike's still back at the clubhouse. They'll be pulling up in a cage.

Dismounting, I pull my keys from my pocket and trot up to the porch. One step, two steps, three, the tap of my boots reverberating against the wood. I step on something that crunches. Squinting in the dark, I glance down. The streetlight isn't enough to see by, so I pull out my phone and swipe for the flashlight.

Glass.

I throw the light in an arc up to where the porch light used to be. Shards of glass pierce the covering, the bulb busted. I reach for my gun.

It's then that I notice the door is ajar.

Without thinking I push inside, gun drawn. "Lucy!" The house is darker than dark. Unbelievably dark. I use one hand to shine my phone's light around. Furniture lies in splinters on the floor. I scream her name again, so loud my throat and chest split.

I run into the kitchen, more glass crunching beneath my feet. "Lucy!" Everywhere I shine my light, everywhere a light used to be, is just smashed glass. Every piece of furniture lies in ruin. White noise, hot and fearful, floods my head, racing through my veins.

"Lucy?"

I hurtle toward the stairs, taking them two at a time. Halfway up, I see her. She slumps against the wall at the top of the stairs, her eyes wide and staring. The light from my phone captures her in a slow flare. The flap of hair and flesh hanging above her eyes like bangs. The blood caked around her scalp. The dent in her skull.

My legs collapse underneath me. I hit the stairs, my chin smacking into a step. "Lucy," I cry, scrabbling up on my hands and knees. I crawl up the remaining steps, pressing fingers to her throat. A pulse flutters, faint beneath my fingertips.

"I'm here, Luce." Tears clog my throat, pouring down my cheeks, soaking my beard. I go to dial 911, then realize I dropped my phone on the stairs. Turning, I reach for my phone, but I stop. My blood freezes.

Where's Bunny?

I stretch down the stairs, my fingers closing around the phone. As I pull my arm back up, the light catches the message written in blood on the wall above Lucy.

It chills the blood in my veins, waking the monster. For a moment, I consider it. If the police see it, it'll kill my club's chance for revenge.

And the monster needs revenge.

I wipe it dry with a towel.

Standing, I dial 911, shouting Lucy's address into the phone even as I walk toward the nursery. Bunny hasn't so much as cried, and I don't know what I'm going to find. Dread slows my limbs, but I find myself standing over her crib. She stares up at me, green eyes filled with a knowledge she shouldn't possess.

Sirens scream closer.

I lift her from her crib and we sit by Lucy while we wait.

On the ride to Lucy's, Mercy is deeply silent. Shannon sits next to me in the back again.

"Do you want me to come in with you?" she asks softly.

I shake my head. "Thanks, but I've got this."

And I do. If I've learned nothing else, it's that life doesn't go as planned. Shit happens, and we just roll with it. I'm lucky. Cliff truly loves me. Through everything, he's never left my side. He's seen me at my absolute worst, and he's still here. I'm scared but I know that somehow it'll work out. We've already been through the worst. Somehow, we'll get through this.

Mercy turns onto Lucy's street. Red and blue lights paint the trees. I scowl, hoping some smartass cop didn't pull over Cliff. This conversation is going to be hard enough. The sight of the ambulance in front of the condo halts my thoughts. Before Mercy even stops the truck, I shove the door open and fall out. Gravel skins my hands and my ribs shift, but I don't feel the pain. All I can see is the ambulance, the gaping door, the infinite black pouring out of the house.

I run toward it.

"Ma'am," a police officer calls out to me, but I throw myself through the door before anyone can stop me.

Floodlights bathe the top of the stairs, blinding me from whatever is upstairs. An officer passes me, a bagged up metal baseball bat in his hands. I gape at the blood and hair clinging to the metal.

"Ma'am, you can't be in here," he says.

"She lives here."

I snap my head up. Cliff sits halfway down the stairs. I stare past him, where EMTs flood the landing, their hands a blur as they work on a figure sprawled on the floor. The only thing I see is her foot, still wearing a fuzzy Christmas sock.

"What happened?" A strangled scream catches in my throat. "Is she alive?" I sway, and arms steady me from behind.

"Let's sit," Mercy says, guiding me to what used to be the living room.

"Can we get another light in here?" an officer calls out.

Mercy sits me down and Shannon throws a blanket over my shoulders. It's then that I realize I'm shivering.

"Cliff?" I call out.

An officer drags another floodlight into the living room, bathing us in stark white light. He turns to me and I stiffen. Finn.

"We've gotta stop meeting like this," he says, taking a step toward me. He lifts a notepad from his pocket. "I just have a few questions—formally."

Shannon stands protectively in front of me. "We're just coming back from the hospital."

"I'll be quick. Do you know of anyone who'd want to hurt your sister?" he asks.

My gaze floats back up to the wall above Lucy. Blood smears the eggshell white. I frown at it.

"No," I tell him. "Was this a robbery?" I think of the home invasion a few years ago, just a couple towns over.

"So far, there doesn't appear to be anything missing. We'll need you to take an inventory. It looks like they came in through the unlocked front door and chased her upstairs."

Upstairs.

I gasp. "She was trying to get to Bunny."

The EMTs slide Lucy onto a gurney, covering most of her with a sheet. Cliff descends the stairs, clutching a bundle to his chest.

I jump up, the blanket falling to the floor. "Bunny! Is she—?"

"She's safe," he assures me.

I meet him in the middle of the wreckage and reach for her. I pull the blanket away from her, checking her for scratches, blood, anything.

"They already checked her out. She's perfect," he promises.

Cradling her to my chest, I nod, unable to speak. I turn toward one of the EMTs, watching as the rest of them carry Lucy down the stairs. They surround her, obscuring her from my view. "Is she alive?" I ask again.

"We need to get her to the hospital immediately," the paramedic says.

"I'm her sister," I say. "I'm going with her. But . . ." I look down at Bunny, then back up at Cliff.

He holds his arms out. "I've got her," he says.

"Go," Finn says. "I'll call you when we have more information."

I follow the EMTs to the ambulance.

"You can sit right here," one of them tells me, pointing to a seat inside the ambulance. I catch a glimpse of her, a paramedic squeezing what looks like a bottle that's taped into her mouth. "We need to work on her, so you'll need to stay out of the way."

I nod, clambering in after her.

"We're right behind you," Shannon says.

An EMT slams the doors shut, cutting us off before I can respond. As if I even have a response. I stare at Lucy's foot while the paramedic squeezes the bag. Her pulse beeps, slowly, faintly. I can't tear my eyes away from that Christmas sock, even as the ambulance screams away from Lucy's street.

43

CLIFF

"I'm gonna need that inventory," Finn says the second the ambulance is out of sight.

I press Bunny into Shannon's arms and wheel around on him, almost in one fluid motion. "It'll have to wait. We're going to the hospital." I take a step toward him.

He holds his hands up. "I'm just doing my job. I know this is emotional."

Mercy catches me by the arm, dragging me back. He's surprisingly strong, considering his age and condition. "Cool it," he says, his voice a low warning.

"Let's get to the hospital," Shannon says, putting her hand on my other arm. Her touch is soothing, a mother's reassurance. She sets Bunny back into the crook of my arm. The sweet weight of the baby, the soothing brush of the club mother, the stern grasp of Mercy all anchor me from dropping off the edge.

"Let's go," I say, bowing my head and turning from Finn. I walk out the front door without looking back, going through the motions because they're all I have. I take the car seat from Lucy's car and toss it into the backseat of Mercy's truck. I fumble with one hand trying to buckle the seat in, Bunny nestled in my other arm. The buckle of the seatbelt snaps back, smacking me on the bone of my wrist. "Fuck," I howl, tilting my head back and shoving the pain and anger down. Bunny shouldn't see me like this. I have to stay calm, for her.

"Here," Mercy says, crawling across the seat. "Let me."

"They've changed a lot since you last hooked one up," Shannon says.

I look down at Bunny, her wide green eyes locked on my face. She hasn't made a sound, not since I found her safe in her crib. Just looks at me with a heavy understanding she shouldn't possess.

"All set," Mercy says, tossing a smirk at Shannon. "I'm not *that* old."

"Older than me," she says. "Cliff, do you want shotgun?"

"I'll stay back here." I strap Bunny into her seat, then jog around the pickup and climb in on the other side.

Mercy peels out of his spot by the curb.

Shannon twists around in her seat, those old soul brown eyes searching mine. "Cliff, what can I do for you?"

My mind skids, skips, blanks out. I'm supposed to tell them something—something important. I can't think. I can't breathe. My lungs crush inward, something inside me vacuuming them. I press my head against the cool glass of the window. I've got to get it together. Got to keep it together.

"Dio," I say. "We've got to go back."

"Pull over, Merce." Shannon unbuckles her seatbelt.

"What? Why?"

"Let me out here. I've got to make sure Olivia's cat is okay."

"She has a cat?" he asks, pulling over.

"Cliff, I've got him. I'll hold it down here, handle Finn's inventory, clean up a little. And I'll call Ravage." She kisses Mercy's cheek. "Go." She slips out of the truck and into the night, hurrying back toward the condo.

Mercy steps on the gas. The engine revs and tires scream against the asphalt, kicking up gravel and debris. We race to the hospital, and I brace myself.

I RUSH into the emergency room, one fist gripped around the handle of Bunny's car seat. "Lucy Demmel," I blurt to the nurse at the front desk. "She came in an ambulance."

She taps at her keyboard, pulling up Lucy's information. "I can walk you back," she says, glancing from the baby, to Mercy, to me, "but there's a two visitor maximum, and there's already family with her."

Olivia.

"Is there another waiting room back there?" Mercy asks.

"Mm-mm." Shaking her head, she stands from the desk.

"I'll stay with the baby," Mercy says, holding his hand out for the car seat. I can't pass her to him. He's my family, but I can't bear to leave her right now.

"You can bring her with you," the nurse says. Then she takes off toward the back, and I leave Mercy in the waiting room.

I follow her through pastel blue halls crammed with patients and family, doctors and nurses rushing back and forth between them. The swell of voices blurs in my ears, the florescent lights amplifying the white noise. I stay on the nurse's heels, nearly stepping on her when she stops suddenly in front of a trauma room. She says something, but I don't hear her.

Olivia stands behind the glass, her face pressed against it, eyes wide as she watches the team work on Lucy. I join her, my hand moving right to the small of her back. She doesn't look at me, just leans into my touch. I grip Bunny's car seat tighter. We stand like this for what could be hours or minutes. I watch them put Lucy back together, stitching cuts and pumping her full of medicine.

Finally, a doctor emerges, streaks of gray through her hair betraying her youthful face. "She's stable," she reports, "for now." She says something about swelling in Lucy's brain and a medically-induced coma and waiting to see and moving her to the ICU in the meantime. "A social worker will be coming by to speak with you," she tells Olivia, glancing at Bunny.

"Who did this to her?" Olivia whispers.

Red swarms my vision. Inhaling, I steady myself.

We walk beside Lucy while they wheel her up several floors to the ICU. A nurse plants us in a softer waiting room, one where they keep people calm while they wait for bad news.

Finally the social worker comes.

"I *knew* it was you, kid," a man with a handlebar mustache says to Olivia. He runs a hand through dirty-blond hair that's more gray. "How're you holding up?"

Olivia blinks away his question. "This is Harrison, Cliff," she says, her voice wiped clean of emotion.

"Hey, man," I say, my tone equally empty. I pump his hand, and we sit down.

"I'm meeting with you as a formality," he says to Olivia. "As Ms. Demmel's next of kin, we're placing Leigh Demmel in your care. I don't have to do a home visit or background check. You're one of us."

She nods, the gesture sharp and robotic.

He glances at me. "From my understanding, the home is currently unavailable. Is there somewhere else you two can stay?"

"With me," I say, my nod just as automatic.

"Good." He checks off some boxes on a form and scrawls his signature. "Just throw down the address and his name, and sign," he says, passing the clipboard over to Olivia.

Bowing her head over the forms, Olivia fills them out. Even her handwriting is as foreign to me as everything else right now.

"Let me know if you need anything. Anything," he emphasizes. "I'm here for you, kid. We all are."

She nods again and then he's gone. She turns in her seat and we just look at each other, alone in the waiting room together.

44

OLIVIA

I stare through Cliff and he stares through me, neither of us seeing each other. The room around me, the man beside me, the baby between us—none of it feels real. I lift a hand through the haze and brush limp hair back from my face. A barrier separates me from everything, including myself. Usually when this happens, I fight to ground myself again. This time the relief is a sweet and warm alternative to reality.

"Hey," Rui says, sweeping into the waiting room. He stops in front of us and crouches down. "Abraham asked me to check in. The whole club's down in the ER. What can I do?"

I turn toward him, a slow blur of movement in the frame of the movie that my life has become. "Hi," I reply.

"They're getting Lucy settled down the hall," he tells me, even though I already know this, even though I don't want to hear it again. "Do you want me to get the club or do you want to wait?"

Cliff and I look at each other.

From our feet, Bunny lets out an abrupt wail. I reach for her diaper bag, then realize there isn't one.

"You need formula? I'll get you formula. Be right back," Rui says, dashing away.

We stare at each other again.

"Who the fuck would do this to her?" I ask.

Cliff's eyes are black, an abyss of fear and anger. I hover at the edge of it. It would feel so good to step in. It also feels good here in the gray.

"I forgot her diaper bag," he says.

"It's okay," I reply, the robot that is playing me in this movie taking over. "Rui will get us whatever we need."

"He's a good nurse." Cliff places a hot palm against my face. His touch sears my skin, but I don't pull away. It's better than the nothing I feel. "What did he say about your ribs?"

"My ribs," I repeat, and it all comes crashing back. Blood levels, referrals, certainty. I dig for it, the certainty, but now is not the time to share. I give him a weak smile. "All good. Just got to rest them."

"I'll get you ice," he says, standing. "Do you want ice? Or maybe some Advil. You need Advil. You should be resting."

"I'm good," I assure him. "I don't even feel it. Really."

"I should've been there with you." He paces in front of me. "I should've been here, with you." He runs a hand through his hair. "I should've been at Lucy's."

"She wanted to come down here," I say, chewing at a hangnail. "I told her not to." I gnaw at it, ripping flesh, tugging, pulling. It won't come free. Examining it again, I try another angle.

He falls to his knees in front of me. "Olivia, there's something—"

"I've got formula," Rui announces, bustling back in. "I also brought diapers, and wipes, and some ice for those ribs." He gives me a pointed look, setting down a small tub of items. "I checked with the ICU nurses. They said the club can come up here, but only the two of you in the room." He eyes Bunny. "Or three."

"Thank you," I tell him.

"Do you want me to get the club?"

I look at Cliff.

"Yes," he says, his eyes never leaving mine. "There's something I need to tell you."

"Okay," I say, busying myself with opening a bottle for Bunny.

"I'll be right back," Rui says.

The foil around the mouth of the bottle sticks, refusing to peel away. I scrape at it with my nail, grateful for the distraction.

"Liv," Cliff says, his tone too gentle. So soft, as if I might break just from hearing my name.

"Yes," I reply, scraping, scraping, scraping.

"I want to tell you this before the others get up here." He kneels in front of me, taking the bottle from my hands. In one neat tear, he removes the foil, then twists a nipple on with a practiced flick of his wrist. He hands it back to me.

"Okay." I reach for Bunny, unbuckling her seatbelt and gathering her into my arms. Even now, all these weeks later, I still find it so awkward, maneuvering her.

"The wall," he blurts, as I hold the bottle to the baby's lips. "There was something written on it, when I found Lucy. I swiped it away so the cops couldn't see."

I glance up, giving him a sharp look. "What the hell did you do that for?" I hiss, checking the room to make sure we're still alone.

"Listen," he begs, his hands on my knees.

Bunny takes the nipple, and I watch her gulp down the formula. Her green eyes staring up at me, accusing.

"It was a message for us. I think they thought she was you."

"Who?" I ask.

"It said 'A biker whore for my son's ankle,' and then they wrote 'Bastard Brothers remember' underneath it."

"No," I say again, as if I can just make him take it back.

"That kid," he says, stroking my knees. "He's one of the Bastard Brothers' sons. This was retaliation, Liv." His eyes go black, my mind goes white.

45

CLIFF

I watch her face go slack with shock and self-loathing, and I hate myself. I didn't want her to be blindsided, and I have to tell the club. I will never forgive myself for putting that hurt on her face, in her heart.

She blinks and it's gone, her attention back on Bunny.

"Liv?" I run my hands over her knees again. Even through her jeans, her skin is ice. Must be the air conditioning in this place. Or shock. "Talk to me. Tell me what you're feeling, baby."

Her eyes latch onto mine for a moment, then she looks back down.

I rub, trying to warm her, to draw her back to me. She keeps her head bowed. Straightening, I return to my seat beside her. I shouldn't have said it like that. Lucy would tell me I'm too matter of fact—such a guy. The thought jars me, reminding me why I'm here in this waiting room instead of Lucy's living room. Rage shoots through my veins, sweat beading on my skin from the boiling pressure underneath. I resume my trek back and forth in front of Olivia and Bunny, both of them and the room lost to me.

"Son? Cliff!" Ravage all but yells in my ear.

I come back to myself, feel his hand on my shoulder. Blinking,

I clear the fog. I find Bunny back in her car seat, eyes heavy, the bottle empty in Olivia's listless hand. My club stands fanned out around me. I skim faces until I land on Vaughn's. I reach out, grabbing the collar of his shirt. I drag him across the room, slamming him against a wall of locked cabinets.

"Why didn't you know?" I shake him, rattling his head against the fake wood. "Why didn't you connect Chad to the Bastard Brothers?" I give him another shake.

He grabs at my hands. "What're you talking about?"

More hands pry me off him, pull me back. I thrash against them, growling. "Chad is one of their sons!"

"What?!" Vaughn gapes at me, the color draining from his olive skin.

"You heard me!" I rip away, lunging at him again.

Donny throws himself in between us. "Chill out, brother!"

Beer Can catches one of my arms, Abraham wrapping his thick hands around the other. They haul me away from Vaughn, tossing me into a chair. The entire club forms a wall between us, Ravage in the middle.

He kneels in front of me. "Why don't you fill us in?" he asks calmly.

Out of the corner of my eye, I see Shannon sit next to Olivia. She lifts the empty bottle from her hand, Olivia's fingers remaining limply curled in the air.

I glare past Ravage at Vaughn. "Lucy was retaliation for that kid's busted ankle," I seethe. The anger keeps coming in waves, rising every time I shove the fear down.

"How do you know that?" Abraham demands.

"There was a message on the wall, written in her blood!" I jump up, but Ravage presses both palms to my chest, easing me back into the chair.

"What did it say?" he asks, that eerie calm still in his tone.

I fall silent. I don't want to say it again. I've already hurt Olivia with it. My chest rises and falls, blood acid in my veins.

"'A biker whore for my son's ankle,'" Olivia recites, her head still bowed. "They signed it 'Bastard Brothers remember.' They thought she was me."

Ravage's eyes flash. "Vaughn," he says, ice in his voice. "Did you know Chad was related to them?"

"He doesn't have the same last name as any of them," Vaughn stammers.

"Find out whose son he is," Ravage growls, "and then check the cameras at the clubhouse. Now."

"Of course. I'm sorry. I'm so sorry," he says over and over.

Reaching up, Ravage clasps my shoulder. "They *will* answer for this," he promises.

"We should vote," Skid says.

"What the fuck is there to vote for?" I demand.

He holds up his hands. "I'm just saying."

"All right," Beer Can soothes. "Everybody's freaked out. Let's not take it out on each other."

"It's my fault," Olivia says from her seat.

"This is *not* your fault," I say.

She scoffs.

"It's not," I insist.

"Beer Can's right," Ravage says. "We're all on edge. Let's take a breath."

"Clubhouse is clear." Vaughn holds up his phone, where multiple angles of The Wet Mermaid flash across the screen.

"And Chad?" I ask, standing.

"He's Malcolm's son."

Ravage runs a hand down his face. "Of course he is."

"Malcolm's the one who led the exodus," Mercy explains.

I curl my hands into fists. "How the fuck did you miss that, Vaughn?"

He scrubs at his face. "Fuck. I thought I checked every angle. I . . ." He hangs his head. "I fucked up. I've been so busy. I—This is on me."

I look away. "So what are we gonna do? Because we are *not* letting this go. I'm not."

"We're not," Ravage promises.

"We need to be careful about this," Beer Can says. He stands in the doorway, arms crossed over his barrel chest. "We need to pause, take a breath."

Rui appears behind him. "Sorry for interrupting," he says. "Cliff? Olivia?"

Olivia rises from her seat. I cross the space between us, joining her. "Yes?"

"You can see her," he says.

I bend to pick up Bunny, but Shannon stills my hand.

"I've got her," she whispers. "You go."

I bite my lip, teeth digging into the tender flesh. "She doesn't know you."

"It's okay." She smiles. "She's fast asleep. She won't even know. Go see your sister."

"It's okay," Cliff assures me. His hand slides to the small of my back, grounding me for a moment. I close my eyes, leaning into him automatically. He is the magnet and I am the needle.

"Oh," Shannon says. My eyes flutter open. "I forgot to tell you. I found Dio at the house."

My heart plummets into my stomach. Dio. I haven't even given him a thought. I sink my teeth into my tongue, keeping the panic and tears away. "Is he okay?" I whisper.

"Perfect." Reaching out, she rubs my arm. "I gave him lots of cuddles and had Pru pick him up and bring him to my place. Then I locked up."

"The police didn't stay?" Cliff asks.

She shakes her head. "They said they had all they need."

"It's fine." I touch his arm. "We'll take care of it."

My voice is still so vacant, the words stiff on my lips. It reminds me of the time I joined drama club my freshman year of high school. I could never get comfortable on the stage. Except now the stage is my life, and I am the girl who dropped in without bothering to look at the script.

Rui leads us from the soft waiting room to the bright hall. At least, the light should be bright. To my lying brain, it looks dim. He brings us down to the end and then around the bend. Finally, he stops at a private room. A cart of gloves, gowns, and masks stands sentinel outside. He gestures to the hand sanitizer on the wall. "I've got to make you sterilize and cover up," he says, almost apologetically. "There's always a risk for MRSA and pneumonia."

Cliff and I glance at each other. The black in his eyes shifts from anger to fear, then back. We copy Rui, donning gloves and tugging on gowns over our clothing.

"Masks, too," Rui says. "But if you want to give her a kiss, you can." He pauses, looking down. His chest rises as he comes to a decision. "This might be your last chance."

"What do you mean?" Cliff asks—the lines *I* should be delivering.

Instead, all I can do is blink. It's like I'm standing in the control room, far away from the action, eyes riveted to the dirty window that lets me see. I can only watch the girl on the stage, powerless to help her in any way.

"I thought she was in a medically induced coma. She's going to wake up . . . right?" His mask moves in place of his lips.

"We hope so," Rui explains gently. "You never know, though. If I were you, I'd treat every time like it's goodbye—just in case."

I peer past him into the room, then rip my gaze back into the hall.

"There are a lot of tubes and wires," he continues. "Don't be afraid. Just talk to her, tell her you love her. Remind her of happy memories. I've gotta get back downstairs now. If you need anything, ask for Whitney at the nurses' station." He gestures for us to go in.

I want to go back to the waiting room.

My feet remain rooted to the floor, all feeling gone from my legs. I rub my lips together, summoning strength. The fire that once kept me going is now cold coals.

Cliff steps inside like it's nothing, his body cooperating. He doesn't even look back for me. Maybe he thinks I'm right behind him. I pinch the skin at the inside of my wrist, but I don't even feel that.

"I'm going out for a cigarette," I say, but instead of stripping down, I look back into the room.

Lucy lies on the bed, a ventilator covering her mouth and the bottom half of her face. The exposed part is bruised and swollen, her scalp sewn back on in neat stitches. From the mask runs a thin tube, all the way to a machine. The hiss and pump of air is the only sound in the room.

My numb feet take me to her side. I find her hand underneath the blanket. Her fingers are warm, but not as warm as they usually are. Maybe it's the gloves. Avoiding the oxygen monitor on her middle finger, I wrap my fingers around her hand.

I stare at her eyes, willing her to open them, to tell me it's okay, she's okay. Her eyes remain closed and her face remains foreign to me. The lashline of her eyes, the cheekbones—all of it is unfamiliar, a mannequin lying in place of the woman I grew up with. Even her hair is weird in the low light of the room. All of its fire is gone, reduced to a murky non-color.

The last brittle piece of me snaps.

Releasing her hand, I turn away, tearing off the gown. I stalk from the room, fury blazing in my belly. I dump the mask and gloves into a bin and storm back to the waiting room. He says nothing, but I feel Cliff on my heels.

I burst into the room, lips trembling. I don't need to remember the lines, because they are written on my heart in her blood. I stand in the center, and my club forms a circle around me. Cliff joins me, his hand finding mine. His fingers are so warm, it hurts, but I let him scorch me.

I take a deep breath.

"I don't want to wait," I tell my family.

Cliff gives me a squeeze, his agreement.

"I'm hitting them back tonight," I say, "whether you help me or not."

"That's fucking crazy," Abraham mutters.

I fling myself at him, standing on the balls of my feet to get closer to his face. He shakes his head, looking down at me. I curl my hands into fists, bringing them to his chest. "How would you feel if that was Rui?" I grip his cut, nails digging into the leather.

He flinches. Bowing his head, he shuts his eyes.

"Call a vote," Cliff says softly.

Releasing Abraham, I turn to Ravage, pleading. "Call it."

He folds his arms across his chest, cold eyes surveying me. "Do you know what you're asking?"

"We know," Cliff says.

"They hit us first," Donny adds. "There's no other move here, Pres."

Ravage sighs, shoulders falling. All fifty-three of his years spring forward in the etching around his eyes and mouth. "I wanted to make things better," he says softly. Then he raises his voice to a growl. "But they keep pushing us."

"There's only three of them," Donny says. "One of them takes a bed down the hall from Lucy."

"This isn't hauling a bunch of kids down to the PD. We're talking about going to war," Beer Can says. "Is that really what we want?"

I clear my throat. "I want to wipe them all out."

"We should've done it twenty years ago," Donny says.

"Let's finish what I started," Cliff says.

"Son," Ravage says, lifting his chin, "you didn't start this. Bastard did." His gaze sweeps the room, pausing on each of us before he lands on me. "Let's vote. Who's in favor of retaliating tonight?"

47

CLIFF

I stand at the prescribed fifty feet from the hospital, leaning against a guard rail, a cigarette clamped between my teeth. Every muscle remains clenched while I burn from the inside out.

I spent twenty years doing nothing; it's still the hardest thing.

Movement across the street catches my eye. Beer Can skirts the line of cars across the street, then crosses over. I look away.

"I'm sorry, son," he says, lighting a thick blunt. He takes a hit and holds it out to me.

I wave him away, my anger strangled in my throat.

"We just want to be careful. The Bastard Brothers are all ex-mil. We can't just go rushing into this."

"You, Ravage, and Mercy are all veterans," I say, my voice low, careful, measured.

He nods. "Yeah. I'm old and fat. Mercy is disabled from the Gulf War. Ravage . . . Well, I think he bench-presses instead of sleeping." He exhales a plume of smoke. "We just need time to plan."

"Like they took time to plan?" I scowl. "That kid was barely discharged from the ER before they went to Lucy's." I grind my teeth, chest tight and aching. This white hot anger is all I have, all that's holding me together before I detonate. The memory of Lucy in that bed, wired and tubed to the nines, is burned into my brain.

"I know you're hurting." He takes a step closer, but I pace away. "Cliff, we didn't vote no to retaliation. We just want more time."

I laugh.

"We *need* more time," he says. "Olivia's ribs are busted. Don't you think she needs to rest and heal a little?"

I stand with my back to him, run a hand over my face. He's got me there.

"We're angry, we're emotional. We need to be clear-headed. That's the only way we do this right."

Scowling, I run through the list of names in time to the blood pumping in my ears.

Malcolm, Zed, Gavin.

Patrick, Alex, Kyle, Chad.

Skid, Mark, Stixx, Abraham, Donny, Beer Can.

It's hard to hate my own club, but everyone who voted nay is my enemy right now, as far as the monster is concerned. I take a long drag, trying to shove it back into its cage. I can't get rid of what is in me, what makes me who I am.

"I'll leave you be," Beer Can says.

I turn, but he's already walking away. I let him go.

Olivia passes by him, lugging Bunny's car seat on her good side. Mercy and Shannon trail behind her. I rush forward, but Mercy gives me a quick head shake.

"What are you doing?" I reach for the car seat. Her fingers remain curled around the handle, her jaw set.

"Mercy's gonna bring us to your place," she says. "Bunny is exhausted. I'm exhausted. We should rest." She watches me with heavy eyes.

"Of course." I reach for the car seat again, but she holds fast.

She descends the stairs to the parking lot without giving me a second glance. I look back at the hospital, torn.

"She isn't going anywhere tonight," Shannon says, placing a gentle hand on my arm.

"You don't know that."

"No," Mercy agrees. "We don't. But I do know it's been a long day." He rubs at his face.

"Thanks for your vote," I tell him.

He sighs, his breath visible in the cold air. "Yeah."

"All right, well . . ." I gesture toward the pickup down in the parking lot, where Olivia stands, her back to me. "Let's go."

I yearn for the comfort of my bike, for the wind from the road washing over me, cleansing me. But it's back at Lucy's, and there's no way I'm going back there tonight.

"I'll have one of the guys ride your bike over," Mercy says, as if reading my mind.

He drives slowly, and my thoughts churn three times faster than the engine. I should've been there at Lucy's. I know, logically, I had to take care of my club. We had to go over everything at the factory, make sure our asses were covered.

We just didn't think to cover Lucy.

I tighten my fists in my lap. It's history repeating itself. The table is split almost fifty-fifty.

I don't speak until after we set up the Pack 'n Play that's been sitting at the back of my closet. "In case she ever sleeps over at Uncle Cliff's," Lucy had said, so cheerily I almost believed one day she'd let go of Bunny long enough for a sleepover. I just never thought she wouldn't do it willingly.

When it's just Olivia and me in my living room, I drop to my knees in front of where she sits on the couch. "She's gonna pull through," I say, placing my hands on her knees. "She has to." My voice breaks, my jaw trembles.

"What if she doesn't?" she asks, and I crumble.

"What are we gonna do?" I whisper, my eyes still closed. I fumble for his hands, squeezing my eyes shut. The tears slip through my lashes, dripping onto our hands. "How can we just sit here and wait?"

"I don't know."

I take a shaky breath. There are so many things I need to say. First I need twelve hours of sleep, another week to sort through my head, and copious amounts of alcohol. I won't get any of those things.

I swallow. "I wanted to wait until we were alone." I force my eyes open, let in the sting of mascara.

"Ah, shit." He runs his hands over mine, shaking his head. "I knew this was coming."

I lean forward, catching his face between my hands. I make him look at me. "I'm not going anywhere."

His chest rises and falls rapidly, his pupils eclipsing his irises. "You're not," he repeats, stunned.

Three words burn on my tongue, but now is not the time. "I'm not," I say instead. I lick my lips. "But when you were outside, when I was wrapping things up at the hospital . . ." Releasing his face, I hold my hands out to him. "Come on. This is a smoking conversation."

Instead of letting me help him up, he sits back, planting himself on the floor. Then he reaches behind him, grabbing an ashtray from the coffee table. He drops it onto the floor in front of him. With shaking fingers, he lights a cigarette.

Planting my palms on the seat of the couch, I ease myself down to the floor. He reaches for me, steadying me until I'm seated.

"You good?"

I nod, afraid to speak. Now that all the adrenaline has worn off, my ribs feel exactly as they should. Every breath, every movement, even just lifting a finger is too much. Distantly, I wonder how I can even still be pregnant.

This is one tough baby.

"I'm sorry for freaking out," he says, his voice gruff. "I just can't lose you, too."

"You don't have to apologize," I soothe. I'm not even sure who this person is, speaking for me, saying all the right things. Two hours ago I couldn't even step into my own body. Now I see things very clearly.

Too clearly.

"Cliff," I continue, twirling a cigarette between my fingers. I'm not even sure I should be smoking. If I don't, he'll know something is up. I'm not ready to have *that* conversation right here, right now.

I light the cigarette. It's not like I can do any more damage than was already done.

Exhaling, I watch the smoke curl into the air, remembering all the times we snuck cigarettes in his room at Lucy's—the room that's mine now. If I can even go back. Who knows if anything is even salvageable.

I take another drag, smothering my frazzled thoughts with

nicotine. Clarity. I need that clarity back. I focus on what I need to say.

"I didn't want to spring this on you in front of everyone," I say, lifting my eyes to his, "but I think we should put Bryce and his mom under our protection. The Bastard Brothers were bold enough to go after Lucy, and they won't hesitate to silence Bryce now, too."

"Yes," he says immediately.

"Is this something we should bring to the table first?" I ask. "Or do we just go get them ourselves?"

He runs a hand through his hair. "We should at least run it by Ravage."

I lean forward, taking Cliff's free hand with mine, even though it hurts to stretch that far. "I want him to stay here, with us. I don't want him out of my sight."

"What, are we just collecting kids now?" A hint of a smile lifts the corners of his mouth, smoothes the furrowing around his eyes.

"Pretty much," I say.

Now is the time to tell him, when the mood is lighter, when it's just us. But then I think of Lucy fighting for her life in the ICU, and Bryce shrinking more and more inside himself every day, and it just doesn't feel right.

I stub out my cigarette. "I need a shower." Biting my lip, I peek over at Cliff. "Join me?"

"Of course," he whispers. He finishes his cigarette and stands. "Want help up?"

"Please," I say with a scowl. "This blows."

He surveys me for a moment, his brows furrowed. "I don't wanna hurt you."

"I feel like it's gonna hurt no matter what I do. Why did I sit down here?" I grimace.

"At least you're not pregnant," he jokes.

I freeze. "Why would you say that?"

"It wasn't a dig," he says quickly. "I know you don't want kids. It's just that you remind me of Lucy. She hated needing help."

Tears sting my eyes. By the time she was full-term with Bunny, we had to help her off the couch. Sometimes she'd sit on the living room floor, I think out of spite. *I can still do it*, she'd tell us through the stubborn set of her jaw, trying and failing to get up on her own.

I tip my head back, squeezing my eyes shut. She might not make it to see Bunny ever again. She might not meet her niece or nephew. I might never hear her laugh again or be surprised when she pulls out a secret blunt.

"*Hates*," Cliff corrects himself. "I'm sorry."

Tears stream down my cheeks. "I can't do this," I whisper.

He sits down beside me, touching my shoulder, cupping my knee. "She'll be okay. She's Lucy. You know how stubborn she is. There's no way she's going out like this."

Leaning over, I rest my forehead on his shoulder. I try to believe him. He kisses the top of my head, his hands finding their way to mine. Our fingers lace together. He lays his head over mine and strokes his thumb across my skin, smoothing comfort into me.

"Come on," he says. This time his hands hook under my arms and he gently lifts me to my feet. I wince but give him a weak smile. "You okay?"

"Good." I make a face. "Just wish I had stronger painkillers."

He frowns. "What do you mean? What did they give you?"

"Ibuprofen 800." I roll my eyes.

"The fuck? Your rib is broken." He grits his teeth.

I give him a little shrug. "Well, you know how it is now. Nobody wants to prescribe the hard stuff."

I hate lying to him.

"But your rib is broken," he repeats.

"It'll heal."

"Liv." He gives me a hard look. "You don't have to be tough. I can call Donny, see what he's got."

"I thought we were mad at him for his vote," I say, the guilt clawing at my heart more painful than my ribs.

"We are, but he's still my best friend."

"I'm not taking drugs from him." I lift my chin. "Lucy would kill me if I popped street pills." Even if they came from Vaughn's mom.

"Good point."

"Grab my phone for me?" I ask, leaning against him. "I want to text Ravage and Bryce."

He hands me the phone. "You should call Ravage. He might not hear a text. You know, us old people and our phones."

I snort softly, pulling up Ravage in my contacts. As the line rings, I meet Cliff's eyes. "I want to get him tonight, if we can."

He nods.

"Yeah?" Ravage answers, his voice thick from sleep.

"Sorry to wake you, Pres." I get right to it. "I want us to bring in Bryce, just in case the Bastard Brothers go after him, too."

The silence stretches over the connection while he thinks. "We can't just take a seventeen-year-old," he says finally.

My phone buzzes in my hands with a text.

"Hang on."

Still supported by Cliff, I open my messages and frown.

Bryce: Please help. I don't know what to do. My mom never came home from work.

"Ravage, we gotta get him now. His mom's missing."

"I'll send Donny," he says, and hangs up.

Olivia: We're on it. My friend Donny will bring you to me. Text me your address.

I stare at my texts, holding my breath until he replies with his address.

I tip my head back and look up at Cliff, who's been reading over my shoulder.

"It'll be okay," he promises, doing his best to hold me together.

All while I hold in the truth.

I don't want to put any more weight on him than I already have. Between Lucy, Bunny, and Bryce, he's got enough to worry about. I don't want him worrying about me.

When Lucy wakes up, I'll tell him.

I LIE in Cliff's arms while we wait. Neither of us speaks, but I sense him awake behind me, his frame curled around mine. When Bunny stirs, letting out a hungry coo, I push the blankets back.

"I got her," he says.

Ignoring the sharp pain that accompanies every movement, I struggle to sit. Nausea roils my stomach, the room spinning around me. It could be the pain or the pregnancy. Maybe both. I have no idea how this is supposed to work, and I can't exactly ask Lucy.

Using my knees, I haul myself out of bed. Then I limp toward the Pack 'n Play. Bunny's coos grow more frantic, a questioning pitch to them. "I'm coming," I promise her.

"Here," Cliff says, hurrying beside me. "Let me at least pick her up for you."

I stop in front of the Pack 'n Play and throw him a glare. "I can do it."

He cocks an eyebrow at me.

Making my own cocky face, I start to bend down . . . and

immediately regret it. Pain shoots through my ribs and sternum. Smiling tightly, I straighten. "You can get her."

"Uh-huh," he says. He lifts the baby with both arms, cradling her to his chest for a moment. He bows his head, swaying her from side to side. She is so tiny in those massive arms, her cheek pressed against his Tool shirt. A tender expression relaxes his face as he takes her in. Rocked in his arms, she calms for a moment, her startled green eyes latching onto his. They gaze at each other, already old friends. A small smile tugs my lips as I watch them.

"Here," he says, passing her to me.

I accept her, wincing when my arm moves wrong.

"Got her?"

"Yeah." I shift her around so that she's more comfortable. She squints up at me, her little lips forming a disappointed O. A second later, she parts her lips and releases a long wail.

"Come sit," Cliff says, guiding me out to the living room. "I'll get her bottle." He eases me onto the couch, then goes into the kitchen.

I stare down at her for a moment. I don't know what to do. Lucy always comforts her. I try to rock her, but even the slight movement sends sharp slashes through me. The baby wails, tears beading at the corners of her pinched eyes. Her face blazes red, her fingers curled into tiny fists.

"It's okay," I say, trying to get my voice down to that soft level Lucy uses. It cracks instead, and she only cries harder.

"She can sense you're in pain," Cliff says, lifting her from my arms. The moment she's away from me, the crying stops. He gives her the bottle and she takes it, settling into content.

"Yeah," I say, taking a shaky breath.

"You want to finish feeding her?"

"She looks comfortable." I give him a smile and stand. "I'm gonna go get dressed."

He closes his eyes. "Shit."

"What?"

"I forgot to put your clothes in the washing machine."

"Oh." I smooth the front of the River Reapers tee I jacked from him. "I'll just wear them again," I say, even though the thought of wearing yesterday's underwear kind of grosses me out.

"I'm sorry," he says, his expression pained.

"Don't even sweat it." I give him another smile. I don't want him to beat himself up. It isn't his fault. None of it is. "You know what? I've got to check in with Donny, anyway. He should be here soon. I'll see where they're at and have Esther grab clothes for me."

Circling the couch, he strolls over to me. "You sure?"

"What are best friends for?" I duck into the bathroom for my phone. "I hate this," I mutter, finishing the text. "Everything is so out of control."

"We'll figure this out." He watches Bunny eat for a second, his eyes going distant.

My phone vibrates with a text, Esther letting me know she's got my back. "They've got Bryce," I say. "They've just been caught up. Esther's littlest sister is sick. But everyone's safe. She'll be by soon."

He lifts the now empty bottle from Bunny's lips. "Things are looking up. We've got this."

He paces away, into the bedroom. Through the open door, I watch him lay Bunny down. Her legs kick into the air but she doesn't protest.

When he comes back out, I light a cigarette. He gives me a look but closes the bedroom door.

"Instead of lying around last night, I could've taken care of all this," he says.

"Just you? All by yourself?" I tease.

A knock on the door cuts off his reply. "Esther?" He gives me a questioning look.

I shrug. "Probably."

He pads into the darkness of the hall, pulling open the closet door. A moment later, he retrieves his gun, clicking the safety off.

I glance around the apartment, suddenly feeling the weight of the situation. A lot of people want us both dead.

"Quit fucking and let me in," Esther says, knocking again.

Cliff puts the gun away, shaking his head. He unlocks the door and she darts inside, ushering her youngest sister and Bryce with her.

At least we're not the only ones who are paranoid.

"Donny told me I got twenty minutes before he comes looking for me," she says.

I frown at her. "What do you mean?"

She rolls her eyes at me. "We're at war," she says, the "duh" clear in her tone. "He's out looking for . . ." She flicks a glance at Bryce.

"My mom," he says, his eyes red, dark circles hanging beneath them. A backpack hangs over one shoulder, stuffed full.

"Here, put your things down," I tell him. "Are you hungry?"

I don't know what else to say to him. I don't want to make false promises.

He shrugs and drops his backpack to the floor, kicking it aside so it isn't in the way.

I glance down at Ximena, Esther's youngest sister. "What's going on with Jimmy?"

She clicks her tongue. "Stomach thing." Before I can stop myself, I make a face. "Don't worry, it's not contagious. It's always been a thing with her. She picks up on anxiety and it makes her feel yucky, huh, baby?" She ushers the little girl over to the couch, setting down a tote bag. "That's why we took so long. I didn't even get a chance to text. I'm really sorry."

"It's all good," I assure her. "Everyone's whole." I sneak a peek at Bryce, who doesn't look whole at all. I bite my lip, aching for him.

A text buzzes my phone in my hands. I glance down at a picture of Dio eating tuna.

Shannon: Don't be mad. He gave me snuggles and I caved.

I rub my eyes. I completely forgot about my cat.

"Come on," Esther says, taking my arm. "Let's get you dressed." Cliff steals my cigarette, and she tugs me into the bedroom. Once the door is closed behind us, she dumps the tote bag out on the bed. "I grabbed your comfiest shit." Her dark eyes lock onto mine. "How are you? Really. No bullshit."

I look back at my best friend, and I want to tell her everything. It's bad enough that Shannon knows. Cliff can't be the last to know. He just can't. So I focus on Lucy. "I'm terrified," I say. I sort through the clothing until I come up with a gray cardigan, gray T-shirt, and olive joggers.

"And playing Mommy." She nods toward the Pack 'n Play, where Bunny is out cold. "What's that doing to you?"

"It's not that bad." I stare at the joggers, a little uncertain about going commando.

"Bullshit," she says. She follows my line of sight. "Oh!" Reaching into her purse, she pulls out a brand new package of panties. "You didn't have anything clean, so I stopped at Walmart." She hands me the package and a stick of deodorant.

"I love you," I tell her. "I don't deserve you."

I couldn't have imagined our friendship growing into something so precious to me. Esther's proved I can trust her, time after time. She's earned those three words.

So has Cliff, but I want it to be special when I drop them.

With her help, I get out of Cliff's T-shirt. I glance down at my stomach, still flat, and wonder how long until I start showing. Esther sees me staring but says nothing. She helps me into my clothes, patiently navigating my ribs.

"I almost forgot," she says, digging into her purse. She holds out a small baggie of white pills. "Present from Donny."

I stare at the pills, tempted. I just need to get through this day. I need to be able to carry Bunny without wanting to scream. I need to be able to blank out the pain and focus on my sister and her little baby. I bite my lip.

Esther gives me a look. "They're just Perc fives."

"It's weird to see you muling," I say to distract her.

"I'm *not* muling." She glances at the door. "I just didn't know what the hospital gave you."

"Ibuprofen 800." I sigh, but still don't take the baggie from her.

Her frown deepens. "All they gave you was Advil? I thought your ribs were broken."

My eyes skitter toward Bunny.

"They're only fives," she says again. "You can still function."

I accept the pills, tucking them into the pocket of my joggers. "Thanks."

"Sure," she says, eyeing me. "No problem."

We stand there for an awkward beat.

"Not to peer pressure you, but you should take one now. Let me get you some water."

"It's not too bad," I say, waving her away.

"Girl, I just had to help you get dressed. I saw your cooch!"

I shrug. "Sisters from another mister?"

"Yeah, but it's still weird."

"You're saying my pussy's weird?"

"Do not use that word with me!"

I crack a smile. "Don't be a pussy about it."

She slaps her hands over her ears. "You're evil."

"Thank you," I tell her, sincere.

I wrap my arms around myself, cold even with the cozy cardigan.

"I don't know what I can possibly do to make this better," she says, "but I'm a good listener."

"I know." I reach for her hand. "Trust me, you don't want to know."

She nods. "I do try to remain oblivious, usually. This is an exception, though. I mean, Lucy? What the F happened?"

"Esther, you know she's just a baby. You can swear in front of her."

"I know. It still feels wrong." Releasing my hand, she walks over to the Pack 'n Play.

I join her, and we both watch Bunny sleep. "What if Lucy doesn't wake up?"

"She will." She wraps an arm around me. "She will."

"What if she doesn't? They were looking for *me*."

She lets out a shaky breath. "I kind of figured."

"She wanted to come to the hospital, while I was getting checked out. I didn't want Bunny to get sick, so I told her to stay put."

"This is *not* your fault, Olivia." She takes my shoulders and gives them a gentle squeeze.

"Nothing is ever my fault," I mutter.

"You know what? Donny had Vaughn bring Cliff's bike a while ago. He said he's got a meeting with his P.O.?"

Shit. I forgot about that. Cliff probably did, too.

"I'll take you to the hospital while Cliff goes to his meeting. I'll check in with Donny so he doesn't freak."

I hesitate. There's something else I've got to do while Cliff's out. "Jimmy doesn't need to be there. I'll take an Uber," I assure her.

"All right. You'll feel better when you see her," she says.

I nod, but I don't believe her.

49

CLIFF

"I wish you could skip this," Olivia says, stretched out next to me in bed. She lies on her back, her nipples hard and dark.

"Yeah, me too." I roll onto my side and rest a hand on her waist. She watches me, all wide eyes and lashes. I place a quick kiss on the corner of her mouth. "I'll meet you at the hospital later."

"I could use some pain relief," she says. She lays a hand on my face, touching her nose to mine. "You sure you have to leave right now?"

I grin just as her lips brush mine. "We've got a little time."

"Good." She presses me back onto my back. Swinging a leg over me in tiny, careful movements, she seats herself, taking all of me inside her.

"Holy shit," I breathe. "Are you sure—?"

"Shh." She leans forward, sealing my mouth with hers. Then she sits up again, rolling her hips against mine, squeezing me tight.

I groan. If she keeps this up, I won't last long at all. I run my fingers from her hips to her ribs, stopping when my hands meet the soft, supple flesh of her breasts. I part my first two fingers, kneading her and squeezing her nipples. Her back arches and she gasps.

I grin.

"Fuck," she whispers. She rides me harder, reaching around and dragging her nails across my balls.

"Are you trying to make me come?" I thrust up into her, smirking.

"You're the one who said there wasn't a lot of time." Her words are cut off by her cry of pleasure. Her head lolls back and she quakes around me. Releasing her breasts, I take her hands, lacing my fingers through hers. And I go with her.

Eyes hazy, she leans forward again and latches her mouth onto mine in a slow, tender kiss. "Hurry back," she says. Then she rolls off me.

In the living room, Bunny fusses.

"Want me to get her?" I ask, sitting up.

"You need a shower." She twists her hair into a messy bun and pulls on a silky robe Esther brought her. The fabric cascades around her ass, filling in the crevices and hugging her curves in all the right places.

"That robe is mandatory here from now on," I tell her as she steps out of the bedroom.

She tosses me a wink over her shoulder.

As much as I want to stay in this bed and let her have her way with me in the name of pain control, I do have to go see my parole officer. I get up and get into the shower.

When I get out, I find her in the kitchen making a pot of coffee. I wrap my arms around her and kiss her cheek. "See you when I get back."

She twists in my arms and brushes my lips with hers, then punctuates it with a quick kiss. Taking a deep breath, she tips her head back and gazes into my eyes. Her lips part. She hesitates.

"What?" I ask, kissing her again.

She blinks, smiling. "Nothing. Just get back."

"Yes ma'am." I kiss her one more time, then head out the door.

I RIDE through the gray streets, working out how I'm going to tell my P.O. about Lucy without alarming him. He's the one who set me up with the bouncer job, connecting me with the club. He's also the one who could pull the plug on it in a heartbeat, if he thinks that I'm in danger of violating my parole.

I roll past wisps of fog, my thoughts just as clouded. I *have* to tell him that Olivia and Bunny—and maybe even Bryce—are staying with me, and he's going to ask why. I'm going to have to lie. There's a chance that he'll check, though, and it won't take much for him to find out about Lucy.

I roar into the fog blanketed parking garage, turning my high beam on. It barely cuts through. Slowing to a crawl, I search for an empty space where my bike won't get scratched or knocked over. It's a loaner, after all.

I find two spots side by side and pull into one of them. Just as I shut off the headlight, a van lurches into the spot next to me, its brakes squealing as it slides in only inches away from me.

I turn toward the driver, my mouth already twisting as I prepare to tell him to be more careful. The doors slide open and two men jump out, their bodies brushing against my bike.

"Watch it," I demand, yanking off my helmet. One of them grabs my arm, stealing the helmet from my grip. He swings it toward me, and the dome of the helmet connects with my head.

I fall to the side, the pavement rushing up at me as I tumble from the bike. Thick arms catch me, and a fist catches me in the skull again.

Everything goes black.

50

I shower while Bunny naps and Bryce watches videos on his phone, then strap us all into an Uber with the driver's help. He takes us to the gynecology office on Meadow Street, where I've been going since I was a teenager.

I stand in front of the building, my arm shaking against the weight of the car seat. I could've asked Esther to come with me. But I don't want Cliff to be the last to know.

My feet carry me to the office, my head still wrapped in the fog outside. I've never been so exhausted in my life. I sign in and then sit in the waiting room, a pregnant woman with two other kids who aren't mine.

Life is weird.

"Olivia?" a nurse calls.

Standing, I reach for the car seat. My rib and muscles protest. I squeeze my eyes shut, shoving it down.

"Want me to watch her?" Bryce asks me.

I hesitate. He might be my responsibility, but he's still a stranger. I read nothing in his eyes other than the need to help, and I nod gratefully, urging him to stay put before following the nurse.

She leads me through the hall of exam rooms. "Are you all right?" she asks over her shoulder.

"I might've fractured a rib." I follow her to an exam room, pausing in front of the table.

"Oh, jeez," she fusses. "Do you need help climbing up there?"

"Yes," I say with a sigh.

"Not used to asking for help, are you?" She pulls out a step and helps me up.

I sit with a groan. "Not really."

She folds up the back half of the table, giving me something to lean against.

"Thank you."

"Just undress from the waist down," she says, handing me a paper blanket. "I have your lab results from the hospital, so I won't make you give me a urine sample. The ultrasound tech will be right in, and then the doctor will be in." She pulls the curtain, then leaves the room, closing the door behind her.

Kicking off my boots with a groan, I peel my leggings off, dropping everything onto the chair. I spread the giant paper towel over my lap, then fold my hands. I'll worry about getting down and getting dressed later.

Someone knocks at the door.

"Come in."

A short and thick woman with ringlets down to her ass rolls a cart into the room. "Olivia Reynolds?" she asks with a warm smile, opening the curtain again.

"That's me."

She pushes the table back down, helping me lie down. "I'm just here to bug you with cold gel and a wand. This will be trans-vaginal," she explains.

I grimace. "Great."

"Just take a deep breath for me and relax," she soothes, covering the wand with gel. "Little cold, little pressure . . ." She gently inserts the wand. I grimace anyway. It's cold and hard, an invasive presence after Cliff's warmth this morning. "So at this stage, we *might* not be able to detect the heartbeat, which is normal," she assures me.

"Okay." I hold my breath, caught between hoping she tells me the hospital was wrong and hoping she tells me I *can* listen to the heartbeat today.

"We're just going to confirm the pregnancy and measure the size of the fetus to get an estimated due date."

"You can do that already?" I wish I'd been with Lucy when she did this. I wish she could be with me now.

"I can." The tech smiles, then goes quiet for a moment. She turns the screen toward me and, making several clicks, isolates a fuzzy egg yolk and sac. "This is your uterus. This is the fetus. Congratulations."

I give her a stiff smile. "Thanks."

"Sorry," she says quickly. "I assumed . . . The doctor can discuss your options with you, if you'd like."

"I'm good. I just . . ." I stare at the screen, turning my head slightly. "It's just hard to believe *that* is a baby."

She chuckles. "Technically it's a fetus. But it will be a baby, if you want it."

I close my eyes. A year from now, Lucy, Cliff, and I will be making Halloween plans with our babies. If she wakes up.

Our babies.

If she wakes up.

Tears sting my eyes.

"You're about six weeks," she says, "which means . . ." She clicks away for a few seconds. "You'll be due around May twentieth."

"Wow," I breathe. "That's forever away. And also tomorrow."

She smiles and turns up the volume. A soft, rapid whooshing flows from the speakers. "That's the heartbeat."

I close my eyes, tears burning. I want this, I realize.

A printer whirs and I open my eyes. The tech hands me a

sonogram, and I stare at it in my hands for a moment. I don't know how I'm going to tell Cliff. It should be special. It should be with Lucy right there, too.

The tech slowly eases the wand out of me. Handing me another paper towel, she turns and cleans the wand. "The doctor will be in just to go over everything with you. Congratulations again. You can clean up and get dressed."

She helps me sit up and then she's gone, leaving me to gather my clothing and my thoughts.

I slide down from the table, and bend slowly, plucking my leggings from the floor. Now that I have a concrete due date, I'll tell Cliff when he gets home. I can't keep this from him any longer. Not when it's happy news.

Everything is about to change.

51

OLIVIA

Luck is on my side, because I get the same Uber driver. He helps me get the car seat strapped in again, and then we're off. I sit in the back, between Bryce and Bunny, touching her sweet face and talking to her.

I can't wait to see Lucy, to tell her my crazy news. I don't want Cliff to be the last to know, but I don't want her to be left out, either. Hell, it might shock her into waking up.

"I can carry all that," Bryce says, motioning to the car seat and base.

I don't know how to comfort him. So I let him help, because I think he needs something to do, and neither of us know what else to say to each other.

After I pay the driver, I lead us into the hospital, a little bounce in my step. For most of my life, everything has been a hurdle to get over—or worse, through. Nothing turned out like I thought it would, but that doesn't have to be a bad thing. Maybe life is what we do during and after the storm.

I've come miles. I'm not the same person I was a few months ago. I'm still me, but a reborn version. A stronger version.

Certainly strong enough to grab this next chapter of my life and make it a good one.

The elevator dings and the doors slide open. Gritting my teeth, I lug the two souls in my body into the hall, Bryce shuffling behind me with Bunny. If I can do this with a busted rib, I can do it in any condition. I can do anything.

I turn into the ICU and hit the button, announcing myself and giving them Lucy's name. The nurse on the other end hesitates.

"Can you stop by the nurse's station?" she asks.

"Sure thing." My hand already hurts from just the thought of filling out more paperwork.

I stagger to the desk. "Hi. I'm Lucy Demmel's sister. You wanted me to stop by."

The nurse glances up from the computer, her brown eyes guarded. "Did you get any of our messages?"

"Messages?" I shake my head. "I had my phone on silent. I had a doctor's appointment."

She takes a deep breath. "You should prepare yourself."

My heart beats twice then falters. "Prepare myself?"

Rui rounds the corner, speeding toward me. "Olivia. Glad I caught you." Giving the nurse a sharp look, he takes my elbow and steers me away from the nurses' station.

"What's going on?" I stammer. "She's freaking me out."

He nods. "Lucy has pneumonia, Olivia."

I blink. "Oh." Exhaling, I relax my shoulders. "So what, no babies allowed?"

"Maybe we should go sit." He reaches for Bunny's car seat.

I grab his hand. "What is it?"

"Pneumonia is serious in coma patients, Olivia," he explains in a gentle tone, the kind people use when someone is dying.

"Okay. So you're going to give her IV antibiotics and she can't have visitors?"

"We really should go sit."

"Rui," I say sharply, "just give it to me straight."

He bows his head for a moment. "Of course we've started her on antibiotics," he says, looking me in the eye. "The problem is, her body is already weak and might not be able to fight the infection. You . . ."

I tilt my head away from him, giving it a tiny shake.

"You should say goodbye, just in case."

I rock back on my heels. "Just in case? In case she dies?"

"Yes. In case she dies." He takes my elbow again, steadying me. "Do you want some water?"

"I'll be in the waiting room," Bryce says softly, touching my arm for a moment before retreating.

"I want to see my sister." I reach for Bunny and my rib shifts. My lips split apart and a sharp gasp pours from my throat.

"Olivia, let me call someone for you. Where's Cliff?"

I hold up a shaking hand. "It's just this rib. I'm fine. Can you just carry her?"

"Of course." He lifts the car seat and base with ease, then ushers me toward Lucy's room. "Hand sanitizer, gown, mask, gloves. I'm serious, Olivia. She doesn't have a good chance."

"You keep saying that," I say, putting my hand under the dispenser. "You haven't met her." I rub my hands together, then pull on the ICU uniform. "Am I good to go?"

He nods. "You should call Cliff, anyone who'd want to see her before she goes."

I hold up a gloved hand. "She's not going anywhere. She has a baby." I look down at Bunny. "Can you unbuckle her and hand her to me? I can't bend."

Rui passes Bunny to me, then carries the car seat into the room. I trail in after him, ignoring the tingling shake in my hands, willing them to instead feel the weight of the baby. The here and now. I stop at the foot of the bed, my breath ragged in my throat.

"I've got some good news, relatively speaking," Rui says from beside me.

"Oh?" I hug Bunny to the good side of my chest.

"The swelling in her brain has gone down significantly. So *if* she gets through this, we'll be able to take her into surgery to repair the damage and remove any blood clots."

"Told you, she's a fighter. Tell him, Luce." I drag my eyes to her face, ignoring the swollen ashen flesh and searching for anything familiar. The only thing that's still *Lucy* is her lashline. "Can I just have a moment?"

"Of course." He touches my shoulder. "I'm going to have Abe call Cliff for you."

"I'll call him myself," I promise. Cliff can't hear this from Abraham, of all people.

I watch Rui leave the room, sliding the door closed behind him. I turn back to Lucy.

"Jeez, woman, you're making me nervous." I take a few steps closer. "Let me just text Cliff." I wrestle my phone out and peck out a message one-handed.

> **Olivia:** I took an Uber to the hospital. Call me as soon as you get our of your meeting.

I hit send, then notice the typo.

> **Olivia:** *out. Holding Bunny.

I switch my ringer back on, then move to Lucy's side. "You have to fight this," I whisper to her. "Because this little girl needs you. And . . ." I glance at the door again, making sure we're alone. "Cliff knocked me up. I'm going to tell him later, right after I tell him . . ." I take a deep breath. My voice wavers. "I love him, Luce." Tears drip from my eyes. "And I love you. So you need to get better so you can laugh at me."

I sit down, resting Bunny in my lap to give my arm a break. "Come on, Luce. Wake up and laugh at me," I beg.

Her eyes remain closed.

52

OLIVIA

———

Every minute I spend in this hospital room is another sixty-second wish that I weren't here. When I leave, all I want is to come back. No one ever talks about how excruciating it is to watch someone you love suffer. You don't want them to die, but your pain is only beginning. Death is a mercy, but only for the dying.

Two hours pass, and I've had enough for today. I stand, leaving Bunny asleep in her car seat. I tiptoe over to Lucy and run gloved fingers across her cheek, then lean in close.

"It's okay if you have to go," I whisper. "We'll be all right."

Just in case she does go, I add, "I love you, Luce. You made my life so much better. Thank you."

Closing my eyes to dam the tears, I kiss her cheek. Then I straighten up. "I've got her," I tell Lucy. "Whatever happens, I've got her."

Turning, I shuffle to the empty chair and car seat. I check my phone for what feels like the thousandth time. Still nothing from Cliff.

I frown. This isn't like him. We're not the couple that needs to be in constant contact, but we always check in. Mark gave us indefinite time off, and Cliff took time off from the shop. He said he'd be here. I don't know where else he could be.

Sighing, I grab everything and drag myself out of the room, stripping off the gown and gloves. I collect Bryce from the waiting room and we step into the elevator. Maybe Cliff didn't get my texts and crashed at his place. Neither of us slept last night. While I wait to reach the ground floor, I fire off a text to Esther begging for a ride.

So much of my life has changed and yet so much is the same.

I shamble out of the hospital, into the designated smoking area. This is the real world. I'm going to need a car, not just a motorcycle. There's no way I'll be able to schlep around one baby on a bike, never mind two.

Two babies. I set down the car seat, gasping for air. Doubling over, I pant, quick rapid-fire huffs. Two babies. I suck in lungfuls, but it makes no difference. I can't slow down. I can't breathe. Two babies. Lucy is dying. I claw at the air, searching for something to hold onto, someone, but there's nothing there, no one. I could wake up tomorrow and Lucy could be dead. My favorite person in the whole world.

"You okay?" Bryce asks, uncertain.

Nodding, I stagger to the stairs. I sit down hard, the impact jolting my rib. I howl, my diaphragm still spasming, my brain still ignoring my lungs. Two babies. I can't raise any babies. And I have no idea where Cliff is.

Hands shaking, I fumble for my cigarettes. I light and inhale, trying to slow my breath. It doesn't work. I take a longer drag, exhaling through my nose, ignoring the burn. It jars me just enough that I can focus. I check my phone.

Esther: Don't stress it! I'm on my way.

I swear I've been sitting here panicking for an hour, yet barely two minutes have passed.

I chainsmoke, keeping the smoke away from Bunny and wearing a brave face for Bryce until Esther pulls up. She leaves the car idling on the hill and dashes out of the driver's side.

"Are you okay? Where's Cliff?" She sits down next to me, wrapping her arm around me.

"I don't know," I say, my voice breaking. I sob, covering my mouth with the back of my hand.

"Okay," she soothes. "Let's get you home."

"I don't have a key to his place," I wail, my heart fluttering in my chest, banging against its cage.

"Do you think he's home?"

"I don't know," I sob again.

"Okay." She looks around the parking lot. "Let's go to Cliff's. If he isn't there, I'll take you to my place."

"Bunny," I gasp, "needs a crib."

"Girl, I have three bunnies. We'll make it work."

"I just wanna go home," I cry. My heart cracks a little more with each word. I can't go home. Half of my home is in the ICU. The other half is . . .

I shake my head. "This doesn't make sense."

"Is there something you wanna tell me?" Her voice is so gentle, I cry harder.

"Don't." Straightening, I hold up a hand. "Don't tell me he left. He wouldn't. He wouldn't." I shiver, the tears cascading down my cheeks.

"Come on." Esther stands and picks up Bunny in her car seat. She carries her to the car and straps her into the backseat. I lean against the railing, watching her through bleary eyes. Then she comes back for me. "Come on," she says again, helping me up. She straps me into the passenger's side, closing the door softly.

Bryce hops into the backseat, his hood pulled up, earbuds in.

"Pendejo," she says, then walks to the driver's side as calm as I've ever seen her. She slides in with a deep sigh. "Okay. Let's go check the apartment."

Urging the car up the hill, she swings into the valet circle, pausing only long enough to let a woman in surgical scrubs cross. Then she guns it out of the parking lot. Neither of us speaks as she drives to Cliff's place. She doesn't say a word when we pull into his apartment building's driveway and I scan the parking lot for his bike.

"It isn't here. He isn't here."

She bites her lip. "Is there something you want to tell me?" she asks again.

"Tell you?" I turn toward her. My rib protests, sending shooting pain throughout my sternum. "Fuck," I gasp.

She holds up a finger, ticking it with her other hand. "You refuse to take pain medicine, even though you're clearly in pain." She holds up another finger. "You cut back on smoking, until a few minutes ago." She puts up a third. "Cliff is MIA." She gives me a kind but stern look. "Olivia, are you pregnant?"

"Did Shannon tell you?" I demand.

She makes a face. "Olivia, the writing is on the fucking wall. Just tell me so I can help you. I want to help you."

"He didn't leave me," I insist.

"Maybe it just got to be too much for him," she says. "Maybe between Lucy, taking care of Bunny, all this club shit, now a baby on the way—"

"He doesn't know!" I shout.

She jumps, jerking the wheel a little.

"He doesn't know," I say more calmly. "I was going to tell him tonight. You can't tell anyone."

"I knew it," she says, making a U-turn out of the parking lot. "The second you turned down drugs when you have a sprained rib."

"It might be broken." I stare at the side mirror, as if any second Cliff will pull behind us on his bike. "I don't know."

"We'll find him," she assures me, patting my leg without taking her eyes from the road.

"Where the fuck could he be?" I pull out my phone. No new

texts. "Should I let the club know? Do you think something happened?"

"Maybe he took a shift to get his mind off things."

"Or maybe his P.O. sent him back to prison," I mutter.

"Could that really happen?"

"I don't know. Maybe if his P.O. found out about Lucy." I rub my temples. "But would they just ship him right back? Wouldn't he get a phone call or something?" I tap the phone icon and scroll through my voicemails, just in case he called and I didn't have service but his message snuck through.

There's nothing.

"We'll find him," she promises me, pulling into her driveway. She parks behind Donny's motorcycle, then shuts the car off.

"He wouldn't just take off. Something is wrong." Unbuckling myself, I open the door and push it open with my foot. With a grunt, I drag myself out of the car. Before I can open the door to get Bunny, Esther appears at my side.

"I've got her."

I let her, lighting a cigarette while I wait. "Something happened."

Bryce ducks out of the car and stands next to me, his face concerned.

"Never a dull moment with us," I try to joke, but it falls flat.

The front door opens and Donny steps outside. "What's going on?" He descends the porch stairs as he lights a cigarette.

"You texted him?" I ask Esther.

"Of course." She lifts the car seat and carries it toward the house. "Right after I strapped Bunny in."

"Lucy would kill me if she knew everyone is calling her Bunny now," I muse.

"Olivia, focus." Donny cups my shoulders. "Did Cliff say where he was going?"

"His parole officer. Do you think he went back to prison?" I latch onto him with my free hand, clutching his sweatshirt.

"Prison?"

"Lucy," Esther and I say at the same time.

"If his P.O. found out about the attack," I explain, "he could say Cliff violated his parole by engaging in gang activity."

"Fuck." Donny shakes his head. "Wouldn't he get a phone call?"

"That's what I said." My lips tremble.

"A'ight. Let's get you inside, get you a drink." He puts an arm around me, flicking his cigarette into the street. I flick mine away, too, then let him shepherd me in.

Inside, Esther sets Bunny down and then starts rummaging through a closet. "I swear I brought Jimmy's old Pack 'n' Play with us. Babe, do you remember?"

"I have no idea," Donny says. He walks to a locked china cabinet full of books and booze, and takes a set of keys from his pocket.

"I'm good," I say, just as he fits a key into the lock.

He twists his head, frowning at me. "You're 'good.' You're shaking. Esther, tell your girl she needs a drink."

"I'll take one," Bryce says.

"Not happening," I tell him.

Esther sets down a box, exchanging a glance with me. "I found it. The thing for babies," she says, her voice too high.

I slide her a sharp look, but Donny follows it.

I sigh. "I can't have that drink because I'm . . . pregnant."

He grabs a bottle of blackberry brandy. "This is for me." Twisting off the top, he brings the whole bottle to his lips.

"Cliff doesn't know," I say before he jumps to conclusions.

He nods. "I wasn't even thinking that. I know him better than that."

"So do I," I say, giving Esther a meaningful look.

She holds up her palms at me. "Sorry."

I sit on the couch and unbuckle Bunny. I rock her back and forth, more for me than for her.

"How's Lucy?" Donny asks.

I suck in a deep breath, keeping my eyes on Bunny. "Pneumonia. It's not good. Rui said to tell her goodbye, just in—" My voice cracks. "Just in case." I lift my eyes to his. "Cliff doesn't know that, either. That's why I was trying to get a hold of him."

"Call Mark," Donny says. "He'll have Cliff's P.O.'s number. We call the P.O., check in. Maybe they ran late."

Bryce reaches into the diaper bag and hands my phone to me.

Mark picks up on the first ring.

"Are you in the office? Give me Cliff's P.O.'s number," I tell him. "Please. It's important."

He rattles it off and I memorize it, thanking him before hanging up. I punch in the numbers, listening to it ring and ring.

"Ntshiza," the officer answers.

"Hi." I chew the inside of my cheek. "I'm just checking to see if Clifford Demmel is still with you?"

"Demmel?" He sighs. "He didn't even show up."

"You're sure?" I ask.

"I've been trying his cell. Who is this?"

Fuck. "His girlfriend," I say, raising my eyes to Esther's. I shake my head, and she bows hers.

"You tell him I'm not playing," Ntshiza says. "He needs to get down to my office, or I'll have to put out a warrant for him."

"Can you make an exception?" I beg. "He's never missed a meeting with you."

"He's got one day," he says, and hangs up.

"He didn't show," I say, stunned. "They're gonna put out a warrant for him."

"If he didn't take off and he isn't back in prison, then where is he?" Esther asks.

Donny shakes his head.

I lick my lips. "Maybe he didn't want to wait."

"What do you mean?"

"Maybe he went after the Bastard Brothers on his own." I sway the baby.

"Dude's stubborn," Donny says, "but not stupid."

"Then something must've happened," I insist. I hold Bunny out to Esther. "Take her and give me your car keys."

She lifts Bunny from my arms. "For what?"

"I'm going to his P.O.'s office." I stand.

"His P.O. told you he didn't show," Donny says gently, guiding me back to my seat. He sits down next to me. Esther places Bunny in the Pack 'n' Play, then sits on my other side. They stare at me with twin sympathetic expressions.

"Don't look at me like that. He wouldn't leave me."

"Maybe we don't know him as well as we thought," Donny admits.

"He went to fucking prison for Lucy. He wouldn't just skip out on her."

They both nod. Esther reaches for my hand, but I yank it away. I turn to Donny.

"Take me to the fucking P.O.'s office. I can't—" I swallow a sob. "I'm in too much pain to drive."

"I think you need some sleep," Esther says, smoothing my hair.

"One of you better fucking take me, or I'll call a fucking Uber!" My voice echoes off the walls of the house. Too late I remember the little girls upstairs, Bryce next to me. "I'm sorry." I press my palms together, pushing them against my nose. I take a deep breath. "I just have to see. I can't accept that he'd just leave. After everything? No." I shake my head, and stand.

"He never gave up on me. Never. I'm not giving up on him. So who's going to drive me?" I look from Esther to Donny.

He sighs. "Okay. Let's go."

"I don't know what you're expecting to find," Donny says as he drives us to Scovill Street in Waterbury. Chelsea Wolfe plays through his iPhone, doing nothing to calm my nerves like she usually does.

I say nothing. Right now I might be *that* girl, clinging to desperate, false hope. Cliff disappearing does *not* make sense.

Which is why I have to see for myself.

The evening presses down on me, the streets sinister and heavy. It's so much darker than usual. We drive into downtown Waterbury, the buildings unfriendly but vaguely familiar. I've only been through here a few times.

Donny pulls into a parking lot shared by the parole office and a dive bar called The Thirsty Goat. "That's convenient," he mutters.

"Huh?" I unbuckle my seatbelt.

"A bar, right next to a parole office." He shakes his head. When I give him a shrug, he sighs. "What if one of your parole conditions is abstinence? You walk out of that parole office one day, you're having a rough day. Right here, right now there's a bar you can get a drink."

"It's fucked up," I agree, distracted.

"The system is designed wholly to *get* you to fuck up," he surmises.

"Yeah." I stare at the barrier gate arm of the parking garage. Cliff's Screamin' Eagle waits, sandwiched by a Honda Civic and a Jeep. I push open my door.

"Wait, I gotta park."

"Then go park." I climb out of the car. Closing the door behind me, I walk toward the bike as if in a trance. I cross the street, step around the barrier gate arm, and drift to the bike's side. Reaching out a hand, I run my fingers across its cool body. "Where did you go?" I whisper.

It makes no sense. The keys are gone. The helmet is upside down beside the rear tire. I lift it, turning it over in my hands.

"That your bike?"

I jump, spinning around, clenching the helmet, my muscles coiled to strike. A guy around my age whistles, completely oblivious to me, openly ogling the motorcycle. He turns his head this way and that, his dreads brushing his back as he moves.

"Damn, she's a beauty." Straightening, he grins at me.

I lower my arm. "It's not mine," I say. I hold the helmet at my side, my arm dangling, my rib throbbing.

"Hey, man." Donny jogs over to us, his arm already out. "Maybe you can help us with something," Donny says. "Where you at? The Goat?"

"Yeah, just having a few drinks with some people. I saw this bike when I was coming in and wanted to take another look." He gives it a wistful glance. "I was hoping it might be yours," he says to me.

"It's my boyfriend's. How long have you been here?" I ask him. "Did you see anything?"

"Like what?"

"He's a big white dude," Donny says. "You couldn't miss him.

He had a meeting first thing this morning with his P.O. and never came home. It's after five now. This ain't like him."

"Shit."

"Did you see him?" I press.

"Nah. I've only been here about half an hour. Sorry."

I bow my head, clutching the helmet with both hands. Light catches the black shell, exposing a crack. "Donny." I hold it out to him. "There's a crack."

Frowning, he takes the helmet from me. "This is fiberglass. You'd have to hit it hard to crack it like this."

My eyes snap to his. "Or someone would have to hit you."

Cliff didn't leave us. Someone took him.

Just like someone took Bryce's mom.

It had to be the Bastard Brothers.

The guy admiring the bike takes a long step back from us. "Well, good luck with that."

"Thanks, man." Donny sighs. He watches the guy walk back into the bar, then he turns back to me. "You were right."

"Something happened," I say again.

"Something happened," he agrees. He takes out his phone. "I'll call Ravage. He'll have someone take the spare key again and pick up the bike."

"What about Cliff?" Hugging myself, I look around the parking garage. "The Bastard Brothers hate him. They knew he'd have to come here. Somehow they knew *when*. They must've waited for him."

"We'll find him," he promises.

I nod, my hands numb. I hope it isn't too late.

55

Blinding pain cuts through my skull, jolting me awake. I open my eyes. Hot white light sears my head. The floor tilts, the ceiling whirling. I slam my eyes shut.

I breathe through one nostril, the back of my head pressed against wet, sticky cement. Blood bubbles out of my nose with every breath. Groaning, I try to get my bearings, to remember the last thing before now.

I've woken up in seg, in a cell so tight, barely one man can fit. Lewisburg liked to cram them with three. There have been times I woke up on a cement floor, my face mashed under someone's boot, my hand pressed against the hot exposed pipe.

The before slips to me in a brief flash, the curve of my bike, the crack of the helmet, the black nothing. Groaning, I open my eyes to slits.

The sticky wetness is blood. I don't remember hitting my nose. It doesn't hurt enough to be broken, so I move on. All of my bones feel intact. I move my toes in my boots, twitch my fingers. The only pain I feel is the pounding in my head.

A boot scrapes against the floor, a throat clears. I stop moving. I close my eyes again, feigning unconsciousness.

"I know you're awake," a man says, exasperated. His voice is familiar, tangible only through the thick fog swirling in my mind. It's a puzzle piece I can't quite make fit, no matter how I turn it. It's the last piece in a nearly finished puzzle. I've been here before, too; I've got a concussion.

Right on cue, vomit rockets from my stomach up my throat. I turn my head just in time, unleashing a stream of hot bile. My head throbs along with each heave. I let out a reflexive howl, garbled by the emptying of my stomach. When it's over, I let my head loll back to the concrete.

"I could've killed you," he says with a chuckle. "Hit you any harder, you'd be dead."

I say nothing, just keep taking air.

"You dropped like a fucking sack of potatoes." He laughs. Boots scrape the concrete, pushing the knife in my head deeper. "You got huge while you were inside." His voice is right next to my ear. He must be squatting next to me. Normally, I could take him like this. But I'm so tired. What little energy I had left is gone after puking.

"We almost had you in there," he continues. "Then Mercy had to go and get himself locked up. We've waited twenty years for this."

I toss out a guess. "Malcolm?"

"Zed," he corrects. "I was a nobody back then. Now I'm VP."

"In a three-man club," I grunt.

"We carry on your father's legacy," he says. "Which is more than I can say for you."

"Raping kids. Some legacy."

Two hands close around my skull, squeezing, lifting my head from the floor. I roar in pain, my limbs going limp under the pressure.

"Bastard was a good man," he screams into my ear. He drops my head. It smacks into the floor.

I pant, willing the throbbing to stop. It doesn't. "Good like Chad?"

"Oh, we'll get to that subject," Zed says. "As soon as we find your little whore."

Olivia.

She's waiting for me, maybe alone. I have no idea how long I've been out, but I can't let them get to her.

Zed wants me to panic. He wants me to go into a blind rage, expending all of my energy so that I can't fight back. I remain still, taking slow deep breaths, sending oxygen through my muscles.

"How's your cousin doing?" he asks.

My fists clench. The monster rears its head, stretching, begging to be unleashed.

"She didn't look too good last time I saw her," he says. "Didn't realize she wasn't who we thought she was 'til all that red hair was bloody."

I shove it all down, tuning out his words. I summon every good memory I have in order to keep myself calm. Olivia this morning, her smile, the brush of her hair across my chest, the skim of her fingers on my face. The sweep of her lips against mine.

"I'm sure you're all planning retaliation." He places his hands around my head again, emitting a small amount of pressure. "You're going to tell me when, where, and how."

"Hadn't got that far yet." I thrash through the fog in my brain, searching for a way out of this. I need more time. I need to get out. I need to get to Olivia.

"Let's start simple," he says, squeezing just enough to break my next thought. "Where's your bitch? She isn't at the condo."

I grit my teeth, sucking in air through my nose.

He presses harder, digging his fingers into my scalp. Blinding pain flares through my skull, punctuated by a quick slice of gray.

"You're going to kill him if you make his head injury worse," another man says. Another familiar voice.

I flip through my memories, sliding faces against his voice. When it clicks, I open my eyes.

Finn stands over us, looking down at me.

"Finn," I grunt. "Man, I'm glad to see you." I stretch out a hand. "Get me outta here."

He steps on my hand, grinding my fingers into the cement. White hot pain shoots through my joints and tendons, radiating up my arm. "I don't think so," he says, putting more weight into his boot. "We're just getting started. I've got a lot of questions for you."

I swallow rage and save my strength.

"So," Zed says again, releasing my head just enough so that I can focus on the pain in my hand. Handcuffs clink around my wrists and I hear the swish of a switchblade. "Why don't you start talking?"

56

OLIVIA

I toss and turn on Esther's and Donny's couch all night. When I do fall asleep, flashes of Cliff being tortured and Cliff being murdered wrench me awake. I fall into another frantic five minutes, only to be yanked awake by a screaming Bunny.

I tumble from the couch, stumbling over to her. Sharp pain shrieks through my rib and chest as I reach down and lift her up. "Hey, hey," I soothe, rocking her in the dark. "It's a strange place, I know."

She wails louder, at least to my exhausted ears.

"You hungry?" I carry her into the kitchen and grab a saucepan from the rack. "Okay, okay." I rock her with one arm, clumsily filling the pan with water and setting it on the stove. "It's coming, baby. It's coming."

While I wait for the water to simmer, I find a clean bottle and fill it with formula powder and water from the tap. "It's like making mac 'n cheese," I quip.

She isn't having it.

Curling a tiny fist, she shakes it in the air. She misses her mother, and I am not Lucy. I'm not even Cliff. I'm the last person in the world she wants right now.

"I know." I shut the burner off and drop the bottle into the pan. "We'll figure this out, little one. You and me."

I heat the bottle exactly like Lucy and Cliff showed me, squirting a little onto my wrist to test it. Satisfied, I carry the bottle and the baby back into the living room. I sink into the couch, pulling a pillow under my baby arm for support. Then I offer the bottle to her.

She turns her face away.

"So, not hungry?" I set the bottle on the coffee table. With both hands, I hold her up and sniff at her bottom. "You don't smell like you need a change, but fuck it."

I strain for the diaper bag, plucking out the items I need one by one, each motion excruciating. Somehow I manage to hold onto Bunny.

Forehead damp, I lay her on the couch and unbutton the bottom of her onesie. Her feet kick at me, the siren scream never ending. "I know it," I soothe. I peer inside her diaper.

"You're dry." I sink my teeth into my lower lip. "Oh, little Bunny, I wish you could tell me what you need." Aside from the obvious.

I change her anyway, in the hopes that maybe the old diaper was just chafing her or something. But she never stops crying.

I'm pacing the living room and kitchen, rocking her, when lights flick on. Esther trails me in her bathrobe, her eyes bleary.

"What's wrong?"

"I'd love to know," I reply, almost in tears myself.

"Want me to take her?"

I lift a shoulder. I've already run through all the options—the ones I know of, anyway. I pass her to Esther, who curls her arms around her like a natural. She paces the kitchen, rocking the baby while making a shushing sound that reminds me of the ocean.

"Nothing is working," I say with a sigh, dropping into a chair.

She shushes me, continuing to rock the baby. "She can feel your distress."

"You and Cliff," I grumble. Just the sound of his name on my lips is enough. Hot tears slide down my cheeks, splashing onto the pajamas I borrowed from Esther. I rest my head on my arms on the table, my shoulders shaking with my sobs. I just want to know he's okay. I just want to bring him back. I can't stand this waiting, this sitting around in Esther's house, doing nothing.

After leaving the P.O.'s office, I called Ravage, who sent every River Reaper out looking for Cliff and Bryce's mom. *I* should be out there with the rest of my club, bringing him home. Yet here I am, and I can't even do the one job I was given.

The baby's cries quiet while mine reach a crescendo. Esther rubs circles on my back, soothing both Bunny and me with her shushing. I claw at the tablecloth, everything in me dying for a phone call, something, anything.

"Be right back," Esther whispers.

I rest my head on the table, taking deep breaths through my nose. Except the air is hot and catches in my lungs. I lift my head, staring into the bright light of the kitchen while breathing the cooler air.

Esther pads into the room, her arms empty. "She fell asleep," she explains. She fills her kettle with water and sets it on a burner, turning it on high. "What kind of tea do you want?"

I make a face. "Whiskey."

"They'll find him," she promises. "Chamomile?"

"Makes me nauseous."

"Really?" Her eyes drop to my stomach.

"It *always* makes me nauseous." I blot at my wet face with a napkin.

"Donny promised me he'd call the second he had news," she says, sitting next to me. The kettle spits on the stove as the water heats. "No news is good news."

"I hate this." I crumple the napkin in my fist. "Why couldn't they just let me go?"

"You know why. You're already injured. You're a liability. Those were Donny's exact words."

I roll my eyes. "He *owes* me for not listening to me. I knew something was wrong. I knew Cliff didn't just leave."

She lifts her shoulders. "Guess he felt more like he owes Cliff. Come on, Liv. You know Cliff would kill him if he let you go. Especially like this."

"Like this." I make a face. "This isn't the 1950s."

"No," she agrees, "but what if someone cracked you in the ribs again? Then you're down, and they've got to worry about *you* instead of finding Cliff and Bryce's mom, and killing the Bastard Brothers."

I bare my teeth and growl at her. "I hate when you're right."

She laughs.

The kettle lets out a whoop, then starts to whistle. She stands and hurries to the stove, lifting it from the burner before it wakes Bunny.

"How did you get her back to sleep, anyway?" I ask while she makes us some green tea with jasmine.

"I used to have to do that with Jimmy—the shushing. It reminds them of being in the womb. Works almost every time." She carries two mugs over and sets one down in front of me. "Don't freak out," she says.

I scoff. "I never freak out."

"While that was going off, my phone went off in my pocket." She dips a hand into the pocket of her bathrobe and wakes up the screen. There's a text from Donny.

I jump up, intending to get my phone from the living room. She catches my arm.

"The baby," she reminds me.

"Call him back." I remain standing, the muscles in my legs poised, ready to sink or run.

"Of course." She taps at her screen.

"Put him on speaker."

"The baby," she reminds me again.

"I don't care. I mean, I do care. Just . . . please." I bring both hands to the top of my head, digging my nails into my scalp. "Please," I sob.

I hate this version of me. This frantic, pleading thing with fucked up ribs. I am not the girl who sits at home waiting for her boyfriend. I'm the girl who goes out and gets him, blasting everyone in my way. I don't do this sit by and wait shit.

Esther puts the call on speaker. The line rings, a drawn-out trill that sets me even more on edge. Each subsequent ring rattles my teeth, stealing my breath. Our eyes lock.

"Essie," Donny answers, his voice hollow and calm.

"You're on speaker," she warns him.

I cut in. "Put Cliff on."

He takes a deep, sharp breath. "We didn't find him."

"What?" I stare at the phone. I'm exhausted. I barely slept. I'm probably hearing him wrong. "Did you go to their clubhouse?"

"Olivia." The way he says my name send a chill down my spine. My legs turn to heavy ice. "Someone must've told them what we were doing."

I swallow. "What do you mean?"

"They knew we were coming, Olivia." His voice is flat.

I stare at Esther. "W-what happened?" I choke out the words, tugging them past the bile rising up my throat. "What does Ravage want to do now?"

He takes a sharp breath. "Ravage is dead."

57

OLIVIA

I don't hesitate, and Esther doesn't stop me. I take her keys and I fly to The Wet Mermaid. My hands shake the whole way there, an unlit cigarette clamped between my teeth.

Ravage is dead.

I pull up to a red light, staring at it. Ravage is dead. They didn't find Cliff, or Bryce's mom. I was out the door before Donny could tell me more. The last time I saw Ravage, he tried to protect me. All this time, he's been looking out for me, and now...

I slam the heels of my hands into the steering wheel until numbness rings from my wrists to my elbows. The light changes and I stare at it through wet eyes.

Ravage is dead.

A horn blares behind me. I lift my foot from the brake and press on the gas, speeding the rest of the way to the clubhouse.

I don't want to go inside. I don't want it to be true. I park Esther's car at the end of the row of motorcycles. Where there should be eleven, there are only nine. Both my bike and Cliff's huddle together at the end of the line.

I shut off Esther's car and push open the door, but I don't move.

Donny rushes out of the strip club. "Where are Esther and the kids?" he demands.

I tilt my head. "At your house."

"Jesus, Olivia. You didn't think to bring them with you?"

I blink at him. "I didn't want to take the kids out in the middle—"

"You didn't think," he snaps. Turning away, he shakes his head.

"Donny, I'm sorry." Grabbing the frame, I drag myself out of the car.

"They shouldn't be alone," he says over his shoulder.

"You're right."

"I'll send someone to get them." He runs a hand over his head. "I don't even know who to send."

"Everybody . . . else is here?" Except Cliff and Ravage.

Suddenly Donny wraps his arms around me, pulling me into his chest. "I'm sorry for going off on you."

I hug him back. "You don't have to apologize."

"Olivia, there's more."

I close my eyes, willing him to shut up. I pretend everything is fine. We're having a party. That's why everyone is here.

I open my eyes and step away. "Okay."

"Ravage took Beer Can, Stixx, and me to their clubhouse to look for Cliff. He sent Skid and Vaughn to try and find Bryce's mom."

My stomach roils. I press my lips together.

"Their clubhouse is on the Naugatuck-Waterbury line, up off Sheridan Road, in the industrial park," he explains. "It looks like a nothing warehouse, but they have an after-hours bar. Ravage and I went in through the front, Stixx and Beer Can went in the back. Our plan was to light it up while Stixx and Beer Can hopefully found Cliff and got him outta there. But they were ready for us."

My stomach clenches.

Lighting a cigarette with shaking hands, he takes a long drag. "There was nobody else there. Just the Bastard Brothers. Malcolm shot Ravage point blank in the head. Stixx and I fired back, and Stixx took a bullet in the fucking leg. I wanted to take Ravage with us, but we couldn't. I had to get Stixx out of there. I threw him in the van, and I laid on the horn."

"No," I say.

"One of them must've been waiting in the back. Beer Can is dead, too."

I lean over and vomit, bile rushing up my throat. Donny lays a hand on my back, steadying me. When my already empty stomach is even more empty, I swipe a hand over my mouth and straighten. "So Cliff wasn't there?"

"He couldn't have been. It's too tight a place. We would've seen him." He leans against Esther's car.

"How did they know we were coming?" I whisper. "Abraham?"

He takes a deep breath. Chills run down my spine. "Abraham didn't know a thing, Olivia."

I bend over and throw up again.

58

OLIVIA

I let Donny walk me inside. What's left of our club sits around the bar. Stixx lies across two tables, Rui stitching up his calf.

"I'm not a surgeon," Rui warns Stixx. "This is going to scar. You need to take the antibiotics I'm giving you."

Stixx waves him off. His gaze lands on me, and relief washes over his face. "You're here."

"I am," I say, puzzled.

"He's wasted," Donny explains.

"We didn't find Cliff," Stixx laments. He shakes his head. "I promised her, but we didn't find him."

I frown. I don't remember Stixx promising me anything. Before I can dig into that, a sob cuts through the bar. I whip around. Shannon sits in the corner, sobbing into Bree's shoulder.

"Vaughn, I need you to go get Esther and the kids," Donny says. "I'd get them myself, but . . ." He looks around helplessly.

"You need to be here," Vaughn says. "I've got her."

"Take Mercy with you. He's the only other person here who's sober."

Mercy pushes off from the bar. He limps toward us, his eyes locked on me. He swallows. "Hey."

"Hey," I reply. I don't know what to say to this man. I barely know him. I do know that he and Ravage were close. No words can suffice. "How are you holding up?"

I now understand where the phrase "long face" comes from. His entire face droops, as if his bone structure lengthened. Grief is a dripping mask.

"I don't know," he answers.

I'm taken aback by his reply. No one is ever honest. They say things like "I'm fine," or "As good as I can be."

"You?" he asks.

"I don't know." I glance around the strip club again, my gaze landing at the door as if any second, the three of them are going to walk in. "I'm not sure this is real."

He puts a hand on my shoulder. "You stay put," he insists. "Don't even think about running off anywhere."

I open my mouth to tell him I can't promise anything when Donny interjects.

"She won't."

I start to roll my eyes at them.

"I'm serious, Olivia," Mercy says. "We're in over our heads here."

I leave them where they stand, drifting over to the bar. I can't drink, but this bar is sort of another home. I stand behind it, my hands resting on the lacquered wood. Back here, I always felt safe, in control. I could make drinks and listen to people's problems. I don't know if I ever really helped anybody, but I like to think that by giving them an ear and a properly made drink, I helped in some small way.

I can't help but feel like this is all my fault. I thought I was doing right by Bryce. If I'd known that all this would happen, maybe I would've done things differently. I still wouldn't have turned my back on him. That's not who I am. But now two people are dead, people who are my family. As for Cliff . . . I don't know. I don't know what the Bastard Brothers have done to him.

I sense eyes on me. I look up to find Abraham and Skid staring at me. Mistrust reflects in their eyes. I look away, busying my hands. I pour a Crown Royal neat for Shannon, then hesitate. I have no idea what Bree likes, and I don't even know if I should be giving her alcohol. I settle on pouring her a glass of ice water, and one for myself. Setting everything on a tray, I add a bowl of pretzels. There's no way Shannon wants to eat right now, but it can't hurt to try.

I carry the tray over. My hands shake, and I set it down the second I reach the table. "Hey," I say softly. "I brought you a drink." I pass the whiskey over to Shannon.

She wraps both hands around it, her red eyes trained on mine. "Thank you, sweetheart. He loved you, you know. He loved you so much." She takes a sip.

"I know," I say, because there's nothing else to say. I hand a water to Bree. "I didn't know what you wanted."

"This is fine," she says. "I'm staying sober."

"Yes, you are." Shannon wraps an arm around her. "That's what Ravage would want. It's what we all want."

Bree's eyes drop to the other water. "I appreciate the gesture, but you don't have to drink solidarity tap water, you know."

"This isn't because of you," I snap. I sink into a chair opposite them, ashamed. Maybe it's my nerves, or maybe it's the hormones, but I need to do better than this with Bree. "Sorry," I say quickly.

"We're all on edge." She watches me for a moment. It's almost like she knows exactly why I'm not drinking.

"How's Lucy doing?" Shannon asks.

The fact that she's even asking right now brings fresh tears to my eyes. I wish I could tell her that Lucy's doing fine, if only to give her some kind of comfort. I sigh. "Not so good. I'm going back to the hospital as soon as visiting hours open."

"The hell you are," Skid growls from behind me.

I glance over my shoulder to find him and Abraham flanking me, their arms crossed. "Who the fuck are you to say?"

"We're not letting you out of our sight," Abraham adds.

I push my chair back. "Then I guess you're coming with me," I say, standing and facing them. "Because if you think I'm leaving my sister to die alone, you're fucking crazy."

"If you think we're letting you leave, *you're* fucking crazy," Skid sneers.

I ball my hands into fists, the muscles in my calves tightening. "I've fucking had it with everybody telling me what to do, telling me to sit tight."

"*Someone* gave us up," Skid says. "And now Ravage and Beer Can are dead."

"Cliff would never," I say, the words slow and measured. "Even if he did, what the fuck do I have to do with that? I'm going to see my sister."

"I'll fucking chain you up onstage myself," Skid says. "You're not going anywhere."

I gape at him. "Who the fuck even are you right now?" I clench my fists, poised to take a swing at them if I have to.

"Whoa." Stixx limps over, babying his bandaged leg. He holds up his hands, placating Abraham and Skid like wild bulls. "I'll take her myself, if you're that worried about her *safety*."

I look him up and down. "I appreciate it, but you're wasted, *and* you've got a bullet wound."

"It's a scratch. *You* have a broken rib," he counters. "Besides, I'll be sobered up at first light. I had just enough to take the edge off while Rui stitched me up." He slings an arm over Abraham's shoulder. "Your man has quite the gentle touch."

Abraham softens. "He really should be a surgeon," he agrees.

Skid peers at the three of us through narrowed eyes. "Fine," he says. "I'll take you."

"John," Donny says, joining us. "You can't drive them. We

need you here. As VP, you're our interim President 'til we can hold a vote. We're not voting on anything until Cliff is back." He gives me a meaningful look. "He *will* be back."

Skid scowls. "It's Skid." He sighs. "You're right, I do need to be here. But this fool *is* wasted."

Stixx scoffs. "Am not."

"Let him sleep it off," Donny says in a soothing tone I've never heard him use. "Give him a few hours, he'll be good as new." He passes Stixx a medical-grade vape pen. "This'll help."

"Help? It'll just get him high," I say.

He gives me a look. "It's CBD."

"Can I have some, then? My rib's killing me."

"I ain't a doctor, if that's what you're asking," Donny says.

"Let's smoke some non-weed weed," Stixx says. He motions for me to sit.

"Let's go have a drink," Donny says to Skid and Abraham. He leads them away, glancing back at me over his shoulder for a moment.

Bree props her chin on her hand, studying me.

Clearing my throat, I turn to Stixx. "Are you sure you want to come with me? Shouldn't you rest?"

"I'll rest later," he promises. He takes a hit of the CBD pen, then passes it to me. "This is no fun."

"No," I agree, avoiding Bree's curious gaze. "It's not." I inhale the CBD, tasting pineapple. I make a face. "Super *not* fun. Anybody else?" I hold out the pen to Shannon, who shakes her head. "It's not really helping, either."

"I think the CBD and THC work better together," Shannon says, her voice hoarse. "For pain relief. At least, that's what Beer Can always said."

We all bow our heads, staring at the table. I can't imagine never seeing jovial Beer Can again, that warm twinkle in his eye forever snuffed out.

"What the hell was his real name, anyway?" I blurt.

"Reese," Shannon says softly. "Reese Davis."

I hold up my glass of water. "To Todd and Reese."

The murmurs around us stop. Everyone holds up a glass, toasting Ravage and Beer Can.

I check Shannon's face. No sense in sugarcoating it. "The Bastard Brothers have their bodies. We should at least have some sort of funeral. And what about the police? Should we go to them?" I look around the room, from face to face. "Shouldn't we have Church?"

Donny nods once. He turns to Skid. "Pres?"

Skid straightens, setting down his empty glass. "Church, then." Giving me a dirty look, he sweeps out of the bar and into the Chapel.

I let out a long exhale. "Sorry," I tell Shannon.

"Don't be sorry," she says. "Those were good questions."

"Shouldn't *you* be the one deciding?" I ask her.

She sighs. "Ordinarily, you bet your ass. But what do I know about any of this? We've never been in a situation like this."

"The closest to it was that night," Bree says.

"What night?" I ask, looking at her for the first time tonight.

"The night Cliff killed Bastard." She drains her glass of water.

I gape at her. "Are you saying this is all Cliff's fault?"

"No," she says quickly. "Of course not."

"Well, everyone else is acting like he's a traitor." I watch Stixx, hoping he'll tell me I'm wrong.

"Olivia!" Donny barks from the door. "Stixx! Let's go."

Sighing, I stand, getting ready for Church.

59

Skid sits in Ravage's old seat at the head of the table. Taking my usual seat next to Cliff's empty place, I frown. I know Skid's only interim President, but it still feels wrong. Ravage should be in that seat. Maybe even Mercy—but he doesn't want it.

Beer Can's seat is empty, too.

Nothing is as it should be.

With Vaughn and Mercy still out getting Esther and the kids, only six of us sit around this table.

Skid sits staring at nothing in particular, his brow furrowed. "I liked being Ravage's VP. I was happy there. I never wanted to be President, and I have no idea what to do right now." He shrugs. "How's that for honesty?"

"It's okay, brother. We're all just doing the best we can," Donny says.

I pull out my pack of cigarettes, trying not to think about how empty this room feels. How empty the seat to my left feels.

Beside me, Stixx reaches over and takes my hand, giving it a gentle squeeze. I glance at him out of the corner of my eye, stunned.

He's been practically hovering over me since I got here. He was damn near thrilled to see me. His words earlier loop through my head: *I promised her, but we didn't find him.* He jumped at the chance to drive me to see Lucy, even though he's no better off than I am.

Now he's holding my fucking hand.

I slide it away, disturbed. I've never had any issues with Stixx —I never thought anything bad about him, the way most people do. But Cliff hasn't even been gone for twenty-four hours, and might be dead, for fuck's sake.

I'm too exhausted to make any sense of this, but something isn't right here.

"I know you all want answers," Skid goes. "You want revenge. No cops if we want that."

Everyone nods around the table. Riding around the law seems to be the only thing we can agree on.

His eyes land on me. "Two of us are gone now, a third maybe turned."

I scoff. "Are you fucking kidding me?" I look around at everyone. "Do you all really think Cliff sold you out?"

Skid lifts a single, defiant shoulder.

"Cliff obviously didn't now about the recon mission," Mark says, "so we can rule out some people, anyway."

"*I'm* the only one y'all kept in the dark," Abraham says. "Why the fuck is that?"

Hot blood burns through my veins. I could kill Skid for even thinking it.

"I think that we don't have enough information to jump to any conclusions," Donny says.

"Cliff loves this club," Stixx adds. "He has the most reason for revenge. Olivia's right. He wouldn't sell us out."

"We'll find him," Skid says. "Then we'll hold a vote."

"Hold a vote for what?" I seethe.

"Voting is how we do things." He explains it calmly, as if I'm a toddler.

"We sure as fuck didn't vote on keeping the retaliation a secret," Abraham mutters.

I slam a fist onto the table, rattling the ashtrays. "We kept it secret because we thought *you* might be a problem." I lift my chin.

"Me?!"

"You voted nay on taking out Bastard back in '97," I say. "Everyone else wants to tiptoe around this, but I won't. Why didn't you go with the rest of them?"

"Because *this* is my club," he says. "Why do you think Rui's been looking out for you? He's doing it for me, because I asked him to."

"You've gone against every move we've tried to make." I pin him with a glare.

"Because I didn't want anything like this to happen!"

"Maybe the Bastard Brothers beat Cliff so badly, he told them everything they needed to know," Skid says. "Or for all we know, he's dead. We'll table this for now."

Rage floods me, my head flaring with white and red. "We're not tabling anything."

"We have bodies to collect," he lashes at me, "decisions to make about retaliation. You're upset, Olivia, and I get that. We all are. We still need to look at the bigger picture."

"It sounds like you just want to abandon him."

"We're not abandoning anybody. Your emotions are getting in the way."

My emotions. This is the first time anyone at this table's made a dig at me for being a woman. I want to argue that it's completely normal to feel this way when two Reapers are dead and a third is missing. Instead I let his comment go.

He's got to be just as rattled as I am, even if he's not showing it. He's doing the best he can. We all are.

He grips the gavel. "We're going to hit them back hard," Skid continues. "I think we should do it tonight."

"That's a mistake," Donny says. "That's what they'll expect."

"We definitely can't hit them at their clubhouse," Mark adds.

Stixx clears his throat. "You know what? I don't even think we should be discussing this without Mercy and Vaughn."

I cast him a grateful look. "That's the most sense I've heard in here so far."

Skid passes a hand over his beard, his nearly translucent blue eyes zeroed in on the table. Those eyes are nothing like Ravage's. Where Ravage's could be outright glacial, there were still traces of warmth. Skid's actually give me chills.

"Let's not be so hasty for revenge that we do something stupid," I add.

He chuckles coldly. "Says the woman who keeps doing stupid shit, dragging us along with her."

Chills run down my spine, dread pitting in my stomach. His words confirm what I feared, that all of this is my fault. I swallow against my roiling stomach.

"Whoa." Donny snaps his fingers, dragging Skid's attention away from me. "That's not fair. You *know* how this all started."

"You're right about emotions," Mark adds. "We're *all* emotional. We're running on fumes. I say we get some rest. Have Church first thing in the morning and decide then."

"That's too long," Skid says.

The doors open. Mercy and Vaughn traipse inside. Mercy's gaze lands on Skid at the head of the table. His brow furrows minutely, but he takes a seat without comment.

"What'd we miss?" Vaughn asks.

"We were just discussing how to handle striking back," Mark says.

"I really think they're gonna expect us to hit back tonight," Donny reiterates. "Don't you think so, Mercy?"

Mercy reaches into a pocket of his cut for his cigarettes. "I just can't seem to quit," he says with a sigh. Lighting up, he looks down the table at me. "I think we should hit back hard and fast," he says. "They killed our fucking President *and* our Sergeant-at-Arms."

"And they have Cliff," Vaughn adds.

"We think," Skid says. "We don't know."

"Bullshit, we don't know. His helmet had a crack in it!" I argue.

"You don't crack fiberglass by dropping it," Donny agrees.

Mercy studies the cigarette between his fingers. "Then I think we should go into lockdown," he says finally. "Nobody leaves, nobody comes in."

"Wait," Stixx says. "I promised Olivia I'd take her to see her sister."

He shakes his head. "I'm not okay with that."

"I have my gun," I interject. "We'll be fine."

"I agree with Mercy," Mark says. "They had no qualms about taking Cliff and that kid's mom, and killing Ravage and Beer Can. Olivia, it's not safe."

I shove my chair back, standing. "Then you're going to *have* to chain me down, because I'm going to see my sister."

"That can be arranged," Skid says.

Mercy clears his throat. "I don't like it. Donny?"

"I wanna say yes," Donny says, looking at me. "But I agree, it ain't safe."

"Let's vote on it," Vaughn says.

I glare at him.

"What?" He lifts both hands. "Isn't that how we do things?"

"It's supposed to be," Abraham grumbles.

"Then let's vote," Skid says. "I think it's a stupid idea. Nay."

"Nay," Mark agrees. "I'm sorry, Olivia, but I'd rather you stay here where it's safe."

"Where it's safe," Skid echoes. "We can't afford to lose any more people."

I bite my lip. Even when we disagree, these men are still my family. They want what's best for me. But Lucy is my family, too. I could never forgive myself if she died while I'm locked down here.

"Olivia just lost two people," Stixx says. "Let her at least say goodbye to Lucy. Yea."

"Thank you," I whisper. He jerks his chin at me. Clearing my throat, I raise my voice. I look straight at Skid. "You say Cliff could be dead." My voice catches on the word. Tears burn my eyes. I can't begin to think about that possibility. "If that's true, Lucy is all I have left."

Next to Skid, Mercy flinches.

"You're all my family," I say quickly. "But Lucy is my . . ." I search for the right word to sum up everything she means to me.

"Home," Stixx says.

I blink at him. "She's my home—exactly. I have to go, no matter the risk. I *have* to." I swallow. "Yea."

Abraham shakes his head, swiping at his eyes. "Fuck," he mutters. "This is a nightmare. Olivia, I don't want to rob you of that. I also don't want anything to happen to you or Stixx, or any of us left sitting here. I'm sorry. Nay."

Letting out a long exhale, Vaughn splays his fingers on the table. "You're right. This is fucking impossible. I love you, Olivia. I don't want you to get hurt in any sense of the word, but I like you better alive. Nay."

"Y'all are gonna make me cry," Donny says. "You know my vote, Olivia. Yea."

"Four to three," Skid says to Mercy. "Your vote decides it or splits the table."

I turn my eyes to Mercy, silently pleading with him. *Let me go.*

He gives me a minute shake of his head. "Even if I vote yea, that splits the table and you stay," he says.

"I'll never forgive you if you vote nay and she dies," I tell him.

He closes his eyes, his brow pinched. I stare at him, nostrils flared. No matter what he votes, I'm trapped here—unless I sneak out or walk out. If I leave like that, I might not be able to come back. I'd lose everything this club has given me. I'd have to take Bunny, too, endangering her.

"Proxy," Mercy says.

"What?"

Everyone stares at him.

"Proxy," he repeats. "As far as we know, Cliff is still alive. Olivia, you can give his proxy."

Skid scoffs. "We don't know he's alive."

"And we don't know how he'd vote," Mark adds.

"I know how he'd vote," I say. "He'd be trying to go with me. He went to prison for Lucy. Do you really think he'd sit nice and safe here while she's dying?" I spit out the word.

"She's not dying," Stixx whispers. "She's not."

"Let Olivia give Cliff's proxy," Mercy says.

"We can't protect you out there," Skid shouts, looking at me.

"I'll do my best," Stixx says.

Skid clenches the gavel. He shakes his head. "Fine. Mercy?"

"Yea," Mercy says. His eyes, round and sad, meet mine. "And Cliff's proxy?"

"Yea," I say, hoping he knows that I'll never forget what he did for me today.

Skid drops the gavel onto the table. "It's decided, then. Stixx will accompany Olivia. We'll go on lockdown." He shakes his head at me. "I hope I don't regret this."

I give him a nod, afraid to speak. I hope I don't regret it, either.

60

OLIVIA

Mercy cuts me off before I can leave the Chapel. "I'm going, too," he says.

I feel everyone's eyes on us. I swallow. "Skid said only Stixx."

"I want to go with you," he says, eyes begging me. "Just let me see you safely there and back."

"Okay," I agree. "Come on, Stixx." I rush back to the table where Esther, Bree, and Shannon sit with Bunny. I so badly want to lift her from her car seat, but she's sleeping, so I leave her be. Instead I touch a finger to her tiny curled fist. "I can't take you with me, little baby."

"I've got her," Bree says.

"We'll watch out for Bryce, too," Esther promises.

I nod. "If anything happens to me—"

"It won't," Mercy says from behind me. I turn with my whole body. He tightens an underarm holster, then slides a gun almost identical to the one Donny gave me into place.

"Where are you going?" Bree asks, a hint of panic in her voice.

"Just visiting at the hospital," Mercy says. He leans down and kisses her forehead. "We won't be long."

"You know you can't go in with that, right?" I glance at the slight bulge under his cut.

"You can in Connecticut, but I'm not going in. This is insurance in case they're bold enough to come after us during the day."

"I don't need both of you." I glance at Stixx. "Sit this one out, get some rest."

"No," he says, too quickly. "I'm not leaving your side."

"Then it's decided," Mercy says.

Bree clears her throat. "Can I come too? I'd like to . . . pay my respects." Her eyes meet mine.

"It's not safe," Mercy says.

"The hospital's just as safe as it is here. Too many eyes on both places." She crosses her arms and lifts her chin. She reminds me of *me*. I stare at her for a beat too long. "What?"

"Nothing." I give Bunny one last long look, guilt churning my stomach. She's only a baby, so it's not like she'll remember Lucy, anyway. She won't remember whether she got to say goodbye. She won't even remember how inadequate I've been. I close my eyes for a moment, squeezing them tight against the panic rushing at me. Once again, I'm overwhelmed by this nightmare. I want to go back to lying in Cliff's arms in Lucy's condo while she makes coffee and Bunny cries for a feeding. But I can't go back to the way it was before, no matter how much I wish I could.

Taking a deep breath, I open my eyes. "Everyone who's coming, let's go before Skid changes his mind." Then I turn away and walk out before I change *my* mind.

I step out at the same time as Stixx. Our eyes meet, and the grief on his face is as deep as mine. I blink. "Whoa."

He swallows. "Yeah. I know."

61

CLIFF

The ringing in my ears drags me into consciousness. A cement floor tilts up at me. I blink my eyes open, greeted by a trail of blood. I stare at it, trying find some familiarity in the flooring, to figure out where the blood is coming from: me or the other guy?

Instead of the constant cacophony that fills the pen, even in solitary, I am enveloped in silence. Jolts of memory hit me: the quick kiss I gave Olivia, the crack of my own helmet hitting my skull, the punch of steel-toed boots in my ribs. The same questions over and over, until black nothing.

Adrenaline floods my system, my pulse pounding in my ears. I have to get out of here, to warn them. I twitch my fingers and toes, assessing, scanning. My head pounds in time with my pulse. My hands are still cuffed. My ribs ache, and I think Gavin's switchblade is still in my leg.

Groaning, I roll onto my back. The basement whirls, my stomach roils. I turn my head just in time. Bile rushes up my throat and splashes the cement.

Add "concussion" to the list.

It doesn't matter. I have to get to Olivia and the others. Even if it kills me. Their Enforcer sure did a job of making me want to die, but I didn't tell him a damn thing.

With another soft groan, I roll onto my side, then plant my hands and knees on the floor. I raise myself slowly, squeezing my eyes shut and gritting my teeth against the pain and nausea. I have to get out of here.

Nothing else matters.

I fucked up so badly, I have to make it right. I shouldn't have left her side, not when I knew the Bastard Brothers were looking for her when they went to Lucy's.

I push myself to my feet, legs wobbling. Bending over, I pat around for the knife. I wrap my fingers around the handle. I *think* he missed the artery. If I'm wrong and I pull it out, I could bleed out. If he hit the artery, I'd probably already be dead.

Too bad there's no Wi-Fi down here. I'd Google it the way Olivia and Lucy are always looking up shit they don't know.

I clench my teeth and yank the knife out. Hot blood trickles down my leg. I rip off my shirt and use the knife to cut a section from it, the cuffs digging into my wrists. Then I wrap the fabric tightly around the wound. It's too dark to see, but I think it's okay, as long as I don't put my full weight on it. I think. I really have no fucking clue.

"Easy there, Rambo," Finn says.

I scan the darkness, knife clenched in my fist.

He chuckles. "I'm not even down there. This is a nanny cam. See that red light?"

I turn in a slow circle until I find it. A pinprick of red up high, as if over a doorway at the top of stairs.

"Don't be in any rush," he continues. "You slept through the whole thing."

"What whole thing?" I rasp.

"Oh, that. Your club stopped by, and we were ready. They

were looking for you, by the way," he says dryly, as if we're discussing fantasy picks. "We picked off . . ." His voice trails off. "Two of them, I think."

My legs buckle.

"Yeah, two," he continues. "Your President. I gotta say, I liked him. Todd, is it? You know him by Ravage. Yeah, I think he and my father went to high school together. Isn't that weird?"

"Ravage is dead?" I sway on my feet.

"Reese 'Beer Can' Davis, too," he says cheerfully. "I didn't really know him. Anyway, if you need any water, it's around there somewhere. Hopefully we'll finish off the rest of your club soon. I made a deal: I'll save you for them if they save Olivia for me. I have it on good authority that she's the one who killed my brother, and that tattooed motherfucker of yours set the fire to cover it up."

My leg gives out and I pitch forward, stretching my arms out to grab something, anything to break my fall. The meat of my forearms hits the cement, the blow radiating up that bone.

"You're not looking too good," Finn says.

Ravage is dead.

Beer Can is dead.

They were here, just feet above my head, and they're dead. My head throbs, my leg throbs. I pat around for the knife, but it's out of reach.

Everything is out of reach.

"That God damned strip club is untouchable," Finn says. "Being right on 63. But don't worry."

My lids droop over my eyes. I wrench one open. I have to stay awake. I have to get out of here.

"Your rat told me your girl is out right now, paying a visit to . . . Lucy, is it?"

My eyes bolt open. Adrenaline floods me again, but it's only a spark. I rest my cheek against the concrete.

"I'm sure you're missing Olivia," Finn says. "Maybe they'll let you watch me kill her."

His laughter is the last thing I hear before he kills the connection.

I sprint through the hospital to Lucy's room, Bree and Stixx trailing behind me. None of us speaks a word, not even in the elevator. I get us buzzed into the ICU, then turn around.

"They only let in two at a time," I say, glancing from Stixx to Bree. "Who wants to go first?"

"You're more family than I am," he tells her.

I want to argue. Instead I step inside the ICU, letting them decide for themselves. I put one foot in front of the other, legs heavy as I approach Lucy's room. A nurse smiles at me as I pass, glancing up from her charting for a brief moment before returning to her work. It's easier to chart stats than it is to comfort the family of the dying.

I reach the sanitation station outside her room and start suiting up.

"Hi," a nurse greets me. "Olivia?"

I pause halfway through pulling on gloves. "Yes?"

"Good news. The swelling in Lucy's brain has decreased enough so that we could get a good picture of what's going on in there."

"So she's awake?" I try to peer into the room, but the nurse blocks my way.

"Not yet." Her smile remains in place. "We were able to see that there are no clots. If the pneumonia clears, we can take her into surgery to repair the damage to her skull."

"If it clears?" I repeat. "I thought she was on IV antibiotics. Don't those work fast?" I tug a gown on, pulling my hands through the sleeves.

She grabs a nearby computer on wheels and taps several keys. "They weren't having any effect, so the doctor switched her to a different one this morning." Her smile brightens. "Sometimes that happens."

"Any idea when she'll wake up?"

"We've taken her off the medication that kept her sedated," the nurse explains. "It's all up to her now."

"What's going on?" Bree asks, approaching me slowly.

"She's doing very well, considering," the nurse says.

I take a deep breath. "I thought . . . So far, it's been explained to me that I should say my goodbyes."

She gives me a patient nod. "There's still so much about the brain that we don't know. Some patients come out of head injuries unscathed, and others never wake up. Your sister is fighting a head injury, multiple body injuries, and now pneumonia. We hope that she'll make a full recovery, but we have no way of knowing for sure. If she wakes up, we'll have a better idea of the damage done."

"Thank you," Bree says.

The nurse gives us another bright smile, then wheels the computer away.

I snatch a mask from the box, hands shaking. "They made me think she was dying. Now they're telling me they have no idea. No one can give me a straight fucking answer."

"I know it," Bree says.

I busy myself with looping the mask over my ears. I want Cliff.

I can't do any of this without him. I don't even know if he's dead or alive. I close my eyes, shoving down the panic again.

"What can I do to help you?" Bree asks.

My eyes snap open in surprise. "I don't know," I answer honestly. "Let's just go in." Straightening the mask, I turn and march into Lucy's room.

I sink into the chair at Lucy's side, studying her face. Where her cheeks were once flushed, her skin a soft peach, she's now pale and gray. She doesn't look better. She looks worse.

"Please, Lucy. Please wake up. Bunny needs a mother. She needs you. She can't be stuck with me."

Someone whines, a long, high-pitched keening. Hot tears singe my cheeks, and I realize the sound is coming from me.

Bree tiptoes into the room. I swipe them away.

She stands at the foot of Lucy's bed, shoulders drawn. "We never met," she says.

I say nothing, my eyes on Lucy, my heart begging her to just open her eyes. I'd even settle for a twitch of her fingers.

"When I heard Bastard's brother was adopting you, I thought I was going to lose my mind," Bree tells me. "I didn't have a leg to stand on."

I reach for Lucy's hand, wrapping mine around her limp fingers. She used to swat at me with this hand. Once she even plucked the cigarette from my mouth. Now her fingers are still, heavy in mine.

"Ravage assured me it'd be okay. He said he saw you with their daughter, and he knew she'd take care of you. I was sick when DCF picked them over me. It wasn't fair. Collin and Nora were drug addicts, too—Bastard sold them pills for years. They ignored Lucy when she tried to tell them what he was doing to her. Shannon said she thought they saw you as a second chance, that they were trying to do better."

I hold up a hand. "Just . . . stop, Bree. Why are you telling me this?"

"Nobody's perfect, Olivia. Everyone has skeletons. If you wanted the perfect mother, you picked a bad species for reincarnation."

I scoff. When I was little, I loved listening to my mother tell me about how when you die, you get to come back again, as anything you want. I always wanted to be a cat. Now it all seems so juvenile to believe in a fantasy. This is the one life we get. If I fuck it up, that's on me. There are no do-overs. All I can do is the best I can.

She sighs. "I'm saying I'm sorry. Or trying to, anyway." She takes tiny steps closer, stopping at arm's length. "I fucked up, Olivia, and Lucy was there for you when I should've been. I owe her more than I can ever repay for everything she did for you."

"Lucy wasn't doing you a favor," I say. "She's a good person who does nice things for people because she *wants* to, not because she wants anything back for it."

"I'm never going to be able to say what I feel in the right way." She shakes her head. "Or maybe it's that you're never going to be able to hear me."

"Can you just stop? I can't do this right now. You heard the nurse. I have to keep saying goodbye, just in case this is it." I blink away tears, turning back to Lucy.

"Okay," she says. "I'll go get Stixx."

"You have so much explaining to do when you wake up," I tell Lucy when we're alone. "Stixx? How did this even happen?" I smile, blotting at my eyes with a tissue. "He was being so weird, I thought he was hitting on *me*."

The monitor continues its steady beeping, the oxygen continues its whoosh and flush.

"Cliff is missing, Lucy." I wait, letting it sink in. "They took him—we think. Aren't you pissed?"

No response.

"I'm pregnant," I try. "Didn't you hear me the other day? Aren't you going to tell me what an idiot I am?"

Whoosh. Flush. My sister has been reduced to Darth Vader.

"Come on," I beg. "Wake up. Please."

The door slides open, and Stixx steps into the room. Like me, he wears the required gown, gloves, and mask. Like me, he also wears a crease between his eyebrows and shadows under his eyes.

I can't believe I didn't see it before.

"So how long have you been dating my sister?" I ask, keeping my voice light.

"Almost a couple months," he says.

I just want to go back. I want double dates we can laugh about and late-night wine sessions where we gripe about our men. I want to hear how they met—if it was at the Sip and See, or some other time. I want to know what their first date was like and how serious they are.

Judging by Stixx's face, it's serious.

"I wanted to come sooner," he says. "I just didn't want to take any time from you."

I shake my head. "She'd want you here, too. Jesus, Luce. You are *so* good at keeping secrets."

He chuckles. "Yeah, she's the most private person I've ever met."

"Right?" I clear my throat. "Anyway, I'll leave you two alone."

"You don't have to go," he says.

I stand. "Of course I do." As I pass him, I touch his shoulder.

I strip off the gown and gloves, then toss them into the garbage. Before I leave, I catch a glimpse of Stixx taking Lucy's hand in his. My lungs tighten. I run out of the room before I lose it.

I wander to the waiting room. There's a TV, so there's bound to be something mindless on I can lose myself in. If I can turn my brain off for three minutes, it'll be an accomplishment.

I know this is where Cliff would want me to be. He'd tell me family is more important than anything. What he doesn't realize is he's my family, too. Whether I'd been adopted by Lucy's parents or Ravage and Shannon kept me—hell, even if Bree stuck around and raised me herself—at one point or another, our paths would've crossed.

Cliff and I are meant to be.

While my club plays by its lame ass fucking rules, he's being held prisoner somewhere, tortured or worse. I should be out there looking for him, especially now that Bunny is safe with Esther.

I can't just take off from here. My gun is in the car because I don't have a permit. Going in without a weapon would be suicide.

Besides, if Cliff knew I went after him knocked up, he'd be pissed. This is, after all, everything he wants.

It's crystal clear to me: Cliff would want me to stay here with Lucy, to keep watch over her and keep both our babies safe. I'll respect his wishes, but it doesn't mean I have to like it.

I shuffle into the waiting room, hitting the brakes when I see Bree—the only other person in here.

"I'll go," she says quickly, standing.

Of course she wants to leave. I sigh.

"Or I could stay, if you want me to?" She blinks hopefully at me.

I drop into a seat, conflicted.

She gazes at me for a long moment, her eyes full of regret. "I fucked up big time, Olivia. I know nothing about being a good mother. I do know one thing: you'll be a hell of a lot better at it than I was." Her gaze drops to my stomach for a fraction of a second before she turns away.

My mouth falls open, my mind racing with what to say. Maybe I imagined it. Or maybe Shannon told her. Either way, too many people know before Cliff.

Stixx bursts into the room, his mask hanging from one ear. "She's awake!"

63

CLIFF

Slow sharp laughter floats to me in the darkness—"Ha! Ha. Haha!"

It's Steven again. Has to be. I close my eyes tighter, as if that could block out the sound. Most of the time, I feel sorry for him. He's a schizophrenic who stole a car. He thought aliens were chasing him. The problem is, when he ripped the driver out, an oncoming car hit her and she died.

Steven should be in psychiatric care. Not Lewisburg. Certainly not seg.

They keep him down here "for his own safety," unmedicated and crammed in with three other men in a cell smaller than a broom closet. I'm sure being chased by aliens was terrifying, but for Steven, *this* must be hell.

It's hell for all of us.

But it's the middle of the night, for fuck's sake, and for once, I'd like to get some sleep.

"Shut the fuck up, Steven!" one of them yells.

"How about *you* shut the fuck up, Roberts?"

"How about you *all* shut the fuck up," a guard suggests.

The hole settles back into silence—except for Steven.

"Ha! Haha. Ha!"

I open my eyes, defeated. Except it's still dark. A complete, impenetrable black envelops me. I stretch out a hand in front of me, my arm scraping against concrete. It's so dark, I can't even see my hand moving.

I listen for Steven, for the other guys in the hole with me. Deafening silence boomerangs in my ears. I can't even hear the scuff of the guard's footsteps, the snarl of men snoring as they try to get comfortable in seg. The sour smell of vomit hits my nose, and reality comes rushing back, the flashback receding.

I roll onto my stomach, scanning the room for any light, any at all. Even a sliver from underneath a door would do—anything to tell me I'm not buried alive somewhere. There's nothing but the red light from the nanny cam.

What I wouldn't give to hear Steven talking to himself. Being in the pen would be better than this.

Finn's last words snap me out of my despair. Olivia. I need to get out of here and get to Olivia.

First things first: I have to get up.

Planting a knee on the cement, I lift myself onto hands and knees. Even though it's pitch black in here, the room spins. I squeeze my eyes shut, but it's pointless. My stomach churns.

I take a deep breath in through my nose, keeping the rest of my body still. Just breathing hurts, probably from the hit my nose took at some point. Still, the pain distracts me enough to settle my stomach—for the time being.

I decide to start with sitting. When I go to shift my weight, my leg protests, sharp pain slicing through the muscle. I forgot about that. Gritting my teeth, I put my weight on the other side and slide the bad leg out in front of me. Then I drop onto my ass with my legs stretched out, panting.

I assess the damage, sliding my cuffed hands down my leg

toward the throbbing. My fingers touch rough gauze instead of denim, crusted with dried blood. Someone came in and bandaged my leg at some point. I feel around some more and find that someone sliced up the leg of my jeans to get to the wound. I rip off the bandage, fingers probing the area for any wetness. I've got to know if it's still bleeding, if I'll be able to walk on it. Instead I find two neat stitches.

No extra thread hangs from the knots. In fact, it's not thread at all, which is what they used in Lewisburg when they ran out of infirmary supplies. This is medical grade stuff, that thin fishline that looks like thick hair when done right. The knots themselves are small and tight—professional level.

Someone patched me up real good.

I wiggle my toes, realizing someone took my boots. They're steel-toed for work, but they also make a great weapon.

Then again, so do my fists.

I don't need anything else.

I stand up, my movements slow, being careful not to put my full weight on my bad leg. The last thing I need is busted stitches. Easing forward, I start walking, arms stretched out in front of me. My fingers only meet empty air.

I keep walking until my hands find stone wall. Grazing my arm along the wall, I my hands in front of me and use the wall as a guide. I count my steps: one . . . five . . . fourteen . . .

I hit a corner.

Turning, I keep moving, still counting steps. I count thirty when I reach the next turn. I count another thirty before I reach another turn.

That's three walls. I keep going, making it nine steps before my shoulder brushes smooth wood. It's raised from the stone, going flat for about the width of my palm, then dipping down into more smooth wood. I trace a seam.

It's a door.

Despite the seam, no light filters through the cracks. Whatever is on the other side could be more of the same.

Either way, I'm getting out of here.

I've been a prisoner for so long, in so many ways. First it was the dark that both Bastard and Ruth kept me in. My mother made my father shrug off his cut before he walked in the door so that I'd never know what he did for a living.

After that it was haven that held me, the draw of Aunt Ruth's warm kitchen when my own Ruth was gone. That sunny kitchen kept me from learning what Bastard was doing to Lucy until it was almost too late.

Then there was the pen itself, a forgotten hole where I was supposed to repay my debt to society, never mind society's debt to girls like Lucy.

When my time was up, I fell into another kind of prison. Meeting Olivia was fate. Falling in love with her was more repentance. It's a special place in hell to love someone who can't love back. It's made me question where I came from, but in the end, it doesn't really matter.

I am here.

I am not being chained. I choose to love her, to receive whatever she has to give, even if nothing at all.

I am more than the monster that runs through my veins. These hands are capable of holding rather than crushing, loving rather than destroying.

These cuffs may bind my hands together, but they can't keep me here.

It can't be this simple, but maybe it is. The Bastard Brothers left me alive, after all. I step to the left, hands scanning for the knob, when my foot brushes something. It tips over, rolling over my foot and then hitting the floor with a soft thud. Spreading my feet for balance, I bend down. My fingers close around a plastic water bottle.

Someone wants me alive.

Maybe that's the point. Maybe they had trouble grabbing Olivia, and they need to keep me alive long enough to get her. Both Finn and the Bastard Brothers want her dead, but they also want me dead. They just need me alive long enough to suffer.

I kick the water aside. I won't be needing it. I'm getting out of here.

Straightening up, I run my hand along the door until cold metal bites into my skin. I reach for it, then hesitate.

I don't know what I'm going to find on the other side. I need to be ready.

I summon all my adrenaline, bouncing on the balls of my feet. It washes away the pain and nausea, floods me with energy. I close my right hand into a fist, ready to clock the first face I run into.

Then I twist the knob and yank the door, stunned to find it open.

Bright light fills my vision, sending blinding pain through my skull. I hadn't accounted for the sudden change in light. I hadn't even realized it'd be bright out here. I squeeze my eyes shut and reach out blind. My fingers mash into something solid and warm —a shoulder swathed in leather. I grab it with one hand and swing with the other, estimating where the head might be. I aim for what I think is a temple, but my fist cuts through empty air.

I wrench my eyes open. A boy with a face I've only seen on the screen of a phone blocks my path from the short hallway and the foot of stairs. He grips an assault rifle in both hands, the barrel pointed down, his eyes wide and his nostrils flaring.

I smirk.

He isn't going to use it.

Someone wants me alive, which means he's only holding that thing to keep me here. And I'm no prisoner.

I bulldoze past him, shoving him hard against the wall.

"Pat!" he yells.

I shoot up the stairs, gritting my teeth against the pain

shooting through my leg. I'm so close to the door. I don't know why they left a couple of boys to guard me, but it's my luck. I fly up the remaining steps, hand stretched toward the knob.

The door flies open. A pair of hands shove into my chest. Surprised, I lose my footing and tumble down the stairs.

I pace the waiting room, Stixx pacing in the opposite direction. We cross paths for the sixth time, awkwardly going around each other. I glance at the door again.

"What's taking so long?" I grumble.

It's been about twenty minutes since I rushed down the hall, only to be blocked by a nurse and escorted back to the waiting room.

"They're taking her vitals," Bree reminds me. "They're just doing their jobs."

"Can't they do it faster?" I switch directions and pace alongside Stixx. "How did she look?" I ask again.

"She opened her eyes," he says.

"But how did she look? Was she scared? Did she recognize you? Was she groggy?" I chew the inside of my cheek, wishing they allowed smoking in here.

"She looked . . . I don't know!" Stixx throws his hands up. "She opened her eyes a tiny bit and then closed them. I thought I imagined it until she started choking—fighting the tube, I mean."

"I'm sure she's okay," Bree says.

"We don't know that," I say, preparing myself. "They said there could be brain damage."

"I'll take her however I can have her," Stixx says.

I stop. "Oh, Stixx." Reaching out, I touch his arm.

He gazes at the door, his eyes soft and distant. "I love her, Olivia. It's way too soon to be saying that, but I do. I love her."

My stomach tightens. What I wouldn't give to be able to say that to Cliff. "She's going to be fine. Then you can tell her, and she can tell you off."

The corner of his mouth lifts. "Yeah." He ducks his head. "I'd love for her to tell me off."

A nurse sticks her head into the room. "Come on down, guys."

I take off after her, Stixx on my heels.

There's a rush in my veins, hope in my blood. Up until twenty minutes ago, everything seemed hopeless. Now Lucy is awake, and for the first time in days, it doesn't feel so dark in my head.

Everything will work out, I tell myself.

The nurse leads us back to the gloves and gown station. "She's awake and alert," she informs us. "We've removed the tube and her vitals are good, considering." She takes a deep breath.

My heart lurches in its usual rhythm. Stixx's eyes latch onto mine. "What is it?" My voice shakes. I fight to remain calm.

"We'll have to do further testing to determine the extent, but she's sustained at least some minor brain damage."

Stixx slips his hand into mine.

"What does that mean?" I stammer.

"Her speech, memory, and some movement are affected," the nurse says. "The doctor will be able to tell you more, after we run some tests."

My world shatters.

"But she knows who she is and . . . ?" I can't say it. It's almost better if she doesn't remember what happened.

"She's a little confused. Many patients with TBI make a full recovery." She smiles. "You can visit for a few minutes. Please keep it light. She's been given some medication to calm her, but she's very disoriented."

She hesitates again, and I tense for the blow.

"I also have to warn you that sometimes, coma and TBI patients experience what's called a surge."

I stare at her blankly.

"They become awake and alert shortly before passing."

She gestures for us to gear up. Neither of us move.

65

OLIVIA

Time stops.

The hospital keeps moving around me. Monitors beep, slow and steady. Nurses pass, families in tow. An attendant wheels a meal cart down the hall.

"We have no way of knowing for sure," the nurse adds. "I just had to mention it, given her previous condition."

"So you're saying," I stammer, staring down at the linoleum, "that this *could* be a last hurrah."

"Could be," she says, her voice low and comforting.

"How long?"

"It could be a few minutes, or a few days."

"Then I need to bring Bunny here." I turn, nearly smashing into Stixx. "I have to get Bunny. She has to say goodbye."

Something warm drips onto my cheeks. I tilt my head back, trying to keep the tears contained.

"Hey," Stixx says, touching my shoulder. "Hey."

I whip my head around, still scanning the tiles above me.

He snaps his fingers in front of my face. "Olivia."

I flinch. "Yeah." I tear my eyes from the ceiling, meeting his gaze. His pale blue eyes are red and haunted. I take a shaky breath. I need to be strong for him. For Lucy. For Bunny.

"Let's go see her," he says, his words hushed.

Nodding, I step toward the cart. Gloves first. Or maybe it's hand sanitizer. I can't remember which. I close my eyes, envisioning myself through the routine. Hand sanitizer, gloves, mask, gown. I follow the steps in robotic movements, my arms just two sticks moving in front of me while I watch. All the while, I take deep belly breaths, willing oxygen and calm back into my limbs.

I wait while Stixx gears up, averting my eyes from the room. Part of me wants to rush in and throw my arms around her. The other part of me just wants her to go already, if that's what this is coming to.

It's a deeply selfish thought, and I hate myself for it, but there it is.

"Ready?" Stixx asks.

I nod. He wraps his gloved hand around mine and we step into the room together.

Lucy sits, the bed elevated. Her eyes zip straight to mine, widening a little when she sees Stixx beside me.

"Shit," she says, clear as day.

I burst into tears, giggling. "You're okay!" I run to her side, my palms pressed together and resting against my lips. I don't want to hurt her, but all I want to do is hug her.

"Okay," she agrees. Her voice is raw, likely from the tube and lack of use. It's the same sweet huskiness I've loved almost my entire life.

Stixx goes to the other side of her bed. He leans forward and touches his forehead to hers. "Hey."

Tears soak my mask. I watch them for a moment, my heart swelling just seeing them together. She lifts her hand, laying her palm against his cheek.

"Okay," she soothes. Her other hand remains limp at her side. I stare at it for a moment, biting my lip behind my mask.

It doesn't matter. A little bit of physical therapy, and she'll be fine. I brush her hair back from her face, careful not to put too much pressure on her bruises and stitches.

"Luce, I'm so sorry," I whisper.

"No," she says, putting as much force on the word as she possibly can. She scrunches her face in concentration. A tear drips from her eye. Then her face relaxes. "No," she says again with a sigh. She turns to me, green eyes pleading. "L . . ." She frowns again, closing her eyes. "L . . . ?"

"Leigh?" Stixx supplies.

She nods.

"She's with Esther," I tell her, sitting on the edge of the bed. "She's doing great. She misses you, though. I'll try to get her here this afternoon."

I have no idea how I'm going to do that—not with Skid and Mercy watching me like a hawk. I'll figure it out. For Lucy, I'll do anything.

Her eyes slide to my stomach. The corner of her mouth twitches up. "Heard . . . you," she grunts.

"You . . . heard me?" I glance at Stixx and my cheeks flush.

She grins, the smile quickly falling. Her eyes close, and she lets out an exhausted sigh.

Stixx kisses her forehead.

She raises her eyelids a fraction. "Cliff?" she rasps.

Stixx and I glance at each other. She should know, but I don't want to distress her any more than she already is. I don't think there's a drug strong enough to calm her if I tell her.

"He'll be by later," he lies, kissing her forehead again.

"Good." Her eyelids fall once more, her shoulders relaxing.

I give Stixx a meaningful look. He heard the nurse. It might be now or never.

He swallows.

"Lucy? I'm actually going to step out." I blink away tears.

Leaning in, I lower my mask and kiss her cheek. "I love you, bitch. Don't you ever scare me like that again."

"Try," she grunts, eyes still closed.

"I fucking love you," I tell her again. "You're the best thing that ever happened to me."

She shakes her head, but she smiles. "Cliff."

Just the sound of his name is a knife in my heart. I blink away tears, relieved she can't see my face. "I'll be right back," I promise. I wave my hand in a *Go on* motion toward Stixx. Then, my heart a little lighter, I tiptoe from the room.

Now that both Lucy and Bunny are safe, I can focus on the next task at hand.

It's time to go get my man, and I know exactly who can help me.

66

OLIVIA

I jerk upright, disoriented for a moment before I realize I'm in the waiting room. Rubbing the sleep from my eyes, I struggle through the fog. I'm supposed to do something, but I must've stopped to rest on my way.

Pregnancy and busted ribs are a mega battery drain.

"Olivia?" Stixx calls from the doorway. His face is paler than usual, the shadows under his eyes even longer.

"What is it?"

"I think . . . something's wrong."

I sanitize and suit up while Stixx waits, then we shuffle back into Lucy's room.

I feel the change right away. There's a heavy silence punctuated by the steady beep of the machine. Lucy lies with her head tilted back, her mouth gaping open—I've never seen her sleep like that.

"Luce?" I call softly.

Her eyes remain closed.

Her chest rises and falls in jagged breaths. Stixx and I face each other.

"She's just sleeping. Right?" I've never seen his eyes so vulnerable.

"She's breathing," I reason, moving to Lucy's side.

"It just feels . . . wrong."

I nod in agreement. Even her coloring is off. The light that glows from within her is just gone. She didn't even look this bad when she was in the medical coma.

"Luce?" I call again. I wait for her to stir, for her eyes to open. Instead she just takes another one of those horrible breaths.

"I . . . I'll go get a nurse." He darts from the room, leaving me in stunned silence.

Lucy doesn't move a single muscle.

"What the fuck, Luce?" I whisper.

She draws another jarring breath. Though she doesn't open her eyes, she gasps out a single word.

"Help."

I jump back despite the pain in my ribs—the pain in my heart.

The door slides open and Stixx returns, a nurse on his heels. Her face remains unreadable while she checks Lucy's vitals.

"Well?" I demand.

"I'm going to page the doctor," the nurse says. "It'll just be a few minutes." She takes slow, deliberate steps out of the room, and I think it's so that we aren't alarmed.

"She said 'Help,'" I tell Stixx.

His face clouds over. "'Help'?"

I nod, my head bobbing on my neck. "What does that mean?"

"Maybe she's dreaming."

"Maybe. She looks wrong," I admit.

"Yeah." He taps his thumb and finger together at his side. "Let's . . . let's just wait for the doctor."

We drop into the chairs side by side, both of us staring at Lucy. It might be my imagination, but I swear her breathing has slowed even more. I shake my head. She was just awake and talking to us. It's gotta be my anxiety on overdrive.

I've never felt so inadequate. I can't find Cliff. I can't save Lucy. I have no idea what made me think I could help Bryce.

I close my eyes. I will not freak out. I have to stay strong, especially while in this room.

A petite woman in a doctor's coat sweeps into the room. She gives us her name but it barely registers. I blink up at her, waiting while she reviews the same vitals the nurse checked. She presses a stethoscope to Lucy's chest, listening to her heart and lungs. Her lips flatten into a tight line. Then she straights, removing the stethoscope from her ears and slinging it back around her neck.

She murmurs several sentences, none of it direct, none of it hopeful. Finally, she gives us a smile that is supposed to be comforting. "Hospice will come in and we'll keep her comfortable."

Lucy is dying, and there's nothing they can do.

"Hospice?" Stixx takes a step toward the doctor. "Hospice?"

She moves back slightly, so little space regained that at first I think I imagined it. Then she draws her shoulders in, and I know I didn't.

I grab his arm, pulling him toward me. "Yes," I soothe in a voice I do not recognize. "Here, sit." I guide him into a chair, watching myself sit down the grieving boyfriend and give the doctor a nod.

She mentions something about hospice and social workers, then exits the room.

Stixx stares up at me. I stare back.

"She said 'hospice'?" he asks.

I take a deep breath in through my mouth and let it out, lips trembling. I feel no steadier, but deep breaths are supposed to help calm someone having a panic attack. Except there is nothing wrong with my brain. It's everything around me that is wrong.

I settle a hand on Stixx's shoulder, not sure whether I should give it a pat or hug him. I end up just laying my hand there. "I think it's time to say goodbye one more time," I say, again in a voice too calm to be mine. "One of us should go down and tell Mercy we're not leaving."

I don't want to be the one to go.

Thankfully Stixx doesn't even make me pretend to offer. He nods, swiping at his eyes. "I could use a cigarette." He stands and takes small shuffling steps back to Lucy's side. I watch him, swallowing hard.

Leaning down, he brushes Lucy's hair from her forehead and presses his lips to her skin. "In case you go before I get back . . ." He shakes his head, voice breaking. "I love you. I'll see you later."

Head bowed, he flees the room.

I stand there, alone with my dying sister. I got fifteen years with her, and Bunny's only had weeks.

I will never forgive myself for this.

A nurse and social worker slip into the room, one removing the oxygen monitor and injecting medication, the other explaining how hospice works. I hear none of it. The nurse tells me to let her know if I need anything, and the social worker tell me she's going to call Bunny's case manager and put him on standby for support.

I hear none of it. I'm barely aware of either of them slipping back out of the room.

I tiptoe to her side, and the cracks in my heart deepen to fissures. I can't think of anything to say that I haven't already said. I can't sum up fifteen years of good memories and how sorry I am for ruining it, for robbing Lucy, Bunny, and Stixx of the happiness they deserve. So instead, I sing, even though I can't carry a tune and Lucy laughs when I try. I used to get so mad at her for laughing, but I'd give anything for her to tease me now.

I sing the song from my favorite childhood movie, "Somewhere Out There." The lyrics give me what I feel in my heart but can't put into words. I tell her that even though we're about to be separated by life and death, at least we have this one moment, under this gray sky, in this room. By the time I finish, tears are running down my cheeks.

Lucy takes a slow, shallow breath. Her chest remains suspended, and for a moment I hold my breath along with her. Then she exhales in a quick whoosh. Several moments go by before she takes another breath. I watch and listen, each time sure that it will be her last.

Minutes that feel like hours pass. I'm so fixated on her breaths, I almost forget her parents again. I forgot to call, and they weren't on her emergency contacts, or else the hospital would've called them. They should be here, regardless of their feelings for me, Cliff, and even Lucy—the daughter who wouldn't just get married. I turn, scanning the room for my phone. It isn't on the tray, the heater, or either chair. I must've left it in Mercy's truck.

Turning back to Lucy, I start to speak, to say something just for the sake of filling the empty space. That's when I realize it's indeed empty.

Lucy lies on the hospital bed, her chest still. Both hands rests at her sides.

I strain to hear Lucy's breath, but there's nothing.

She's gone.

68

OLIVIA

I'm frozen in the chair when Stixx returns. He takes one look at me, glances at the bed, and freezes mid-step.

"Oh."

I stand. "The nurses said we can take as long as we need," I say in a hushed voice too soothing to be mine. Not when all I want to do is scream. "I didn't want to let them take her away before you got back." My voice is still so steady.

"Oh," he says again. His lips tremble beneath his blond beard, making it look like his entire beard is fighting tears.

I bite my lip. My arms long to hold someone, my body longs to be held and comforted. I go to Stixx, wrapping an arm around him. It isn't hard. He's a beanpole, not at all as solid as Cliff. I hug him, summoning the last of my strength and giving it to this broken man. This man who loved my sister and didn't get nearly enough time with her.

None of us did.

He wraps two long arms around me, and we stand there clinging to each other. Neither of us moves to break the embrace. Neither of us wants to leave, and neither of us wants to be here.

Someone clears their throat from the door, a short, gruff sound.

I crane my neck and peer past Stixx. Harrison stands with his head bowed, hands tucked into the pockets of his jeans.

"Hey, kid."

I don't know whether it's the sight of him or the way he greets me, but I burst into tears.

"Now, now," he whispers. "Don't get me started, too." He walks over and wraps his arms around the two of us. I am both surprised and comforted by his embrace. He's told me to suck it up more times than I can count. Yet here he stands, trying to comfort me even when there isn't a single thing in this world that could make any of this better.

Clearing his throat again, he steps back. Stixx and I release each other, too, and I'm left holding myself together.

"I know it hasn't been very long," Harrison says, "but I wanted to get rolling on everything right away for you."

I nod, numb.

"Shall we go sit in another room?"

I nod again. Glancing once more at Lucy, I try to superimpose the memory of her that I want to have rather than the broken, cold remnants of her. I turn to Stixx. "Are you staying here?"

He nods, his eyes fixated on the linoleum.

"Just let them know when you're ready." I give his arm a squeeze, then follow Harrison out of the ICU.

He opens the door to a room that I haven't seen yet—a small and quiet space with similar muted blue walls, but much more privacy.

He peers at me. He seems like he wants to say something, or even ask me something, but he just nods. "Okay."

We both sit at the small table decorated by a plastic succulent, grief pamphlets, and a plain folder labeled "Leigh Demmel." I bite my lip.

"This should all be fairly straightforward," he says, "with a couple caveats."

"Like?"

He shakes his head. "Sorry. Let me start over. I thought I'd keep it sterile, for your sake, but I can't, kid. Not with you." He sighs. "First of all, I'm really sorry for your loss."

"Thank you," I reply automatically.

"Diane and everyone at our office extend their sympathies, and Diane said flat out, you can take all the time you need."

"I'm going to need a lot of time," I agree, my thoughts racing. Everything has changed now.

Everything.

"There's no father listed on the birth certificate. About a month ago, Lucy filed to make you both her and Leigh's next of kin. You are by right her legal guardian."

I think of her green-eyed baby, this little girl who is already so like Lucy. Delicate yet strong. Stubborn yet sweet.

"Because you're one of us and there's no other parental claim, we can fast track this and appoint you as Leigh's legal guardian. Or," he says, drawing out the word, "we can expedite adoption."

I nod. All of this I know. "But?"

He taps the fingers of his hand against the folder, frowning. "But," he continues, "she cannot live with a convicted felon until it's finalized." His cornflower blue eyes meet mine.

I swallow. "You mean Cliff."

"Christ, kid. I mean all of them." He waves his hand, gesturing at my ribs. "You're suddenly badly injured, your sister was beaten to death . . ." He tilts his head sternly. "What the fuck's going on, Olivia?"

He's right.

Bunny is now my responsibility. She has to be my priority, before anything else—or anyone. It's now my job to keep her safe.

I lift my shoulders. "I'm still waiting for the police to find a suspect," I lie, even though I haven't even heard from Finn.

"Oh, come on, Olivia. I read the police report. It's part of my job. Evidence was literally erased." He makes a wiping motion with his hand.

I stare back at him.

"Fine. But I'm telling you right now, this child cannot live with your boyfriend. It's the law. Don't make me have to take her away."

No way in hell I can stay away from him.

"Got it," I mutter. If I follow the rules, I can't even stay at the clubhouse. I can't stay at Mercy's or Esther's, and the last place I want to go is back to Lucy's—especially not alone. I take a shaking breath. "What else?"

"That's it," he says with a sigh. "You just have to tell me what you want to do. Guardianship, or adoption? It's a big responsibility, Olivia. Think carefully."

69

I don't even have to think about it. The main difference between the two is money from the state, and I don't need it. "Adoption."

"Okay." He slides me the paperwork and I sign. "Any chance your adoptive parents might fight you on this?"

Shit. I still haven't called them.

"No," I say, standing, "but they might have something to say if I don't call them. Excuse me."

I flee the room. I will do anything for Lucy's baby, *anything*. I can't stay away from Cliff any more than I can keep her from him. He's her family, too.

And he is mine.

There has to be another way.

I hurry back to Lucy's room, not bothering to glove up. I start to ask Stixx if I can use his phone when I realize he isn't alone.

Lucy's parents occupy the chairs, each talking on their phones as if they're making business transactions.

"The flowers better be fresh," her mother says. "Not like last time I ordered with you."

"The condo is in her name, yes," her father says.

Stixx stands off to the side, a baffled expression on his face. I try to get his attention, to sneak us out before they see me, but he doesn't see me.

"Olivia," Collin says. "Good. You want the condo, yes?"

I open my mouth and a strangled "Uh" pops out.

"Which would she like better?" Nora asks me. "Calla lilies or white roses?"

They aren't sad. They aren't even angry that I didn't call them. They don't even ask about Bunny. I turn to Stixx. "How did they . . ?"

"He called me," Nora says, waving her hand at me. "Lilies or roses?"

"The condo's yours," Collin says. "We'll just need to meet with the lawyer."

"The condo is a crime scene," I say, rubbing my temples.

He makes the exact same hand gesture, brushing me off.

"We'll have the wake tomorrow night, the funeral service the morning after," Nora tells me.

I shake my head. "No. We have to wait for Cliff. He's—"

"Not here, is he?" Collin says, hanging up.

"He must've had something better to do," Nora adds with a sniff.

"Like join a biker gang and get our daughter murdered," Collin says, looking directly at me.

My lips tremble. "Your daughter? I'm your daughter, too."

Both of them shake their heads. "The wake is tomorrow night," Nora repeats.

They're done with me.

I don't know what I expected. They weren't the warmest parents, growing up. They were always there, though. Bree never was.

"Come on, Olivia," Stixx says quietly. "Let's go . . ." He hesitates. There's no home for us to go to. "Let's go."

Nodding, I let him guide me from the room and down the hall on numb legs.

"They're grieving," he says when we reach the elevator. "They don't mean it."

"Oh, they mean it. This has been coming ever since Cliff got back." I lift my chin, blinking away tears. "It's fine. I don't need them."

"You've still got me," Stixx says. "I'm not going anywhere. Neither are Donny and Esther, or Mercy and Bree." He fixes me with a hard look. "You've got all of us."

In an instant, everything has changed. In just a few weeks, I will be Lucy's baby's mother. I am the only parent she has now. She comes first, no matter what.

We meet our group in the parking lot. I find Bree, wrapping my fingers around her arm.

"Thanks for waiting." I lead her away from the group.

"Of course," she says. "Olivia, I'm not leaving you. Never again."

"I need you," I say. "I need—" Terror strangles me, and she wraps her arms around me.

"I know, baby. I know. Let's go home."

"Home?"

"Well, I—" She bites her lip. "I thought you'd be more comfortable at our place—if you want."

I nod, too empty to argue, and let her take care of me.

For the first time in days, I am floating in numb bliss. The pain is still under the surface, clawing its way to the top. I hover at the edge of consciousness, only aware of how heavily my body sinks into the mattress. Someone's hand sweeps back and forth across my forehead, and I fall asleep.

I wake up in the room at Mercy's that used to be my nursery. The room is dark and I'm alone—at least, I think I am. When I go to move, I elbow someone.

"Ouch," Bree groans.

"What are you doing in here?" I fumble around for a lamp, but my hands come up empty.

"I didn't want to leave you."

A beat passes, and then a warm, gentle light breaks up the darkness.

I sit up in bed, the pajamas too loose and my body aching. "Where's Bunny?"

"Right outside," she assures me.

I lean back against the pillows. "Bryce?"

"He's here, too," she promises.

Heaviness begins claiming my limbs all over again. "Good," I murmur. "How long was I out?"

"Just a few hours. It's after nine now. You can rest some more. It's okay."

Except it isn't. Bunny and Bryce are safe, but Cliff isn't. I try to swing my legs over the side of the bed. All my body wants to do is sleep. I fight through the fog.

"Olivia," my mother says.

I manage to throw her a glare. "I need to meet with the rest of my club."

She inhales sharply, as if to say something, then thinks better of it. "Everyone's out in the living room. I have no idea where you get this stubbornness from," she says, her words thick with sarcasm.

I scoff. "You don't have a stubborn bone in your body."

The door opens. "I beg to differ," Mercy says. He steps to my side and helps Bree help me out to the living room. They guide me into a recliner and then step back, giving me space.

Esther's younger sisters fuss over the baby while Bryce and Cierra huddle over his phone.

I feel Donny, Stixx, and Esther staring at me, waiting for me to speak. I tap my fingers against the soft leather. Why is everyone looking at me? When the fuck did I become the one in charge? I want someone, anyone, to take control of this. At the same time, I don't trust anyone to do it right.

Oh, PTSD, thank you for ruining me.

I turn to Mercy. "Can we get the rest of the club here for an emergency Church?"

He and Donny exchange a dark look.

"What?"

"Skid wants us to come in as soon as you're up to it for a vote . . . to stop looking for Cliff," Mercy says. He flicks a glance at Bryce, and I read it in his eyes.

Skid doesn't want to find Bryce's mom, either.

"He's convinced Cliff is dead," Donny explains.

"We don't know that," I insist. "We have to try again."

"I agree with you," Donny says gently. "Neither of us like the way Skid is running things."

Fatigue curls its fingers around my brain, making my thoughts sluggish as it squeezes. "Who wants to vote yea?" I ask in a whisper.

"Skid, for sure," Donny says. "He's really pushing hard on this, Olivia. He wants to focus on revenge for Ravage and Beer Can."

"Don't we all?" I snap. "How can he turn his back on Cliff?"

Bree stands from her perch on the arm of the couch. "She needs rest," she says firmly. "Church can wait."

No one argues with her. Not even me.

I look at Bunny lying on the floor next to Bryce. "Can you hand me her?"

Bryce reaches for the baby, but Bree swoops in and lifts her into her arms, cradling her protectively to her chest. She carries her to me, relinquishing her into my arms. The sight is almost too much. When did she last hold me like that?

"I'm here," I tell Bunny, wondering if she even noticed I was gone. I'm not sure how much comfort I can give her. Someday I'm going to have to tell her that it should've been me, not her mother. They were looking for me. If I'd let Lucy come down to the ER, things might be very different.

Bunny stares up at me, her green eyes uncertain. She kicks out a leg and lets out a sigh.

"She missed you," Esther says.

Yeah, right.

"We'll all stay here and get some rest. I'll tell Skid we'll be there first thing in the morning," Mercy says.

"It has to be unanimous," Donny reminds me. "We won't stop looking unless everyone votes yea."

"Yay," I intone.

Bree strokes my hair. I don't recoil from her touch. She stayed by my side the whole time I slept. It isn't everything, but it counts for something.

"Can you take her?" I ask, my arms aching.

"I'll set up the Pack 'n Play in your room," Esther says.

Bree takes Bunny and I blink away tears. If Cliff isn't alive, I'm not all she has left in this world. At least I can sleep knowing that.

Stixx's eyes meet mine across the room. He gives me a nod. Without exchanging a word, I know he's feeling what I'm feeling. Lucy left behind a gaping hole, and if it's the last thing I do, I'm going to make the Bastard Brothers pay for it.

Bryce draws his knees to his chest, tucking in his chin so that all that's visible is that tuft of soft pink hair.

I'll make them pay for all of it.

71

OLIVIA

"Vaughn's gonna call in a few," Donny says, passing me a cup of coffee the next morning. "He texted me some cryptic shit, asking us to hold off going over to the Mermaid."

I nod, too exhausted to speak. I sip the coffee with one hand and rock Bunny with my other arm. I've been rocking her all night; the second I stop, she cries. My ribs ache, and I keep rocking her.

Donny and I sit across from each other, the kitchen table littered with gun parts. I watch him clean his pieces while I sip and rock, sip and rock.

"Donny . . ." I search his eyes. "Do you think Cliff's . . . alive?"

"I think if he wasn't, we'd know by now," he tells me, his eyes gentle. "They'd have dumped him off at our doorstep as a message. Right about now, they're probably torturing him to find out where you might be, since they can't hit the clubhouse without lighting up Naugy in red and blue. He hasn't served his purpose, so they still got him."

I nod, clinging to his logic.

His phone rings as he reassembles both guns. "Grab that," he says. "Put it on speaker."

I take the call, holding the phone between us. "Vaughn."

"Olivia," he says. "You okay?"

"Eh." I wave him off even though he can't see me. "Everybody already in the Chapel?"

"What's left of us," he says darkly.

"What's going on?" I ask him. "Donny's here with me. Stixx, too," I say, glancing at the man in the doorway.

"Skid's a rat," he says, his tone hushed. "He's been in touch with the Bastard Brothers for months—probably longer, but I couldn't get phone records going back that far."

"Phone records?" My mind races, throwing all the pieces together. As VP, Skid was privy to *everything*.

"He's been texting them everything we discuss in Church. He warned them, Olivia. He told them we were coming, the night Ravage and Beer Can were killed."

All the fight drains from me, leaving my limbs weak.

"Motherfucker," Donny says.

Stixx's eyes meet mine, mirroring the sick fury roiling in my stomach.

I inhale, trying to organize my own thoughts. "Skid was a Prospect during the split."

"Guess who brought him in?"

"Bastard?"

"Yep," he says. "They were tight. Olivia, Skid wants this club. He'll do anything it takes." He pauses. "There was another text."

"Do you have copies of all these texts?"

"Backed up on an external hard drive. Listen, there was another text that seemed weird. It said something like, 'Don't go faking any more suicides.' Does that mean anything to you?"

I start to shake my head. Then I remember the night I rode out to Mercy's place and Cliff followed me. We sat at the metal table in the backyard and he told me he suspected his father killed his mother.

"It's more of a hunch," Cliff had said. "The official cause of death was a suicide, but I've always wondered. Mom didn't have any trouble with depression. She wasn't even on medication or anything." He'd taken a long drag, blinking away the horrifying memory of finding his mother dead. "They didn't bother to look into how she got ahold of the fentanyl and Ambien in her system."

I grip the phone in my hand. "Cliff suspected his mother's suicide was staged. He thought it was Bastard."

Donny and I stare at each other for a beat.

"It was Skid," he says, and I nod.

"That means he's been after that seat for a long time," Vaughn says. "He probably hoped Ruth's death would unravel Bastard all the way—and it did, just not in the way he thought."

"Fuck," Stixx says. "How do we play this?"

"I have to tell Mercy," I say. "Can you leave the Mermaid?"

Vaughn sighs. "Shannon is in the room Ravage kept here for late nights. I can't leave her, Olivia."

Mercy has no interest in being President again, which leaves Cliff as Skid's only threat. Cliff . . . and me.

"You need to stay away," he says. "I'll keep Skid busy. If you're going to do something about Cliff, you better do it soon."

"And we better find someplace else to stay," I say, taking a long drag. "Fuck."

"I hate that we're split." Vaughn exhales into the phone. "I hate this, Olivia."

"Just keep that hard drive safe."

"Who do you think I am? Gotta go." He disconnects the call.

Donny, Stixx, and I stare at each other, and I'm pretty sure the look on my face matches theirs.

One way or another, Skid is going to the river.

I run through my To Do list.

Bring Cliff home.

Keep the kids safe.

Make the Bastard Brothers pay for Lucy, Ravage, and Beer Can.

Kill Skid.

With broken ribs and a baby inside me, it should be a piece of cake.

72

I strap on the gun Donny gave me what feels like forever ago, tuck a knife into my boot, and strap another to my wrist. While I suit up, I fill Mercy in on what Vaughn told us.

"Motherfucker," Donny seethes. "It never even occurred to me. This whole time, we were worried about Abraham's loyalties."

"Where do you want to look for him?" Mercy asks, his eyes hard.

"I want us to go back to the warehouse," I say.

Mercy, Donny, and Stixx stare at me.

"The after-hours bar," I say.

"We know what you meant," Donny says, "but we were there. He wasn't there."

"You weren't there long enough to be sure." I bend down, careful not to put too much pressure on my abdomen, and tighten the laces of my boots.

"We'll look again," Donny says, but I can tell he thinks it's a waste of time. "Mercy, you drive. We'll take Essie's car again. Stixx, you're in the back with Olivia."

"Just a minute," Stixx says. "I've got to bring my kit."

I lift an eyebrow at him. "Your kit?"

He strides to the shelves in the garage and plucks items from each, stowing them in Esther's trunk. "Accelerant," he mutters. "Zippo."

"Ah. Your kit." I grin.

He grins back. "I never leave home without it."

"Sure, just shop at Mercy's," Mercy jokes.

We pile into the car. None of us bother to remove our cuts. I want them to see us coming and know who we are. I want to see their faces when I put bullets between their eyes. I want this leather on my skin when we carry Cliff out, Stixx's set fire to their warehouse blazing behind me.

When this is over, I want everyone to know not to fuck with the River Reapers.

Mercy drives to the industrial park, Donny messing with Esther's Bluetooth. "I need to get hyped," he explains.

Not me. I don't need music. My heart pumps adrenaline through my system.

As we get closer, Donny lays out the plan. "I'll go in through the front. Stixx will take the back. Mercy, you'll stay behind the wheel, and Olivia, you'll hang back."

"Fuck that," I say, rolling my neck. "I'm going in the back with Stixx."

"I'm not sitting in this car while you all go in there," Mercy says.

Donny sighs. "Y'all realize this is the stupidest goddamn thing we've ever done, right?"

"I'd rather do something stupid than sit on my hands," Mercy says.

"You'll come in the front with me, then. One of you better pray we have time to get away."

Mercy pushes the car up the hill, rolling it in front of the warehouse. The tires spit gravel everywhere, announcing our

presence. Except there's no one to announce it to. The lot is deso-
late, not a single motorcycle or car in sight.

A frown creases Donny's forehead. "This ain't right."

"I don't like it, either," Mercy says with a sigh, "but we're
here."

"Let's go." I fling my door open, planting a boot on the
ground.

"Olivia," Donny warns.

I look at him over my shoulder.

"He might not be here."

I nod, blinking away tears. I can't think about that, or any
other alternative. I step out of the car and pull my gun from its
holster. With Stixx on my heels, we run toward the back entrance.

"This is for Lucy," Stixx whispers. I give him a curt nod, and
wrench open the door. I expect it to be locked, but it opens easily.

Stixx steps in front of me, gun pointed into the dim hall. The
front door bursts open and Donny and Mercy charge inside. The
four of us stand in the small space, peering through the gloom.

Several scarred bar tables are scattered across the floor. A
battered old bar sits in the deep shadows. The scent of stale beer
and booze stings my nostrils. It's a familiar, almost comforting
smell, except for the sharp tang of blood and vomit beneath it.

"There's no one here," Donny says, disappointed.

I spot a door off to the side. Gun pointed, I inch toward it.

"Wait," Donny says, but I wrench the door open before he can
stop me.

I blink against bright light. A steep set of stairs plunges into a
bright hall. A figure stands halfway up the stairs, another stands
near a door at the foot of the staircase. I blink again, recognizing
them: Patrick and Kyle. Both of them wear Bastard Brothers cuts
decorated with Prospect patches.

Kyle shouts, and Patrick lifts his gun toward me. I don't hesitate. My gun is already pointed. I aim with my eyes and I kill with
my heart, pulling the trigger once, sending a bullet through

Patrick's chest. From behind me, Donny sends a bullet into Kyle's forehead.

Both drop to the floor.

Donny whistles behind me. "Nice shot."

"Ravage taught me," I whisper.

The door at the foot of the stairs opens, bumping into Kyle's crumpled body. "Shit," Alex breathes.

I catch a glimpse of his pale face, and float down the stairs, stepping over the bodies. I am the grim reaper. Alex slams the door shut, and his footsteps skitter away. His shout is muffled from behind the door.

I descend the stairs and throw the door open, Donny, Stixx, and Mercy behind me every step of the way. They draw their guns, but none of them shoot.

I step into a dank room where the scent of blood and vomit and sweat and fear is stronger, no longer dulled by alcohol and cigars. Cliff holds Chad immobile, the metal of his handcuffs digging into Chad's throat.

Alex stands with his gun pointed at Cliff.

Relief floods through me at seeing him alive and mostly in one piece. "Sorry it took me so long," I greet him.

"Better late than never," he grunts.

"For Lucy," Stixx screams from behind me. He fires his gun, and Alex drops to the floor.

Chad's face pales. Tears streak his dirty cheeks. "Please. Please no. Please." His voice is strained as his eyes search mine for mercy.

I have none.

I look him dead in the eye. "For Bryce," I whisper. I fire into him, once in the ribs. He screams in pain, no longer sounding like a man. Now he resembles a child, but it's too late for him to go back. It was too late when he stole Bryce's innocence and when his father murdered my sister.

I'd pull the trigger again, but I don't want to risk hitting Cliff.

"This the one who broke your ribs?" Cliff asks me.

I give him a single nod.

Using his handcuffs, Cliff lifts Chad from his feet, and the life drains from his face. I wait for what seems like extended minutes, watching Chad's feet thrash, his fingers clawing at Cliff's. As his face goes from pale to blue, he stops moving. Cliff squeezes tight, tighter, until he goes limp. He crumples to the floor, blood pooling around him.

I step over the body.

"We're gonna sweep the rest of this place, see if there's some-where they might've stashed Ravage and Beer Can," Donny says. "You two good down here?"

"Perfect," I say, never taking my eyes from Cliff.

"Here," Mercy says, pressing a small key into my hand. "I found this upstairs. Might fit those cuffs."

Stixx gives my shoulder a squeeze, then the three of them leave us alone for the first time.

Cliff and I take each other in for a beat. There are so many things I want to say—need to say—but all I can do is stare. He swallows, then takes a step toward me.

I meet him in the middle of the basement, the dark split only by the light from the hall. I motion for him to give me his wrists, and fit the key into the lock. The cuffs fall to the cement floor with a soft clink.

"Hi," he says, brushing my hair back from my face.

I tip my head back, gazing up at him. "Hi," I reply, my voice soft. Even though I don't want to wait even one more minute to tell him about our baby, my nerve wavers.

"Watch out," he calls, but it's too late.

Patrick's arms close around my middle, wrenching me away from Cliff. He makes a grab for my gun, but his bloodied hands are clumsy. It drops to the floor.

I thrash against him, kicking wildly, but his arms tighten,

crushing the breath from my diaphragm. Fear floods me, not for myself but for the tiny heartbeat inside of me.

"Let her go," Cliff says, his voice low, dangerous.

Patrick freezes, and I look up.

Cliff picks up my gun from the floor and points it at Patrick. "Let her go," he says again.

I tell him with my eyes to just do it, to shoot, but he gives his head a small shake.

He won't risk hitting me.

Patrick drags me backward, staggering into the wall. His labored breathing steams against my ear.

"You're bleeding out," I tell him. "Let me go, and I'll call an ambulance."

I feel him hesitate. He isn't even twenty yet. He wants to live. Bullies have no power when their own lives are on the line.

He releases me, and I stagger forward, ducking behind Cliff.

"Call," Patrick begs, sliding down to the floor. In the dim light, I make out a wide streak of blood left on the wall.

Cliff's face twists into a leer, his eyes cold and black. He holds the gun, his own breathing controlled. "Bryce begged for you to stop."

Sweat drips down Patrick's face. "Please." He stretches out a hand, and again I think of that fuzzy sock on Lucy's foot.

"Say hello to Bastard for me." Cliff pulls the trigger, putting a bullet in his temple. Patrick jerks against the wall, then slumps over, still.

Cliff turns to me, switching the safety on and tucking the gun into his waistband. "Are you okay?" He runs his hands up and down over my arms.

I start to nod, to tell him I'm fine.

A wave of cramps crashes through my belly, bringing me to my knees on the floor. Every beat of my heart threatens to flush the life inside me.

73

CLIFF

Olivia gasps in pain and fear, and I scoop her into my arms. My head pounds and my fingers throb and my leg shrieks, but none of it matters. I take her to the door, using the light to look for wounds. There aren't any I can see.

She looks different.

Something is missing from her eyes.

She buries her face in my shoulder.

Donny appears at the top of the stairs.

"We gotta go," he yells.

"They went to find you," I tell Olivia, still in awe that somehow, she's alive. The sound slowly bleeds back into my ears, the ringing from the gunfire still present but no longer drowning out my every thought.

I carry her to the stairs, all but dragging my leg behind me.

"I've got her," Mercy says. He pushes past Donny and meets me at the foot of the stairs. I pass Olivia to him, too weak to argue. My arms immediately feel empty. Now that I have her again, I'll never let go.

"I told you it was a good idea to take Essie's car," Donny tells

Mercy as he helps me up the stairs. "They've been on a wild goose chase." He grins.

"Ravage? Beer Can?" Olivia asks as we leave the clubhouse. We stumble into the night, and I breathe in my first taste of freedom.

Stixx joins us. "We combed the whole place. I don't know what they did with them, but they're not here," he says.

Olivia sags against Mercy. "We should go," she reminds us, her voice weak.

"Bree and Esther are alone with the kids," Mercy agrees. "They haven't thought to look for us there yet, but they will."

"On it." Donny presses his phone to his ear. "I'll have Esther and Bree meet up with us."

Mercy sets Olivia down, and she leans against me. I wrap my arms around her, soaking in the scent of her.

"Stixx?" she calls softly.

I turn. Stixx stands staring at the building, his head cocked to the side.

"Do it," Olivia tells him.

I want to ask her how she even knows what he's thinking. A tiny flare of jealousy lights me up. I dampen it before it can catch. I'm just glad she had him while I was gone. I'm glad she had all of them.

"There's no time," Donny says. He takes Stixx by the arm and hauls him toward the car.

Stixx wrenches his arm away. "We'll make time." He breaks into a run, looping around to the back of the building.

We stand, frozen in the moment to bear witness. A few minutes later the windows light up with an orange glow. As glass shatters and flames spit through the windows, Stixx runs back into view.

"Go, go!" he screams, waving us forward.

Olivia and I squeeze into the backseat next to Stixx, everyone slamming their doors shut in unison. As Mercy backs out of the lot, tires screaming, I study her face again.

"Are you sure you're not hurt?"

"Yeah," she says, still not meeting my eyes.

I've never seen her like this, so hard and yet so afraid.

I want to crack a joke, to say something to lighten the mood. Instead, I press my forehead to hers, breathing her in, just grateful that she is whole and that we have a second chance, that we can face whatever happens next.

She makes a sound somewhere between a sob and a whimper, and suddenly I'm not so sure. Then she cups my face with her hands and presses cold lips to mine. "I thought you were dead," she whispers against my lips.

"Not yet," I grunt.

The building behind us explodes, the eruption shaking the car. All of town must've felt it.

"I told Essie to get everybody ready," Donny says. "We've got to keep moving."

"Where are we going to go?" Olivia asks.

"The Mermaid?" I suggest.

I've missed a lot, but I can tell by how everyone falls silent that our clubhouse is not an option.

"Where?" Mercy repeats, speeding out of the industrial park. I catch glimpses of it through the dark, amazed that I've been so close to home this whole time and had no idea.

Olivia sags against me. I wrap an arm around her, pulling her closer to me. I don't want to ever let her go again.

"Bunny?" I ask.

"With Esther," she whispers. "Bryce, too."

I nod, relieved, grateful for some good news. I don't want to ask this next question, but I have to. "Lucy?"

She closes her eyes, tears spilling from beneath her lashes. The heavy silence in the car is all the answer I need.

I want to go back to the warehouse, to wait for the Bastard

Brothers and make them pay. But adrenaline has long worn off and my limbs are heavy and useless. I need to see Olivia to safety, to hold Bunny. We need to regroup, we need to plan, and then we'll have our revenge.

"How did you do that?" I ask Stixx.

"Secret recipe," he says.

Normally this would be the part where Beer Can would turn to me and say with a wink, "Accelerant and upward flame."

Beer Can, of course, is gone, along with Ravage. I know that, even if we never find their bodies. There's a soul to this club, comprised of all the breathing individuals that make up this family. I can feel its empty spaces in my own bones.

"I know where we can go," Stixx says.

I sit in numb shock. So much else is gone or changed, the monuments of my life dwindling.

At least I still have Olivia.

"Someone call Rui," Olivia says. "I think something's wrong with the baby."

"The baby?" I repeat, and the hollowness and fear in her eyes finally makes sense.

74

CLIFF

"The baby?" I echo. I blink away the basement, Lewisburg, and Bastard, and zero in on my love, where I hold her in the backseat of Esther's car.

"We can't call Rui," Donny says, his eyes worried in the reflection of the rearview mirror. He grips the steering wheel.

I cup my queen's face, noting how her hands settle protectively over her belly. "Talk to me, Liv." I damn near choke on the words. I'm afraid to hope.

"Surprise," Olivia whispers, her voice hoarse. "I was waiting for a better time to tell you." She closes her eyes, and I hold her close.

"Just hold on, baby," I say, and I'm not even sure who I'm talking to.

We made a baby.

We made a baby, and it might not even be okay. I brush back her curls. I've got about a thousand questions. When did she find out she's pregnant? Hasn't she been punished enough? Are they going to be okay?

Her eyebrows furrow and she clamps her lips together like she can hold onto our baby if she just fights hard enough. My chest swells with love for this stubborn woman, aching with fear that I can't show.

"It's gonna be okay."

We take back roads into Watertown, Bree following us in Mercy's truck with Esther and all of our kids. A month ago I didn't think I'd have any. Now I'm responsible for Bunny and Bryce, and this baby I didn't even know about.

Stixx leads us to a house I've never seen before, pulling into the driveway and opening the garage doors. We squeeze both vehicles inside, and once the engines are off, Stixx shuts the doors.

"I never even told Ravage about this place," he says. "It ain't mine. It's my godmother Margit's."

"We left our bikes at my place," Mercy says, "so hopefully that'll keep them off our backs for a while."

I follow him inside, supporting Olivia despite the pain in my leg and the dizziness from what I'm positive is a fucking concussion. I brush past huge leaves. This place is a jungle, full of plants I've never seen.

"You've got her?" Olivia asks Esther, who holds Bunny.

She nods.

"I need to get cleaned up," Olivia says. "See if everything's . . . okay."

"Come on." Stixx leads us upstairs to the main bedroom, Olivia and I supporting each other, Bree and Mercy on our heels.

"Are you okay?" Bree asks Olivia.

"I think something might be wrong with the baby." Olivia looks at Mercy. "Is there any way we can get Rui here?"

I sit her down on the bed, kneeling before her. I cup her knees, run my hands over her thighs. I'm so fucking lost. There's no target for my fists.

"It's not safe," Mercy says. "I don't know if we can trust Abraham."

"Mom?" She reaches for Bree.

Her mother's face goes through a whole range of emotions as she takes Olivia's hand. "Let's get you cleaned up and in bed," she says, real soft.

"Don't go anywhere," Olivia tells me as Bree leads her into the bathroom.

"I won't," I swear.

While the shower runs with the door closed, Mercy and I stand in uncomfortable silence. I can't tell if he wants to kill me for knocking up his little girl, or if he's just as worried as I am. Maybe both.

"I'm dying for a smoke," I say finally.

With a glance at the door, he opens one of the windows and hands me his pack. "I've got first aid from the service," he says. "I can look at your leg, tell you what to do for your head. I just don't know how to help her." He bows his head.

"I get why you don't wanna call Rui." I stare out the window, where the sun shines and the world keeps moving despite how much we've lost. "I guess we're just gonna have to wait and see."

I've never felt so useless.

"We've got a lot of shit to handle," he says, and catches me up on everything I've missed while the water runs and we smoke. His dark eyes meet mine. "This is your club now. I don't want that gavel, and I sure as fuck don't want it in Skid's hands."

"We'll vote him out," I say, eyes darkening. "Vaughn's got those texts. Ain't no way any Reaper will back him." I rake hair that needs washing back from my face.

"Let me look at that leg."

I kick off my jeans, crusted with blood, and sit on the edge of the bed. Mercy peels off the bandage and prods my injuries, but all I can think about is what's going on behind that bathroom door. Stixx comes back with a first aid kit, and the water stops running, but the door remains closed.

"Looks good," Mercy says, taping me back up with a clean bandage.

Stixx rubs at his beard. "I've, uh, got some of Lucy's clothes here that Olivia can use." He ducks out of the room and returns a moment later with a folded bundle. "We missed the services."

I close my eyes. I never got to say goodbye, and that'll haunt me for however many days I've got left.

Standing, I shove down my grief and limp over to the door. "Liv? I've got clothes."

"We'll be downstairs," Mercy says, leading Stixx out.

The door opens and Olivia steps out wrapped in a towel.

"You need to rest," Bree tells her. "You're bleeding, but it's light. I don't think you lost the baby, but you've been through a lot." She sits Olivia down and starts helping her dress.

"I'm gonna get Bunny," I say. Now that I know Olivia and our baby are probably okay, I need to hold Lucy's baby, to make up for all the time I lost.

"Stay." Olivia grabs my hand, and turns to Bree. "Can you get her? I won't be able to rest if you're both downstairs." Her fingers squeeze mine.

When it's just the two of us, I help her finish dressing. "We really know how to keep the fire in a relationship," I joke.

Her mouth curls into a half smile. I lift the covers and she slips underneath them. "I'm so sorry you're the last to know. This is *not* how I wanted to—"

"I know now," I soothe. "I just want you to rest."

For once, she doesn't argue.

While she sleeps, I tend to Bunny, rocking her, changing her, feeding her, soaking her in after so long apart. I stare down at her tiny face and saucer green eyes, my heart aching for Lucy and this little girl who won't remember her. I whisper stories to her about her mom, my first best friend. Talking to her gives me something I can do.

While the baby sleeps, I wrap my arms around Olivia and press kisses and strength into her, telling her to take all the time she needs. She held it down while I was gone. She kept Bunny and our baby safe.

While she sleeps, I whisper into her ear knowing she won't hear me, but maybe my words will reach her dreams and make *her* feel safe.

"I love you."

Because I do.

I've loved her for a long time, for as long as I've known her. I didn't know it at first. It crept up on me, slowly filling me until it was all I could taste.

No one disturbs us. They give us the day and the night. I lie awake, my hands full with responsibility. Ravage thought I needed more time, and now there isn't any left.

This club is mine now.

I leave the room only once to find Donny downstairs. The whole house sleeps around us and he gives it to me straight. Vaughn called him while Olivia was in the shower.

There's a warrant for my arrest.

We've got a thousand problems and few solutions.

I should turn myself in. By being here, I'm putting everyone in even more danger. If the police find me, they'll lead our enemies right to our door. DCF would take Bunny. The Bastard Brothers would kill us all.

I should leave, but my woman clings to me, rendering me immobile. When Bunny wakes, Olivia releases her grip on me. I leave her in bed while I pick up the baby.

"You're awake," I say.

Olivia opens her eyes, just a crack, then closes them again.

"I'm right here. Just sleep."

I rock the baby, pieces of my heart raw and jagged. We're all safe, but for how long?

Olivia sighs and opens her eyes again. "You're here."

"I'm here." Still swaying the baby from side to side, I sit on the bed.

"She okay?" she asks. She doesn't look at me. Heavy-lidded eyes watch the baby.

"She's perfect." I move to put Bunny back in her Pack 'n Play, but Olivia sits up, limp curls falling around her face, arms stretched out.

"Can I?"

"Of course." I set Bunny in her arms, bleeding out from the inside as I watch my love hold our niece.

In just a few short months, she'll be holding our own baby.

She lowers her nose to Bunny's head, breathing in deeply. "God, she smells so good."

The corner of my mouth twitches. "Right?"

"Her little head is like crack."

Some of the light bleeds back into her eyes, and some of the tightness in my chest eases.

"It really is."

Her eyes meet mine. "Cliff . . . If we have a girl, I want to name her Ruth. After your mom," she whispers.

"Really?" I move closer. "That . . . I'd love that," I say, throat tightening.

"I'm adopting Bunny. Harrison started the paperwok." Tears spill down her cheeks, dripping onto Bunny's head. "She'll be a good big sister."

"She will," I say with a smile. I climb into bed behind her, favoring my bad leg, and draw her back against my chest. The three of us sit like Russian nesting dolls. "Bunny and Ruth," I say into her ear. Their names sound good together, like fate.

Olivia leans back into me, quiet.

Bunny glowers up at both of us. Olivia's shoulders shake, and I start to soothe her before I realize she's laughing.

"This baby is grumpy."

"She takes after you," I say, running my hands up and down her ribs.

"Does not." But she tips her head back and tosses me a wink.

"I missed you so much," I tell her.

She stares up at me for several beats, blinking under long wet lashes. Then she swallows, the lump visible in the stretch of her throat. "Cliff . . ." She purses her lips, hesitating. Rubbing her lips together, she looks back down at Bunny, then gently sets her down in the middle of the bed. "Hand me those pillows."

I do as she says, and watch her block the baby in from rolling. Just weeks ago she wouldn't touch Bunny. "You're doing great," I tell her softly. "You're a natural."

Her shoulders tighten but she nods. Turning around on her knees, she faces me. "I . . ." She swallows again. "I missed you, too," she whispers. Stretching out a hand, she touches the cuts on my face. "I thought . . ." She blinks and tears dribble onto her lap. "I don't know what I'd do if something happened to you. I . . ."

Her eyes meet mine. Her lips part. She blinks once, twice, and then cradles my face in her hands. "What time is it?"

"A little after four," I tell her. "Sun'll be up soon."

She starts to climb out of bed. "I can't believe I slept that long. If Harrison wants to check in, and he finds you here—"

I pull her back into me. "There's something I gotta tell you." I rub my palms on my jeans. This is a smoking conversation, but aside from the bathroom, we're in close quarters.

She waits, those eyes I love so much wide.

I swallow. "We missed the services, for Lucy."

"I know." She sighs. "It probably wouldn't have been safe, anyway. I just hate that you and Bunny didn't get to say goodbye."

"I'll never forget Lucy," I say, "and we'll make sure Bunny doesn't, either."

She nods, and I give her the rest of it.

"There's a warrant out for my arrest." I exhale.

"Mark," she says. "Mark could call your P.O., cover for you—"

I shake my head. "It's too late for that. Either I keep moving, or I turn myself in. And if they come for me, they'll take Bunny, too." I lift my eyes to hers. "Bunny can't live with a felon."

"So *we* keep moving," she says, lifting her chin. "The adoption will be final in a few weeks. I'll hold off Harrison from a home visit, and when it's official, there won't be anything they can do. I'm not letting you turn yourself in. We stay together."

I love the steel in her eyes. "Whatever happens, Bunny's gotta be your priority. Our baby, too," I say, the words catching in my throat.

Her brown eyes meet mine, wide and vulnerable. "I lasted seven months."

I cock my head at her. "Huh?"

"I tried not to love you. It only took you seven months to break me down."

A grin spreads across my face. "Sorry, what?" I mime cleaning out my ear. "It's just, I'm so 'old,' I didn't hear you."

She rolls her eyes, but a faint smile touches her lips, and I know she'll be okay. We both will. "I said I love you, asshole. Don't make me say it again."

I lean in, still smiling. "Come again?"

"I said . . ." She fights a smile and loses. "I—" She moves closer and presses a kiss to my lips. "Love—" Another kiss. "You." She goes to give me another quick kiss and I catch her chin, holding her in place.

A warmth I've needed since I walked out into this cold, lonely world back in February swirls through my chest. "I love you, too," I say against her lips.

She smiles, and the warmth in my chest spreads through me. "I love you."

I wrap my arms around her and we curl around both babies, one nestled between pillows, the other safe inside her.

I finally got everything I wanted, but at what price?

~

Cliff and Olivia's story concludes in
A Lasting Prospect
February 28th, 2022

Pre-order Now: books2read.com/alastingprospect

Read Lucy and Stixx's story in
Burning for Stixx
June 2nd, 2021
Pre-order Now: books2read.com/burningforstixx

GET RIVER REAPERS MC SERIES UPDATES

The final book in the River Reapers MC series is under way, and there are more spinoff novellas coming!

You'll also get Bree and Mercy's story for FREE when you sign up.

Visit **bit.ly/HerMercyNovella**

BODY COUNT

12

ACKNOWLEDGMENTS

Every book release is stressful, but everything that could possibly go wrong went wrong while I was writing and then revising this book.

From the loss of my own Lucy in 2019, to a monster flare of my UCTD that had me in and out of the hospital in 2020, to a pandemic and my own COVID-19 infection in 2021, and more dark nights of the soul than I can count, I pushed myself over and through every hurdle, victoriously hitting publish.

So many people bandaged me up along the way.

I'm so freakin' grateful for Traci Finlay, who took over editing at the last minute and gently and expertly helped me whip the wild draft I had into shape. Any remaining issues with this book are on me.

Molli Moran and Katy Young beta read early drafts, giving me valuable feedback, even if they laughed at me every time I re-wrote the ending.

My work wife J.C. Hannigan also busted my balls about changing the ending a million times, let me bounce ideas off her over FaceTime, and patiently patted my head every time I swore I'd just burn the thing.

Natasha Snow as always designed a gorgeous yet gritty cover that fits the aesthetic of this series, while making my books stand out in the ever-growing biker romance community.

My friends and family held me down while I fought through chronic illness and resumed treatment under the best rheumatologist in the world.

My IRL book boyfriend and OTP Mike . . . What can I say, babe, after all we've been through together? I'm just grateful that our story isn't over.

Two stories ended while I worked on this book. Noni was my grandma and my first reader. Squirt was my furbaby and my writing buddy. Life isn't the same without either of them, but every time I sit down at the keyboard, they're with me in spirit. I really hope we meet again.

I'm proud of myself for pushing through and never giving up. It took my whole life for me to realize I'm my own hero, and I really, really like the person I've become.

I twirl.

Finally, I'm thankful for each and every one of my readers for taking a chance on my offbeat stories, unconventional couples, and prickly heroines. I'm still scared every time I publish a new dark romance that it'll be the one that crosses the line, yet you continue to support me and instigate my insanity.

I'm far from done . . .

ABOUT THE AUTHOR

Elizabeth Barone writes dark biker romance with a body count and contemporary romance with badass belles because life isn't just heavy or light, it's both.

Before publishing her debut novel, she was a web designer trapped writing code instead of stories. It took a debilitating autoimmune disease to shove her toward the path she was always meant to be on.

Elizabeth has published over a dozen novels, and has so many ideas for more, she'll be employed 'til she dies. She lives in Connecticut with her husband Mike and more coffee mugs than she'll ever need.

Connect with Elizabeth
Website: https://elizabethbaronebooks.com
Reader Group: https://facebook.com/groups/baronesbelles

www.ingramcontent.com/pod-product-compliance
Lightning Source LLC
Chambersburg PA
CBHW031608100726
47898CB00006B/1692